THE SHADOWS IN THE STREET

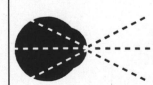

A SIMON SERRAILLER MYSTERY

THE SHADOWS
IN THE STREET

SUSAN HILL

THORNDIKE PRESS
A part of Gale, Cengage Learning

GALE
CENGAGE Learning™

Detroit • New York • San Francisco • New Haven, Conn • Waterville, Maine • London

GALE
CENGAGE Learning™

LIBRARY OF CONGRESS CATALOGING-IN-PUBLICATION DATA

Hill, Susan, 1942–
    The shadows in the street : a Simon Serrailler mystery / by
Susan Hill.
        p. cm. — (Thorndike Press large print crime scene)
    ISBN-13: 978-1-4104-3620-7 (hardcover)
    ISBN-10: 1-4104-3620-9 (hardcover)
    1. Serrailler, Simon (Fictitious character)—Fiction. 2.
Police—England—Fiction. 3. Serial murder
investigation—Fiction. 4. Large type books. I. Title.
PR6058.I45S53 2011
823'.914—dc22   2010051909

Published in 2011 by arrangement with The Overlook Press, Peter
Mayer Publishers, Inc.

Printed in Mexico
1 2 3 4 5 6 7 15 14 13 12 11

To
the old familiar faces

ACKNOWLEDGMENTS

I am again indebted to Detective Chief Superintendent Paul Howlett of Wiltshire CID, who has answered my many questions in most helpful detail and with both authority and alacrity, and spared time and thought to my fantasy cases when he had plenty of real ones on his hands.

Dr Robin Birts answered my medical questions with clarity and patience, while the anonymous members of the police999.com forum were always willing to come to my aid with professional information on police procedure.

Barrister Anthony Lenaghan has advised me on legal points. Sheila Finlayson drew on her many years of experience in social work to reply to my queries and passed others on to those still toiling in the field who gave me up-to-date information.

My grateful thanks to them all. Any errors that may remain are my own.

ONE

Leslie Blade stopped in the overhang of the college entrance to put up his umbrella.

Rain. Rain morning and evening since the beginning of the week.

He could drive to work, but it was only a couple of miles so he didn't qualify for a college parking permit. He could get a bus, but they were infrequent and unreliable and there was still a ten-minute walk from the stop nearest to his house.

People were dashing down the steps and out into the downpour. Students crossed the courtyard with anorak hoods pulled over their heads.

Leslie Blade lifted his umbrella and stepped out.

Until the last few months he had always followed the same route along the main road and around by the Hill, but now the Old Market Lanes had opened he some-times walked through them, liking the cobbles and the less garish lights, looking into the windows of the bookshop and a couple of galleries, buying a piece of cheese or some salami from the delicatessen which stayed open until seven. It made him twenty minutes or more later arriving home, which his mother did not like, so he had taken to buying her some chocolate or a bag of butter toffee. It was a bribe, and it wasn't what she really wanted, which was his company, but it worked. She enjoyed the sweets.

By the time he reached the Lanes this evening, rain was sluicing off the gutters and there were deep puddles at the side of the narrow cobbled way. The deli was closing early.

He saw her at the end of the Street, where the Lanes decanted onto the market square. She was standing just inside the light that spilled out from the pub, the collar of her jacket up, trying to shelter from the rain but still remain visible. Leslie quickened his step. This was a new place; he had not seen any of them here before. It was too near the main shopping streets and cars were not allowed to stop in the square — only buses, and taxis on their way to the rank at the far end.

But it was Abi. He was sure it was Abi, even from the other end of the street. Abi or just possibly Marie?

He skirted one puddle but hit the next and felt the cold water slosh up the front of his leg, soaking his trousers, and he almost fell as he reached the corner.

'Abi?'

The young woman did not glance round, but instead went to join the man for whom she had clearly been waiting. Took his arm. Went into the pub.

Not Abi. Not Marie. Not one of them after all.

Leslie felt angry and he felt a fool. But there was no one to notice.

He crossed the market square and headed away from the shops and the lights, towards the Hill.

Hilary, his mother's carer, left at four thirty and he tried to get home just after six. Tonight, it was nearer twenty past because the rain driving into his path had slowed him down. It was Thursday, one of his two nights for going out, but if it didn't clear up, he wondered, was there much point? Would any of them be out in weather like this?

He opened the front door.

Hilary always left the porch light on for him, the kettle filled and ready. If he wanted

11

her to do anything else, peel potatoes or put
something into a low oven, he had only to
leave a note and she would do it willingly,
though he rarely made any requests. She
was his mother's carer, not a domestic help.
He and Hilary almost never met, but com-
municated, if they needed to, by a series of
notes — hers always cheerful and decorated
with funny faces and little pencilled stars or
flowers. He was lucky. He had heard stories
of the other sort of carer — the Chief
Librarian's secretary had had a few bad
experiences with her mother's carers,
women who had been brusque or even
downright unkind, and one who had been a
thief. Hilary was dependable, strong, cheerful, reliable. Leslie knew good luck when it
came his way. Norah Blade was not difficult,
but rheumatoid arthritis as bad as hers did
not make for an even temper.

'Leslie?'

'I'm here. But I'm going up to change,
I'm soaked.'

'It's poured all day, I've watched it
through these windows and it hasn't let up
since you went out this morning.'

He could tell everything by her tone of
voice. Good day. Bad day. Painful day. She
sounded bright. Not a bad day then.

They could have a nice evening, and she'd

be settled in bed before he had to go out. Sometimes, if she was in a lot of pain, he had to stay up with her, play a game of cards, help to make the night a bit shorter. On those evenings he couldn't go.

The strip light was on above the kitchen worktops, a pan of peeled carrots on the cooker, a chirpy note from Hilary on the pad. He felt better for dry trousers and his slippers, poured himself a lager and checked on the casserole. The curtains were not yet drawn and, as he reached up to close them, he saw that the rain was no longer teeming down the windows and the wind had dropped.

'There's nothing much on,' Norah said, after they had eaten supper and he had helped her back to her chair.

She watched quiz games, wildlife and travel programmes, *Midsomer Murders* and reruns of the gentler comedy series.

'*University Challenge?*'

'They all look so scruffy.'

'Goodness, Mother, you should see some of our students. The ones on television are quite presentable.'

'There was a boy with green hair.'

'That was years ago.'

'All the same.'

13

They could continue bantering enjoyably in this way on and off until bedtime. It had taken Leslie some years to understand that Norah pretended to be grumpy and dissatisfied about small things — television programmes, the noise the neighbours made, bits and pieces in the local paper — as a safety valve. She was in continuous pain, she was limited in movement, confined to a couple of rooms, and about those things she never complained. Grumbling over the scruffiness of the young on TV was a way of letting out a scream of anguish and misery at her condition.

So he indulged her, let her grumble on. The actor who played the young detective in *Midsomer Murders* wasn't as good as his predecessor; some of the wildlife programmes had too much chat from presenters and too little focus on the animals. He was used to it. He didn't mind.

'Hilary's sister is expecting a baby, did I tell you?'

'You did. When's it due?'

'Spring sometime. Ages yet. But of course Hilary's thrilled to bits. They live only a few streets away from her.'

'Yes, you said.'

Norah Blade never spoke a word against her carer and had never fallen out with her, even over something trivial.

They watched half of a vulgar new sitcom before Norah decided to go to bed.

'I've got three new library books Hilary changed for me. They can't be worse entertainment than this.' She snapped the remote control button and the television died.

It was half past nine by the time she was settled. Leslie went into the kitchen and opened the window. He could see a few stars in the clearing sky. He cleared away the supper plates, then took out a fresh sliced loaf, cheese, tomatoes and a pack of ham, made the sandwiches, cut a bought fruit cake into slices and wrapped everything in foil. He put the food into a carrier bag, with half a dozen Mars bars, some apples and a flask of coffee. He always made enough for four, and if there were more, they had to share it.

He sometimes wondered if Hilary ever saw the large blocks of cheese and packs of butter in the fridge, the chocolate and biscuits in the cupboard, and wondered who ate so much food, and usually overnight; but his mother always said one of the best things about Hilary was that she was never nosy, never commented, waited to be told things and if she was not, did not ask.

15

He tidied up, then watched the news headlines. When he switched off the television, the house was very quiet. A car went past. Quiet again. They were at the end of the row, and the neighbours on the other side made little noise. He wondered if Norah might prefer to live in a livelier street, with more families passing by, children going to and from school; she spent a lot of time in her chair by the window. But she had lived in this house for fifty-three years. It had been his home all his life. There was no question of moving now.

The front room, which had once been the dining room, had been made into a bedroom, now that Norah could no longer climb the stairs; there was a bathroom in a small extension. He went into the hall. There was no light coming from under her door, but he called her name softly a couple of times. Waited. Nothing. He opened the door slightly and stood listening to her soft breathing. The numbers glowed a strange alien green on her radio clock.

'Goodnight, Mother.'

She did not reply.

But ten minutes later, hearing the soft click of the front door closing, Norah Blade opened her eyes. The house was settling

16

back into itself. She listened. Leslie parked his car on the small piece of waste ground between their house and the block of flats. Sometimes she asked him why he bothered to keep it, whether it wasn't too much of an expense, as he didn't use it for work.

'I take you to the hospital, I use it for shopping, we go out in the summer. You'd miss it.'

'You could hire one.'

'No, once you stop driving regularly you lose the skill.'

But he used it more often than that, Norah knew; he took the car at night, twice a week, though where he went and what he did she did not know nor would she ever ask. He was a grown man. He had a right to a private life. She felt guilty enough.

She strained her ears waiting until she heard him drive away down the road. The pain was never bad during this early part of the night because she was warm and comfortable propped on her special pillows, and the medication she took with a hot drink blurred the sharp edges for a time. But she never slept until Leslie came in, just lay in the darkness, strangely comforted by the green glow of the bedside clock. He would be out for a couple of hours and when she heard him return, she would fall asleep at

17

once, until the pain and the stiffness in her limbs woke her again in the early hours.

TWO

Abi Righton pulled the sleeping bag further up round Frankie's neck. He mumbled and chewed his lips for a moment, but did not wake. Next to him in the camp bed against the wall, his sister Mia coughed, stirred, coughed again and opened her eyes.

'It's OK, go back to sleep.'

The child coughed again and struggled to sit up. They were in sleeping bags because Abi thought they were safer and warmer, and because apart from a large knitted blanket she didn't have any other bedclothes for them.

She sat at the mirror that hung from a nail on the wall, stretching her eye from the outer corner to get the black liner round, trying to look only at what she was doing and not at her own face, the sepia shadows under her eyes, the crack in the corner of her mouth where a cold sore had just dried.

Mia coughed again and started to whimper. Abi didn't have any cough medicine but there was some orange drink at the bottom of the plastic bottle; she could tell Hayley to give her that warmed up if Mia coughed too much. Where was Hayley, anyway? It was ten past nine, she was supposed to come at nine, that was always the arrangement. Three nights, Hayley came here to stay with Abi's two; and three nights, Abi took them to Hayley's. She couldn't go out until Hayley had arrived, that was a given. Leaving their kids alone was something they had both said they would never do. That was how the arrangement had started, over a year ago. She turned her head and started on the other eye. At least it had stopped raining. Rain was the worst, though the bitter cold last winter had been something else — she'd had flu and then a cough she couldn't get rid of for weeks, Frankie and Mia had been ill on and off the whole time and she hadn't been able to afford the gas fire more than a couple of hours a day. That had been her rock bottom. If she hadn't had Hayley she wouldn't have got through it. They had kept one another going, and if one of them had money they'd help each other out that way too. Once or twice they'd stayed here, all the kids sleeping together, she and Hayley next to them,

20

for warmth. It was like being kids themselves again. One night they'd had no money for the meters, so Hayley had gone over to the Catholic church and nicked a couple of candles from the stand. They'd lit them and talked about ghosts with the light flickering up the walls. They'd wet themselves laughing, woken the kids, made jam sandwiches with the last of the loaf.

I was happy, Abi thought suddenly, putting down the eyeliner. That was what it was. It was being happy.

She heard Hayley coming down the steps. If they could just be like that, have a laugh, be with their kids all together and not go out. Not go out ever again. Only, she had to go out, she was saving. Her savings were in an old biscuit box and every time she looked into it they'd grown a bit. Not enough. But a bit. She thought three years, maybe four, the kids would be in school, and she'd have enough to move into somewhere else or maybe her name would have come up for a house — either way she could get something better than this.

Four years, maybe five. Then not go out ever again. Not once.

'Hiya.'

Hayley came through the door and Mia started up coughing.

'Thought you'd got lost.'

'He was sick.'

'Oh bloody hell, you haven't brought him sick, have you? He'll give it to mine, and that's all I need.'

Hayley stood in her jeans and parka, holding Liam by the hand. He was the colour of wax.

'Well, you've got to go out, what else was I supposed to do?'

'OK, OK. Only maybe put him over there. Put him on the other side.'

'Make it sound like he's got fucking mad cow disease or something. He can't help it, you know.'

Hayley muttered on, dumping Liam on the old sofa up against the window, pulling off her jacket.

'Anyway, it's stopped raining. Can't be bad.'

'My luck, it'll start again five minutes after I get out. And I ran out of tea bags.'

'Great.'

'If I'm quiet I'll go to the all-night, get some. There's a bit of milk.'

Abi got her fleece from over the chair back, checked the pocket for her mobile. It wanted topping up, and she didn't have enough cash for that either. Another reason she had to go out. You could do without a lot before you did without the phone. The lifeline.

'Lend us your mobile, Hayles.'

'No way. What's wrong with your own?'

'Nearly out. Go on, I'll leave mine here, there'd be enough on it to call an ambulance or something if you had to.'

'Same goes for you then.'

Hayley stared her out. When she was in this mood, it was best to leave her. Jump down your throat, yell, bang her head on the walls, chuck something at you, all of that, it happened, and they both knew why. Abi wasn't risking it when all the kids were here with her.

'OK,' she said. 'Anyway, the van might be out, they'll give us some tea bags.'

'Not seen it for a week.'

'Or Loopy Les.'

Hayley let out a snort of laughter. Mia woke, coughing, and Liam threw up a stream of pale vomit that went arcing across the floor.

Twenty minutes later, Abi was on the street. The sky was clear and a sneaky wind had got up, the sort that went through your clothes and out the other side. But it was dry. Rain was the pits. If you stood somewhere you could be seen properly, you got

23

soaked. And cars didn't stop so much in the wet. Nobody came by on foot when it rained. Not that you got too many of them anyway, apart from Beanie Man, unless you went right into the town when they were turning out of the pubs. She used to do that quite a bit, but lately it had been hopeless. Four girls had turned up one night, brought by a van and dropped off near the Lanes, foreign girls, across from Bevham where there were too many of them now. A couple of nights after that there were three more.

The police had started moving them all on, no messing, whereas before they'd left you alone.

She walked quickly, cutting across the car park and then along the main road to the grid of streets between the canal and the bypass, short cuts for motorists heading to Bevham. On one side, there were the posh apartments carved out of the Old Ribbon Factory, expensive but now with several For Sale boards cluttering up the front. Who could afford those? Yuppie couples, buy-to-lets, only the bottom had dropped out of all that. She could picture them, all the same, from glances up into the lighted windows and photos in old magazines, guess what they'd be like inside. Space. Lots of wood on the floor. No kids. You didn't live here if

24

you had kids. But why shouldn't you? Why didn't she have the right to live with her two in a place like this instead of in her dump of a room?

She knew why.

She reached the corner opposite the snooker club. There were a couple of girls nearby. The foreigners. Another two round the corner. Abi turned away, cut through a side alley, came out into the last street before the main road. It ran alongside the locked gates and high fence of the print-works, but it wasn't bad — there was shelter and the Reachout van sometimes stopped in the works entrance. And the men knew this part, knew which girls were generally here. The police didn't seem to bother either, not like they did in the town centre.

She saw Marie leaning on the street lamp near the corner, smoking. Nobody else. Abi pulled the collar of her jacket up tighter. Her legs were cold, but they always were, you had to wear a short skirt and some of them wore low tops as well. But in winter it made sense to look after yourself a bit. If she got sick, she was no use. The collar of a fleece wasn't a lot but it helped. It was quiet. There weren't even many cars going down the main road. She walked up and down a couple of times, then went towards Marie.

'Y'all right?'

Marie shrugged and threw her cigarette butt onto the pavement.

'Nobody else been around?'

'I saw that van go by. Foreign girls. Think it was that one.'

'They better not stop here.'

Marie shook her head. 'Going towards town.'

'They'll get moved on.'

'Yeah, but there's more people about in town, isn't there? Dead here, I tell you.'

'I'm sick of them.'

'We never had any of that, you know. It was us. That was it. Maybe a new one now and again . . .'

'That girl with the dead white face.'

'Melissa.'

'Right.'

'She didn't last.'

'No. Them foreign girls just better not stop here,' Abi said again.

Marie looked at her. 'British jobs for British workers.'

They both cracked up.

A car came round the corner and they separated, Marie crossing the road to wait by the warehouse. It didn't stop. Ten min-

26

utes more and three girls came down the street, girls they knew. They separated too, one of them walking down towards the canal end, the others crossing over.

It was colder. Abi banged her feet on the path. Then, two cars, and another, slowly round the corner and gliding up the street. Abi felt herself caught in the headlights of one, saw Marie go towards the kerb where another had stopped. Maybe it wasn't going to be a dead night after all.

But it was another twenty minutes before there was anyone else, this time on her side of the street. She moved forwards but it stopped a few yards away and doused the lights. Engine off. Driver's door open.

Bloody hell, it was only him. She moved quickly away. Marie was getting out of a car further up, pushing money into her inside pocket.

'Keep walking, it's Loopy Les down there.'

Marie glanced. She looked young, Abi thought, young in the half-light, not like she looked under the street lamp. Like they all looked. She knew Marie lived in a caravan on a patch off the Starly Road. Her mother was with her on and off, when she wasn't locked up or drunk in a ditch somewhere.

Footsteps.

'Abi? Yes, I thought so. Abi and . . . who's

that . . . ?'

'Marie.'

The girls glanced at one another. They didn't mind Les. But he wanted to stand and chat and that put off any punters driving down.

'Hiya.'

'Come here, nearer the gate.'

They followed him to where there was a bollard by the turn-in to the factory. He had his usual canvas satchel, plastic bags of sandwiches, the chocolate bars, the flask of coffee.

'Cold for you tonight,' he said, unwrapping the packets. 'Too cold to be out on the streets.'

'Yeah, yeah. Thanks anyway.'

Abi wasn't hungry but the coffee was OK, still quite hot, and she took a couple of bites of the chocolate, before putting the rest in her pocket to take home.

'That's a good bit of cake.' Marie was scoffing the food down as if she hadn't eaten all day, which, Abi thought, she probably hadn't. She was thin as a rake, bony-thin. She smoked instead of eating. She stuffed another half of ham and bread into her mouth.

He'd been coming out like this for the best part of a year. He just turned up, brought the food and the flask, chatted a bit about nothing. She'd wanted to ask him why he did it but had never bothered. He wasn't one of the Reachout lot, wasn't Sally Army or any other Church, so far as she knew, and besides, he never preached at them, never mentioned anything like Jesus. He chatted about the weather and asked them if they were all right, asked after anybody who hadn't been out for a while. Once, when he knew one of the girls who'd used to come was ill, he'd offered to get her a medical appointment, take her to the hospital. She hadn't gone and the next week the word was out that she was dead of an overdose. Les had asked about her but they hadn't told him anything.

Just lately, he'd been coming out a couple of nights a week. Hayley had seen him as well.

'I thought you'd be nearer town. Bit warmer, bit more shelter.'

Abi shrugged.

'Safer as well.'

'We're all right. We look out for each other.'

They could never quite decide if he was OK or not. He wasn't weird. He wasn't anything. All the same . . .

One of the girls had asked him if he was

looking for payment in kind but Leslie had been horrified. He'd jumped in his car and driven off fast, leaving the flask behind on a bench, and nobody had seen him for a couple of weeks after that.

'Say what you like,' Hayley had said, 'not normal.'

Only he seemed normal, watching them eat the sandwiches he'd made for them, pocket the chocolate bars he'd bought out of his own money, finish off the hot tea or coffee. He had a normal coat, normal trousers, normal blue wool scarf. Normal black shoes. Normal. He was clean, he shaved, he hadn't got anything special about him or anything peculiar either. Just normal.

Only not.

Abi handed back the plastic cup. 'Thanks.'

Not normal. How could it be?

'Oh, Christ.'

'What?'

'I remembered I have to get tea bags. I've got to go to the all-night. Fuck it.'

A car turned round the corner.

Marie walked quickly away, sensing it would stop further down. Abi swore.

'Cheers, Les,' she said, and went, not wanting to mess around there keeping him company or whatever and waste the rest of the night. She hadn't even earned the money to pay for the tea bags yet.

But as she got to the top of the street, a car came off the main road and flashed its lights at her.

Her last punter dropped Abi off by the printworks just after midnight. Things had got a lot busier, she had more money than she'd expected, but that was it, she'd had enough. She'd always had enough, had enough before she started out, but it wasn't going to be forever. That was what kept her going. Knowing it wasn't going to be forever. Four years. You could put up with anything for four years. Or if she did really well maybe three.

The street was empty. The others had gone. She'd take a cut along the canal towpath and over the footbridge. She didn't like going that way usually but it saved ten minutes.

As she passed the bollard by the factory, she saw something. Maybe Les had left his satchel behind, though that wouldn't be like him. Neat and tidy, that was Les.

She couldn't make it out until she got right up to it. It was a plastic carrier bag from the supermarket on the Bevham Road. She hesitated. You never knew.

'Les left it for you, I was going to text you.'

Marie appeared out of the shadows. 'He went but then he came back with it.'

'You OK?'

Marie sounded odd. She had her head turned away.

'Nothing that won't go away. I'm off, Abs, I've had it. You walking back a bit my way?'

It was a couple of miles to the field and Marie's caravan. She carried flat shoes in her pockets, put them on instead of the heels once she was ready to go, and as she bent down to pull one on, Abi caught a glimpse of her face.

'You want to get that bash seen to, Marie. Did you take his number? You don't have to put up with that stuff — you can go to the cops, you know, if you get their number.'

'Yeah, right.'

'You can.'

'That's what you'd do then?'

'Only saying.'

'Well, fuckin' don't.' Marie wobbled as she put on the second shoe.

'I don't mind going to the top with you, only I've got to get back to the kids.'

'Nah. You're all right.' Marie waited.

'What?'

Marie pointed to the carrier.

'Yeah.' Abi picked it up. Reached inside.

Two Hundred Tea Bags. Full Flavour. Economy size.

THREE

Nothing happened for a day, sometimes, miraculously, even a couple of days. Everything went on as usual; she got up, made breakfast, drove the children to school, did her job, shopped, collected the children, made supper. It was dry or it rained; it was cold or mild. The world turned. And then the grief roared up towards her again quite without warning, hit her so hard it took her breath away and left her sobbing or shaking, sick or terrified, a tidal wave of recollection and misery and hopelessness.

Cat Deerbon opened the door of her car and then leaned against it for a moment, head on her arm, trembling with tears that seemed to come from somewhere in the depths of her body, another wave with the power to knock her off her feet. Behind her, the lights of Imogen House fanned out onto the tarmac. It was twenty to ten.

She had been fine for the past half-hour

or so, altering the dosage of a patient's pain relief, talking to a family, even fine while she had been examining Cassie Porter and sitting by her bed, listening to her, holding her hand. Fine discussing Cassie and another two cases with the night sister. Fine having a cup of tea with Lois, the receptionist. Fine. And all the time knowing that she would not be fine once she had left the building and stopped being a duty doctor and could let her guard drop. Fine, until she was alone.

Cassie Porter was twenty-seven and dying of a brain tumour.

People did. This was a hospice. Cat was a doctor.

A year ago, her husband, Chris, had died of the same type of brain tumour, though not here but at home, in their bed, as she lay with her arms around him. He had sent plenty of his own patients into Imogen House, he was hugely supportive of the place and encouraged Cat to do more palliative care work. But he had refused to be admitted there himself, refused to die anywhere but at home. Cat did not know whether the fact that at least there were no memories of his death held forever in the hospice made it easier to work there or not. Nothing affected her either more or less. It got worse. That was all. Time passing made it worse. People told her it got better and people were wrong.

She wept on, tears running down her arm and onto her hand. Tears were infinite and the well was bottomless. She had learned that now. In a few moments they would cease, but there was always, always, the next time, in an hour or a day. Tears were exhausting, uncontrollable and ultimately pointless, but now they were as much part of her life as hunger or the need to breathe.

The only thing time had done was teach her to accept that.

A car turned in through the gates and parked in the visitors' area. Cat had encouraged Cassie Porter's family to come in now. She didn't think Cassie would die that night but it was better to doubt her own clinical judgement, have the relatives there, ensure that there was time for things to be said before a patient slipped into a last unconsciousness. Better to be wrong, better that they had time to talk again, to say the loving words over and over, than that the chance was missed forever. Because Chris had died at home it had been easier. She had been there most of the time, the children in and out. Yet not everything had been said. They had talked, but last things had been left unspoken because Chris had preferred it, cut her short if it had seemed she was trying to say what he refused to hear. In the end, she thought now, Chris had never been able to face the fact that he was dying. That was why he had not allowed her to say some of the things that she would now never be able to say. It had been his choice, his right, but it was unfinished business and somewhere half buried within her, Cat knew, was anger and frustration because of it.

Perhaps that was partly why she was crying now, why the tsunami of grief had swamped her so that she would have to wait in the car until she felt sufficiently in control to drive home. Perhaps. Or perhaps there was never a specific reason. Missing Chris, feeling totally bereft of him, wanting him back, sinking to the depths every time she remembered that he would never come back, longing for him so that she felt ill and incapable of functioning as a human being — all of it needed no prompting, like some memories that were touched by a piece of music, or a chance remark, or going into a particular building. All of it was now part of her, wrapped around her like a second skin. The best she could hope for were some periods when she was occupied and preoccupied enough to be unaware, as one can sometimes be unaware of pain for a short time during sleep.

She watched two women and a man walk through the entrance. The Porters. At the moment, every bed in the hospice was occupied, and the day unit could barely cope. This was how it ebbed and flowed, though the place was never really quiet. Too many people dying, Cat thought, too many people in pain. Too many.

The car smelled faintly of disinfectant. Felix had been sick on the way home from nursery and she had had to scrub out the back seat. Disinfectant, 'the horrible hospital smell', Hannah had once said. When Chris had been dying, Cat had made sure there was no 'horrible hospital smell' in the house and kept his drugs in a separate locked cupboard in the bathroom, not wanting the paraphernalia of illness and dying to invade the house because he had so desperately needed to remain 'home'. She had succeeded. The one pain she did not have to endure was that of having to send him to die anywhere else — even this hospice.

She wiped her eyes. Felt quieter. For the time being it was over. She was better able to save her bouts of grief for when she was on her own now, concerned above all not to distress the children. At the beginning, they had cried together — save for Felix, who had been too young to understand what had happened, and that had been nothing but good, she was sure. But after a few weeks, Sam did not cry at all, or if he did it was, like her, in private, and Hannah's tears, though they still came, were short-lived. Hannah responded to comfort, some cheerful words, an assurance that sadness about Chris's death was right and good, but that she did not have to feel guilty about allowing this sadness to pass.

'I don't think I'm worried about Hannah, you know,' Cat said, talking to Chris as she reversed out of the car park. She talked to him all the time, asked his advice, told him this or that, as easily as she had done when he had been physically present. She had often reassured bereaved patients that, no, they were not going mad, yes, of course it was fine to talk as if the person were still alive, it was a good thing — how could it be otherwise? She was taking her own advice. She had taken it when her mother had died too. Sometimes, even now, she caught herself asking Meriel Serrailler what she would do about a patient or a concern with one of the children.

'No,' she said now, 'it isn't Hannah, is it?

She'll be fine. Oh, Chris, it isn't Hannah, it's Sam, you know it's Sam. And I have no idea what to do about him.'

The streets were quiet. As she stopped at a traffic light a pair of girls ran across in front of her, miniskirts, high heels, bleach-blonde hair, and as Cat glanced after them, she saw two others on the far corner. Lafferton had never had a visible prostitute presence until the last year, but then the drug dealers had moved in from Bevham and started to target the clubs and pubs in the centre of town. There had always been a few, peddling in the underpass leading to the Sir Eric Anderson Comprehensive, but they had been small fry and local. The new ones were more serious dealers, linked together and also to trafficking. She looked at the girls again as they stood by a street lamp lighting cigarettes. They were probably no more than twenty, thin, hollow-eyed, their legs without tights under the short strips of skirt. Sexual disease. Drug-related illnesses. Every sort of violence. Even just exposure to the cold. Those were only a few of the risks they ran every night. But they went on running them, hooked on crack and heroin, or in thrall to the men who controlled them. The lights changed to green. Cat wanted to pull in, tell them to go home, protect them, but she knew it would do no good, they would be back in ten minutes unless she gave them money, which would go straight on the next fix. The street lighting threw hard shadows, but when they turned their faces to it, they were the faces of children.

'What should I do?' she asked Chris. 'Somebody needs to do something for them. Help me out here.'

When Simon got back she would talk to him. He was not directly involved with the vice squad but he had a vested interest in containing the drug and prostitute problem that was spreading so fast through Lafferton. He might know of initiatives that were taking shape.

She thought of Hannah, bright, chirpy, almost nine and living in a fluffy cloud of Barbie pink, in spite of her beloved father's death.

Hannah. Those girls had been Hannah when Hannah was born. She sped along the bypass towards the country road and home, anxious, angry and lifted for the time being out of grief.

Ground-floor lights were on in the farm-house, but the bedrooms were dark, the children long asleep. Judith had switched on the porch light to welcome her back.

Thoughtful, kind, practical Judith. Every Friday night for the past few months, when Cat was on call to the hospice, Judith had come over to help, hold the fort if she had to go in, or simply be company for her if she did not. She slept over. On Tuesday nights, when Cat went to the St Michael's Singers practice at the cathedral, the children went to Hallam House. Usually, Cat slept there too, after choir. It had helped. Her father, Richard Serrailler, never a natural family man, seemed surprisingly sanguine about both arrangements. His new marriage, which Cat welcomed and Simon still resented, had changed and softened him. But why? Cat asked herself again now, why was it so different with Judith from with her mother? She understood why Judith had had the effect she did, but not why her father and mother had been so distant from one another and, she now knew, so unhappy.

'Hi.'

Judith was curled up in her dressing gown watching the late news. 'Doom and gloom and pestilence,' she said, 'so I shouldn't think you want to watch.'

'No thanks. I feel like a drink — they won't call me out again tonight. Glass of wine?'

'I'd rather a whisky.'

Judith followed her into the warm kitchen, where the dishwasher was humming and the cat, Mephisto, had made the corner of the sofa his own. Nothing changes, Cat thought. Nothing changes. But everything has changed.

A finger painting was pinned on the cork noticeboard. F.E.L.I.X done in bright blue across the bottom. He could paint the letters of his name and Chris did not know, would never know, would not see this stage, or later his son's name written in pencil and then, gradually, other words and then paragraphs of writing, the small, brown-haired boy leaning over the paper, his hand moving carefully, his head the same shape as Chris's own head.

She drew in her breath.

Judith touched her arm briefly.

'He brought it home today,' Cat said. 'It's a JCB moving a dinosaur. I think.' She pulled the cork hard out of the wine bottle.

'How was IH?'

Cat shook her head. 'Cassie Porter,' she said, 'twenty-seven and she has Chris's sort of brain tumour.'

She sat down next to Mephisto and scratched his ears. The cat curled and uncurled his front claws briefly but did not deign to open an eye. Judith leaned against

43

the fridge, swirling the whisky round in her glass.

Judith did not mouth platitudes, did not try to give hope and consolation when they were not to be had. Her first husband, a medical colleague of Richard and Meriel's, had died suddenly while out fishing. She knew. She was probably the only one who had never said the wrong thing, or left the right one unsaid. Cat had liked her very much, before Chris was ill. Now, she loved her.

Simon, of course, thought differently. His attitude to Judith had got even worse since she and their father had married, and the fault was entirely his own. Whenever Cat thought about it, she forced the thought to swerve off the kerb of her anger and fall away. There was no room for it. Nothing else had ever cast a real shadow between her and her brother, nothing in their lives until this.

'This was always going to happen,' she said now. 'I don't think it makes any difference.'

'Of course not. You don't need a patient with a brain tumour to bring it all back.'

'If anything — it's better. Better walking in through the doors of Imogen House than walking into the surgery. Every day, in the surgery I see the door to Chris's room and the plate says Dr Russell Jones and I want to kick it down. Russell has rearranged things — of course he has, why wouldn't he? I want to scream at him to move it all back because it's pushing Chris out. It's making Chris not exist.' She gripped the stem of her glass. 'I know this isn't rational.'

'Since when did any of it have to do with reason?'

Cat leaned back and closed her eyes. This is what happened. Grief. Tears. Rage, sudden rage at what had happened. And then exhaustion as the wave rolled away, leaving her beached and drained of feeling.

'I've been thinking a lot about the practice,' she said after a moment. 'It hasn't got easier, it's got harder. I like Russell, he's a good doctor. He just isn't my sort of doctor, and general practice has changed so much. I don't feel part of it. But when I go into the hospice . . . the moment I walk through the doors something happens. I do feel a part. I feel I belong and I can still make a difference.'

'You make a difference as a GP. Don't underestimate yourself.'

The dishwasher had finished its load and stopped humming. The kitchen was quiet.

'When Chris died, I said I would keep

things ticking on. No big changes, no decisions. I think that was right. I couldn't have functioned at all if some of it hadn't been automatic. But now I'm not sure how much longer I'll want that — things just ticking on.'

'Follow your feelings.'

'Yes. My mother always said that.'

Judith smiled. 'By the way,' she said, 'Felix was sick.'

Cat groaned.

'And Hannah said she felt sick. I'm not entirely sure if she did.'

'Hmm. Sam?'

Judith frowned. 'No,' she said, 'Sam wasn't sick. And if he felt sick he didn't say so.'

Sam. More silent than ever. Closed within himself, oyster-like, private. Thin. Too thin.

'I wish I knew what to do,' Cat said. 'I can't make him talk — really talk. I can't get through to him at all. He lives like a sort of shadow in this house, he's here and yet somehow . . . he isn't. What did he do tonight?'

'Some homework. Maths. Watched *Doctor Who*. Then he went upstairs. I looked in after I'd sorted Felix out. He was lying on the bed with his book but I don't think he was reading. I asked him if he was all right and he said, "Yes, thank you, Judith," in that way he does — rather formal. I so wanted to go and give him a hug, Cat.'

'But you couldn't. I know. He prickles if you go too near.'

'I think so long as he knows that it's there when he wants it . . .'

'The hugs.'

'The hugs, the love. The listening. All of it. So long as he always knows.' Judith stretched. 'I'm going up. I put Felix's bedding through the wash and it's dry and folded. Hannah has a bowl by her just in case. I didn't dare suggest a bowl to Sam.'

'Thanks, Judith. I couldn't function without you.'

'As I said — don't underestimate yourself. Goodnight, my dear.'

Cat sat on, sipping her wine, stroking Mephisto. She felt peaceful. Wondered if any of her children would be sick in the night or if whatever bug Felix had brought home from nursery had run its course. Wondered if Cassie Porter would die tonight. Thought that soon she would change something, she would decide something.

Move on. She would never say it, never even think it. She would not move on, because moving on was moving away, from

Chris, from Chris's dying and death, from their life together, their marriage, the past, and how could she bear to do that? How could she leave Chris behind?

'No,' she said aloud, 'no. You'll come with me. You will be as close as breath for the next ten or twenty or fifty years.'

She realised suddenly that she could make changes and yet not move away, not leave him behind. The realisation made her smile.

Sometimes, when she asked Chris a question, the answer would come at once. She talked to him about Sam almost every day, told him what troubled her, asked him what he thought she should do, and now, locking the door and switching off the lights, 'putting the house to bed' as Hannah called it, she talked to him about it again. Sam. What to do, what to say, how to help him. Sam.

'He's always talked to Simon,' Chris said. She might as well have heard his voice, aloud in the quiet kitchen. *He's always talked to Simon.*

She stood still. 'Yes,' she said. 'You're right there.'

Sam might talk to Simon again. If he did, she would stop worrying.

If Simon were here.

FOUR

The worst thing you can do is run. That
warning floated in her head when she heard
the footsteps behind her, crossing the canal
bridge. 'The worst thing you can do is run.'
Who said that and why and were they right?
Why not run? Because in your high heels
you could slip over and fall? Because if you
run he'll run too, only he might run faster?

The other thing was: don't look round.
But when Abi got to the other side of the
bridge, she did look round and then she
groaned slightly, no longer from fear but
because of who it was, the last person she
needed. She wanted to get home. She'd got
nearly £200 in her pocket. She didn't need
this.

'Wait,' he said.

Beanie Man.

She hesitated. £200 could be £250 but
she hated him not having a car, or if he had
one, not letting them go in it, hated having

to go into one of the shelters on the rec or break into a shed on the allotments. Once, it had been the cemetery, the place where they put stuff, mowers and bins for dead flowers. She'd been scared witless, terrified he'd want them to lie on a grave. She had never been past the cemetery again.

Here, there were just wooden benches. It was cold. Too cold.

Beanie Man.

One of the girls had said he was mad, but Abi knew better, knew that it was an act. Sone punters did that. They put on an accent, Scottish or Irish, and they kept touching their hand to their face, half hiding it. As if you'd ever know them again in daylight, even if you walked into a shop where they stood behind the counter, or a pub where they were barman, or a bus and they were driving it. You didn't look at them, tried not to, you blotted them from your mind even when you were with them, they left no trace. Except Beanie Man, because he was never without the black wool beanie, pulled low over his forehead, even in summer. He tried to act daft, but you could see through the act like you could see through the Scottish and Irish voices. They were thinking: if you ever see me you haven't seen me, you don't know me. And you wanted to say: don't fucking flatter yourself.

'Abi.'

She stopped. There was a moon, washing the stone of the footbridge pale, making the canal black silk.

Abi shrugged. 'OK.'

She put the carrier bag with the box of tea bags in it on the ground under the bench.

Forty minutes later, letting herself in through the door of her room, she found Hayley smashed out on the bed and Liam throwing up for what looked like the twentieth time. She reached for the short bread tin on the top shelf, stuffed the money inside, put it back. The room smelled of dope and sick.

She went over and started to pull at Hayley, by the arms, by the hair, to shake her until she mumbled and sat up, eyes all over the place.

'Cow!' Abi screamed at her. 'Cow. What did you say, what did you promise me?'

'I'm OK, I'm OK.'

'You are — what about them? Liam's been sick everywhere, he's crying, he's filthy, he could have choked. Look at him.'

Hayley rolled off the bed and half knelt on the floor. 'I'm sorry, I'm OK, Abs, it's

OK . . .'

'Oh, get out, go on, leave Liam here, you're in no fit state.'

'I'm sorry, it's OK.'

'Shut up.'

The anger subsided as exhaustion hit her. But she cleaned Liam up, gave him a drink and an old clean T-shirt of her own to wear, then put him down again. His face was still white. Frankie and Mia had not stirred.

She undressed, sluiced her face and hands in cold water. She'd put money into the meter tomorrow.

'God, Hayley, I thought you wouldn't do this to me. Now sleep it off.'

She threw a cushion down. But it was cold. A cushion wasn't enough. She got up again and found the knitted blanket.

'Here.'

'Thanks. Thanks, Abs. I'm OK.'

Abi switched off the lamp and pushed her feet down into the bedclothes. It was only later, waking as a dawn like sour milk seeped into the room, that she remembered she had left behind the carrier with the tea bags.

FIVE

The last patient left and Bronwen, the duty receptionist, tapped on the surgery door and came in.

'Cat, here's that note from the orthopaedic consultant and I'll bring your coffee, only the thing is . . .'

Cat groaned. Her surgery had booked double the usual numbers, and there were seven patients to ring — Lafferton's norovirus epidemic was in full spate.

'I know, I know, but can you see one more?'

Bronwen had a sixth sense when it came to who to let in and who to send away, and Cat trusted it.

As the girl entered, carrying one child and leading another by the hand, Cat thought: I've seen you, I know you.

She glanced at her computer screen as the name and address came up, but they were not familiar.

'Abi Righton? Hello I'm Dr Deerbon. Come in.'

She was worryingly thin, pale with dark hollows under her eyes, bad skin. Her denim jacket, short skirt and trainers were not adequate for the bitter weather outside, but her children were well wrapped up.

The screen showed the record of her last visit, two years before, and to Chris.

The consultation was straightforward enough — both children had the winter vomiting bug, the boy an ear infection as well. The young woman got up.

'Thanks, Doctor, thank you. I'm sorry. I know I didn't have a proper booking, thanks. Say thank you, Frankie, you got medicine to make you better, go on . . .'

The boy looked unhappy and turned his head away.

'Frankie . . .'

'Don't worry. He's feeling rotten. Keep him indoors and warm, won't you?'

The girl heaved the now sleeping toddler onto her other arm and opened the door.

'Abi . . .'

She glanced round. It was a child's face, a prematurely old child, anxious, wary, masked in worldliness. But a child.

Cat remembered.

'Are you looking after yourself? I know

how it is when your children are ill . . . Are you eating properly?'

'I'm fine, I haven't had it, can't afford to, can I? Anyway, it's the kids get these bugs, it's all around them. He goes to a playgroup, he got it there.'

'You need to look after yourself as well, Abi.' She glanced at the white bare legs. 'Keep warm.'

Her eyes were defensive. 'I'm fine. Thanks anyway, Doc.' She sailed out, head up, the boy hanging on to her hand. Cat looked at the address. How had she got here? It was a good mile's walk from the bus route. She would have to get the child's medicine, trail home.

And it had been her, Cat was sure, crossing the road at the traffic lights, looking out for punters. Where had the children been then?

Bronwen's instinct had been right. Cat needed to have Abi Righton on her radar.

And the others, she thought, going through to the receptionist's office. Because there were others, too many others, on the streets, at risk.

'We don't know the half,' she muttered. Bronwen nodded, understanding, keeping her counsel.

Cat went back to her room, Abi Righton's notes were still up on the screen. They were sparse enough. Both children had been born in Bevham General and she had moved to her present address in the same month in which she last visited the surgery, when Chris had prescribed an antibiotic for a chest infection. She had attended the ante-natal clinic once only, the mother and baby clinic for immunisations, but not otherwise. It was a thin record but probably not one to ring any alarm bells. All the same, Cat picked up the phone.

'Lynne? It's Cat Deerbon. Can I just run a name past you?'

Lynne had been the practice health visitor for over nine years, until the team had been split up. She now worked with the other community nurses out of the social services department, her workload doubled, her colleagues fewer and mainly young and inexperienced.

She came back to the phone. 'Abi Righton doesn't ring any bells with me and there isn't anything on the SS register about her or her children. What's worrying you?'

'Nothing specific . . . just a hunch.'

'Usually worth following.'

'I know.'

'I'll make a note. I would say I'd call and see her but random visits for no reason aren't part of the job any more. How are you?'

'Fine,' Cat said. She wanted to mean it, did not want what Judith had once called a 'widowhood conversation'.

'You?'

'Counting the days.'

'Sorry?'

'I'm taking early retirement — didn't you know? Can't stand it any longer. Let's meet sometime. I have to go but I've flagged up Abi Righton on my system.'

'Thanks.'

Another one the NHS could ill spare, Cat thought, closing down her computer. Another reason for looking hard at where she herself stood. She picked up her list of visits. Once, she would have spent three hours or more on house calls, now they were discouraged as not cost-effective. Russell Jones did almost none, thought them rarely necessary. But the three elderly, frail patients she was going to see now would not dream of wasting her time, and would be better, emotionally as well as physically, for her visit. In her book, that was reason enough.

As she headed for the grid of streets known as the Apostles, though, it was Abi Righton who stuck in her mind. Abi Righton, thin, pale, malnourished, trying her best with her children, and working, Cat was sure, as a prostitute. It troubled her.

SIX

Abi had a cappuccino, Marie a strong tea. Frankie and Mia were asleep in the double buggy, Frankie still pale. She had given him the prescription medicine straight away, in the chemist, expecting him to throw it back up, but he had turned his face to the inside of the buggy and slept.

'There's a load of girls go to the new place,' Marie said, looking round Dino's, which was crowded, steamy and small. 'They meet up there, every morning nearly.'

Abi had seen them. The 'new place' was in the Lanes, dark wood tables and chairs and polished floors and about a hundred different kinds of coffee.

'Yeah, well, I don't know how they can afford it, believe me, two fifty, three quid a coffee? Anyway, I don't know them.'

'You do — there's Sandy, there's Melanie Liptrott, there's . . .'

Girls who had been in their year at the

Eric Anderson. Yes, she knew them. Only she didn't.

'Well, I like it here. You go if you want.'

Dino's was friendly. They didn't make you leave the buggy outside and the coffee was one pound ten a big mug. If the kids had toast or a bun, they'd get a drink free. Besides, nobody looked at you in Dino's.

The coffee machine hissed.

'Jonty's back,' Marie said.

Jonty. He beat Marie up, he drank, he did coke, he sent her out to work when she felt like death, he threw a fiver at her and expected a three-course dinner every night for a week out of it. He'd been inside twice since she'd met him five years before. He was a lowlife and if he was at the caravan Abi wouldn't go there because he tried it on with her if Marie turned her back.

'I'm not saying anything.'

'It was one in the morning, it was pissing with rain. What was I supposed to do, tell him to sleep in the ditch?'

'Yes.'

'He's not that bad.'

'Yes, he is, Marie, he *is* that bad. What are you thinking? Is your mother there as well?'

'No. She's not been back for weeks.' Marie stirred more sugar into her dark tea. 'Probably dead and a fat lot I care.'

Her mother was a drunk and a junkie and another one sponging off Marie, but harmless next to Jonty.

'Not your mother, Marie,' Abi said. 'You don't mean that.'

'You don't know anything.'

'I know one thing. I'm getting out of it.'

'Out of what?'

Abi turned to check on the buggy. Frankie had pulled the blanket up over his face.

'What're you on about?'

'What the fuck do you think?'

'Oh. Yeah, right.'

'I mean it.'

'Course you do. And then what? Get a proper job?'

'Maybe. Maybe go to college.'

Marie spluttered so that the mouthful of tea sprayed over her coat and the table.

'Why shouldn't I do that? I got four GCSEs, didn't I?'

'Listen,' Marie put her hand briefly on top of Abi's own until Abi pulled it back. 'College costs money, and what would you do with the kids? College isn't for people like us.'

'Speak for yourself.'

'I do. And for you.'

'There's a nursery. They look after them there.'

'What, free?'

Abi bent her head and stared into her mug because she had no answers and because she wasn't about to let Marie make her feel stupid. She didn't know how much it cost or if the kids could go to the college nursery or what she would do even supposing she got in, she hadn't made plans like that, you couldn't, you didn't.

'Here, did you know they raided a house in Bevham? Took loads of girls and then they went on to another, some flat, got the pimps, well, a couple of them. Dawn raid. It was on the news, cops battering the door down and yelling. Everybody yelling.'

Abi raised her head. 'So maybe we get our streets back for a bit, till they ship in another load of illegals and it all starts over.'

Frankie woke, and as he woke, let out a wail and flailed his arm across Mia's face so that she wailed as well.

'I better go.'

'See you later.'

'Maybe. I dunno. I don't want to leave these two with Hayley, I can't trust her.'

'You got someone else lined up?'

'I told you —' Abi manoeuvred the buggy in the small space between the tables — 'I'm packing it in.'

Marie looked at her, her face half a sneer,

half a question.

'See you,' she said.

Abi slammed the café door without responding, but Marie was peering through the window, wiping the steam away with her arm. Staring.

'I mean it,' Abi mouthed at her.

She stopped to pull the blanket round the kids, wipe Mia's mouth.

It was as if saying it could make it happen, which it couldn't, but it could make her listen to herself and try to believe it.

When she got back, she'd check the money and then she'd take half and put it in the post office, now, today. She had said she would give it up, always said so, and meant it, only somehow, now, she meant it more.

It had started to rain. She pulled up the collar of her denim jacket and walked faster. Frankie was grizzling. The buggy didn't have a cover and the blanket would be soaked by the time they got back, but she knew there was over an hour left on the electric, she could put the fan heater on to dry things.

Abi felt a dart of something run through her, something she recognised after a moment as a sort of excitement. It caught her off guard. She had glimpsed something ahead of her, something about her future. Let Marie think what she wanted.

SEVEN

June Petrie had an irritating habit of whistling slightly under her breath to signal the start of coffee and tea breaks, and the lunch hour. It was perfectly possible that she did not know she was doing it, and more than likely that she had no idea how close Leslie Blade sometimes came to attacking her because of it.

Usually he went outside to eat or, if it was raining, to the staffroom. But once the college heating went on in the middle of October, he took his lunch box down into the basement stacks, where the pipework warmed the whole area and he was usually undisturbed. But occasionally, because the lunch break was staggered, other librarians had to come down in search of a book, even among the old stock that was housed here, and then he felt acutely self-conscious, found sitting on a high stool with his sandwiches and fruit and plastic cup of tea spread out on the ledge in front of him. The basement windows were always slightly grimy, but they only looked onto a side alley leading to the stores. He was perfectly happy with that, not wanting a view as he ate and read his paper. When librarians came, they never spoke to him. They walked along until they had located the required book and then walked out again.

Only June Petrie sometimes came, not to find a book, but to find him and only June Petrie whistled so irritatingly under her breath.

'Mind if I join you, Leslie?'

Yes, he thought. Yes, I mind, yes, yes, yes, and yes, stop whistling under your breath, yes, yes.

'Of course.'

Meaning, of course I mind, but that was not how she chose to take it.

She settled down at the bench, exuding her lunch vapours of Bovril and cheese.

'Tuna?'

Leslie nodded.

'I don't care for fish.'

How often had she said it? How often had he promised himself that if she said it again he would kill her?

He smiled slightly and turned the page of his newspaper. But she had ruined that too.

She opened a packet of crisps and now the smell of chemical onion puffed out.

'I wanted to catch you because we had a committee meeting last night to vote on the final choice.'

He turned his head away from the onion smell.

'It's *The Mikado*! I can't tell you how pleased I am. There was a strong movement for *Ruddigore* on the grounds that it wasn't often done, but there is a very good reason why. It isn't often done because it isn't really very good.'

'No?'

'Not one of the best by a long chalk.'

Where did that come from? He stopped reading about the plans to convert the Old Gaol into workshops to go over it in his mind. *Not by a long chalk.* Sport, it must come from sport, surely.

'Anyway, it isn't *Ruddigore,* it's *The Mikado.*'

Or some old taproom term? Chalk marks on beer barrels? Why did he think it might be that?

He took the second half of his tuna sandwich out of the polythene bag and bit neatly into it.

'You know, you really should join us, Leslie. I've been saying it for ages I know, but with *The Mikado* coming up I don't see how you can bear to refuse.'

'I did see it once,' he said. 'Some years ago now.'

'And?'

'I'm afraid I remember very little about it, June.'

'But you enjoyed it?'

'I don't remember that either.'

'Of course you did. How could anybody not enjoy *The Mikado*? Once you heard the tunes again it would all come back to you. Do think about it, Leslie.'

'I can't sing. I've said so before. I can't sing. Or play any instrument. What use would I be?'

'There are plenty of jobs backstage. We always need extra hands.'

Why did she do this to him? Twice a year, it seemed, she sought him out in these book stacks, barging in on his lunch hour, to try and persuade him to join the Lafferton Savoyards, choosing to forget that he told her each time that he could not sing or play an instrument and did not wish to lug scenery.

'You do need to get out, have a life, you know.'

She had a small, pale mole on the side of her nose. He would have liked to take a

68

razor blade to it, slice it off, watch the blood flow.

He turned the page of his newspaper but he had come to Classifieds and Property.

'I have a perfectly happy life, thank you.'

'Meet new people.'

She didn't listen. She never listened. He could have used a chain of obscenities, shouted them into her face one after the other, and she would wait until he had paused and then continue, telling him that his mother would be glad if he joined something, she could surely not expect him to give up a social life for her. June Petrie had made it her business to find out as much as she could about him and about his mother, dripping small questions like drops onto a stone over the months and years, wearing him down.

Well, she had found out little enough.

'You might have a voice, anyway. You don't know till you try. You might surprise yourself.'

He folded the empty sandwich bag and took out a small bunch of seedless grapes. June Petrie ate the last of her onion crisps, making a loud rasping sound.

Today, tomorrow, or the next day, he would kill her.

'You know where we are, the Baptist Hall.

You know where that is.' It was not a question. 'Thursdays at seven, until it gets nearer the production, then it's Thursdays and Fridays.'

Leslie stood up. He folded his paper. He crunched down viciously on the last grape.

'Then I'm afraid that's that, June,' he said. 'I'm busy every Thursday and Friday evening. What a pity.'

She came fast behind him, down the stacks, through the swing doors, up the concrete staircase. She would not do so yet, but before long Leslie Blade knew that she would ask him, in some roundabout way, what exactly it was that he did, where he went, every Thursday and Friday evening. He smelled the onion crisps as she panted up the stairs. He could make one slight move, turn sharply and push. He pictured it, her soft marshmallow body tumbling backwards down the flight of concrete to the bottom.

She had started to whistle 'A Wandering Minstrel' softly, under her breath.

EIGHT

Dear Cat

I'm sorry it's been so long and I feel bad about that, and about simply disappearing and not telling anyone what I was doing and why. But the truth is, I didn't know myself. I was confused and uncertain and I couldn't talk about it. In the end, I decided I needed to get right away so I came here — a remote and very strange and beautiful part of Nepal and an orphanage in the foothills of the mountain range. (See enclosed photo.) I am helping generally, teaching a little, spending much time in thought and self-assessment and prayer, and also exploring as much as I can — places, people, culture, life — it is all so totally unlike anything I have ever experienced.

I felt very constrained in Cambridge, and didn't quite know which way to turn. I was enjoying my own work but found college life claustrophobic. And where else could I have gone? Not back to London, and the convent wasn't right — it for me or me for it. And I knew really that this sort of personal chaos — emotional and career was a hopeless place from which to launch into a relationship. Simon's life and mine were never going to be anything but parallel, there seemed no real meeting points. I don't think I was ever what he wanted and, I am sure, not what he needed.

I wish it had been different. I do miss England and I so miss my friends. My address is below. I can't email as there is no connection but letters do arrive, if a little unpredictably, so I would love news of you and the children. I hope you are finding things easier, and I hope you are all right, though of course you cannot be. I think of you and you are in my prayers, and I send love.

Jane

Cat turned the photograph to the light. Snow-capped mountains. Mist. A few bent trees lower down the slopes. A pinkish light. Beautiful. Jane Fitzroy had simply evaporated from their lives for half a year —

Cambridge said they had no forwarding details — and now she had reappeared here, in this remote, exotic and rather random place.

Cat shook her head. Jane was right, she and Simon would never have worked, if she was as unsettled and undecided as this — one minute a chaplain, then living among nuns, then doing medieval theology in a Cambridge college, but always unsure if this was 'it', the thing she most desired, the round hole into which she might fit, or if she was destined to be a square peg yet again. Whether she had loved Si or he her, Cat had no idea. They had seemed in some vague sense to be right together but Jane had too much baggage, life baggage, faith baggage and emotional baggage. Simon had the last. He did not need someone as complicated and unpredictable as Jane.

Cat set down the photograph. She would send a postcard — Lafferton Cathedral, a reminder, a bit of the past — but she did not feel able to write anything too personal or too revealing. Besides, she did not think that was what Jane wanted. Perhaps Jane would find herself in Nepal — how many had tried? But probably not, Cat thought. She was the kind of person who might walk into the farmhouse next week asking how one became a doctor.

Or not.

She put the card into a pigeonhole in her desk, wondering if Simon knew about Nepal, guessing not, unsure if he would even be interested. Jane Fitzroy was not a subject she had been able to broach with him.

The farmhouse was quiet, the older two children at school, Felix upstairs having his nap. Cat had cut down her GP work to three days, extended her hospice hours and hoped to do more, but before she did so she needed to do a further specialist course in palliative medicine. She should find out more about what that would entail, when, where, how — and could not summon up the energy to do so. Bereavement, she had discovered, was about many things, but one of those, and the one which few people seemed to know or warn about, was a long-lasting, overwhelming physical and mental tiredness. Even now, a year after Chris's death, she felt exhausted for much of the time, with an exhaustion that seemed to be bone-deep and to bear no relation to whatever else she might have been doing or even to how much sleep she got. To start researching courses in palliative care, filling in application forms, reorganising her life around it, she needed an alertness and an energy she never seemed able to summon.

Now though, she said, now, today. She switched on her computer. Outside, the autumn sun was bright, the sky brittle blue, the branches of the oak tree tinged with yellow.

Today. She would start to look. Focus. Concentrate. After she had checked her emails she would make a start.

From aisling.petty@laffertoncathedral.org.

Dear Cat

Canon Hurley asks if you could possibly make 4pm on the 3rd, for the first meeting of the Magdalene Group? If so, please note that the meeting will now be in the Precentor's House. Would you kindly let me know if this date / time are convenient for you?

Many thanks.
Aisling

There were a couple of other work-related messages to which she replied. Emptied the washing machine and put in another load. Made fresh tea. 'Displacement activity,' she said aloud. But why? She had got as far as this — why was she avoiding the next step?

75

Because it was just that, a step, a step forwards, a step into the future, a step in the dark, a step into the unknown. All of those. A step further away from the way life had been. From Chris. She did not want to take that step.

'Come on,' Chris said, 'do it. I'm telling you.'

She took the tea back to her desk.

King's College London
MSc, Diploma and Certificate in Palliative Care
Course booklet in PDF format

She clicked to start the download.

NINE

Frankie had gone from white, floppy and silent to roaring round the room like a tank. The medicine had worked. It was Mia who was quiet now, having been sick three times. Abi sat with her on her lap watching an old video of *Bagpuss,* which had been her own. There was a little pile of them on the window ledge, along with half a dozen books she'd loved, kept and taken with her from flat to flat. Mia was hot and sticky.

'Frankie, quit pulling the curtain, you'll have it down. Come and watch this and sit still, you'll be sick again.' But he wouldn't. He was made of cast iron.

She could've done with those tea bags now. Lurky Les. He'd probably be round tonight as well with his sandwiches and cakes, trying to make conversation, asking them stuff. Hayley said he was weird, Marie said he was bonkers, some of the others laughed at him. Abi wasn't sure. He gave her the creeps and she wondered what he got out of it, why he did it, if he was lonely or religious or what. The Reachout van people were religious but they didn't push it at you. There were leaflets and posters in the van but nobody preached. Loony Les — they had plenty of names for him — was always alone. So why'd he come, bringing the sandwiches? Why buy her a box of tea bags?

Frankie was making a high noise, partly a whistle, partly a screech.

'I said, pack that IN.'

He went on.

It was boys, everyone said that, you couldn't do anything with them, they got out of control, they were like permanently revved-up engines, even at this age. When Frankie was born she'd been depressed for two days, wanting a girl if she'd wanted anything, wondering how she'd cope. Yet Frankie was the soft one too, the one who crept into her bed and put his arms round her neck, the one who always offered her half his sweets or his biscuit.

He'd roar round like this but then he'd crash. He was still pale. She knew the signs.

It didn't matter because she wasn't going out, even if Hayley turned up. She couldn't forgive Hayley for getting stoned when she had all three kids, couldn't stop imagining what might have happened. They had an agreement, it had been solid, and Abi had trusted her. Abi wouldn't even have drunk a glass of beer when it was her turn and Hayley went out to work. She felt betrayed and let down, furious whenever she remembered. The trouble was, she couldn't leave Frankie and Mia alone, and who else was there? It had been a good arrangement with Hayley, suited them both, meant they could both of them work enough and the kids were all safe. Now what?

The wind-up music was playing at the end of the video and Mia was slumped and heavy in sleep on her lap. Abi carried her to the bed and laid her carefully down as her mobile beeped.

CU soon. H xx.

As if nothing had bloody happened then. She replied. *Don't bother.*

But by the time she had washed out Mia's sicky clothes and started to cook sausages and toast, Hayley was up the stairs and in the room, shoving a bunch of garage flowers at her and trying to give her a hug.

'God in heaven, Abs, it won't ever happen again, hope to die. It never will.'

Liam was already down on the mat with

Frankie and two beaten-up metal cars, both of them making motor noises.

'Shut up, you'll wake Mia.'

'I don't know what I was thinking and I was out of order, but give us a break, Abs, nothing happened, did it? I was fine.' Hayley took out the toast and started to scrape butter onto it.

'Get your mitts off.'

'Oh, come on, I'm starving, Liam's starving, we've got nothing to eat, Abi.'

'Don't give me that. I know you, I know what you spent it on.' She snatched the toast out of Hayley's hand.

'Cow.'

'Right.'

The room smelled of frying sausages and she went to open the window and put the shoe in to keep it propped up. Hayley stood miserably staring at the toaster.

They'd been here before enough times, Hayley without ten pence, Abi feeding her and Liam. But it had been the other way too, when Abi had been ill and couldn't work for two weeks and Hayley had helped her out with money and taken the kids off her hands. That had been last winter, when Hayley had been clean for four months, even started saving a bit. They'd talked about getting a decent flat together, two bedrooms, a garden for the kids. They'd laughed.

'Oh, Christ. Frankie, get up to the table and eat this. Liam as well.'

Abi shook the ketchup bottle and tipped it upside down. Behind her, Hayley was putting more bread in the toaster.

Abi sighed.

'It'll be OK, Abs,' Hayley said.

'Will it?'

Abi walked out and down the corridor to the shared toilet. But she knew that, for now, Hayley meant it. It would be all right. She'd scared herself. She'd look after the kids properly tonight, no problem, and for the next few times, weeks maybe, till it all started up again. It was a risk but Abi knew she'd have to take it. She always did.

When she got back, Hayley had put the rest of the sausages on and cracked two eggs into a cup. Frankie and Liam were throwing bits of chewed-up toast at each other.

'Happy fucking families,' Abi said.

In the end, though, it was Hayley who went out because both Frankie and Mia were sick again.

After she'd gone, Abi opened the window and leaned out, smelling the night. It was colder. She was not looking forward to

81

winter, when the punters got fewer and the streets were bleak, but this was the last one, she told herself, the last winter. She'd go to the post office tomorrow, put more money away.

Liam was asleep wrapped in the old blanket, Mia too, but Frankie came crying to her, pale again and miserable. She picked him up and closed the window to keep him warm, then sat in the armchair with him until he too slept and the room went quiet. Occasionally, there was a racket from somewhere else in the house, someone shouting or dropping something, sometimes a car went by. But even that all settled eventually, so that Abi was left listening to the soft sounds of the three children breathing and stirring and mumbling now and again, and thinking about Hayley, out on the street.

TEN

The dawn was coming up a little later every day now but it was still the same soft, pearl-coloured light that sifted gently in through the window. He never drew the curtains and the bed faced the gentle slope of shingle that ran down to the silver water and the huge pale sky. Serrailler wondered how he could ever have woken to anything else.

He turned slightly. Her bare shoulder was towards him, her hair fanned out finely against the pillow.

She must have sensed him looking at her. She stirred slightly, murmured, turned. 'What time —'

'Twenty past six.'

'Christ!' She shoved back the duvet. 'The boat'll be here in half an hour, I've got to move. I said not to let me sleep in.'

'I don't call twenty past six "sleeping in".'

But Kirsty McLeod was already on her way to the shower. Simon rolled onto his back and crossed his arms behind his head, propping himself up to look at the water, and at the heads of two seals which were bobbing close to the shore.

He had been on Taransay for six weeks and it felt like half a lifetime, remote from everything and everyone, in its own time that was somehow out of time. It had taken two days and a night of driving, a ferry and then a helicopter to get here, and it seemed as if he had fallen off the edge of the world. The last SIFT job he'd headed up had been exhausting, draining, terrifying and ultimately successful, but when he'd got back to his own CID the Chief Constable had taken one look at him and told him to take some leave.

'Five young men were brutally murdered, one of them in front of you, Simon. You've been living like a rat in a sewer for weeks, you've been short of sleep and in some danger, and if your nerves aren't in shreds they damn well ought to be. I'm extremely proud that you belong to us and you've done an amazing job, but I don't want you back on my force until you've had a proper break. That's an order.'

Sitting in the Chief's office, he had suddenly felt all the wind go out of him, and as if he might be about to faint, throw up or burst into tears. Paula Devenish was right. He needed to get away. He had spent half an hour on the Internet tracking down this small, isolated cottage on the remotest Scottish island he could find, booked it, packed and set off. He had brought a single bag of old, rough, favourite clothes, some books and his rucksack of pencils, pens, inks and sketch pads. He had even thought of leaving behind his phone, but only for a moment — work wouldn't call him, but family might. No one else. He had recently changed the number.

Kirsty was out of the shower, still damp, pulling on jeans, shirt and sweater which had been thrown across the back of the chair. He watched her. Thick, light brown hair with a deep wave at the end. Long legs. Blue eyes. A laughing face. That was what he had first noticed. A laughing face. She tied her hair up quickly in an elastic band.

'See you,' she said. She did not come over, did not kiss him goodbye, just waved and was out the door.

A minute later, Simon got up and went to the window, but by then, Kirsty McLeod was halfway up the track and away. In fifteen minutes she would be at the small cluster of houses, pub, shop and quay that was Taransay Village. Other than that, the islanders were scattered in single cottages and small houses across the island, overlooking other stretches of water, different fields and tracks, and the low violet and brown hills.

Kirsty was in a rush because the weekly ferry was due in with supplies and mail, and she was an essential hand, needed to carry boxes and crates from the boat to the one small hotel-cum-pub and the shop, in both of which she worked.

Kirsty McLeod. Serrailler shook his head, smiling, and wandered into the neat, small kitchen to make coffee.

There were virtually no trees on the island, which took the winds from all corners of the earth, so he did not have the usual markers for the onset of autumn, but the light had changed subtly, and everything seemed to be slowing gradually, like a creature moving towards a long winter. Not that anything ever moved quickly on Taransay. Life was lived at a steady, measured pace, quite different from the one he was used to; people did not hurry and there was little noise other than the sounds of nature. For the first few days here he had slept, taking sleep in great draughts like cool water after a drought, and had soon lost much sense of time and the progress of the weeks. Coming to, he had wondered briefly if he would become bored or restless. He need not have worried. He slipped into the life and the pace and floated on its surface, never for a moment missing anything about his usual life, other than his family. He sometimes woke late, sometimes early, sometimes went to bed before nine, hardly able to remain upright, sometimes went out walking on the shore at three in the morning. He ate and drank when he felt like it. And then, going across to the village pub for supper one evening, he had met Kirsty McLeod.

It was the most uncomplicated relationship he had had since the early days of Diana — more so because Kirsty had made it clear that she was not likely to fall in love with him and certainly would not want to follow him when he left the island for home. She was a local girl but she had left to study biology at the University of Glasgow, stayed to do teacher training and worked in schools in the city for three years before realising that she was homesick at too deep a level to stay away any longer. She had returned to the island to help the various members of her family run the hotel, pub and shop, and, more recently, had taken a business studies course online. She was no fool, she was even-tempered, cheerful, pretty, without baggage and they had fallen into an easy friendship. But it had been Kirsty who'd stepped the friendship up a level when she'd appeared at the cottage late one night.

Simon enjoyed having her in his bed, liked her company, found her straightforwardness and slight stubbornness attractive. But that was all. It was all for her, too. The whole thing worked pleasantly and easily, and when he eventually went home, it would end in the same spirit. He had found out, in any case, that a farmer on the other side of the island regarded Kirsty as his own for the future, if not just for the present, and Simon guessed that he was right — when Kirsty was ready to settle she would do so with Douglas and that would be for the best too.

He opened the cottage door and wandered out onto the strip of thin grass which was all the place boasted as a garden. From here there was an uninterrupted view down to the water. The seals had gone but they would reappear later, sleek dark heads surfacing and diving. There was barely a line between sky and sea and little colour but different washes of grey, soft brown, faded green.

He had spent hours walking about the island, sitting on outcrops of rock to draw the landscape, the hills, the bobbing heads of the seals, cormorants, gulls, divers. He had brought back sheeps' heads picked bare and whitened by the wind and salt air, strangely shaped stones and pieces of driftwood, and had drawn those, sitting in the clear light at the table in the window, or, when it was warm enough and not too windy, outside. His drawing books were almost full.

He had met a few people, enjoyed his trips to the pub, bought what he needed from the shop, and avoided the visitors. Taransay was a paradise for birdwatchers and walkers, but had little else to offer. The cottages dotted about the island, like this one, were rented out for five months of the year — otherwise, the island was too difficult to get to, too bleak and windswept.

It was the end of September. He had another week, though he could extend the rental for as long as he chose, but he knew he wouldn't enjoy a winter here even if he could stay. The Chief had been generous with the leave but he would not take advantage of that, though there were days when he was so content to sit in the open air, eating a sandwich, drawing, happy in his own

89

company, that he wondered how he could go back.

He had had the time, space and solitude to clear his head as well as sleep away months of exhaustion, and, equally important, to think about his life — whether he still wanted to do his job, as a DCS and as head of the Special Incident Flying Task-force, whether he wanted to try and take up again from where he had left off with Jane Fitzroy — wherever that had been. When he had first arrived on Taransay both had seemed complex, difficult areas of life, but, to his surprise, they had sorted themselves out rather quickly. He did want to carry on with his job. He enjoyed it, he was still challenged by it, he found it satisfying. He would never be content as a full-time professional artist, though by now he could have become one — the London gallery wanted to mount a new exhibition of his work, he was illustrating a private press book, and he had more than enough plans for what he wanted to do next, after he had sorted out the Taransay drawings. But he needed the other half of his life, the balance of the two, he was quite sure of that now. And Jane he would not see again. Jane had too many uncertainties and anxieties And, increasingly, he felt that he would never need, want or find a lasting close relationship. The Kirsty Mcleods of this world suited him fine.

When Kirsty had discovered what his job was she had shrugged and said 'Great', but shown no real interest, asked no questions — that was refreshing too. 'You'd have nothing to occupy you here,' was the only other thing she had said. It was true. Taransay was crime-free and only boasted occasional visits from the police during the season. They checked gun licences but were otherwise severely underworked.

An hour later, he walked down to the village. The wind had got up again, pushing at his back. He would find that tiresome through a long winter, the moaning and battering of the gale as it scoured the island for weeks on end.

The ferry had come in, the only contact with the outside world other than a small passenger helicopter which came twice weekly in the summer. Serrailler had a friend from training days who was now heading up the local force on the mainland and had called in a favour, to get his car mothballed at the police station pound while he was on Taransay. He would fly back soon, to pick it up and start the long drive home.

But for now, there might be mail and he needed bread, eggs and coffee. As he neared the landing stage he saw Kirsty carrying a couple of large cartons off the boat and offered to help her.

'I'm fine,' she said, laughing, 'you just get the next one.'

He joined the others who were unloading, lifted a heavy box of groceries and headed across the shingle to the post office and shop.

There was no mail for him. He had hardly had any during his stay, and that suited him perfectly well. In any case, though there was no mobile phone signal here, Taransay, like many other remote places, had been parachuted into modern life and global communication with the arrival of wireless broadband. He had come down to the café a couple of times a week to access emails, mainly from Cat, though quite often from Sam too, and once or twice from his father. He had even received a flurry of them from his brother Ivo, who was a flying doctor in the Australian outback. Ivo wrote no letters, only the very occasional laconic postcard. His emails were equally terse but they were often funny, and Simon realised that he'd had more communication with his triplet during his weeks in the distant Scottish isles than he'd had for years.

But it was Cat he needed to keep close to him, Cat about whom he worried. He had been so concerned about how Chris's death had hit her, how she would cope, he had almost decided not to come here at all. She had been the one to push him into it, insist that he needed the long break, and of course she had been right but it didn't stop him worrying. Physically, managing work and family, she would be fine — she was competent, she would grit her teeth and get on with it, and she had plenty of friends and willing help. She also had Judith, with whom she had formed a close bond that Simon should not have resented — but did. But emotionally, he knew, Cat was only just holding herself together, was more vulnerable than she would admit. He was the one to whom she always turned.

He spent the next half-hour helping to unload the ferry, then got a mug of coffee and paid for access to one of the Island Café's two computers. The shop was busy and noisy, the café quiet.

From
samuelchristopherdeerbon@hotmail.com

I am sending this from the school computer in lunch hour. Thanks for the pictures of the island. I wish I could come up theyre and see you. Im OK, school is OK. I have not been picked for the rugby or soccer teams but I don't mind. I am liking hockey which I didnt play b4. Cricket is better. If you go to the Scottish island again can I come with you? I miss talking to you about things. I miss you being here, when are you coming home? Have you been fishing if so what kind of fish? I am reading a very good book called Northern Lights. Did you know the other name for Northern Lights was aurora borealis? Can you see those on your island?

Love from Sam.
PS Hannah still likes puke pink everything. Judith bought her a puke pink new bed-cover. It is puke.
PPS I really wish you were here.

There were no other messages.

Simon spent the rest of the day on the other side of the bay, drawing two of Taransay's ancient cairns and the hollowed-out section of rock behind them, which had been excavated a few years previously and found to be an Iron Age burial site. It was windy but he was well sheltered. He had been here several times, trying to capture the roughness and textures on the stones, the intricate overgrowth of lichens, the shading of the ground. There seemed to be so little in this bleak landscape and yet, the more closely he looked, the more detail he saw.

He was only stopped by a great sweeping veil of rain that soaked him before he had gone fifty yards. It was forty minutes of hard slog back to the cottage. The sea was whipped up to a frenzy, the sky pewter. He changed, had a shower and lit the fire. Rain and wind hurled themselves at the stone walls and made a drumbeat on the roof. He stretched out on the sofa in front of the blaze and picked up an old John le Carré novel which someone had left behind. He had first read *Tinker, Tailor, Soldier, Spy* twenty years ago, when what had seemed to matter was the story that he had raced through to reach its denouement. Now, what delighted him was the prose, the sense of place, the richness of a text which he had not appreciated before.

He was still on the sofa, book on the floor and the fire burnt down to a small red core, when Kirsty McLeod came banging in and woke him just after six. She bore a wide smile and a small carrier bag containing two large steaks. An hour later, Serrailler wondered why he had thought he might ever leave Taransay at all.

ELEVEN

There was no light on in the caravan but Jonty Lewis kicked at the door anyway. He knew she'd be in there. It was too early for her to be working and she didn't have many other places to go. But it was several seconds before she answered and by then he'd kicked harder.

'For Christ's sake, do you have to do that?' Marie stood back to let him shove his way past her into the dingy space. She'd tried to make it like a home, put curtains at the windows and a weird-looking plant on the cruddy work surface, and there were some cushions on the bench that did for a seat. But it was still a manky caravan.

He pulled open cupboard doors above his head and slammed them shut.

'Stop doing that, will you? I haven't got any bottles — you want to bring your own.'

He switched on the television which sat above the worktop. The picture was fuzzy but he sat down and started watching anyway.

'I could do with a brew.'

'Brew it then.'

But when he caught Marie's eye, she put the kettle on the hob, not wanting to start anything, which with Jonty was never difficult.

She had the beginning of a cold, her mother was still on the run which meant she had the van to herself, and she had planned to lie down under her blankets and watch both episodes of *Corrie* and *EastEnders*. She had a boil-in-the-bag curry and a block of Galaxy. She was sorted.

Only now he was here, sprawling his legs out, tripping her up, filling the small space. But she was frightened enough of him to say nothing. She handed him his mug of tea and found a half-packet of Custard Creams.

'When you going out?' he asked, looking at the screen. The voices and the laughter coming out of it were fuzzy like the picture.

'I'm not.'

He looked at her then, a long, steady expressionless look, dunking his biscuit as he did so.

'I was out last night and my throat's sore.'

'Sounds all right to me.'

'Yeah, well, it doesn't feel all right.'

'When'd a sore throat stop anyone?'

She hesitated, wondering if she would bother making herself tea and deciding against it. She just stood, staring out of the plastic window into the darkness.

'I need to pay someone,' Jonty said.

His dealer. There was never anyone else he had to pay.

She said nothing.

'Or else I won't get any gear.'

She wondered if anything was beyond the window in the dark field. Rabbits or a fox or someone's cat. Funny thing, but she was never bothered here on her own at night, though she put the bar on the caravan door. She was more bothered by having him here.

'So get yourself done up. I'll mind the van.'

Marie shivered. She would have to go. The best she could hope to do was keep some money back for herself, but most of it she'd have to hand over. When Jonty was around he called the shots, he was the one she worked for. She remained looking into the darkness, thinking about what Abi had said — that she was getting out, saving up, looking to the future, this was the last year. She wouldn't make it of course, none of them ever did. Marie would watch her struggle and sink under, watch her kids go into care and her hopes blotted out. All the same, she wished she had some of Abi's guts even to think of it, make the plans in her head that were never going to come to anything. Because the difference between them was that she had long since given up on anything except getting from one day to the next and sometimes dreaming that Jonty Lewis would be found dead in a ditch with his head kicked in.

He had turned up the television. The hissing, crackling laughter blasted out of the set and filled the fetid space inside the van, along with the sound of him slurping tea. He had finished the biscuits.

She went to the cardboard box where she kept her clothes. She couldn't wait to get out after all.

It was a busy night. By half past eleven she had been picked up by four punters, the last of whom must have been high on something, though he hadn't seemed it, because he gave her £90. She stood on the corner at the top of Old Ribbon Street. It was mild. There was a moon. Traffic was quiet. But it didn't matter, she'd earned plenty. She'd go back. The only thing stopping her was that Jonty would be there, feet up, guzzling everything there was to guzzle, filling the van with smoke, and waiting. If she had a place she could stash the extra money she'd do that, but there was nowhere that someone wouldn't find. A couple of other girls had been out working but she wouldn't trust them, and anyway, they'd gone now. The road was empty.

She started to walk, not going down onto the canal towpath and over the bridge, which was the short cut, but sticking to the main route. Abi said the only thing to worry about on the towpath was if it was muddy and you slipped, or if you met Beanie Man, but it bothered Marie. She would walk the long way, round by the Hill. A car slowed beside her but she kept her head down and the collar of her anorak up and walked faster. The car drove off. She'd had enough tonight. But then, she'd always had enough. Which one of them hadn't? But which of them could get out, even Abi and her great ideas?

It was as she crossed over to the road that ran alongside the Hill that Marie heard something behind her. She looked round quickly, thought she saw something, a shadow or a movement, but when she stood still, there was nothing. Moonlight and an empty road. Someone went by on a scooter, buzzing like a gnat.

She walked on fast. But then it was a definite sound, footsteps, someone running to catch her up, and as she glanced over her shoulder again and saw a figure, she remembered where she was. The Hill. People had been caught and murdered on the Hill, a serial killer had made it a place of danger for months until he was tracked down, and then he had come to the Hill and found a tree on which to hang himself. It had all happened before she came to Lafferton but she'd heard about it often enough and now the thought of it made her blood freeze. She didn't know why. She told herself it was not only ages ago but the man was dead — not even in jail and alive somewhere, stone-cold dead. He couldn't hurt her or anyone else.

But the person following her could. He had not overtaken her, he was not someone making quickly for home, with no interest in her. He was there, keeping behind, and nobody else was in sight or earshot. To her left reared up the dark outline of the Hill; to her right, the railings of the park. Houses were on the far side of that — she could not even see any lights, people had gone to bed by now.

She prayed for someone to drive by, for the gnat whine of the scooter, a late-night van, even a police patrol, even just one person walking a dog last thing.

But there was no one, except whoever was now a couple of yards behind her and closing in. She could hear breathing, a soft pant, in and out, in and out. Quiet footsteps. Marie broke into a run. The footsteps behind her quickened too.

But then a car came, from the opposite direction, its headlights picking her up in a wide and welcoming arc of brightness.

In the caravan, Jonty Lewis found a single can of cider, drank it standing up, then smashed the can against the wall. He felt strung up, he was sweating and his stomach churned. The television picture changed from a row of faces to fizzing snow again. He thumped it and the snow went black. There was no food, nothing left in the milk carton, no coffee in the jar.

He lay down on the bench but he didn't sleep, there was too much going on inside his head and jangling in all the nerves of his body. He ached and sweated and sweated and ached his way through what felt like a lifetime of darkness until the moon swung in through the window above the sink.

Marie should be here and she wasn't. When she did turn up, he was going to kill her. He lay, seething, waiting, being leered

at by the moon with mould and pockmarks
all over its face.

TWELVE

'Just to recap, then, before we close. The next meeting is on Thursday 24th of October, and we'll be here again because the building work on the Deanery still won't be finished.'

'If you'd rather not host two book club meetings in a row, I'm happy to do it next time.'

'Thanks, but it's fine. I'm in New Zealand during November anyway, so it'll be you to host it then. Our book for October is *Learning to Dance* by Michael Mayne and I have two copies so if anyone would like this spare . . . ? Cat?' Ilona held out the paperback.

'So — that's it.'

'And I propose the thanks to you, Ilona, from all of us.'

'Seconded,' Cat said. 'The best coffee and cake in the Cathedral Close.'

'And the best sofas.'

'Ah, no, you haven't visited my brother's flat. He has two white leather sofas to die for.'

'Your brother?' Ruth Webber, the wife of the new Dean, said sharply. 'Why does he live in the Close?'

Ilona, wife of the cathedral Precentor, caught Cat's eye before turning quickly away.

'A few houses are rented privately,' Cat said.

'I thought all those were used as offices.'

'They are, mainly. Simon lives on the top floor — there are three offices below him.'

'So what's his cathedral connection then?'

'He doesn't have one. He's a policeman.'

Ruth raised her eyebrows. 'I'd have thought everything available in the close was needed for clergy. Miles Hurley is looking for somewhere better than that bungalow at the end of the Precentor's garden.'

'I think it's a rather nice bungalow.'

Cat bent down in a gesture of clearing coffee cups and plates from the low table to avoid continuing with this interrogation, but brief acquaintance with the wife of the new Dean had taught her that Ruth Webber was nothing if not persistent.

'Is your brother married?'

Cat shook her head and picked up the tray

of crockery.

'Aren't there police flats?'

Ruth was hard on her heels out of the room, carrying a plate with a single biscuit on it towards the kitchen.

'Though I suppose it helps us with security. Don't you find it odd having a policeman for a brother?'

'Why on earth should I find it odd?'

Ruth shrugged. She was looking around her. 'Did you ever see the old kitchen in the Deanery? I mean, I'm not much of a cook but honestly, it came out of the ark, how on earth they managed . . . I'll be hosting the book group the minute all the work's done — not in the kitchen, obviously. Which service do you and your family come to, Cat?'

She was a tall bony woman and it was difficult to tell her age, though Cat guessed at early forties. The previous Dean had retired only three months ago, and Stephen Webber had already started making major changes, not all of which met with the approval either of the rest of the chapter or of the congregation. St Michael's Cathedral people were not, Cat thought, backward-looking or, as Ruth might have put it, out of the ark, but if there were to be changes they needed to be made over time, with tact and care. So far, they were being made at speed and without much consultation. There was a new canon residentiary in Miles Hurley — someone else Cat had not yet got the measure of.

'Nice garden,' Ruth said, looking out, 'though the Deanery's is nicer. Where do you live, Cat?'

'Out of Lafferton. A farmhouse.' She could hear Ilona talking at the front door and willed her to come to the kitchen.

'You didn't say which service you come to?'

'No. I didn't. It varies.'

'In what way?'

'I sometimes come on my own to the early Communion.'

'Why?'

Good God, this was an inquisition.

'I like the 1662 order, I like the quietness.'

Ruth snorted. 'I'm not sure how long 1662 is going to last here, so you'd better make the most of it. We can't be doing with it at all. You have a family, don't you? The ten thirty is a big family service now of course.'

'It always was.'

'Yes, but Stephen is putting much more emphasis on being family-friendly. And then evensong is going to be very much for the young, the students and so on. We've got some great preachers lined up. Quite a few of Stephen's old colleagues of course, and some very exciting rising stars. Have you done the Alpha Course?'

She has a very wide mouth, Cat thought, and I wish she would shut it. And a rather large nose and I wish she would keep it out of my business. She felt uncharitable and unrepentant. Ruth Webber wore jeans with Mary Jane shoes.

Ilona came into the room, and said brightly, 'So sorry, we had to talk about the dreaded flower rota.'

'Isn't that utterly typical,' Ruth said, taking the remaining biscuit and crunching it. 'Flower rotas! That says it all about the Church of England.'

'Well, as I'm sure you'll have seen, the cathedral has very talented flower arrangers and the job takes some doing — just look at the size of those stands and the stone vases. It's a great skill — some would call it an art. It isn't just a case of bunging things in. Don't you like flowers, Ruth?'

'Oh, I don't mind flowers, I know they brighten up the place — just don't ask me to join a flower rota.'

'We wouldn't,' Ilona said, not catching Cat's eye, 'dream of it.'

'Help, look at the time, I'm supposed to be somewhere else. Thanks for the coffee and so on.'

She went clattering out on her Mary Janes, but spun round in the doorway.

'I've forgotten the book we're supposed to be reading.'

'*Learning to Dance*. Michael Mayne. He was Dean of Westminster Abbey. I'm sure Stephen will know his work.'

'Oh, I doubt it,' Ruth said, waving her hand in Cat's direction. 'By the way, do we get to discuss novels and things or is it all religious? If it's novels, you'll lose me, never read them, but I'd like to have a hand in choosing the Christian literature.'

Not wanting to leave at the same time as Ruth and risk further questioning, Cat carried on clearing up, putting cups in the dishwasher and emptying the coffee dregs, until Ilona came back from seeing Ruth out, counting aloud.

'. . . Nine, ten. Cat, will you give your lovely brother a message from me?'

'He's away, but when I'm next in touch, yes of course.'

'Tell him if that woman is found with her neck wrung I'll have done it.'

'I doubt it, Ilona, because I'll have got there first. God, I'll never be the Dean's best friend and I hate some of the things he's doing here, but I can sort of bear him, only . . .'

'Only *not* Mrs Dean. Now, Cat dear, Duncan's in London at the RSCM so I'm entirely alone. Stay and have a cheese salad with me, I need you.'

Cat glanced at her watch. She had made herself come to the St Michael's book group, as she made herself do a number of things she had felt like ducking since Chris's death. She liked the people — or had until Ruth had arrived — she read a lot and enjoyed discussing her reading and she knew it was important to make a social effort when it would be easier to curl back into her shell and never emerge again, other than to work and for the domestic round. The club had been set up to discuss books which were in some way, however loosely, related to faith, not to chatter about the latest fashionable fiction. There were, as Ilona said, plenty of other book groups which did that. They had roamed widely and tackled some difficult titles, not always with success, but Cat would come away feeling that her mind and sometimes her beliefs and principles had been challenged, as well as having enjoyed the company of the others. It had also helped her through bad patches by giving her something to address outside her own unhappiness.

'I only have to call in to Imogen House, then pick up Hannah and Felix. If you're sure . . .'

'Thank God. I think I might explode.' Ilona held up a bottle of sherry but Cat shook her head. 'Pity. You're quite right though, it might loosen our tongues.' She started setting out plates.

'Oh, mine doesn't need any help.'

'No. You don't mind eating in here, do you? Even if our kitchen hasn't been done up and has come out of the ark. Cat, stop me, stop me. She is a woman I am never going to like, and OK, that's my problem, but what he is doing is far more serious. How they could have appointed him I can't think. He doesn't fit in, he isn't right, he's hell-bent on destroying everything that's been built up over years, he has no sense of what is fine, what is excellent, of tradition, of . . . It's making Duncan ill you know. And as for David Lester — I really fear he will leave. Apparently he was talking about other cathedral organist posts that might be coming up.'

'He can't! We can't lose David. We need them both to stay put and fight.'

Ilona shook a plastic colander of salad so

angrily that drops of water sprayed onto the wall behind her. 'Are we stuck in the past, are we out of touch, does the cathedral need a shake-up? In some areas, yes, it does — we have to accept that. Not everything can just go on as it always has, there are some cobwebs, and we should welcome a new broom to help us sweep them away. But not to destroy the liturgy, the music, the high standards of the choir and the organ, the great services of the church. Yes, add to those, and do look at attracting more young people — the students for instance — but to vandalise what there is, to kick out 1662 altogether, dumb down the choral services, to have the lowest common denominator of modern hymns sung to an electronic keyboard, to . . . Oh, Cat, stop me. But it's breaking my heart.'

'I know,' Cat said, taking the colander from her and shaking the salad into a bowl. 'And mine and those of most of the congregation. Vandalise is the right word.'

'And when madam talks about the flower rota in that patronising, supercilious way, I . . . I think I will kill her.'

'No, Ilona, you won't. Let me grate that cheese — you slice the tomatoes. And nor will I. But she is going to try our tolerance and forgiveness to breaking point.'

'I don't think I have any tolerance and forgiveness left,' Ilona said sadly.

'I do wonder what sort of books she'd choose for us.'

'I can imagine.'

'Are there happy-clappy books?'

'Of course there are. They're all about what Lewis Carroll called "writhing and fainting in coils". Did you know she speaks in tongues? They go to some huge evangelical holiday camp and do it there apparently. And of course we all have to learn how to arm-wave properly.' Ilona sat down. 'Am I going to laugh hysterically or cry?'

Cat looked at her. 'You have first go, laugh or cry. I'll do the other. Shall I get some bread?'

'Please . . . and let's talk about something else or we'll get indigestion from all that bile. Only just before we do, have you had a message about this new bee Webber has in his bonnet? The Magdalene Group?'

'Yes. The first meeting's on Friday the third. I think I ought to go. You?'

Ilona sighed. 'I don't know. I feel like just steering clear of everything, to be honest. Who else got that email from Aisling?'

She took a carton of apple juice from the fridge and started to pour it absently into a jug until she caught Cat's eye and dumped it as it was onto the table.

'Miles Hurley obviously, Sally from St Hugh's, me, I think someone from the police as well but I've no idea who . . . Miles ought to invite the Baptists because they run the Reachout van.'

'What's on the Dean's mind, do you suppose? Why is this a cathedral thing?'

'Well, there are girls working in the Lanes round here, you know.'

'No. I didn't know. I'm stupid, aren't I?'

'Of course not. You wouldn't necessarily realise they were prostitutes. The red-light area is mainly out beyond the canal bridge and the Old Ribbon Factory. I see them if I'm coming back late from the hospice.'

'Dear God! I had absolutely no idea.'

'It's nothing new here. Don't kid yourself that there is a city in this country without its prostitutes and its drugs. The girls being trafficked from Eastern Europe have made it a lot worse — especially in Bevham. I think Stephen Webber is right actually — the cathedral is in the heart of the city, the centre of the community, we should be trying to do something. I'm just not sure what. But I'll be at the meeting.'

Ilona stared at her salad. 'Now I feel ashamed of myself,' she said. 'So let's talk about you. How's the beautiful Sam?'

115

'Not sure,' Cat said. 'He's got an away hockey match today and is staying with one of his friends which will cheer him up.'

'Does he need cheering up?'

'I honestly don't know, Ilona. I don't know what Sam needs. He's an oyster, closed up tight. He's getting more and more like Simon.' Even as she said it, Cat realised how true that was. 'I sometimes wonder if they both intend to stay closed to the rest of us forever.'

THIRTEEN

The Reachout van was parked under the street lamp near the factory gates and already people were queuing at the counter. It had turned cold suddenly, the side streets like funnels for the wind to tear down. Abi had thought twice about coming out, but Hayley had arrived early, it was her turn, and besides, if she wimped out every time there was a breeze how was she going to do as she'd promised herself and make enough money to quit for good? She'd been busy. The punters were out in force, God knew why — there was never much of a pattern to it, except that it was busier on Saturday nights and at the end of the month when people had been paid, and dead when it was raining.

She saw the Reachout van as she got out of the car and headed for it, needing the brightness and the hot drink, but more, needing people, normal people who didn't want anything from her except to give her another leaflet about their church. She had a load of the leaflets. She never liked to refuse or to dump them in the litter bins, though sometimes for a laugh she'd leave one behind in a punter's car.

She knew both people on tonight and the one serving the soup winked at her as she got in the queue. They towed a caravan where you could go and sit, and which had a needle exchange, a lot of posters round the walls and another load of leaflets. Unless the weather was very rough most people sat outside, at the metal table and chairs, or on the bollards by the factory gates.

'Hi,' someone said behind her.

She was small and pasty and was wearing a weird lime-green nylon jacket. Abi had never seen her before, but there were always new ones. Usually new ones came for a night or two, maybe a few weeks, then went again.

'Hi.'

'Is it free?'

'Yeah.'

'What do you get?'

'What you like — tea, chocolate, soup, sarnies. Crisps. You just ask. They have bananas and apples and stuff like that as well.'

'Like a proper café then.' She lit a cigarette, threw away the match. 'Sorry, only
it's my last.'

'You're all right, I don't smoke.'

'Right.'

Her nails were bitten down but she'd
painted them black, as if that helped. Her
eyeshadow matched the nylon jacket.

Abi asked for a hot chocolate and a Wagon
Wheel, which she wouldn't eat, but put in
her pocket for Frankie later.

'You from round here?'

Abi pretended not to hear.

'How are you tonight?' Darren said, wink-
ing again. 'We're having a big open-air rally
— music and that. Sunday week. The old
acrodrome. Can I give you a leaflet?'

'Yeah, right, thanks.'

'You'd be really welcome, Abi.'

'Right. Thanks.'

'Anything else I can get you? Got some
nice satsumas. You should eat more fruit.'

'I know, only I hate fruit. Thanks anyway.'

'Cheers, Abi, God bless, you take care
now.'

She walked over to the bollards. The other
girl followed.

'What's it like here?' She relit the end of
her cigarette. 'Punters. You get many?'

Abi shrugged.

'Don't seem too bad. Don't seem many working this way either.'

'Depends, doesn't it?'

'Only asked.' She half turned away and pulled at her cigarette to get it going.

Abi felt guilty. It was the bloody leaflet. Whenever she took one, she started to feel guilty about something. At least when Loopy Les came round with his little packets of sandwiches he didn't hand out Jesus leaflets.

'Four or five regulars,' she said at last. 'A few others, only they come and go. We look out for each other.'

'Get much work?'

'Enough.'

'No good in Bevham any more, I tell you.'

'Right.'

'Used to be steady, you know, and the same girls. Coppers knew us, punters knew us, no trouble. Then all of a sudden they turned up — Eastern Europe they come from, got pimps, everything. They dumped them on a corner, maybe a dozen or fifteen at a time, it was ridiculous. And I tell you what, at least half of them was kids — thirteen, fourteen? Bloody disgrace.'

'They got raided, last I heard.'

'Right. Dawn raid, yeah, rounded up a load of them, cleared a couple of houses. Il-

legals. They just brought more in. There's
hundreds of them all over the country, they
move them around.' She ground out the
cigarette end under the heel of her boot.
'Bloody disgrace. Anyway, someone said it
was good over here, nicer sort of place. So I
thought I'd come. Try it. Came on the bus.
Get a lift back. See how it goes.'

'Right.' Abi stood up.

'What's your name?'

'Abi.'

'Hi.' The girl put out her hand. It seemed
weird. But Abi took it. It was cold and
small, like a kid's hand, like Frankie's.
'Chantelle.'

'Hi.'

There were cars going by at the top of the
road.

'You better get right away from the van.'

'Why?'

'I dunno. Just better you do. Fan out as
well. No point standing together.'

'There's, like, plenty of space,' Chantelle
said.

'Yeah. Maybe some others'll be out later.'

'Who?'

'Kelly, Amy, Marie . . . there's loads.'

'OK.' Chantelle turned and went down
the road, looking hard at every car that
passed. 'See you.'

'Right. See you later.' Abi crossed over and headed nearer to the bypass. She knew the best corner to bag and, as she reached it, a Renault Mégane slowed beside her. Vince.

'All right?'

'Hi, Vince,' Abi said, opening the passenger door. She didn't know if Vince was his real name but it didn't matter because he thought she was called Bella.

She caught a glimpse of Chantelle, looking towards the Renault as it drove away.

An hour later, she got a text message from Hayley, saying that Frankie had been sick twice and was asking for her. It was worrying that he couldn't seem to get rid of the bug the way the others had. Maybe she ought to take him to the doctor again. He didn't look right either, always pale and clammy-feeling, and whiny, when he wasn't really a whiny kid.

It was a lot colder and she jogged a bit. The Chantelle girl hadn't reappeared and the Reachout van was packing up.

Abi felt suddenly depressed, fed up with everything. If she'd been a drinker, this was just the sort of time when she'd have got in a few bottles. She could see why people did, and why they got onto crack, why it would be easy, because sometimes you needed to get out of it for an hour, times like now, when she was frozen and on her way home to spend half the night holding a bucket so Frankie could throw up into it. But she knew she was right never to start on anything at all, never go down that road. She had sixty quid in her pocket, another hundred in the tin, and tomorrow that would go into the post office as well. This time next year . . .

Passing the corner where she sometimes met Marie, Abi remembered that she hadn't seen her. But Marie's life was all over the place. She had to sort out her mother and her waste-of-space boyfriend. She sometimes took off altogether for a week at a time.

But as she reached home, she stopped under the street light and found Marie's number on her mobile.

Hi kid, u right? c u love abi xx.

FOURTEEN

'I don't see how we could possibly go.'

Judith Serrailler got up from the table. She went to the rubbish bin, pulled out the full black bag, tied the top and carried it out, letting the kitchen door bang. It relieved her feelings, though only slightly. It was bitterly cold and the new moon had an edge like a blade. They seemed to have gone from a serene and golden autumn to raw winter in a couple of days. The air smelled frosty.

She lingered by the door, wondering if Cat's car might swing into the drive, but it was probably too early. When the St Michael's Singers rehearsal finished she sometimes went to the Golden Cross with the rest of them. Judith had persuaded her that she should go, rather than duck out and race for home, as she had done for so many months after Chris's death. 'I can sing,' she had said. 'It's the one thing I have felt like doing — it's kept me going. I just can't go and be sociable in the pub.' But the last couple of Thursday nights she had done just that and said that it had been fine, better than she had expected.

All three children were asleep upstairs, collected from school by Judith. She had suggested to Richard that he might collect Sam but he wouldn't. He didn't find his grandchildren any easier than he had found his children, did not unbend or feel able to throw himself into their affairs. He spoke to them, Cat had said once, exactly as he had spoken to her and Simon and Ivo — as if they were his equals in age and understanding. She had hated it, but her own children responded differently, Hannah telling her grandfather that he made her laugh and sometimes talking to him as if he were deaf and simple, Sam becoming solemn in his attempt to match up to Richard's expectations of him. At least Felix was too young to know, Judith thought now, rubbing her arms in the cold. She was well aware Cat was unhappy that her father still seemed distant and aloof. Richard was not cold, not unbending, she herself knew that, and she thought that she had helped him to be more at ease and happier in his own skin. But he found it hard to let down his guard and perhaps he was too old to change. Tonight

125

he had annoyed her and now she was annoyed with herself as much as with him. She was not by nature a banger of doors, nor a sulker — and what was she doing standing out in the cold if not sulking?

There was no sign of Cat.

The kitchen was empty and there was no sound — Richard had probably gone to bed, but the maps he had spread out were still there.

When he had produced them, she had been interested. Richard's idea was an extended trip, starting in California. But when it became clear he intended to leave straight after Christmas, she had objected and he had become impatient. Their marriage might have gone some way towards mellowing him — but there was, Judith thought now, still a good deal further to go.

She poured herself a glass of wine, wondering whether she should go and find him and try to make peace, or remain aloof, carry on as if nothing happened, or continue with the argument. When she had been married to Don, this sort of situation had almost never arisen because Don had been the most laid-back, easy-going of men, happy to change plans, ideas, sides, almost anything, not because he was weak or any

126

sort of a pushover but because he had believed conflict was generally self-defeating and few things worth falling out over. To him, argument should be reserved for entirely trivial matters such as whether cushions should be set straight-edged or pointed against a chair back. Richard would take a position on cushions and stick to it, expecting everyone else to see his point of view. 'Your father has never been gainsaid,' she had once said to Cat, 'and it is not good for someone never to be gainsaid.'

She was halfway through *The Times* crossword when Cat came in, humming Handel.

'All well?'

'If you mean with the children, all fine, if you mean with your father, so-so.' She indicated the wine. 'Medicinal.'

Cat made a face. 'If it's any consolation, I'm taking to drink myself.'

'Bad rehearsal?'

'Not musically, no, great rehearsal. But for the first time since I have been a worshipper at Michael's, which is nearly twenty years, the place is riven by faction — I mean serious faction. And it's not nice. If the Dean isn't careful he'll be looking for a new organist and master of choristers. The Precentor is seething, a lot of people in the congregation are so unhappy they're seriously thinking of going elsewhere —'

'Dear God, the man's only been in office a few months.'

'All it takes to start tearing down what has been built up over centuries.'

'How? You know if I'm anything it's Catholic and we do things differently.'

Cat took a long slow drink of wine before replying. 'Loosely, Stephen Webber is evangelical-charismatic — what my mother would have called Low Church and I call happy-clappy. I dare say it has its place — but that place is not at St Michael's or any other of our great cathedrals which have a tradition of excellence in liturgy and music. That's what cathedrals are about — excellence. The best. It shouldn't mean being out of date and out of touch — times change, so do people. But change is not the same thing as wanton destruction.'

'You're rather cross.'

'I'm very cross. Nothing like as cross as some though — cross and upset.'

'Did you get my tickets, by the way?'

'Yes.' Cat reached for her bag. 'Two for Saturday, about six rows back . . . I chose with care.'

'Thank you, darling — how much do I owe you? And don't say "oh, nothing". If I come to your concerts, I pay my way.'

'Thirty quid then, I'm afraid. Top price.'

'Fine. Your father borrowed my last cash, I'll give you a cheque.'

'Talking of Dad . . .'

'Don't ask.'

'Ah. Am I to take this seriously?'

Judith sighed and refilled her glass. 'Richard decided he would like us to fly to California soon after Christmas, hire a camper van and tour in it.'

'A *camper van?* Dad? I'm surprised he even knows what a camper van is.'

'Apparently he read an article about them, did some research on the Internet and discovered that they are large and extremely comfortable.'

'They are, we had one when we were in Australia. But why on earth should he want you to do that when you can fly and stay in hotels. Much more your scene I'd have thought.'

'Being pensioners.'

'I didn't mean that and you know it. But if you don't like the idea, say so.'

'I don't mind the idea of a camper van in the least, I think it would be rather fun. What I do mind is travelling round the States in one for a whole year.'

Cat felt as if she were standing on a ledge overhanging some sort of precipice and that

129

ledge had suddenly started to move beneath her feet.

'A year?'

'Which of course we cannot possibly do. There is no way we could leave you and the children except for a short holiday. A year's out of the question. You rely on us and so you should.'

'Judith . . .'

'I mean it.'

'I confess I'm not sure if I could cope. You do such a lot for us.'

'Not a lot but I think what we do is pretty vital.'

'It is. Believe me. But Dad disagrees, I suppose.'

'He'll come round, but in the meantime, he's gone off to bed to read P.G. Wodehouse which, as you know, is his customary defence against the world.'

'God, I feel guilty.'

'Don't be ridiculous. Tell me more about the cathedral. I love tales of internecine strife.'

Cat laughed. 'But it is grim,' she said, 'grim and not funny. A lot of people are being walked over. It isn't just hurt pride or jostling for position, Judith, it goes a lot deeper than that. I don't know how anyone can be so insensitive and it's odd because

130

when you meet Stephen Webber you don't get that feeling at all — he seems very kind, quite gentle, he listens. Unlike his wife. But I hate to see David Lester so upset. It's affecting the music. It was quite noticeable tonight.'

'The Dean isn't trying to close down St Michael's Singers surely?'

'No, no, he can't do that — we're not part of the cathedral organisation. I don't think he much cares for what we sing but that's his problem. I dare say he thinks it's elitist and not relevant. But no, it's the cathedral music he wants to change, and most of the services. He's riding roughshod over everyone.'

'Can he?'

'Pretty much. It is the Dean *and* Chapter, of course, and there are still several from the old regime who are fighting all the way. But there are others — Canon Hurley for instance — he came with Stephen Webber, they've worked together before . . .' Cat got up and wandered restlessly round the kitchen. 'I suppose some of this is just me, isn't it? I can't bear anything else to change, especially not something so important. The cathedral is my shelter — it's a rock, it's there. If that goes then anything can.'

'I remember feeling like that. Just after

Don died they changed the time of the nine o'clock news to ten and it was as if the ground was shifting under my feet. Sounds ridiculous now but that was how I felt, needing the television news to be where it always had been. Bereavement makes you very insecure.'

'I have to sort out what is important from what isn't, though. If things change at St Michael's, I need to decide which I care about enough to fight for and which to let go.'

'Priorities, yes.'

Cat went and put her arms round Judith's shoulders, 'It's this sort of thing, you see? You help me sort things out. If you went away for a year . . .'

'Yes, darling, I do know. Well, it's fine because we're not going.'

'But Dad . . .'

'You leave Richard to me.'

As she got ready for bed, Cat realised that it was true, she could leave her father to Judith. It was one thing she no longer had to worry about and it was a change she welcomed.

She lay awake, listening to the wind in the trees, wanting to still her angry thoughts about the cathedral and her anxious

132

thoughts about Sam and the new worry, that her father was thinking of going away for a year, and was unable to quieten any of them. She felt as if she were entirely alone and fighting a long, exhausting war of attrition. It was a long time before she slept.

FIFTEEN

Leslie Blade slowed as he turned onto Wharf Lane. Sometimes the girls were along here, sometimes by the row of boarded-up shops further on, and he could park on the service road. It was a dismal end of the town, bought up by a developer who had gone bankrupt. There was not much chance of anyone starting a business here now, bringing in work, so the shops would stay as they were, the bookies, the hairdresser's, the launderette, the corner stores, the butcher's, all closed and covered in posters and graffiti. Even the charity shop had gone. He was later than usual. His mother had gone into hospital overnight for a check on her pacemaker, and travelling to Bevham and back to see her after work meant that he did not begin to prepare the food until gone ten o'clock. He had almost lost heart and stayed at home in front of the fire instead. But he had bought the food, the bread was fresh, and besides, they would miss him, it was not a night for the Reach-out van and the weather had turned colder. The girls needed him.

The wind whipped bits of paper and empty plastic bags down the road ahead but he thought he could see a figure near the empty shops as he slowed.

The next minute, a blue light came flashing into view and the police car pulled in front of him, siren wailing.

'Excuse me, sir, would you just get out of the car for me?'

'I haven't been drinking, officer, I assure you, I don't take alcohol at all.'

'Just get out of the car, if you wouldn't mind, sir.'

Leslie got out.

'Thank you.'

'As I say, I haven't had any alcohol, I don't drink.'

'Can you tell me what you're doing here?'

'Doing? I was driving along the road.'

'You weren't driving in a normal fashion, were you? You were driving slowly along this side . . . Another way of describing it is "kerb-crawling".'

'I was going to park over there as it happens. By the empty shops.'

'Why would you want to do that, sir? Got

some business there?'

'I'd like you to tell me why I am being questioned. I'm not aware of having committed any offence.'

'Kerb-crawling is an offence, sir. Are you aware of that? Are you also aware that young women work as prostitutes in this area?'

'I know that.'

'Oh, you know?'

'I know because I come here to visit them. Ask any of them. I come out to bring them a hot drink and some food. I don't know if you are aware, officer, that these girls are on the streets night after night, in the cold, in the dark, on their own, and that nobody gives a damn about it. I bring them something to eat. If you would like to open the bag on the back seat of the car you'll find it.'

Now the other one was out and walking slowly round Leslie's car, examining the wheels, the doors, the bumpers.

'Go on, please . . . open the back door and look in the carrier bag and if any of the girls are about, they know me, they'll vouch for me.'

But the road was deserted.

The PC took out the carrier bag and opened it, nodded to the other.

'Right, sir, well, I've only your word for it

that you were taking this to give to the girls or anyone else, but if that is the case, I'd advise you against doing so.'

'What on earth for? What harm am I doing? Ask them. They're glad enough of it. I look out for them, which is more than the police do, if I may say so. Look . . .'

A car had come down the road on the other side and slowed down. Seeing the police car, the driver barely stopped to let the girl out onto the path and was away, tyres screaming.

'Abi,' Leslie Blade shouted across the road. 'Abi.'

Abi Righton stopped dead.

'Abi, over here, please, come over.'

She walked at an angle across the road, keeping her eye on the police.

'All right, love, not a problem, you haven't anything to worry about. Just a word if you don't mind.'

Abi shrugged, kept her distance.

'He wants you to say you know me, and —'

'Thank you, but if you'd just leave it to me, sir. Can I have your name first please, miss?'

Abi hesitated.

'Like I said, there's no problem far as you're concerned.'

'OK. Abi. Abi Righton.'

'Address?'

'Do I have to?'

'No, but it'd make me happier.'

'11c Barter Road.'

Leslie tried to catch her eye but Abi stared at a spot beyond the car.

'I'd like you to tell me if you recognise this man, please.'

'Yeah. I recognise him. What's he done?'

'Can you give me his name?'

'You arrested him then?'

'No, he is not under arrest. Do you know his name?'

'Leslie. Leslie something. We call him — Les.'

'Just Les?'

'Yes.'

'Know another name?'

'No.'

'Can you tell me anything more about him, to corroborate what he's told us?'

'I don't know what he's told you, do I?'

'Any idea why he's here? I gather you see him from time to time out this way.'

'Oh yeah, he brings us stuff, sandwiches and tea and that.'

'When you say "us" . . .'

'The girls.'

'Any in particular?'

'No. Anyone. I got no idea why he does it but he does. Kindness of his heart, I suppose. He doesn't preach or give us leaflets or anything.'

'Does he, er, how can I put it, do you *pay* him for the food and so on?'

'If you mean, is he a punter, then no, he bloody isn't. He just likes a chat, hangs around a bit, talks to us about stuff.'

'What sort of stuff?'

Abi shrugged. 'Anything. What people talk about. Weather and how nobody's got any money and is the royal family a waste of space and what music do you like. Just stuff.'

'Right. OK, thanks. I don't need to keep you. Only I would just say you'd be better off at home, not on the streets, you know.'

'Better off? How come?'

'Safer, warmer, out of harm's way.'

'Safe enough here. We look out for each other. The Reachout van comes. More than you lot do.'

'All the same. No life for a young girl, is it, Abi? I've a daughter. I wouldn't want this for her.'

'No, right, well, let's hope you don't get it.' Abi pushed her hands into her pockets and turned away.

'I can go as well, I imagine,' Leslie Blade said.

'Just a word though, same as to the girl. Might be best if you didn't hang around here, chatting to them, sandwiches or no.'

'And why would that be? Am I committing an offence?'

'No. All the same, better leave it to the authorities — the Reachout van and so on. Better leave it to them.'

'If there isn't anything else, officer?'

The policeman shut his notebook. 'On your way then, sir. Thanks for your co-operation. Drive carefully.'

Leslie drove down the main road for a couple of miles, turned onto the bypass, left it at the roundabout, skirted the Hill, and in less than fifteen minutes was back beside the empty shops. The patrol car had gone and neither Abi nor any of the other girls was on the street. He pulled in and waited a while, then went round the block and down towards the canal. Still no one.

He could hear the cathedral chimes for midnight ringing round the cold and empty streets as he drove away. From the shadows near the towpath the one they called Beanie Man saw him. Watched. Waited.

■ ■ ■ ■

'The leccy's nearly gone,' Hayley said the second Abi opened the door. 'You got any change?'

Abi pulled thirty pounds in notes from her miniskirt pocket and went to the cupboard over the sink. The cornflakes packet where she kept pound coins for the meter was empty. The room was cold, all three children asleep together under one duvet on the bed, Hayley with her parka pulled up round her neck huddled into the chair.

'There was ten quid in here,' Abi said. 'Where's that gone?'

Hayley's face was pinched, her eyes red.

'You must have used it.'

Hayley had been biting her nails.

'I didn't use it, and nobody else has been in here. Except you.'

Hayley shrugged.

'OK, I'll go downstairs, see if they've got any change. Only I know you had it and I want it back, right?'

When Abi returned and fed the meter, Hayley was making tea.

'I had a good idea,' she said.

'What, like nicking my leccy money? I'm telling you, I want it back. You work tomor-

141

row and you give it me, right?'

'No, listen, where I live, the flat below's gone empty.'

'So? God, I'm bloody frozen. I'm having a Cuppa Soup. You want one?'

'We could have it. It's got two bedrooms, it's got a separate kitchen. We could have that.'

'What do you mean, we could have it?'

'Rent it. You, me, our kids. It's a whole lot better than here and mine, and we could do it up.'

'You're joking, right?'

'No, I'm not, what would I be joking for? It's a good idea.'

'Not in my book.'

'Save me traipsing here with Liam all the time. Save a load of money as well.'

'How do you make that out?'

'Oh, work it out. Anyway, it's a flat that's going and I think we should have it.'

'Looks funny. Two girls living together. People'd think.'

'Let 'em bloody think then.'

Abi poured water into two mugs.

'It was dead tonight,' she said, turning the television on low, 'one punter, nobody else out there. Bloody freezing.'

'. . . her mother, Mrs Audrey Buckley, reported

Chantelle missing. She was last seen five days ago walking towards the bus station. Chantelle, who is seventeen, was wearing a distinctive bright green nylon jacket and short skirt. Mrs Buckley, of Aberdeen Way, Bevham, said that Chantelle sometimes stayed over-night with friends but none of them had seen her this week and . . .'*

'I saw her,' Abi said.

The CCTV picture of the girl walking down a street was replaced by a snapshot of her with a dog, younger, darker hair.

'That's her, deffo. She was on my patch. Naff jacket. Didn't think she'd stay around.'

They watched the rest of the news, eating a packet of Jaffa Cakes.

'See, that's why there's no punters out there,' Hayley said, 'it's this credit crunch.'

'I flippin' hope not. Anyway, you'd think there'd be more of them, not less, cheer themselves up.'

It was as the weather chart came on the screen that it occurred to Abi. 'That girl,' she said, 'that Chantelle with the green jacket.'

'What about her?'

'Only I haven't seen Marie for over a week.'

'Be her mother playing up again then. Or that dosser Jonty.'

'Maybe.'

'You know she goes off, Abs, she went off before, you remember. Last summer.'

'OK.' Abi reached for another Jaffa Cake. 'You're probably right.'

'I'm always right. I'm right about that flat as well.'

Abi chucked the empty biscuit packet at her.

Hayley and Liam left just before nine the next morning.

'Just come and have a look at it, you don't have to make up your mind, only it'd be great, Abs, think how much more room the kids'd have, think of a proper kitchen. Just come and have a look.'

But Abi wouldn't promise anything. She needed to think a lot of things out before she got tempted by looking at any flat and committing herself when she wasn't ready. Hayley wasn't dependable. She was still liable to dope herself up and then wouldn't be fit to work or look after the kids, she was still liable to hitch up with some no-hoper and bring him home. The room Abi lived in was a dump, small, cold, shared toilet and bath and only a corner to cook in, but it was hers, she felt safe in it, and it was cheap. She'd been able to save. She had the kids

144

where she could see them and they were safe as well. Chuck this away to share with Hayley and there'd be a load of what-ifs.

It was playgroup morning for Frankie. After she'd left him, Abi stood on the corner waiting for the bus to the supermarket. She always went when it was just her and Mia, did her shop and then had breakfast, one good cooked plateful. Mia had bits off hers and an egg of her own. She bought a magazine, Mia went to sleep, she had a second coffee. Happy. Sometimes, sitting in the supermarket café, in the warmth and brightness, people all around her, she felt OK, and when she thought about it, she knew it was because she felt normal. She could be anybody, a mum with a toddler, house to go back to. Not doing what she did. Normal. Only this morning, she suddenly knew she had to do something else. She'd woken half a dozen times in the night and each time it was there, churning round her mind, and when she had slept again it had flitted in and out of her dreams.

She crossed the road and caught a bus in the opposite direction, then walked. Mia slept. A raw wind snaked towards her bare legs.

She'd thought it was a short walk but it took twenty-five minutes before she was at the broken gate leading through rough grass into the field. The caravan was on the far side, standing in a patch of mud and nettles. Abi could see the door swinging open. She couldn't push the buggy over the thick grass and ruts, so she lifted Mia out and carried her.

There was no sound. She hesitated, then knocked on the open door. But she knew she wouldn't get any reply, and in the end she just went in, and found the place wrecked, as if someone had taken a sledge-hammer to it, table, cupboards, benches, sink, windows, the lot, everything was smashed and splintered and the floor was covered in broken bits of wood and cushions from the bench. The television was upside down, smashed, and plates and cups had been smashed too, there was crockery and glass all over. But nothing else. Nobody. No sign that anyone had even been living here except for a few clothes, pulled out of a cardboard box and piled onto the mess. She recognised a sweatshirt, and one shoe from a black patent pair Marie wore.

Mia had woken and was looking round, her face bewildered, and the wind blew at them across the field and cut round their heads.

'OK,' Abi said, 'OK . . .'

She ploughed her way back across the field, collected the buggy and went through the broken gate into the lane. Mia had started to cry.

Abi walked fast, to get warm, to get away, and to help herself think about what she ought to do.

SIXTEEN

Marley had his head out of the stable and began to toss it about and whinny with anticipation when Stacey drew up. She thought he knew Saturday and Sunday the minute dawn broke, though it was light later in the mornings now, the long days when they had started their ride at five and six o'clock were over. Still, she liked to be at the stables as early as she could, stretching the weekend out.

Marley was a sure-footed, Coloured horse, the easiest Stacey had ever owned. The livery stables were three miles outside Lafferton on the Starly side so she could ride for a couple of hours without hitting much traffic, across the hill track and out onto the moor. But the weekends were sometimes a problem up there because of the mountain bikers and scramblers, and today she had heard on the early local news about a rally, so she took Marley along the road and through the gate that led towards the canal towpath. They might meet dog walkers and runners, sometimes other riders, but never noisy bikes. Not that Marley was bothered — he was that rare thing, the genuinely bomb-proof horse.

There was no one on the path. Here the canal broadened out and flowed through the fields between pollarded willows. There was a thin mist floating over the water. With luck, Stacey thought, the sun would break through and it would be a fantastic day. She leaned forward to pat Marley's neck.

Marley was always keen to get going, but once out he was never wound up, never over-energetic, happy to canter if she pushed him but otherwise just to amble. He was ambling when she saw it. At first, she couldn't tell what it was — a bundle of clothes or rubbish caught up in the roots of a tree maybe — but she kicked the horse on to go nearer. It looked odd.

He wouldn't go nearer. He stopped dead and tossed his head slightly. Stacey kicked. He wasn't a horse that just stopped. He never did that.

'Come on, come on, boy, what are you playing at? Walk on.'

It took a lot to get him to move. She could feel him, torn between reluctance, the desire

149

to stand his ground, and his usual willingness to do as he was asked.

'Walk on, Marley.'

After a moment or two, he walked.

From where she was, sixteen hands above the dark water, Stacey had a view but not a full view. She waited, looked around, saw no one, no walker, no runner, not even a random dog.

She didn't want to go closer, didn't want to find out, didn't want to get off the safety of the horse's back. But she knew she had to. She couldn't just go. She knew she couldn't.

She slid to the ground and went slowly closer, hanging onto Marley's reins, not because Marley would ever bolt away, but for her own reassurance. Because she knew, she said afterwards, she knew all along really, she didn't think it was a bundle of old clothes from the first second.

She knew.

Thank God for mobile phones, though her hands were shaking so much she could hardly dial. The police were there in ten, maybe less, she heard the screaming tyres, saw them jump the stile and come running, and by then she was sitting on the ground, her head between her knees and the reins hooked over her arm, Marley's reins, her lifeline to the great, steady, warm, breathing safety of her horse, who was cropping the grass beside her.

The body of Chantelle Buckley had caught in the tree roots and the water flowed on round it and away, as if it was somehow abandoning her. She had been strangled and there were cuts about her face, though at first the cuts mingled with the bruising and bloating and discoloration and were not clear. The pathologist would find them later, when she was stripped and labelled and under the cold white lights on the slab. Surprisingly, she was fully clothed, in short skirt, T-shirt, torn green jacket, though inevitably the shoes had gone, pulled off by the movement through the water.

She was face down, one arm out, one bent behind her, her hair wrapped like weed round her head. From the first second of realising what it was, and so forever, Stacey had been grateful that she hadn't seen the face.

SEVENTEEN

'Miles, we were just talking about you. Come in if you can. Shall I be glad when we're out of this!'

Cardboard boxes were stacked against the walls and the small sitting room was crammed. The house had been lent to the Webbers until the Deanery was ready.

'Would you like coffee? And keep to this side of the room if you don't want the plague. Stephen was going to phone you.'

Stephen Webber was hunched into a chair, his face flushed.

'Oh, I'm bound to get it sooner or later — everyone else has. I'd love some coffee, thank you.'

'Now don't start talking till I come back.'

Miles Hurley frowned slightly.

'We won't,' Stephen Webber said quickly, his voice rasping and thick with cold.

Miles smiled conspiratorially at Stephen. They were old friends and sat in companionable silence.

Ruth came back with a tray of coffee, an angular woman who carried herself awkwardly, with severely swept-up hair and a strangely expressionless face. She laughed, often and loudly, but never smiled.

'I can't find a thing. I just want to be settled.'

'I feel settled,' Miles said, 'have done for months.'

'You can't. Impossible. Nobody could feel settled in that dreary little shed at the end of someone else's garden.'

'It isn't a shed, it's a perfectly nice bungalow, and as I have a separate path, I don't have to go through the Precentor's garden at any point. I like it.'

Ruth shook her head. 'No, we can do better for you than that.'

'He just said he was perfectly happy, Ruth,' Stephen Webber said, turning his head away to sneeze.

'And I said he can't be. Did you know the cathedral owned a very nice, spacious apartment at the top of one of the office buildings in the close?'

'I don't think I did.'

'Well, it does and I think you should live there. I gather it's a very smart flat indeed, wonderful tall windows, view down the close, and fantastic fittings.'

'How did you find all that out?'

Ruth held his gaze.

'But it really doesn't matter,' Miles said quickly, 'because I like my bungalow, thank you. Find someone else for the smart flat. I'm sure there are plenty of candidates.'

Miles Hurley was adept at resisting Ruth's manipulation. He and Stephen had known one another since theological college and had worked together at their London parish. Not for nothing had Ruth been nicknamed Mrs Proudie.

'Oh, it isn't empty. Not yet anyway. Some policeman or other lives in it, which is a disgrace.'

'What's wrong with policemen?'

'He isn't even a member of the congregation.'

'Ruth, several of the houses in the close are let out. Offices and flats. You know perfectly well we don't have the huge staff there would once have been. Besides, the lettings have nothing to do with the Dean and Chapter, thank goodness.'

'Why don't they? Now *there's* an abdication of responsibility . . .'

'We have more than enough to do, and they are in the hands of a very good agent. Anyway, how did you find out about the policeman?'

'He's Dr Deerbon's brother. She told me herself.'

'She's coming on to the Magdalene Group, isn't she? Good idea.'

'Which brings us to why we were talking about you when you turned up, Miles. The Magdalene Group.'

'I didn't know you were joining us, Ruth.'

'I'm taking Stephen's place.'

Miles glanced across the room as Stephen turned away, ostensibly to blow his nose again.

'As you can see, he obviously isn't well and frankly he has taken far too much on. This place needs a complete sorting out and the Magdalene Group is the perfect example of something he can hand over to me.'

She got up and went out of the room in the abrupt way Miles Hurley knew well.

'I'll come back,' he said. 'You should be in bed, Stephen.'

The Dean shook his head. 'Have you seen David Lester today?'

'No — should I have?'

Stephen Webber sighed. 'He can't go on avoiding me. I thought he might have said something.'

'I know he isn't happy, but that's not surprising — nobody likes radical change and he's more of a traditionalist than most.'

'He's a very good musician. I just wish he could see that I'm trying to bring new light and life into the cathedral.' He stood up cautiously. 'I'm sorry, Miles, you're right. I'd be better off in bed. Can it wait — whatever you wanted to talk about?'

'Of course. But I think you ought to come to the first Magdalene Group meeting at least. Perhaps suggest that Ruth takes your place from time to time?'

'Oh, I shouldn't think anyone would mind. It's just a question of too much to do, too little time. Ruth can run it just as well as I can.'

'What?' Ruth came out of the kitchen as Miles was leaving. 'What can I run as well as you?'

'The Magdalene Group.'

'I certainly can. And judging by the radio just now it's very timely. That girl who was reported missing — apparently she was working as a prostitute, and they've found her.'

Ruth took a glass of hot lemon and honey upstairs. 'I've had an idea.'

Stephen Webber's head ached and his throat was sore, his breathing came as if through lungs full of rusty nails.

'The charismatic conference in eighteen months' time . . .'

'Some way off.'

'I think we should offer to host it here. It would be great for the cathedral, bring a new lot of people in, and it would be a real focal point for the students — there's been hardly any missionary outreach from here to the college, so no wonder there are almost no young people in the congregation. If we could target the students at the same time as the charismatic conference the place would be shaken to the rafters. Don't you agree?'

Stephen Webber sipped the hot lemon slowly. If he had felt better, he might have agreed, or disagreed, or told Ruth to leave things alone, that it was not up to them to offer to host the conference, that . . .

As it was, he swallowed the two paracetamol tablets she held out to him and then lay back gratefully on the pillow, feeling unable to say anything at all.

Eighteen

'Is there only you I can talk to?'

Abi Righton stood at the counter in front of the duty officer, an impressively tall and broad man known to every criminal within a wide radius of Lafferton as a right bastard and to old ladies with lost purses as 'that nice sergeant'. To Abi he was an unknown quantity, and a male.

'I don't bite. Who else did you have in mind, love?' Sergeant Rayner was also a year off retirement and scathing about political correctness that forbade him to use endearments.

'Can I talk to a woman?'

'Not sure who's available — might be a female CID officer upstairs. Can you give me a clue as to the nature of your problem, Miss? Might help to get someone down here.'

Abi hesitated, glancing down at the pushchair. Mia was chewing an iced bun.

158

'But if you'd rather not tell me I'll get someone, don't worry.'

She looked bothered about something and she wasn't happy being in a police station. She kept glancing round at the doors behind her, as if half thinking of changing her mind and getting out. He had a hunch. The sergeant's hunches were well known and he had been ribbed about them for twenty-seven years in the force, but he trusted them and they didn't often let him down. He thought the girl in front of him deserved treating gently.

Abi decided. 'It's not a woman to talk to so much, it's being private.'

'Ah, now I'm with you. Right, private we can do. If you'd like to take a seat over there.' He smiled.

Abi hesitated again. You couldn't always trust a smile on a man. But she sat down. The bench covering was split and there were crumbs and bits of paper pushed into the crease at the back.

Mia had finished the iced bun and was drinking out of her plastic cup, her eyes over the top of it half closed, uninterested in her surroundings which Abi thought was the right attitude. With any luck, she'd nod off.

Someone had left a newspaper on the bench. There was a photo of the girl in the

green jacket. *Missing Prostitute Chantelle Buckley, 17.*

Abi looked away. Why did they have to do that? She wasn't a prostitute first, she was a girl, just a girl, no need to label her. Would they do that to her? Abi Righton, 23, prostitute. She shook her head to clear the words out of it. That wasn't her, she was Abi Righton, mother of two, Abi Righton any bloody thing, and the same with this Chantelle, same with Hayles, same with Marie. Just people. Besides, she was giving up. This time next year . . .

'Abi Righton?'

Young. Frizzy hair. Big necklace, blues and greens and soft browns. She liked the necklace.

'We'll go in here. Can I get you a coffee or anything?'

'We're all right, thanks.'

'It's OK, bring the baby in. Hello?'

Mia turned her plastic cup upside-down.

The room was better than Abi had expected, sofa and two chairs, table, plants, picture of the sea on the wall.

'We had a makeover,' the policewoman said. 'Interview room was like a cell before.'

She didn't go round the other side of a desk, she sat on the sofa and beckoned Abi to the chair. She might not be much older

than her. The beads of the necklace had a rough surface, like stone.

'I'm DC Mead, Steph Mead.' She had a notebook but she didn't open it, just looked at Abi, smiling. 'So?'

She seemed encouraging. It was like some sort of job interview, not like being with the police at all.

'Look, this is probably nothing, well, part of it is probably, I just got worked up, only the first thing, that's not nothing, I mean. It's that girl, the one that went missing, Chantelle.'

'Chantelle Buckley. Do you know her? Are you a friend?'

'Not . . . no, not a friend, like, only I met her. That's it. I just met her. Last week. And I was going to come when I read about her missing but I . . . well, I didn't.'

'Did you know that we found Chantelle? That we found her body?' She spoke quite kindly, quite gently, as if she was breaking bad news to a relative and didn't want to upset her.

'I heard,' Abi said. 'Just on Radio Bev, this morning. I knew I should have come.'

'Right. Well, you're here now, that's the main thing. Have you got something to tell me about Chantelle?'

'No. I don't know. I shouldn't think I

have, no. Only now it isn't just Chantelle, is it?'

The policewoman looked at her. Then she said, 'Abi, are you sure about that coffee? Only maybe you could do with it. It sounds as if you might have quite a bit to tell me.'

In the end, she was there for an hour and had two coffees. Mia slept without stirring the whole time.

It wasn't difficult, nothing like as much as she'd expected, talking about herself, what she did, all of it, and then about Chantelle. Not that anything she had to say about her was really much use, she knew that, and Chantelle took less time than the rest. It was Marie. When she got to Marie, DC Mead asked her to wait, went out for a bit, and when she came back, had someone else with her, another detective, a man.

'This is my colleague, DC Garnet, he's working on the Chantelle Buckley case, so if you don't mind, I'd like him to hear anything else you've got to tell us.'

He looked all right. A bit small. She didn't think policemen were ever small but maybe it was different with plain clothes.

'Abi, I hear you met Chantelle and there are a couple of things I'd like to ask you. But first, do you want to tell us about Marie O'Dowd?'

'Yeah, right. Listen, I was a bit bothered, only not . . . not like I am now. Now there's Chantelle. That makes it . . .'

They waited. What? She tried to find the right way to explain but her thoughts and feelings were in a mess and they'd got worse since she came here. Only she wasn't backing out now. She owed Marie that much.

'Different,' she said at last. 'It's not a joke, is it, it's not "Oh, that Marie, she's done it before, gone off. Not my problem. She'll be back." OK, well, maybe she has and she will be, only now you've found that Chantelle dead, you ask me, it's different.'

Nineteen

Ben Vanek laid out three ties on the bed — the plain blue, the navy with white spots and the maroon. He discarded the maroon — boring — then the blue — colour good but fabric cheap and shiny. But though the navy with white spots was smart, pretty new and given him by a girlfriend of whom he had quite fond memories, maybe it wasn't right because it was a bit too smart. Maybe none of them wore ties at all.

Serrailler would wear a tie. Definitely.

Ben thought back to his old CID team. Ties? From time to time, but more often open-necked shirts, or T-shirts. Leather jackets.

He took off the navy tie with white spots. Opened his shirt collar. No, too casual, at least to start.

In the end, he put on the boring maroon, left the others on the bed. It was either the bed or the back of the one chair as they were the only pieces of furniture in the room. The rest of the house was not much better equipped. He went down the narrow staircase. The hall was empty. The front room had an old trunk, the back room, an armchair, a card table, a television. The kitchen had a cooker, a formica-topped table, two chairs, a fridge. And that was pretty much that. 27 St Mark's Street. He had moved in three days ago.

But 27 St Mark's Street was his, all his, bought without so much as a mortgage with everything his mother had left him when she had died the year before. She had known she was dying, after three bouts of cancer, three lots of appalling treatment, three remissions. And she had insisted on talking about everything with his father, and with Ben, including how much money she was leaving him.

'Buy a house,' she had said several times. 'Have a holiday on it if you want to, enjoy it — but buy a house. You'll never regret it.'

She had died before he had got the Lafferton job, but she would have approved of 27 St Mark's Street, he knew that much. Victorian terraced cottages, preferably with original fireplaces intact, were right up her street. There were fireplaces in the front room, the back room and one of the bedrooms, though that was blocked and he would never use it. He'd have a fire in the front room, though. There was money left over, he could buy more than the bits of old furniture he had brought with him from the flat he had shared with two other plain clothes in Telford, he just hadn't had a chance, didn't know what would suit the house, what choice there was. He'd find his feet on the job first then ask around. Ikea? Auction rooms? There were curtains in the front room and the bedroom, which the previous owner had left, hideous curtains but they served, like the stair carpet and the lino in the kitchen. He could live with any of it because he had the house. His house.

He took his jacket off the nail behind the door. His stomach was doing what stomachs do the first morning of anything — first day at Big School, at uni, at Hendon — the combo of excitement, anticipation and dread, but this time, excitement was right up there because it was different. It was new and it was the pick, the job he'd wanted and never expected to get. The dream job.

The DC waiting in the station lobby wore pale pink cord jeans, a checked scarf fashionably tied and an anxious expression. Ben

166

decided she missed being pretty but not by much.

'DS Vanek?' She made it sound like Varnek.

'That's right . . . but, er, do you mind, it's pronounced Van-yek. Sorry.'

'Oh God, another weird name. That'll be fun, Vanek and Serrailler — nobody can ever say that either. I'm Steph Mead.'

'Nice and normal then.'

He didn't mind people getting his name wrong, it happened every day, and usually they didn't mind him helping them get it right. He marked pink-cords down as prickly.

'I'm your welcoming party.' She punched in the security number to the door beside the duty desk. 'There you go, one-five-six-four.'

'It changes, presumably.'

'You'll get a text. It happens at random.' They went up the regulation issue concrete stairs. 'Where'd you come from?'

'Shropshire.'

'What, country parish?'

'Telford.'

'Right. Well, you'll find Lafferton much like anywhere, I guess. Only things are a bit hot this morning, we're just going into a case conf . . . Do you know DI Franks?'

'He was on my interview panel.'

'He's taking it.'

She banged through two sets of swing doors and along to the end of a corridor. The conference room was filling up. He could hear the usual hubbub. It was like school playgrounds, Ben Vanek thought. The noise of children out at playtime was the same wherever you were.

'Hi, morning, DS Vanek.'

He couldn't get used to it. He didn't think he'd ever get used to it. Detective Sergeant, no longer just DC. And heading upwards, only it didn't do to make ambition too public, he'd learned that early on.

'Morning, sir.'

'Welcome on board. Interesting case today, listen and learn.'

'Sir.'

He wondered where the Super was. It was Simon Serrailler he had come here to work with, Serrailler whose career path he wanted to emulate.

'Is the DCS in?'

Steph Mead was finding them chairs. There were nine people in the room, and a couple more uniform coming in.

'Serrailler? He's on leave. He headed up the Falmer gang case for SIFT — earned himself a nice holiday.'

'Oh.'

She gave him a look.

'He's a legend,' Ben said, 'that's all.'

'Apparently. I've only been here a month myself. I've never even met the guy. Head up, here we go.'

DI Franks hit the ground running, talking as he walked towards the white board at the end of the room.

'Chantelle Buckley, seventeen, lived in Bevham, had worked there and in Lafferton as a prostitute.' He took them through the photographs — Chantelle alive, wearing the vile green nylon jacket, Chantelle caught on CCTV at the bus station and again in Lafferton Market Square. Chantelle dead, body floating Ophelia-like in the water, caught up among the roots of the pollarded willows. Chantelle on the mortuary slab. Close-ups. Injuries. Franks went on. Last known movements, witnesses, family, acquaintances.

'Motive?' someone asked.

'Good question. None, so far as we know. No enemies, no big debts, no current boyfriend. Bit of rivalry between the toms, always is, you know, "she took my punter", "geroff my patch", all the usual stuff, nothing important. Though there are a lot of new pimps, running very young girls. According to a local prostitute, Abi Righton, Chantelle

169

had come to try her luck over here because there were too many foreign girls in Bevham.'

'Family?'

'Mother, two stepbrothers. Chantelle lived at home and her mother reported her missing. If they knew she was working as a tom they didn't own to it. No family tensions, mother married the stepfather when Chantelle was eight, but he died last year. Gets on OK with the stepbrothers, both married and live elsewhere. Don't think there's anything there.'

'Dead end then.'

'Nothing's a dead end. We're only just started. One person we want to talk to — a man the girls call Loony or Loopy Les. We don't know his real name. Les takes flasks of hot drinks and sandwiches to the girls on the street from time to time . . . I wonder why . . .'

'Religious nutter.'

'Girls don't think so. We need to find him. Description — IC one, medium height, brown hair, in his fifties, no distinguishing features.'

'Well, there you go then, soon pick *him* out of a crowd!'

'Drives a —'

'Ford Fiesta?'

'You read my mind.'

There was a general groan and people started to move.

'Hang on, I know you're eager to get out there but there's another thing. Another prostitute. Marie O'Dowd — local. She was reported missing yesterday by another tom, Abi Righton. Abi went to the caravan where Marie lives and found it trashed. There's a boyfriend, and he's got form . . .' He pointed to the right of the board and a mug-shot of Jonty Lewis. 'Possession, bit of deal-ing, aggravated burglary, vicious assault.'

'Nice.'

'I want him brought in. Last known ad-dress 44 Payton Street but that turns out to be a squat and there's no one in it now. That was wrecked as well.'

'Doesn't sound like there's a connection, does it, sir? I mean, apart from the dead girl and the Missper being toms.'

'I agree. I don't want anyone wandering off after red herrings. I want the killer of Chantelle Buckley. Chances are Marie O'Dowd'll just turn up — apparently she's done this before, gone off for a few weeks. Looks like things turn nasty with the boy-friend so she does a runner. Right, that's it, except I'd like you to welcome your new DS, Ben Vanek, pronounced like that, right?'

'Right, sir.'

'DS Vanek will be working with DC Mead today — try and find this Loopy Les . . .'

Franks went on assigning the jobs — some to liaise with vice squad at Bevham, others to talk to the local prostitutes.

'But I can't spare everybody to this — we've got reports this morning of another big country-house antiques raid, village of Milton Copley, four miles north of here. That's the third in as many months. Uniform are there but I want . . .'

Ben Vanek looked at pink-cords. 'Right,' he said. 'Best get out and about, DC Mead.'

'Steph.'

He nodded.

'Do you know the place?' she asked as they headed for the car. 'Or do you want the guided tour?'

He would have preferred not to be teamed with Steph Mead. She was bouncy and confident and he suspected she would chat a lot.

'You drive,' he said.

'Where are we heading?'

'Out to where the body was found.'

'Won't forensics have finished?'

'Yes.'

He thought she made a slight face, but she took the hint and drove the rest of the way in silence.

There was nothing left to see other than the usual tape and markings at the spot below the willows. It was a cold morning and the surface of the water shone.

Vanek looked upstream as far as he could see, wondering where she had gone in, if she had been killed here or put in somewhere else and floated down. He would check out the pathologist's report.

Steph Mead was standing by the willow, looking into the water. 'No place to end up.'

'Abi Righton,' he said. 'Do you have the address?'

She drove well, he gave her that, competent, smooth.

'Where were you before this?'

'Bevham,' she said. 'Uniform. But I always knew I wanted to be CID. Just had to do my time. You?'

'Same. Though I really liked my first couple of years on the beat. I was in Birmingham. Lot going on in Brum.'

'Why Lafferton?'

'I want to work with Serrailler. Thought I'd said.'

'You said he was a legend. You seriously went for the job because of him?'

'Why not?'

She shrugged, taking a corner and accelerating.

'Hello, again, Abi.' Steph smiled. 'This is Ben.'

'Jeez, what's happened? You haven't found Marie, have you?'

She stepped back to let them into the bed-sit.

It was clean, that was Ben's first thought, untidy, with kids' toys and clothes lying around, but it smelled clean, as if she'd been wiping the surfaces down with something. It was a decent-sized room, but it was just that. A room. A toddler was sitting in a high chair pushing bread around a puddle of liquid.

'You haven't found her?'

She pulled a towel off a chair.

'I'm afraid not. I take it you haven't had any word from her yourself?'

'Well, I'd have said, wouldn't I? I don't like thinking about it.'

'Tell me about this man you call Loopy Les?'

He wandered round the room, looking at CDs on a shelf, a couple of children's books, a pretty china mug. No photographs, he thought. But then, he didn't have any himself.

Steph Mead was sitting at the table, making faces at the toddler who stared back at her, huge-eyed, suspicious.

'Or is it Loony Les?'

Abi shrugged. 'We call him all sorts. He's OK.'

'Lives in Lafferton?'

'Yes, he said so once, it was about the recycling bins thing. He said his street was getting them, said it drove him nuts putting one thing in this, the other in that, only you had to do it.'

'His street?'

'He never said which one, no. Sorry.'

'And he just brings out sandwiches and hot drinks?'

'Yeah. And if you want me to tell you why, I haven't a clue about that either, but I reckon he just feels . . .'

'Sorry for you?'

'I don't want anybody's sympathy.'

'Really? I would.'

She narrowed her eyes.

'If I had to do what you do to put food on the table. Does he bother you?'

'Why should he?'

'Scare you?'

'What, him?' Abi snorted.

'Did he know Chantelle?'

'He met her. He turned up the night she

was working, night I saw her. She thought it was weird. The Reachout van was out as well.'

'Do you know the Reachout people, Abi?' Steph Mead asked. She wanted him to know she was still there, Ben thought.

'How do you mean? I don't know them like friends. I know where they come from, what they're called.'

'Is it always the same ones?'

'There are about four regulars. Damian, he's always on. Nicola, Darren.'

'Know anything else about them?'

'They wouldn't have anything to do with it.'

'With what?'

'Chantelle — with what happened to her.'

'Because they're from a church? Doesn't follow, I'm afraid.'

'Maybe not, but they wouldn't.'

'Les?'

She hesitated. The child looked round at her.

'Abi?'

He frowned at Steph, meaning leave her, let her think, take her time.

'No,' Abi said in the end, 'he's all right. He's been coming out with stuff ever since I . . . I been working and he's never said anything . . . you know . . . never been funny

with us. He likes to chat, he brings the stuff
to eat, but that's it. Les wouldn't hurt any
of us.'

'What does he like to chat about?'

'Anything. Weather. The bloody govern-
ment. Usual stuff.'

'Money?'

'You know, why do some people have all
the money, wanker bankers, all that.'

'Quite serious chats then.'

'Why shouldn't we? I'm not thick, you
know.'

'No,' Ben said, 'I can see that.' Meaning
it. She was not thick. 'Think, Abi. Has he
ever said anything at all which would give
us a clue to where he works?'

'It's in some library,' Abi said.

TWENTY

By the time Cat arrived, the others were already in the sitting room of the Precentor's house. She'd had a call from the hospice, an accident had closed the bypass so that she had a four-mile detour to take Sam from school to Hallam House, and traffic coming back into Lafferton was still snarled up on her return. She had almost rung to cry off the meeting, but conscience pricked her — conscience and curiosity. She wanted to see Ruth Webber in action.

'Unworthy,' Chris said as she parked.

'Shut up.'

But they were having tea and general chat. 'We waited for you,' Ruth said, flicking the pages of a notebook to and fro. She was not on her own ground, which would have made it easier to take charge.

Miles Hurley sat slightly apart from the rest, on a straight-backed chair, looking temporary. I haven't got the measure of him, Cat thought, can't tell which side he's on, which way he might jump on any given subject. Is he the Dean's man or his own?

The only other male was Damian Reeve, young, shaven-headed, enthusiastic, the Baptist who had set up the Reachout van, sitting beside Sally Pitts, vicar of St Hugh's, the ugly Victorian church close to what most of Lafferton would never have acknowledged as its red-light district. Cat wondered about Sally. She never wanted much to do with the cathedral and St Hugh's was not known for its social initiatives. Did she even know that girls worked in her parish? Sally was overweight, buck-toothed and, Cat thought, in her own way as charmless as Ruth Webber. What would girls like Abi Righton make of this roomful?

'You lifesaver, thank you.'

But as Ilona handed Cat a cup of tea, Ruth tapped her biro on the notepad.

'We should make a start now. Welcome, everyone, and thank you for sparing the time. This is the first meeting of the Magdalene Group — I suggested the name in fact, Mary Magdalene having been a prostitute —'

'We don't actually know that,' Sally Pitts said.

'Well, whatever the textual niceties, people

179

will know what we mean, the name fits. Everyone agree?'

'I suppose it depends.' Damian had one leg hitched over the other and was scratching a hairy ankle. 'I mean, when you say Magdalene . . .' But under Ruth's stare, he faltered. 'Don't suppose it matters.'

Miles Hurley had pinched his lips together slightly when Ruth began speaking. They stayed pinched.

'Well, we know why we're here, what we're hoping to achieve. I became aware from the first week we arrived in Lafferton that there were prostitutes on the streets, quite a few of them and very blatant, and that isn't right for anyone. I expect most people wonder why the police do nothing, but meanwhile, these are women in need of someone to help them get out of this dreadful way of life — and in need of some sort of haven while they do that.'

'The police move them on,' Ilona said. 'They have blitzes.'

Ruth snorted. 'And what does that achieve? They're back within the hour. This isn't anything to do with moving them on or ignoring them. We want to do something else. If we can provide shelter, a centre for them to come to, they could get food, it would be safe and warm, there could be things for them to do, and above all we would make sure they knew they were part of the cathedral's wider community. That's surely the beginning of the way back — and the way to grace. This has been one of the great failings here in the recent past, as I see it. The cathedral has stood in the middle of Lafferton but it has stood aloof, distancing the ordinary people. Jesus came to save sinners, and we need these girls to know they can find a safe haven here. There could be all sorts of information for them — about housing, sexual health and screening — that's where you come in of course, Cat — counselling, advice about childcare. And then there's the usual question of drugs. I think —'

'Hang on a minute, hang on.' Damian Reeve was pink in the face. 'This is a heck of a lot you're chucking into the mix all at once. And, you know, there already *is* a lot of this sort of advice available, you can't just take the place of social services.'

'Social services!'

'Ruth, may I make a suggestion?' Miles Hurley looked coolly round, his shoulder slightly turned away from Ruth.

There's a history there, Cat thought. He doesn't like her.

'Far be it from me to try and rein in

181

anyone's enthusiasm . . .' He paused and glanced about, then away again, a man who was saying precisely the opposite of what he meant. 'It's always a good idea to set out a clear agenda, have a few specific, achievable goals.'

'Don't run before you can walk,' Damian Reeve muttered, staring at his ankle. He might have been saying it to himself.

'Indeed. Cat,' Miles said, 'might you have something to add?'

'From a medical perspective?'

'Obviously.' Ruth was tapping her biro again.

'From any,' Miles said with a small smile.

'Some of the girls will obviously see their own GPs.'

'Do you have any prostitutes on your list?'

'I'm sorry, Ruth, I couldn't possibly comment on that.'

'Well, of course I meant in general, not naming names.'

'Even so . . . But to look at it more broadly, there are sexual health clinics at Bevham General — drop-in clinics I mean, not just for GP referrals.'

'But I wonder if they would go,' Ilona said. She was sitting at the far end of the sofa, quiet, alert, tactful. She should have been running the group, Cat thought. But Ilona was involved in a great many things. She wouldn't want to take on another job, even if Ruth Webber would let her.

'Some will, some won't. But Bevham isn't Lafferton of course. We don't have a clinic here — perhaps we should, but that isn't really a matter for us today.'

'Why not?'

'I doubt if the medical aspect of this is any of our business here,' Miles said.

Cat nodded. 'There's no rush. We must get it right. Let's go through things point by point. Shall we begin with trying to decide what exactly we are hoping to achieve?'

There was a silence, and then several voices at once. 'Shelter.' 'Bring them to Christ.' 'Give them someone to talk to.' 'Do what we already do, minister to them where they are, on the streets . . .'

Ruth held up her hand. 'Priorities? Let's get some order going. What's our main aim for these girls? From a cathedral point of view.'

'Or perhaps,' Ilona said quietly, 'from their point of view?'

Forty minutes later they had decided that a drop-in centre was most needed. Ruth determined that it should be housed on cathedral premises, Miles Hurley questioned whether there was anywhere suitable, Ilona and Cat were doubtful if prostitutes would come precisely because it would be seen as part of the cathedral and therefore have a religious agenda.

'Well, of course we'll have a religious agenda!' Ruth said. 'I mean, we *are* Christians, aren't we?'

'Reachout has a Christian agenda,' Damian said sadly.

'Yes, but you're just an intermittent thing, we'd be there all the time.'

'All the time?' Miles asked.

'You know what I mean. Not just a van turning up at random.'

'We have a proper schedule.'

'Yes, Damian, but I'm sure you take my point. They want somewhere they can go to when they need it, not when you choose to be there.'

Cat smiled at him sympathetically, but he seemed to have retreated into himself, unable to deal with Ruth's combative manner.

'So, I'll start finding out where we can put this centre. It'll be the Magdalene Centre obviously. I'm sure there are plenty of places we can use.'

'I'd be glad to know where.'

'I'll find the right place, Miles. Leave it with me.'

'I think,' he said, 'that the purposes and aims of this centre are not yet properly thrashed out.'

Ruth sighed.

Cat looked round. 'This may be the wrong phrase,' she said carefully, 'but what about some market research?'

Ilona nodded. 'As in, asking the girls what they might want? Absolutely.'

'Damian.' Damian jumped as Miles turned to him. 'You know these girls, you talk to them. They come to the Reachout van.'

'Yes.'

'Then it would seem that you are best placed to start asking some questions. Doing what Cat calls — and I think it's exactly the phrase — market research. Any other approach would not only be counterproductive, it would be patronising in the extreme. Let us ascertain the extent and the nature of the need, otherwise, we are in danger of doing something to make ourselves feel good and not for the good of these young women.' He stood up. 'I'm sorry, I have to go. Will you excuse me?'

Ruth Webber's angular body exuded tension. Her long fingers ruffled the pages of the notebook and she met no one's eye, did not acknowledge Miles Hurley's departure

185

nor bring the meeting to a conclusion.

Cat's phone ringing brought them out of an embarrassed silence. As she left the room to answer it Damian jumped up, but she didn't hear anything else that was said. The call was unimportant but she told a white lie about having to go into the surgery and fled, knowing that Ilona had understood perfectly, even if Ruth Webber was too thick-skinned to do so.

Twenty-One

'Deano? You coming or what?'

Deano Whelan lay on the sofa trying to make the Nintendo work with the remote which he knew was broken. He had a bag of crisps and he was all right. He didn't need Tyler yelling at him from the garden and banging on the window.

'Come on, what you doing?'

He tried turning the sound up but that didn't work either.

The next thing, Tyler was kicking the front door open.

'Shut your racket, me dad's asleep. He'll fuckin' have you.'

'He on nights then?'

'No, he's pissed.'

'What, at half past ten?'

'You bunked off?'

'Who's asking?'

'Not me dad anyway. All right, hang on, hang on.'

Deano stuffed the last crisps into his mouth and rolled off the sofa. His bike wheel was bent so he went next door and borrowed one that was up against the side gate. Next doors wouldn't be back till late.

'I got a sore throat,' Tyler Nobes said, doing a wheelie off the kerb.

'Yeah, right.'

'That's what it says on the note.'

'What note?'

'The one I'll have for next time I'm there, dickhead.'

They shot down the slope and fast across the road, quick right and left as they went but there was never much traffic just here.

'That bike's crap.'

'So's yours.'

Tyler headed off. They didn't have a plan. They never had a plan. They just went until they got somewhere and that was the plan.

Somewhere was the canal towpath.

Nobody about. Cold with a drizzle.

'You got any money?'

'I've got a smoke.'

'All right.'

But the drizzle was becoming heavy rain. Tyler turned his bike and skidded off towards the footbridge. Underneath the footbridge they could at least light the single cigarette Deano had and pass it between them, and wait for the weather to clear. Wait for anything.

It was Tyler who saw it first. He pulled the bike up so that Deano nearly rammed into him.

'What? What is it?'

Tyler stared until he made out that it was a person, on the ground, head down, knees up. He saw a bit of face, white face, some dark hair.

He could feel Deano's breath on his neck. He took a step, then another, until he could see better.

'You OK?' Deano asked after a minute.

But Tyler had moved another couple of steps until he was close to the huddled figure.

Then Deano saw it, too. He thought at first it was a dog. But it didn't move. Just a heap of rubbish then.

Tyler bent over.

At first Deano thought Tyler was crying, but then he saw that what he was doing was being sick, retching onto his own shoes, and at the same time backing away, pushing Deano back too so that he almost fell over.

'Shit,' Tyler said. 'Holy shit, holy shit, holy shit.'

'What? What?'

Tyler grabbed hold of Deano's arm.

'There's . . .'

'What? Fuck it, Tyler, what is it?'

'Dead body, dead body, it's there, I saw its head and . . .' He threw up again.

Under the footbridge the thing seemed to sway.

'Christ,' Tyler said, pulling up his bike and swinging it round.

'What you doing, where you —'

'Tell someone,' Tyler shouted over his shoulder. 'Come on, don't stay there for fuck's sake.'

But he was away and almost out of sight before Deano could get himself together sufficiently to climb onto his own bike and follow after him, his hands so wet with sweat he had a job keeping his grip.

TWENTY-TWO

'You lost, mate? That's the fire escape.'

Ben Vanek backed away from the door he had been trying to push open.

'Canteen?' he asked, face blazing and furious with himself.

The PC was grinning.

'Basement,' he said.

'I suppose it would be. Thanks.'

How could you be twenty-seven and a half years old and still blush like a teenager for making a daft mistake?

'Don't know you, do I?' The uniform looked suddenly wary.

'DS Vanek. No, first day — can't you tell?'

'OK, no probs, sorry, Sarge.'

That'll be round the station, Ben thought, racing down the stairs. While Steph Mead was checking out the libraries in search of Loopy Les, he had realised he was starving. The station was like all stations, people racketing up and down stairs, banging

191

through swing doors, phones going. He liked to be out, looking people up, going to crime scenes, talking to strangers. Every hour at a desk tapping at a keyboard was an hour he counted as lost. He wondered whether Serrailler let himself get desk-bound, thought not, wondered when the DCS was going to show his face. Ben hadn't come to Lafferton to work with a plod like DI Franks.

There was the slightest of murmurs as he walked into the canteen. He thought he could hear the 'who'shewhere'd-hecomefromnewDSbityoung'. A bit of him was tempted to stand up on a nearby table and introduce himself to the room. Most of him took a tray and slid into the queue at the counter.

It was only as he was taking his coffee and toast away that he glanced quickly round, clocked a couple of the CID he had seen in the conference but otherwise saw only uni-forms.

'Sarge!'

Ben found a seat in the corner and started to open the small pack of butter.

'Sarge . . .'

He didn't look up.

Then she was at his shoulder. 'DS Vanek?'

He jumped up.

192

'I called you three times. You not answering to Sarge then?'

He prayed that he wouldn't colour up even as he knew he was doing so.

'DC Mead, sorry, I was miles away. Can I get you anything?'

'They found Marie O'Dowd's body.'

He swigged down three mouthfuls of coffee and took the toast with him.

'And I think I've found Loopy Les,' she said as they went up the stairs. 'College of FE. Senior Assistant in the Humanities Library. Leslie Blade. I tried the public libraries — nobody in any of them here or in Bevham called Leslie. Unless he's in a school I haven't tried yet, looks like this must be him. *And,*' she said, as they headed towards the car park, 'uniform have his car number. They pulled him over . . . Kerb-crawling.'

As they crossed the yard, Ben Vanek stuffed the remains of the now cold toast into his mouth and swallowed it in a lump which he knew would sit in the middle of his chest for the next couple of hours.

'Bags I stay on the Chantelle case,' Steph said. 'If the boyfriend gets charged, Marie O'Dowd'll be open-and-shut. Bor-ing. Shall I drive?'

TWENTY-THREE

It was the quietness that woke him. He sat up, puzzled for a moment, then got to his feet and went to look out.

The gale had died down. The cottage had been battered by it for days but now everything was still. The heavy clouds had been blown away, leaving a sky pricked all over with bright stars and a huge moon that rode the surface of the water. The sense of quiet was extraordinary.

Simon half thought of dressing and going out, but he had not slept well for the last few nights, because of the wind hurling itself at the windowpanes until they rattled like loose teeth. So now, glad of the calm, he went back to bed.

When he woke again, sunlight flooded in, and the patch of sky he could see as he lay there was clear silver blue.

He was alone. Kirsty had come down with a heavy cold and though he had much enjoyed her intermittent company during his time on Taransay he was glad, as ever, to be by himself. The subject of his leaving had scarcely been mentioned but she knew that he would have to go before long and had seemed quite sanguine about it. The whole thing had been stress-free, he thought as he dressed — the first time in his history of relationships — and for that he held Kirsty McLeod in great affection.

Twenty minutes later he had put fruit cake, cheese, some of his favourite dark chocolate and a bottle of water into the rucksack with his drawing things, and was heading west across the island. After an hour's walking, he came upon a run-down stone crofter's house. Leaning into its walls was a single small tree, bent half over by the wind. He settled down in the sun.

There was never complete silence here, always some birdcall, or the wash of the sea, but without any wind it was as quiet as he had known it. He worked steadily, doing several small rough sketches of the croft and tree before moving to make a more careful drawing of them from another angle. He ate and drank and got up a couple of times to stretch his legs, and when the sun was full on his face, took a fifteen-minute nap. And for the whole time he was conscious of a deep sense of contentment, a freedom from any petty irritations or discomforts, which made him wonder again whether this was what he should do, where he should be, whether he should resign from the force and spend at least half his year on Taransay, the rest travelling and perhaps with Cat, if he gave up his flat. But it was when he imagined doing that, packing up and handing his home over to someone else, or, more likely, to be turned into yet another suite of offices, that he felt sure he could never do it. It was not the flat as such that he cared about — though he did — but what the flat represented, the privacy and quiet space, his own rootedness.

He was concentrating so hard that at first he did not hear the sound of the vehicle, until it drew up on the track a few yards away and the door slammed.

'Hello?'

Douglas Boyd, Kirsty's farmer friend, was coming towards him, his long Scottish oval of a face reddened by the sun.

'What's wrong?'

Serrailler was six foot four but when he stood up Boyd was of a height with him plus perhaps an inch.

'Call for you — they rang twice then asked

if someone could locate you.'

Simon followed Douglas to the jeep, stuffing things into his rucksack as he went.

'Who? My family?'

Douglas started the engine up as he swung into his seat. 'Your Chief Constable, I'm told. They want you to call straight back.'

He did not speak again for the five-mile journey over the hill and down towards the village.

This is the last day, Serrailler thought, looking out to where the dark seal heads were bobbing up and diving down, bobbing and diving in the silver water.

'Thanks for that,' he said to Douglas, as they climbed out of the jeep. 'Good of you.'

'It was nae bother.'

He faced Simon, blocking his path.

'Just another thing,' he said, and without a split second of warning, swung his fist into Serrailler's jaw. 'That's for Kirsty.'

The line from Taransay to the mainland could be temperamental but he got through within a couple of minutes. He touched his jaw a couple of times. It was tender but a clean hit. Boyd hadn't drawn blood.

He had a seat reserved on the chopper the next morning and was packed and the cot-

197

tage tidied. When he was done he thought of walking across to the pub to have a last drink and say his farewells. But whether or not Kirsty knew about the crack Douglas had given him, he decided better not and instead went for a solitary walk along the shoreline and then to bed early, to sleep to the soft sound of the waves turning over and back on the shingle.

At ten thirty the next morning, he looked down and watched grey-green Taransay recede as they climbed away. He had not seen Kirsty McLeod again.

TWENTY-FOUR

'You know, we really could have done with an extra pair of hands last night, Leslie. Three people were down with this stomach bug and it was touch and go whether to call the rehearsal off altogether. If you knew how welcome you would have been — I mean doing anything, but you could have added your voice to the chorus, it was very sparse.'

Ten minutes. He couldn't go to lunch early. He prayed for a student to come up to the desk with a difficult enquiry that only he could answer, but the library was quiet and those who were here showed no signs of needing anything at all.

'Won't you think about it?'

He wondered what his excuse for killing June Petrie would be. Extreme provocation? People killed for less, those whose neighbours had driven them insane with loud music or a ceaselessly yapping dog, and they often met with understanding from a sympathetic judge. June Petrie grinding on about his joining the Lafferton Savoyards to sing in *The Mikado* when he had made it clear to the point of rudeness that he would never do so must count as extreme provocation over a sustained period.

Eight minutes.

'You wouldn't have to do a full audition, nothing like that, he'd just hear you sing a few bars of something easy like a hymn.'

'I don't know any hymns.'

'Or even a nursery rhyme.'

Fool. He ought to know better than to start an argument with her because she always had a pat answer to whatever objection he raised.

'He'd train your voice himself, he's awfully good at that. You'd be amazed the bricks he's made out of straw in his time. He even had . . .'

Six minutes. He could go to the Gents. By the time he had done that and collected his lunch box, it would be one. He didn't need to go to the Gents but if he did it might spare June Petrie's life.

Afterwards, he realised he had not even seen them come into the library, they were just there at the counter in front of him, a young man, a young woman.

'We're looking for a Leslie Blade,' the young man said.

'This is Mr Blade, the Assistant Humanities Librarian.' June Petrie, in a flash. 'Who wants him exactly?'

The young man ignored her. Showed a card.

'I'm Detective Sergeant Ben Vanek, this is DC Mead. Is there somewhere we can have a word in private please, sir?'

'What's wrong, has something awful happened? Leslie, will you be —'

'There's the office,' Leslie Blade said. 'But I was actually just going for my lunch —'

'If you'd show us the way please?' the young woman said.

'Is it my mother? Has something happened to her? Her carer should be there now, Hilary, if something has happened.'

'As far as I'm aware, nothing has happened to your mother. Is anyone likely to interrupt us here?'

'No, the Chief Librarian is on the late shift and everyone else will be going to lunch. I was going to lunch. If this is about the book thefts, then you would need to speak to Mr Dalton, the Chief Librarian actually, he —'

'It has nothing to do with book thefts. Do you know a young woman called Chantelle Buckley?'

Somewhere, the name was somewhere, he was groping for it.

'Is she a student? I don't know all the new students by name, or even the older ones come to that, we have over —'

'No, Chantelle Buckley was a young woman whose body was found in the canal last weekend. As far as I know she had no connection with the college. Did you know her?'

He had a flash picture of the girl's photograph on the television during the local news.

'Mr Blade?'

'The girl who . . . I didn't know her. No.'

'You didn't know her but you did see her?'

They looked hostile and he couldn't understand why.

'Do you know Marie O'Dowd?'

Marie? If it was the same one.

'I know — I have . . . yes. If it's the same Marie. I sometimes . . .'

'Sometimes what?'

He looked round for a chair. They did not. They did not ask him to sit. They did not sit themselves.

'I see her. If it's the same Marie. I don't know their — her other name.'

'Their? Their other names? Who are *they*?'

The girl now. She had a look he didn't care

for, a pert, cocky look. Authority, it said. I have authority. But she didn't, not here. He had.

'Is it the case that you go to meet prostitutes on the streets, Mr Blade, that you often go out to where they're working and talk to them?'

'I take them food — I take them hot drinks and food. Someone should. They shouldn't just be ignored. People ignore them because they don't want them to be there. People treat them like scum.'

'How do you treat them, Mr Blade?'

'I take them food and drink. I try to befriend them.'

'Why would you do that?'

'Why? I would have thought it was obvious.'

'Not to us,' the girl said.

'They shouldn't be treated as if they were untouchable.'

'I'm sure that's right — but there are voluntary organisations that go out there to befriend them and take them food. You could join them, do your bit that way.'

He didn't reply. He did not want to volunteer on the Reachout van because he was not a churchgoer, not religious at all, and they were religious, they had an agenda. He didn't.

203

'Do they pay you?'

'Of course they don't pay me.'

'I wasn't thinking of anything financial.' The young man was staring at him hard, trying to embarrass him, but the odd thing was, he was the one who had coloured up at the implication.

'No,' Leslie said.

'No? No, you receive no payment or, should we say, no favours from the girls?'

'No.'

'When did you last see Chantelle Buckley?'

'I've never seen her. I don't think so . . . well, yes, her photograph on televison, and it was in the paper. I've seen her there.'

'But not on the streets to chat to, not to give sandwiches and coffee to?'

'Her photograph — she isn't one of the ones I know. One of the regular girls. I don't think so.'

'You were stopped by one of our patrol cars, Mr Blade.' The girl. 'What was all that about?'

'If you know they stopped me, you'll know what it was about, won't you? They made a mistake.'

'What sort of mistake?'

'They thought I was . . . they followed my

car. I was down that road, where the girls go.'

'They mistook you for a punter. A kerb-crawler.'

'Yes. I said. They made a mistake. I told them they had, and then one of the girls, Abi, she knows me, she told them. She put them right.'

'Was Chantelle there that night?'

'No. Nobody. Just Abi. I said, I have never to my knowledge seen the poor girl, this Chantelle.'

'But you have seen Marie?'

'I know Marie.' He felt suddenly giddy.

'Right, Mr Blade. Now I'm not entirely happy with what you've told me or that you've told me everything. I'd like you to come down to the station with us, please.'

'What for? I've told you everything I could possibly tell you. I can't just come down to the police station . . . I . . . have to get my lunch and be back at work. I can't just leave.'

'I'm asking you to come voluntarily, sir, but if you don't, we can arrest you.'

'What for? You can't arrest me for nothing.'

'It wouldn't be for nothing.'

There was a sound at the door. June Petrie, eyes everywhere, trying to see right into the room, trying to see Leslie.

'I just wondered if — if there's anything I can do? I wondered —'

'Thank you, Mrs . . . ?'

'June Petrie. Is everything all right, Leslie?'

He should have killed her. Then there would have been a reason for them to take him to the station.

'Thank you, there's nothing for you to do.' The policewoman closed the door in June Petrie's face. Good on you, he thought. Shut the door in her face. Good.

'Do you have a coat, Mr Blade?'

'Yes. A jacket. I have a jacket. A grey jacket.' He heard himself babbling.

'Right, we'll get that while DC Mead goes to start the car. Lead the way please.'

'But . . . I have to give — I have to tell someone, explain . . . what do I say?'

'That you're coming to the police station, sir. That should do it.'

June Petrie was hovering at the end of the passage. He could see a bunch of students at the desk, another couple by the bag check.

'I . . . Could we —'

'Just get your jacket, Mr Blade.'

Head bent, eyes down, he walked to the staffroom, the policeman at his heels, then following him in, then watching, as he took down his jacket.

'My lunch box . . .'

'Bring it.'

He brought it.

TWENTY-FIVE

Abi Righton's face was as pale as Cat remembered, the circles beneath her eyes darker, and she had spots round her mouth. The child sat on her lap quietly.

'She just isn't herself, know what I mean? She's just not right, she hasn't been right since that tummy bug thing.'

'Is she still being sick?'

'Not really.'

'How are her nappies?'

Abi shrugged.

'Is she eating and drinking as usual?'

'Yeah. Well — maybe a bit off her food. Not — she just seems not right.'

'How's your little boy now?'

'He's OK, he's at the nursery.'

'Would you like to sit Mia on the couch then? I'll have a look at her. Has she seemed feverish?'

Cat watched her carefully. The child smiled. She was clearly not in any pain, her stomach was not tender, neither throat nor ears were pink and there was no sign of any rash. The small eyes watching Cat with some suspicion were bright, the whites clear with a healthy blue tinge.

'Good girl, Mia. You're a star.' Cat stroked the child's hair.

'Shall I put her back?'

'Yes, I don't need to examine her any more.'

Abi bent over, strapping Mia into the buggy, then handing her a plastic beaker. Mia drank.

'Has she still got this bug then?' Abi asked.

'I don't think so. Sit down a moment, Abi — when you've got her settled.'

Abi hesitated, then did so, but when she sat, she looked down at Mia and then towards the window blind. Cat waited. She had long ago learned that if a patient had something to ask about other than a routine physical symptom then being silent and waiting to listen was the only way to give them enough confidence to do it. The little girl sucked on her beaker. Abi Righton sat twisting her fingers together. Sometimes, the silences lasted a lifetime.

'I want to know how to get out of it. I don't want . . .'

Cat nodded slightly, still said nothing.

'Did you know about Marie, Doctor? And that other one.'

'I know what I've heard on the news, yes. Like everyone.'

'I knew Marie, I didn't know that other one, Chantelle, well, I met her once, she . . .' Abi looked desperately at the window, as if she might find a way out there. 'Maybe if she'd listened to us, Marie — we'd all said, we'd told her. Chuck that useless Jonty Lewis. And now look. It's not just him. I want out of it and I can't get out of it, you know?'

'Yes,' Cat said gently. 'I do know and you're right. It's no life, Abi.'

'The thing is . . .'

Once she had opened up, she went on, talking about life on the street, about the children, about her own childhood, her bed-sit, Hayley, things that had happened, things people did, and then what she wanted, what she was planning. She talked very fast, as if she had never done so to anyone before. Cat had only to listen.

The allotted ten minutes ran to twenty-five, the queue in the waiting room would be building up, Mia whimpered a little, then went to sleep in the buggy — and none of it mattered beside Abi Righton's distress and fear and her determination. When she stopped talking she looked limp, as if all the life and energy had drained out of her, and she had cried too, but her eyes no longer seemed dead and the air of defeat had lifted a little.

Cat pushed the box of tissues over to the other side of her desk. Abi took a couple and blew her nose.

'How do you feel now?'

Abi looked at her and shrugged, but then said, 'Better.'

'Yes. It always helps.'

'Sorry.'

'What on earth are you sorry for?'

'I mean — I'm not, like, ill or anything.' She nodded at Mia. 'She's not ill either.'

'I'm still the right person to come to — at least at first. But I'd like to make a suggestion, Abi. Would you talk to a counsellor? I could find someone who had the time to listen and advise you, support you while you get out of all this. She could help with access to courses or whatever it is you decide you want to do — when you feel ready? You could see her every week or so. I think it would help a lot.'

The wariness was back even as Cat had started talking.

'I don't know . . . not sure about that. What sort of a person would it be? I don't want social services poking their noses in, I know all about them, they might want to take my kids away.'

'It wouldn't be social services and no one would have any reason for taking the children. You're a good mother, Abi.'

Abi gave a short laugh.

'You are — those aren't just empty words. You love them, you care about them, you feed them properly and it's their future that matters to you. All of that makes you a good mother in my book, and you should be proud of yourself. It's not easy. But you know that you'd be an even better mum if you weren't working on the streets. I really want to help, Abi, and you can always come and see me, of course, but I think you deserve more than I have time for.'

'Where would I have to go?'

'I'm not sure — I want to find the best person for you. Can you leave me to find out and come back next week? I've got someone in mind but I need to check if she can take on anyone else.'

There was a long silence. Cat heard the phone ringing in the reception area, voices, someone going into the surgery next to hers.

'OK,' Abi said. She got up, took hold of the buggy, looking as if she couldn't leave fast enough now, embarrassed rather than upset.

'Make another appointment at the desk — and can we get in touch with you? It might only take me a couple of days to fix something up.'

'I got the mobile.'

'Would you give me the number?'

Mia jerked awake suddenly and looked around in bewilderment. Abi leaned down to her.

'No,' she said. 'I'll come back. Thanks, Doctor.'

The door banged shut behind her.

Cat added a line to Abi's notes on-screen, jotted a reminder on her memo pad and called the next patient. She was still catching up two hours later.

'One of those mornings,' Bronwen said, coming in with coffee and a sympathetic smile as the last patient left. 'Oh, your brother wants to know if you can have lunch.'

'My brother's on a Scottish island.'

'Not any more. He'll be in the King's Oak at Stanton from one o'clock.'

Cat glanced at the clock. 'I can't,' she said, 'I really can't. Not today.'

'Of course you can,' Bronwen said firmly.

213

TWENTY-SIX

It felt good, he thought, looking round the room, and Taransay was in another life, though he still felt its effects; his energy was up, he was focused. He had driven through the day, stopped in a hotel off the motor-way for supper and a short night and had been back in Lafferton in time to drop his things at the flat and book lunch with Cat. They had caught up but not entirely. He would try and spend part of the weekend with her at the farmhouse. Then he had gone to see the Chief Constable. Now, he was back, in the small meeting room with half a dozen senior CID officers, the sun shining in, the new DS, Ben Vanek, looking, as Paula Devenish had said, bright, alert — and cocky. 'He's very keen to work with you,' she had said, 'so encourage him, Simon — just don't let him run before he can walk.'

Recognising something of his younger self

in the new sergeant, he agreed, knowing how easily the edge could be taken off enthusiasm and ambition by the setbacks of the daily grind. Time he spent with Vanek now could encourage the new boy, as he knew it had encouraged his former sergeant, Nathan Coates — now a DCI in Yorkshire and as committed to the job as ever.

'As you know, the media are all over us at the moment. I've called a press conference tomorrow because I need tonight to get up to speed with all the details. If you have any problems with them, speak to the press officer. I am now OIOC and I want to stress that for the time being and until we have any evidence which may cause a reassessment, the two cases are being kept separate. DI Franks is heading up the Chantelle Buckley investigation. DI Drummond, I want you in charge of the Marie O'Dowd team from now. Of course you'll talk to one another about any common factors but there are just two at this point — both women worked as prostitutes, Marie here in Lafferton, Chantelle only in Bevham, so far as we know, until the one occasion just before she disappeared. And they were both strangled. Marie O'Dowd had some injuries to her face consistent with there having been some sort of struggle. Chantelle didn't.

215

What we don't want is any more stuff in the press about a serial killer of girls on the street. Unofficially, though, I'm keeping an open mind. If anything comes in to link the two killings which is more than just vague and circumstantial, the SIO of each team will want to talk to one another. Right, Dave, what do we have so far?'

DI Franks handed out some A5 sheets on which were a photograph and a few typed sentences. 'This is Leslie Blade. DS Vanek and DC Mead went to his workplace and questioned him, and he was then brought in here, not under arrest, and interviewed by DS Vanek at some length.'

He went through the background.

'Did you get anywhere with him, DS Vanek?' Serrailler said.

'Sir?'

The young man sat forward, almost bursting out of himself with eagerness, his bright blue tie swinging back and forth, his face flushed.

'Welcome on board. What's your take on this librarian?'

'I think he's as guilty as hell, sir, I'm sure he is, I'm convinced he did it.'

'Did what?'

The flush spread up from his neck.

'Murdered Chantelle and Marie, sir.'

'You're investigating the killing of Chantelle, DS Vanek. Leave the other case to the other team.'

'Yes, but, sir, he could easily have killed both of them and I think he did.'

Serrailler paused before replying. He didn't want to nip enthusiasm in the bud or put the new sergeant down before a roomful of more experienced officers. On the other hand . . .

'What grounds have you got for believing Leslie Blade killed Chantelle Buckley?'

Simon sensed an atmosphere in the room. He'd known it often enough before. They were up for a game, waiting for Vanek to be sat on, bear-baiting. It happened, especially in the middle of a difficult investigation. Winding up Vanek would be a safety valve, but he was not about to let it happen.

'Something funny, DC Shastri?'

'No, sir.'

'Good.' Serrailler waited as the mood in the room changed again. He turned back to Ben Vanek. 'You were going to say . . . ?'

'Well, he's obsessed with these prostitutes, he's around them most nights, he's had every opportunity. And he's hiding something.'

'Such as?'

'Not sure. *And* he's the type.'

217

'Ah. The type. Now that's an interesting observation. Have you done a profiling course, DS Vanek?'

'I did work with a profiler in my last force, yes.'

'All right. What type of man kills two prostitutes?'

'Well, this guy is sexually suppressed, he has no relationships, he lives with his elderly mother, he doesn't seem to have many friends . . . a loner in other words. He's buttoned up, but he goes and chats to toms on the street at night . . .'

'All of that may well be true. But we need more. Do we have anything? Blade's movements on the night Chantelle was last seen?'

'Says he was at home with his mother.'

'Have you corroborated that with her?'

'Not yet, sir, no.'

'Better do so.'

'Sir.' Vanek stared down at the floor.

'Any CCTV?'

'Nothing. There's a camera focused at the printworks gate and it does have footage of Chantelle talking to one of the other girls and going to the Reachout van. Nothing with Blade on it.'

'His car?'

'No, sir, not on the night Chantelle was killed. We've got it from the previous night when Blade was questioned by a patrol on suspicion of kerb-crawling. There's actually no indication he's ever picked up any of the girls. The thing is, he just doesn't ring true with me, guv, he's pretty weird.'

'Doesn't make him a murderer.'

'No, sir.'

'He's still here?'

'Yes, sir, but I don't think we've enough to charge him.'

'Anyone else in the frame?'

'A punter came forward — he'd been with one of the other girls that night and he'd seen Chantelle. He didn't recognise her so much as her green jacket, he'd remembered that. He gave us a statement. There's nothing on him — he was on CCTV but much earlier that evening. We're going through every inch of the tapes for the whole week.'

Someone groaned.

'And you go on doing it and if you half spot anything, rewind and look again — this is the sort of case where anything and everything could well be on camera.'

'With regard to the pathologist's report on Chantelle . . .' DI Franks turned over a couple of pages in his folder. Serrailler watched him. Boring copper, dutiful, patient, a bit resentful that he wasn't a DCI but probably realistic about his chances because, once made up to DI, he had shown no further signs of ambition or outstanding capability. Just competence. And they needed competence.

'All right. Let's move on. Marie O'Dowd. She had a boyfriend, Jonathan — Jonty — Lewis. Drug addict, small-time dealer, lots of previous — GBH, assault — he'd apparently been violent towards Marie on and off, never reported but one of her friends confirms it, and he probably wrecked the caravan she lived in. Finding Lewis is a number-one priority.'

'How long had she been dead when she was found?'

'Pathologist reckons three to five days, settle for four.'

'Sir?'

There was another faint frisson through the room. They'd got him down as a show-off, the kid who always has his hand up in class. Serrailler wanted them to be wrong, guessed that they were only partly so, but he didn't want them gloating.

'Sergeant?'

'Look — two prostitutes, on the same beat, both been out there at or around the same time. One goes AWOL, found strangled and her body in the canal, the second one goes AWOL, found strangled,

220

not in the canal but right by it. I know you say we're keeping the two inquiries separate but I'd bet they're not.'

'I'm not a betting man, Sergeant, but all the same, I wouldn't bet against you. It's as I said — the two teams investigate separately but that doesn't mean my mind is closed to the possibility that we're looking for one person. Just to pursue your hunch, Sergeant Vanek — if the same man killed both girls, would you definitely pin it on Blade?'

Vanek looked worried. But the flush was not rising to his face now, he had gained confidence, sensed that Serrailler was more with him than against him. He waited a moment. DI Franks was putting papers into his folder, clearly uninterested in the theories of a very young new sergeant.

'Yes,' Ben Vanek said.

'Thanks, Sergeant. Now — the public. Although we've had a man in for questioning he hasn't been under arrest and he isn't being charged. We need to ensure that the public has confidence in us, confidence in what we're doing and confidence not only that we will find the killer or killers of these two girls but that until we do our priority is everyone's safety — the general public and the girls working the streets. As from tonight, we are putting a large and very visible presence out there — in the red-light district, in the centre of town. I have the Chief's backing on this one for as many as it takes. Here's what's happening.'

They listened as he gave them the outline of what and where the uniform presence would be, including information points, leafleting and stop-and-search patrols. It would not involve CID directly but the investigation teams needed to be briefed.

As the meeting broke up, Serrailler called DS Vanek back.

'Everything all right so far?'

'Sir. I'm really enjoying it actually. This is great for my first one here.'

'From whose point of view? No, you're right. It's interesting now — and it could go either way.'

'Open-and-shut, Blade killed them both.'

'Or Lewis killed them both.'

'Or . . .'

'Exactly. Or neither of them killed anyone. Is that the outcome you're praying for, Sergeant?'

Ben Vanek grinned. 'Not at all.'

'Good. You take your orders from DI Franks of course — but tread carefully with Leslie Blade.'

'Guv.'

■ ■ ■ ■

Serrailler did not leave the station until after seven, by which time the teams were already rolling out, vans packed with uniform heading for the streets, 'a strong visible presence to calm and reassure', as the Chief had put it. He took the long way home, noting the yellow fluorescent police jackets everywhere, the information van setting up with lights, the groups of officers waiting to be sent this way or that. The minute anyone was charged, the temperature would drop and the overtime hours of uniform reduce, but until that happened people wanted to be reassured and to feel safe, to see something being done.

He felt buoyed up as he swung into the Cathedral Close, enjoying being in the thick of an operation, determined to get it right. He wondered about Ben Vanek's hunches. He had them himself, though he had learned never to rely on them alone, only to see them as one small component in a complex set of mainly standard procedures. Hunches were never dull and when they were correct they gave you a lift which saw you through any amount of pedestrian routine. Some people never had them, or if they did dismissed them at once; others he knew had acted on one, it had come good, and they had over-relied on them for the rest of their careers, believing they had some special knack their colleagues did not possess, like a healing touch or the ability to dowse.

He had dropped his things off at the flat earlier but scarcely looked around. Now, when he walked in, he did not put on the lights but went straight to the long windows overlooking the close. The daylight had gone and the lamps were lit, shining gold through the autumn trees that lined the path on either side. The floodlights were on the cathedral tower. He opened the window to let in the cool evening. The air on Taransay had been salty and fresh — here there was no sea, no salt, but the grass had been cut, probably for the last time that year, so that the smell of it came to him as if from deep in the country. But even though the close itself was quiet at night, the sound of traffic was always faintly in the background. He had wondered if it might take him a few days to adjust but he felt immediately at home. No jet lag.

He switched on the lamps and looked around. At home.

Cat had been in every week to sort out his

post and forward the few things that had seemed urgent. The rest was in neat piles on the table and she had even roughly organised the piles so that what was obviously business mail, bank and bills was in one, personal in another, catalogues and circulars in a third. The smallest pile had the personal letters. A blue airmail envelope from an old friend in Canada. A card from Nathan and Emma Coates in Yorkshire. A card from Nepal. He turned it over and read the message from Jane Fitzroy. Read it twice. Looked at the picture of mountains. Jane. A sudden picture of her came into his mind, as vividly as if he had seen her a moment before, Pre-Raphaelite red hair, heart-shaped face, generous mouth. Jane.

The cathedral clock struck the half-hour, the sound reverberating round the close and beyond. Whenever he was away it took him a while to adjust to not hearing it; the moment he returned it made him feel somehow settled and rooted again.

Jane.

He wished her well. But it would not have worked. Nobody would, he thought, nobody could ever break permanently into this world, this private space.

He remembered what the new DS had said about Leslie Blade, unmarried, the

225

loner, and so in his elementary profiler's handbook, a suspect — 'weird'. Simon smiled to himself, thinking of easy-going Kirsty, who had no wish to pry, nor probably even to get his Christmas card — remembering, too, Douglas's swift upper cut. His jaw remembered it as well.

He dropped Jane Fitzroy's postcard into the waste basket along with the entire pile of junk mail, poured himself a whisky, and went to unpack.

TWENTY-SEVEN

'Now is the time for the burning of the leaves,'
Cat said. 'Is that Shakespeare?'

'Binyon.'

Cat and Judith had been raking the lawn
at Hallam House since before tea, and now
the leaves were piled at the far end of the
garden ready for a bonfire.

'My mother loved this job,' Cat said. 'She
loved everything to do with the garden, but
for some reason, this especially. She said
she liked putting it all gradually to bed for
the winter.'

'Do you mind? That I'm here doing it
instead?'

'No. Not now. I mind her not being here
as well — if you follow.'

'I follow.'

The light was almost gone. In the house,
Felix was asleep, Sam in bed reading *Gala-
had at Blandings*. Hannah was staying at the
house of her friend Ellie, who possessed

even more Barbie dolls and their paraphernalia than she did.

'What I could never bear was Dad being here on his own. The place was so bleak and he was so forbidding. I used to put off coming, get him over to us instead. It's different now.'

'Thank you.'

Cat put down the rake and rubbed her neck and shoulders.

'Yes. I think we're done.'

'Dare I ask about America?'

Judith shook her head. 'I told you — all sorted. Perhaps later next year and for a couple of months. Let's go in, I must put the vegetables on.'

But as they went into the kitchen Cat's phone rang. She went back outside to get a better signal, expecting to have to advise on a patient in the hospice.

'Cat? It's Miles Hurley. Is this is a bad moment?'

'Oh. No, it's fine. Is everything all right?'

'Well, I rather wanted to have a chat about all this Magdalene Group business. Do you think that would be possible?'

'Of course. I wasn't altogether happy with how things went at the meeting.'

'No.' He had a faintly sarcastic, dry manner of speaking. 'Indeed not.'

'Were you wanting me to ask anyone else?'

'I rather hoped to keep it between us. Are you free tomorrow evening? I know you're tied up at work during the day. Perhaps you could come by for a drink around half six?'

She agreed, warning him that if she couldn't make arrangements for the children she would have to cancel.

But Judith, as ever, was glad to help her out.

'I can't get used to it . . . I'm a single parent — how can that be me? It doesn't make sense.'

Judith handed her two glasses of wine. 'One for you, one for Richard. Go and keep him company.' As Cat went out she said, 'I thought I'd try asking Simon to supper. Again.'

Cat hesitated. Judith had turned her back and was filling a saucepan with water, moving a pile of beans across to it, being busy, not wanting a discussion.

'Fine.'

Richard Serrailler was sitting at the small desk her mother had always used, marking proofs of the medical journal he still co-edited. Cat put down his glass of wine.

'I gather the wanderer has returned,' he said without looking up. 'I do wonder why we pay our police such large wages to take long holidays.'

'He needed it. And he's plunged straight back in with these two murders.'

'Ah, the street girls, yes. The letters in the local paper are full of moral outrage. Do people go about with their eyes shut?'

'They certainly turn blind ones.'

He put away his proofs and came to sit opposite her.

'You look well,' Cat said. It never ceased to surprise her, that happiness could so transform someone.

He gave her a sharp glance but ignored the comment, saying instead: 'I have started my grandson on his first book by The Master.'

'Wodehouse? Bit old and dated for Sam, isn't he?'

'Neither. We shall see. I heard promising chuckles coming from his bedroom. I decided Lord Emsworth was the right place to start rather than Jeeves.'

'Maybe it's skipped a generation. Neither Simon nor Ivo ever took to him.'

'More fool them. Have you been in communication with your brother?'

'I had lunch with him before he went off to take charge of the murder squads. He looked well too. He's working up to a new exhibition in the spring.'

Richard shook his head. He had never understood why Simon was a policeman, or why he was an artist, or why he had not married years ago. Cat thought the reason was that he had not tried.

He was looking at her over the top of his spectacles, a straight, careful look. As if I were a specimen, she thought. That's the way he's always looked at all of us. But not Judith. He looks at her quite differently.

'How are you, Catherine?'

She was taken aback. It was difficult to know how to answer, whether to tell the truth, or to brush the enquiry off. But with her father, that was never possible.

'The hardest part is trying to find a way of accepting that there is nothing you can do about any of it. Nothing you can do to change it, or to put the clock back, or put things right if they were wrong. Nothing. You probably didn't leave many things unsaid. You knew what was coming,' he said.

She had to read between the lines — that he had not known, that he had been completely unprepared for her mother's death and that there were chasms of unspoken things left lying between them.

'I just feel leaden,' she said. 'Nothing's worth doing but I have to do things.'

'If I were your doctor, I would ask if you

231

were eating properly but I am not and you are sensible in that regard.'

She smiled. He was trying to reach her at least. Judith had changed him — or perhaps, more truthfully, helped him to change — in several ways.

Later, as she was helping her load the dishwasher, Cat said as much. 'Can you work your magic on Si too?' she added.

Judith stood with a plate in her hand. Her expression was not so much serious as deeply sad, as though a shadow of unhappiness had fallen across and darkened it, and at the same time taken something from her usual sense of ease.

'I don't know,' she said after a moment. 'Only so much can come from one side. I think after that it's up to him.' She slipped the plate into the rack and closed the machine door.

The following morning the application forms for her palliative care course arrived, but a hectic day left Cat no time to read them properly and it was not long before six thirty when she left, running late for her drink with Miles Hurley.

When Jane Fitzroy had been attached to the cathedral and had lived in the same bungalow at the end of the long garden of the Precentor's House, to reach it had meant a walk down an uneven stone path, one which was treacherous in the dark without a torch. But now it had been relaid, small lights had been placed the whole way down, and Miles had also left the porch light on and his curtains open to guide her.

It was still strange to come here — she had not been since Jane's time and the bungalow held bad memories of the day when she had been held hostage by one of her own patients.

But as Miles opened the door to her she could see that it was entirely changed, not just decoratively — the wall leading into the sitting room had been taken down, making the whole area open-plan, with only the study still separate.

It was a tidy, bland interior without anything to personalise it as belonging to Miles Hurley rather than anyone else — like a show flat, Cat thought. It had probably been furnished by the sort of person who did these things for a living. Everything was perfectly comfortable, perfectly neutral, a blend of taupe, sand and magnolia, every-thing new but low-cost, the whole lot bought as a package.

He was unmarried, he was out a good deal, as all the cathedral staff were, he had no touch when it came to turning four walls into a home, yet she thought he would probably be quite surprised if anyone had told him so.

'I can offer you wine, gin or a decent fruit-juice spritzer.'

She waited, sitting in a chair covered in taupe linen while he brought the drinks. He was a nondescript but not bad-looking man, hair prematurely greying and tonight he wore a normal collar.

'Right. The Magdalene Group — the putative Magdalene Group. What is this all about, Cat? You see, I thought we were going to start exploring ways in which the cathedral might get the message across to the girls on the street that they are as welcome as anyone else, positively welcome — how we do it, what we say, whether we provide some sort of — I don't know — welcoming space.'

'And you think it won't be welcoming?'

He sighed. 'Can I be blunt?'

She smiled.

'Yes — Ruth. Ruth is the problem. She always has been. Stephen will let her steam-roller him into letting her head-up this committee on the grounds that he already has enough to do — which indeed he does. But with Ruth, in my bitter experience, nothing is up for discussion — a committee is there to rubberstamp her proposals, and for a quiet life many of them do.'

'I won't be steamrollered, Miles. What is a drop-in centre? A bit like a shelter for the homeless, except that most of the prostitutes do have homes. I'm not sure that the cathedral's the right place for it. Of course we shouldn't dissociate ourselves from any moves to provide something, but there are other bodies who need to be involved. We ought to look at being part of a group, a team, with a voice and a role, yes.'

'It's a great relief to hear you say that, Cat.'

'The question is, what do we do?'

'About Ruth? We have to make — certain allowances. That's all I can say really.'

He stared into his drink for a moment. Cat waited.

'She has had — troubles. They have no children of course and that has been something of a hardship for her. If she had, perhaps it would all have turned out differently.' He hesitated, but then seemed to draw a line under making any further confidences. 'Otherwise, we stand up to her — that's a lesson I learned some time ago. Let me top up your glass.'

The spritzer, made with some sort of fruit smoothie whisked up with soda and ice, was

235

good. Most men would have provided weak orange squash as a soft drink. She wondered about him. He was a man who gave out no personal clues, though he was easy and open in conversation.

'How long have you known them?'

'I was at Cuddesdon with Stephen. He met Ruth when he was in his first curacy. He and I were in the same group ministry in south London, then he was archdeacon. One of those men you never quite expected to rise up the Church career ladder as far as he has, to be frank.'

'I sense that you and Ruth have crossed swords in the past.'

His face became set and his mouth twitched at the sides, but he simply said, 'Yes. Which makes it difficult for me. I wanted to hear what you thought, as someone from the outside, as it were. This is quite an important issue, though perhaps not so high up the agenda for everyone else as it seems to be for Ruth. But still, I think it's something we should be looking at.'

'Have you talked to any of the others?'

'No. I decided you were likely to have the most informed opinion.'

'I'm pretty sure Ilona will agree with us.'

'Oh yes. Dear, good Ilona.'

There was something in his tone that she

didn't altogether like, a suggestion of —
what — sarcasm?

'Damian will agree — he has his Reachout
van, why should he want the cathedral
muscling in? Sally — I'm afraid I couldn't
make Sally out.'

'Nobody can.'

He smiled at her, a quick smile that
flashed on and off again, leaving his face
exactly as before.

'I bet we have a majority,' he said.

'I think we should start the next meeting
by making it quite clear we should move
with caution — that everything is up for
discussion, and nothing is going to be
decided in a hurry. It's too important.'

'And Ruth will say that is why the Church
of England never gets anywhere — because
it is always moving cautiously after much
discussion.'

'I've often thought that's one of its
strengths.'

'You are a woman after my own heart.
Now, the other thing I wanted to talk about
— just because I don't have any direct
involvement in it — is the musical life of
the place. Tell me about the St Michael's
Singers.'

They talked for another half-hour, rang-
ing over some of the things that were caus-

ing tensions within the congregation. Miles Hurley listened, and did not come out with clear opinions on any of them, as he had on the Magdalene Group issue. Perhaps he saw himself as a go-between, trying to get rival factions talking to one another, or at least to prevent open warfare. It would not be easy, and she wondered if he was the right person, whether he was likely to keep his counsel. Some people, she knew, say what they imagine whoever they are currently speaking to wants to hear. Miles Hurley could be one of them.

She went away, slightly puzzled as to why he had asked to see her at all.

TWENTY-EIGHT

'Come in.'

DI Franks's head came round the door.

'Sir. DNA reports.'

'I don't need to ask, do I?'

'Afraid not. No leads at this stage.'

Simon got up and looked out of the window. The forecourt was even busier than usual. On the other side of the entrance, the press had set up shop. They wanted somebody arrested and charged. They always did — preferably in time to catch the lunchtime news bulletins. It was easy to be put under pressure by the frenzy they could whip up and he had learned over the years that keeping them on side, telling them the truth wherever possible and then asking for their full cooperation, was the only sensible way.

He had scheduled his statement for eleven thirty and was, as always, punctual to the minute. The conference room was packed.

'Good morning. Thanks for coming.

Right. We have this morning released a fifty-three-year-old Lafferton man without charge, following questioning in connection with the murders of seventeen-year-old Chantelle Buckley and twenty-three-year-old Marie O'Dowd.'

An immediate buzz. Voices called out with questions, arms were waving. Serrailler waited.

'We are looking for a twenty-seven-year-old man, Jonathan James Lewis, generally known as Jonty, who was the boyfriend of Marie O'Dowd. We want to interview him in connection with Marie's murder.'

He pointed to the picture that had come up on the large screen behind him.

'This is Lewis, though I'm afraid the photo isn't very recent. You can get copies from the press officer and I'd be grateful if you could publish it as widely as possible — we want the public to report any sightings or other information. No relatives locally and we've drawn a blank so far among known acquaintances. Meanwhile, separate inquiries into the murders of both women are continuing.'

The questions came from all sides of the room.

'Are you saying the two murders are or are not connected?'

'Can you say why the Lafferton man was brought in and then released?'

'What are you doing to reassure the public?'

'What measures are police taking to protect other prostitutes still working on our streets?'

The two DIs sat beside him stone-faced but Serrailler never minded being challenged by the press — that was their job, they asked questions the public would have asked, and needed to know. They also knew how constrained he was in what he could and could not say. He replied with care, knowing that he had given them little.

'I may be able to give you more information later today but I'm afraid that's it for now. However, I will keep you fully up to speed with any developments.'

They broke up, knowing the score. They also knew Serrailler played fair. When he had any more to give them, he would.

TWENTY-NINE

Leslie Blade walked without stopping or looking back for almost ten minutes. It was drizzling and he had no mac but he barely noticed. A car swerved to miss him, blaring its horn as he stepped out across the road, and when he reached the opposite pavement he wondered what had happened, why the noise, why the horrified stare of a woman watching. He had no sense of time, little of where he was, except that he was somewhere between the police station and home, and he had no idea if he was going home, or going to the college, or of what he was expected to do, who knew, who to ask.

There had been some sort of breakfast but he had eaten nothing and only taken a few sips of the tea and then, suddenly, it was over, they were listing his possessions, handing them back, sign here, sign there, you're now free to go, that way, sir, not this way. Free to go.

There was a café in the row of shops he was passing. Dino's.

The noise from the espresso machine startled him. There were people at a couple of tables and they stared. But perhaps not at him. Perhaps they did not even notice him. Did anyone know? How would they? Hilary knew. He had had to ring Hilary, ask her to stay with his mother, tell her something but he could not now remember what he had told her.

Free to go.

He got coffee and toast and sat with his back to the window. People went by. Anyone might recognise him, anyone might know.

Suddenly, he felt tears prick his eyes. His hand shook as he lifted the cup. The coffee spilled over.

Free to go.

He bit into the toast and it seemed to swell inside his mouth, and turn into some alien substance, soft and choking.

Inside his head a muzz of echoes and sensations but no clear thoughts, nothing he could grasp and hold to. At first, it had been troubling but he had felt that he might be of help. The murder of two girls appalled him, especially of Marie, the one he had known. He could not keep pictures of her out of his mind, could not stop imagining

243

what had happened, how, when, what she had felt and tried to do. He had thought that by telling them everything he possibly could about the girls, the time he spent with them and why, what it was like for them out there, that he would be useful, might lead them to whoever . . . whenever. It had taken some time for the cold realisation to seep into his consciousness, that he was being questioned as a suspect, that they had his name, his details, his private activity, down on paper, that they were challenging him to prove to them that he had not killed either girl.

That was why they had taken swabs from inside his mouth. That was the way they proved things now.

He managed to swallow the soft swollen mass of wet toast congealed with butter but it hurt his throat, as if it were made of hard metal passing down his gullet.

The café door opened. He dared not look round. People went, people came, the coffee machine hissed, and every sound was magnified inside his head, like drumming and shouting and screaming.

He did not know what to do. Perhaps he would not be allowed back into the college. You are free to go. But mud sticks. He had been taken to the police station, after all.

June Petrie had seen everything.

Mud sticks.

He was free to go but not free to go.

He went to the counter and bought another cup of coffee though when he got back to his table he saw that the first was only half drunk. The toast was cold and he pushed it to one side.

The smell of the police station was on him, on his sleeves and his collar, in his hair; an institutional, antiseptic yet grubby smell. He would throw away the clothes he was wearing and bathe until his skin was raw to get rid of the smell. When he got home.

How would that be? Hilary would be there. His mother would be there. He could see them both, looking, waiting, puzzled, as he walked in. What did they know? He had been allowed a telephone call but he had talked only to Hilary and he knew he had not been very coherent, just been anxious to ensure that she could stay with Norah, and Hilary had agreed and sounded worried but had asked no questions, done no prying. That was the way Hilary was.

He took small sips of his coffee, holding the cup with both hands because they were still unsteady. The café was steamy. He had been here before once or twice. Liked it well enough. They were always cheerful, always

245

friendly. He heard the proprietor now, chatting to someone, making a teasing remark to another. The ordinary world, Leslie thought suddenly. This is the ordinary world and I am returned to it. None of them knows me. Nobody knows where I have been nor why, and they will surely never know. He had no idea if his name had been in the paper but had the vague thought that you were anonymous until charged. And he had not been charged. He had not been charged. He gripped the cup so hard he thought it might shatter in his hands.

They had warned him not to go near the girls again, not to take them food, not to drive into the area at night. They could not forbid him, they had said, they could only warn him not to do it for his own safety, to ensure he came to no harm, got into no more trouble.

There had been three of them interviewing him at different times. The young woman had been tough, supercilious, trying to trip him up, the younger man cocky. Only the older detective had been easy, relaxed with him, friendly almost, as if this were not a police station, as if he had not been brought in, as if they were having a confidential chat. But none of it had altered what he had told them. None of them could make him say what he could not say.

The one word that had been repeated like bangs of a hammer on a nail, over and over again, had been 'why.' Why did he go out to the girls on the streets at night? Why try to befriend them? Why take them parcels of food and flasks of drink? If he had no religious motive and he was not wanting to buy their services, why? Why? Why? Why? Why?

How could he answer?

He had no real sense of time but he seemed to sit there half frozen, his thoughts moving more and more slowly so that they seemed to be congealing, for much of the morning. Nobody spoke to him, nobody disturbed him. He did not look at anyone.

But in the end, he simply got up, left a pound coin on the table by the cups because it seemed to him that he should somehow pay for having stayed so long, and went out into the street. Nobody glanced at him. He waited, anticipated a stare, even tried to catch someone's eye, but she walked on.

He felt tired now and it was a fifteen-minute walk home, so he went to the taxi rank in the square, hesitated as he approached the first cab, wondering if the man would know, would look at him, would refuse to take him.

But he just nodded, started the engine. Leslie leaned back in the seat and felt a great weakness overcome him and a tightness in his chest so that he had to concentrate to breathe. They stopped at a pedestrian crossing and a woman glanced into the cab. Perhaps she knew, perhaps he was recognised after all. He slid down in the seat. They drove on. He glanced out of the rear window but she had disappeared. There seemed to be a thousand stops, at traffic lights, at junctions, behind other cars, at more crossings, the journey went on miles into the future, carrying him a great distance. He fell into an odd, half-awake trance and the sound of the engine was like an animal purring.

'Forty-eight?'

Forty-eight.

'Forty-eight, yes. Thank you.'

He noticed the clock on the dashboard so he knew what time it was but what was the day? He could not remember the day.

The street was quiet. Were people at their windows? He felt spying eyes following him as he went up the path to the front door, judging eyes, and heard the whispering tongues. He wondered if he would ever live down the shame. Word would get out. Word always got out. June Petrie knew. He could not imagine June Petrie staying silent.

He was fumbling about for the key with fingers that seemed to have lost all sensation when the door opened.

'Oh, Leslie!'

Hearing Hilary's voice, full of warmth and understanding, he thought he might burst into tears, but he only shook his head and went in as she held open the door for him.

'Come into the kitchen, I'll make you tea. You'll perhaps want to get yourself together.'

Before you see her, she meant, before you have to come up with an explanation.

He followed her and reached for a chair before his legs gave way under him.

'It's quite all right,' Hilary said. 'I told her you'd been called away, you had to go with a work colleague somewhere, you hadn't had time to explain, or else I'd misunderstood, I said, being stupid as I am. You needn't worry.'

He looked at her but could not speak. Hilary. How old was she? In her forties, with, he knew, a husband and two children, boys. What else did he know? Nothing else, except that without her their lives would not have functioned so easily. He felt a wave of guilt, that he knew so little about her. Did he take her for granted? Easy to do so.

He watched her, pouring milk into the jug,

water into the teapot, unused, not making anything of it. A large, fair-haired woman in grey trousers and a brightly coloured T-shirt. Hilary.

'It was all a mistake,' he said. 'Something — some confusion — someone else . . . they made a mistake, you see . . . but they had every right to . . . I had to clear myself, I had to answer the questions, of course. I've no complaints, I can't blame them, they're doing their job, they have to do their job.'

Hilary set down the mug of tea and then, briefly, placed her hand over his. It was a soft hand but her touch quite firm. He felt the tears behind his eyes but they did not show.

'She's watching the lunchtime news,' Hilary said, 'you know she doesn't like to miss that. You take your time.'

She did not watch him or fuss over him, she started to put clothes into the washing machine, and then to fold up a basket of dry clean ones, moving patiently from this to that, so that, after a while, he began to calm down, to drink his tea and feel his heart beat less erratically, to hear the tick of the kitchen clock and the soothing hum of the machine, and realise that he was home and quite free.

'You're free to go, sir.'

Sir.

He had never been further than the reception area of any police station and that perhaps only a couple of times in his life. But that must be true of most people. Most people did not know anything about the rooms and the talk and the procedures and the smells and the noises beyond the front desk. It had been like entering a foreign country, full of people he knew existed, people like actors he had seen on television, dressed in uniforms or none, people going down corridors carrying files and banging in and out through swing doors. He had felt dirty, and guilty, from the moment he'd realised that he was being questioned, 'interrogated', not simply spoken to, from the moment he'd entered the bare room with the table and chairs and linoleum floor. He had understood quickly how easy it would be to agree to anything, become confused, forget things you knew perfectly well, in the anonymous, impersonal, horrible space between four beige walls.

'Why?' The one word they had used again and again. 'Why? Why?'

He heard them now, their voices trapped inside his head, and realised that if he forgot their faces, over time, forgot how many of them there had been and certainly forgot their names, he would not forget the room, and its smell, and their voices asking him why.

'I think I'd like to have a bath.' He had begun to itch with the need to get the smell and dirt from his skin.

'The water should be hot. I had the heater on for doing all this. You go while she's watching her programme and then, you know, she has a nap, so you'll have time to yourself.'

She took his mug to the sink, rinsed it out, put it on the draining rack. The sun was shining through the window. The kitchen was neat and clean. The clock ticked.

He wanted to say something to Hilary, that he was grateful to her for saying nothing, carrying on with what she was doing, not asking questions, but he did not know how.

As he went up the stairs he heard the television, voices, the sound of an explosion, more voices.

The sun was shining into the bathroom, washing across the white enamel and the pale blue wall, highlighting the rim of the toothbrush holder.

He turned on the taps and as he watched the steam rise from the surface of the water, he began to cry, uncontrollably and to his own intense shame. He stayed in the bath for some time, topping it up until the water ran cold from the taps, and went on silently crying.

But in the end, changed into clean clothes, he felt better, as if crying in a way he could not remember having done as a grown man, and rinsing his body, had removed more than simply the smell and dirt and memory of the police station and the interviews.

He came downstairs. Hilary had gone, without disturbing him, but there was a note on the kitchen table about food for supper. His mother would nap for a bit.

He wondered if he should telephone the library, or if he could go out to buy a paper, but he had no energy, his body felt as if he had been awake and lifting heavy weights for a week, and besides, people would be in the street, people would look out of windows, people who might know — would know. So, not going out, or being able to concentrate on anything, he went quietly back upstairs and lay on his bed, and after some time, during which he went over everything that had happened, every detail of what had been said and done, and could not stop himself, he slept, deeply, without stirring or dreaming, and woke uncertain where he was or why the light was fading.

He went into the bathroom and drank two full glasses of water then sluiced his face and washed his hands. From the front room he could just hear the sound of voices from the television. He had to go to her. He had no idea what he was going to tell her, he relied on himself to make up something, but he could not lurk up here as if he were a guilty man.

As he went downstairs, though, he realised that the voices were not from the set, they were those of his mother and Hilary, loyal, thoughtful Hilary, who was not supposed to be working at this hour but who was doing so because she would know how much she was needed.

She came out of the front room now. 'You'll feel better for that,' she said. 'Can I get you something to eat now? There's a bacon and egg flan I was heating up for Mrs B, with some salad, but she won't eat it all of course.'

She went calmly into the kitchen, letting him take his own time, do what he wanted without being fussed.

'Thank you, Hilary, thank you, I can't tell you —'

'You don't have to. But — I think she'd like to see you.'

He had been putting it off, but she was right, of course she was right.

'It isn't any of my business but she has been asking.'

'But it is your business, Hilary. Where my mother is concerned, everything is. I don't think I'm hungry though, I'll just get a bit of something later on.'

'Fine. I'll leave the rest of the pie covered up. There'll be plenty of salad.'

He was more grateful to her than he could express, grateful that she did not tell him he must eat something, did not insist on his sitting down, just got on quietly with preparing Norah's supper and left him alone.

Norah looked round as he went in. She had switched the television on to a quiz programme.

'Oh, Leslie, Hilary's just getting a spot of supper. Do you want to watch this or shall I turn it off?'

She sounded as usual. He might just have come in, as usual.

He sat down. The television chattered away brightly but it might have been broadcasting in Mandarin for all it meant to him.

'Where was it you had to go for the library?'

He stared.

'Manchester, was it Hilary said?'

'Oh, yes.'

So that was what she had said. Manchester.

They watched the screen in silence and she did not look at him again. He wondered what she was thinking, whether she had been worried or just accepted it because that was simpler. She had enough to battle with.

'Hilary's taking me to see the specialist on Thursday, did she say? I'm going to mention this new treatment — there was that programme about it, you remember.'

He began to feel disorientated, wondering if any of it had happened, or if he had not, after all, just returned from a normal day at the college, so little had anything seemed to impact on her. It was only the fact that Hilary was here when she should not be that reminded him of the truth of things.

She came in now.

'Would you like me to help you into the kitchen and eat there or shall I bring your supper in here?'

Norah chose to stay where she was. The evening went on. Hilary set out the food, told Leslie where she had put the remainder. Went home. The television went from quiz to comedy to a documentary about Africa.

It was only when a violent American film was flagged up that Norah flicked about, trying other channels, but found nothing of interest.

When the room was suddenly quiet, he got up, afraid of having to sit with her without any distraction, afraid of the questions that would surely come, afraid that she knew more than she had said. Afraid.

'I think I'm going off to bed early,' he said, 'I'm rather tired. Would you mind?'

He settled her with the reading lamp, her glasses, her drink, a new library book. An ordinary evening. He bent over to kiss her. She said nothing except, 'Goodnight, Leslie.'

He felt uneasy, and restless, not tired after all. He had slept so much earlier, he wondered if he would ever need to sleep again, and everything was churning round in his head, bits of the interviews, odd remarks, the sound of a heavy door slamming, the scrape of the chair on the bare floor.

He waited an hour, lying on his bed fully dressed, until the house settled back into itself, and when he looked down through the stairwell, he could see that his mother had switched off her light.

Then he went out, closing the door very quietly, as he always did.

THIRTY

'Frankie, will you stop doing that to her? Pack it in, you're making her cry.'

Frankie lifted up the plastic car quickly and banged it down again on Mia's arm, lifted and banged it, lifted and banged it. Mia howled.

'I'll put you on the landing and shut the door on you. Now stop it. Why do you have to do stupid things like that? Play with your trucks properly, that's what they're for, not for bashing Mia with.'

Abi turned back to the sink where she was rinsing out a basinful of their clothes, and, seizing his chance, Frankie brought the plastic car down but this time on his sister's head. She ducked, and it scraped her on the cheek, raising even louder howls.

Abi leapt at Frankie, who slipped out of reach round the other side of the table.

The trouble was, he was almost four and growing fast, his energy pent-up inside the one room and ready to break out every other minute. Playgroup finished at twelve but Frankie needed full-time school, needed occupation and other children — or at least a garden in which to let off steam. Mia, normally placid, was now wound up by him to the point where she screamed if he went near her.

And if it was like this now, what was it going to be like when Frankie was six years old, and eight and eleven, growing, frustrated, and even more likely to cause trouble? If they were still living in one room then?

But no, they wouldn't be, they couldn't. She had a boy and a girl so they'd have to give her a council flat soon. Trouble was, a council place would be somewhere scummy like the Dulcie estate, or even as far as Bevham. She was torn between wanting a flat of her own no matter where and dreading what it would be like.

Frankie was banging one of the cars on the underside of the table loudly and rhythmically.

'Frankie . . . look, do you want to watch *Bob the Builder*? Watch anything?'

Bang bang bang bang. Howl. Howl. Howl.

'Jesus Christ, what's going on?' Hayley knocked and came into the middle of the row as Abi reached under the table and dragged Frankie out by his arm.

'He's driving me bloody nuts — I don't know what to do with him.'

'Liam, get over there and play with Frankie and don't start fighting.'

Hayley dumped her tote on the table. 'You heard?'

'What?'

'They're still looking for Jonty.'

'So what's new? They'll find him. He hasn't got the brains to go far.'

'They let the other guy go.'

'Right. Who was it anyway?'

Hayley shrugged. 'They never say a name, do they, not till they charge them. Anyway, obviously wasn't him.'

'Jonty Lewis is capable of murdering a hundred girls if he felt like it. Be good when they catch up with him.'

'I'm not that worried now, are you?'

Abi shook her head as she unstrapped Mia from her high chair.

'Listen, Abs, that flat's still free.'

Abi said nothing. But she had thought about it. She knew where the flat was, there'd be more room until the council did come up with something.

'What?' Hayley looked straight at her. 'Go on, what?'

'I was thinking we should take them out.'

'Where to?'

'Victoria Park, maybe.'

'Well, it's not raining,' Hayley said doubt-fully.

'Come on then, you lazy cow, you never take Liam anywhere. We can get an ice cream if the hut's still open.'

Hayley sighed. 'They're playing all right though,' she said, looking under the table.

'Yeah, for five minutes. Be better for them racing round out there. Come on, shift.'

'It got really disgusting here,' Hayley said as they sat on a bench half an hour later. 'They've made it a lot nicer.'

The paths had been relaid, the flower beds cleaned up and replanted, and the children's play area was full of brightly coloured new slides and swings and roundabouts set on a bed of thick rubber, with a boundary fence.

'We used to swing on that witch's hat thing.'

'Yeah, bloody dangerous those were, a kid got killed.'

'Old wooden seats on the swings.'

'Those iron chains that made your hands go rust-coloured when it was wet.'

'Jeez, look at her face.'

Mia's ice cream was smeared like shaving

261

foam over her chin and cheeks.

'She's all right, she's enjoying it.'

Frankie and Liam were sliding down the small slide, running round and climbing the steps and sliding again.

'You're glad I dragged you out,' Abi said.

'OK. Be nice though.'

'What would?'

Hayley looked at a group of mothers with pushchairs on the other side of the playground.

'What?'

She shrugged.

'You going out tonight?'

'Yes,' Abi said. 'I'm not bothered. I see that Jonty Lewis, I'd kick him where it hurts. Poor Marie. She didn't deserve that.'

'Who does? Who deserves any of it? Liam, you be careful, you'll fall on your face doing that.'

Abi watched them. They'd gobbled up their ice creams, Mia had finished hers and was laughing at the boys.

'I reckon we should do it,' Abi said.

'What?'

'That flat.'

'What, go for it? You and them? All of us?'

'Yeah. They need the space, look at them. I'll go mad much longer in that bloody room. Can you find out about it?'

Hayley was grinning, her arms in the air.

'Only thing,' Abi said quietly. 'You know what.'

'No, I've stopped, I swear, I'm not wasting any more money on it, I'm clean. I'm staying clean.'

'You better mean it. I gotta trust you, Hayles, if you —'

'I said, didn't I?'

'OK, OK.'

She meant it, Abi thought, looking at Hayley, she meant it for now, for this minute, for when she was saying it, like they all meant it, always did. Another year, maybe a bit longer now, depending on how much the rent was. Then out.

'Then out,' she said aloud.

Hayley gave her a sideways look.

'We could get a Chinese on the way back.'

'You never know what's in that stuff, and anyway, it costs a fortune.'

'Fish and chips?'

'No,' Abi said, getting up. 'There's beans and eggs at our place. Saves money.'

She went out earlier than usual, well before nine. The punters were different, not like the midnight ones who'd been in the pub, or were coming off a late shift at the Bevham canning factory and smelled of boiled meat. And a lot of the girls didn't come out till at least ten o'clock, so she could earn more.

The kids had been asleep, apart from Frankie who was playing up, and she'd been worried about leaving them to it. But he was sometimes better with Hayley than he was with her, though Hayley never bothered doing anything with them, never did a colouring book with them or talked, they messed about and then went to sleep while she watched whatever she watched. So long as that was all she did, Abi didn't care. Had she kicked it? Was she going to believe her? She had to believe her. Not believing her wasn't an option when they were going to share. Everything was riding on that.

It was a mild night. She walked down to her usual pitch on the corner near the print-works, but before she got there, she saw the patrol cars parked up, and she doubled back towards the canal. If they were here every night, there were going to be no punters at all. But they couldn't have a police car on every corner, and the punters would soon find out where it was clear, where the girls were. Anyway, what was the point of them? They should be out looking for Jonty Lewis. He'd have done both, Marie and that girl Chantelle.

Loopy Les probably wouldn't be out for a bit though. He wouldn't risk it. He'd been warned once. She felt sorry, in an odd way. He was weird but not so weird that you wanted to run.

She found what seemed like a good place, out of sight of the patrol cars. There was another girl she knew further down on the opposite side. Marie came into her mind again, Marie and the inside of the caravan after he'd wrecked it. That had been her home, whatever it was like, whatever went on there, and he'd beaten it up and then killed her. Scum.

A Toyota slowed down.

After that, it went dead. She walked up, back, up again. Then crossed over to where the other girl was leaning against the wooden paling, lighting a cigarette.

'They're all running scared,' she said. 'You had any business?'

'One.'

'I can't live on this. Bloody cops.'

'Suppose they've got to put on a show of doing something.'

The girl made a face and walked off.

Half an hour. Nothing. Not even the Reach-out van.

Then something. Jaguar. Newish. You

didn't get many like that but when you did it was worth it. Abi went over quickly.

She'd been right. The Jaguar sped off fast, leaving her with a roll of notes. Two hundred pounds. She wondered if he'd even known how much cash he had and how much he'd handed over to her. He'd been smart, smelled expensive, looked nervous. She thought of him pushing off home to one of the big houses behind gates on the other side of town, garage doors opening as he drove up, nice sitting room, drinks tray, wife.

Two hundred quid.

She'd be home before half eleven. She'd cut over the footbridge and up to the all-night shop, get them a couple of bottles of beer, crisps and chocolate. They could pig out watching a late film. You had to have a treat sometime.

Two hundred quid, no trouble. It made her think about the girls who went upmarket, escort agencies in London and stuff like that. Except that they were all beautiful with fantastic hair and skin, classy-looking — Russian and Oriental girls — and how did she think she could compete with them? Abi Righton, poor skin, scratty hair, wonky teeth.

Still. She touched the roll of notes in her

skirt pocket. It wasn't bad.

The other girl had gone. The trouble was, the police scared everyone off, far more than the thought that Jonty Lewis was hanging about somewhere. Scared the girls off, scared the punters off, even scared Loopy Les.

Down the track leading to the towpath, she almost slipped on a muddy patch, and in reaching out to save herself from falling, grabbed at a piece of broken fence and felt something go into the palm of her hand, a jagged piece of wood or a nail, she couldn't tell. It hurt though, enough to make her stop. It was too dark to see anything much but when she put her hand to her mouth she tasted salty blood. OK, so the all-night shop would sell plasters. She sucked on the cut for a minute until the stinging eased.

Then she heard it, the faint low whistle. Or maybe the bushes just rustling. She stopped again and listened.

This time it was a soft breathing, a sighing sound instead of a whistle.

In spite of herself, in spite of her ice-cold nerves and her knowledge that it had been Jonty Lewis who had murdered Marie and probably Chantelle as well, in spite of not caring a toss for the likes of scum like him, down on the towpath or not, in spite of all that, she felt panic rise from the pit of her stomach and run through her until it reached the back of her throat.

'SSSSSSS.'

How many times had she told herself not to come this way and then done it, and always moved quickly, knowing her way and usually sure-footed, easily ahead of anyone who might be hanging about.

Her hand was throbbing where she had cut it.

'HHHHHHAAAAA.'

Right behind her.

Abi spun round so fast she almost overbalanced again. She had reached the steps up to the footbridge. Once on the footbridge, she could outrun him.

'Here.'

After all that, it was only him, not Jonty Lewis, not some stranger lurking, waiting to terrify her. Only him.

'Come here, come on.'

She wasn't going. She'd had enough, she had well over two hundred pounds in her pocket, she didn't need his money, and anyway, even though she knew him he still gave her the creeps.

She started up the steps two at a time, but he was quicker than she expected. She felt him reach out from behind, his hands on her sleeve and then, expertly, as if he had done it so many times before, his arm hooked tight round her throat and his strength, extraordinary strength, she thought with a terrible sense of surprise, dragging her backwards, her feet trailing on the wooden bridge and then down each step, back again, back and back and back into blackness.

THIRTY-ONE

Stephen Webber sat looking down at the letter on the table in front of him. The work on the Deanery was nowhere near finished, so he was having to work on this table rather than at his own desk, and it was not well placed for the light, but then, nothing in this house was well placed and he was beginning to notice the small irritations of being unable to find things, having his papers and books in an unfamiliar and temporary order. In the great scheme of things he knew that none of it mattered, but his life since coming to Lafferton had been far more stressful than he had expected and it would have helped him stay afloat if they had been settled in their permanent home.

He was calmly certain that he was right to be making the changes he had set in train and startled that many of them had met with such ferocious opposition. On some days he felt as if he were holding back a rising tide of anger and resentment, rather than carrying the staff and congregation with him into what he thought of as an exciting new life, and he was not temperamentally suited to battles and argument.

The letter gave warning of more conflict. It was clear, concise, polite and angry, an expression of deep concern from the organist and master of the choristers, David Lester, voicing his regret that the Dean seemed intent on changing the cathedral services so radically that the choir was being sidelined and the high musical standard that had always been upheld imperilled. There might be room for the new and the 'popular', Lester wrote, but there was none for the third-rate, none for the lowest common denominator of music and liturgy, hymns and accompaniment. Unless he could be assured that a halt was called and a return made to former standards, he would be obliged to consider his position.

The Dean felt a surge of what he could only have described as hopelessness in the face of such a letter, whose general cold tone barely concealed both rage and, he understood, great hurt, together with a profound contempt for the new regime. Lester was a man who wore his prickliness on the outside, as liable to cause sharp pain as the spines of a hedgehog, and the thought of having any sort of discussion with him about music was not one the Dean wanted to face. He believed that it was the role of the cathedral to meet the changing needs of the people, not cater to the elitist taste of the existing director of music or the conservative standards of a diehard congregation. He had come from a large London parish in which the average age of those attending all the services had gone down dramatically during his time there, so that when he had left, most people were under forty, and many of them under twenty-five. Lafferton's congregation had an average age of fifty-five, though the family service was well attended by parents with young children. But students, teenagers, twenty- and thirty-something singles and young marrieds were conspicuous by their absence, put off, Stephen was sure, by the formality, the distancing effect of the traditional choral services and the highbrow music, and by a liturgy which seemed to touch their own lives and tastes and concerns at no point whatsoever. He had no doubt that he could do at St Michael's what he had done at All Saints, push through change and a new agenda and pack the building with an altogether younger and more vibrant crowd of people. It would take energy and enthusiasm and a great deal of collaboration with the rest of his team, and it meant, as he knew, hard work. But energy spent in battles with the existing regime was energy wasted and he did not intend to dissipate his own strengths in such a negative and unproductive way.

He did not want to confront David Lester. He thought he would sleep on the letter and reply to it pleasantly and firmly the following day, not giving way but trying to give the impression that he understood his concerns and that he would much prefer him to be onside. Privately, though, he knew Lester would realise before long that things were never going to return to the old way, and he might well want to look for a post elsewhere. Also privately, Stephen would not be particularly sorry to see him go. David was not an easy man and there were others who would see the point of all the changes and be eager to start implementing them.

As he set the letter aside the door was flung open. Ruth came in. Her hair, which was normally tied back in a band or piece of ribbon, was loose and looked as if she had shaken her head vigorously. She was wearing a skirt and a smile which immediately made him uneasy.

'Come on,' she said, going over and taking his arm to pull him up, 'I've had the most fantastic idea, I want to show you now, it's just perfect, I've been wondering about it for ages but suddenly it came to me. You'll see, you'll see.'

'Ruth . . .'

'Oh, stop stuttering. Come on, Stephen.'

'Where is it you want me to go?'

He hung back, reluctant to let her persuade him, whatever her idea was, knowing what was happening.

'The crypt. Come on, Stephen, you'll see what I mean straight away. It's the most brilliant idea.'

She was ahead of him, half running, half dancing across to the side door beside the chapter house and pushing it open, waving for him to hurry.

Apart from a few visitors looking up in awe at the great ribbed roof to where the carved and gilded angels were poised as if about to take flight, the place was almost empty at this time in the morning. A vacuum cleaner hummed over the floor of the chancel, out of sight.

The crypt was beyond it at the end of the west aisle, approached down four shallow stone steps and through an iron grille which was always open. Now, sunlight came slanting in through the high window slits onto the tiled floor. The space was little used. The yeomanry flags were kept here, furled on their poles, and there was a plain altar with a single rail and kneeler in front of it. The whole had an air of neglect, though it was cleaned as regularly as the rest of the building.

Ruth had bounced down the steps and now she stood in the centre of the crypt with her arms flung out, before turning round and round in a solemn little dance.

'You see? Perfect. It's exactly the place.'

'For . . .?'

'The shelter — a place for them to come. The Magdalene Group can take this over and it will be a place where the girls on the street can come to get counselling and where they can be safe and . . . everything I told you. This is a dead space, nobody uses it, so now we can. I knew there'd be somewhere, I asked for guidance and I was led straight here. I'd thought of perhaps a room in the Song School or maybe part of the Chapter House but this is so much better because they won't feel they're being pushed out of the way — this is in the heart of God's building, you see, I thought we —'

Stephen went over and laid his hand on her arm. 'This needs careful thought, Ruth.

I really don't know if this is suitable or even if it would be permissible to turn part of the actual cathedral into some sort of social centre. Now, it would be best if we went. Maybe we could go out somewhere? I can take an hour or so off. Shall we drive into the country, have a walk and lunch?' As he spoke he was guiding her, his hand still on her arm, out of the crypt and back up the aisle towards the side door, feeling her resistance but being quite firm and in control.

'I don't know what on earth you mean, permissible? What sort of word is "permissible"? Honestly, Stephen, you're the Dean, you can do what you like.'

As they neared the door, he noticed one of the cleaners who was dusting the rows of chairs give them a strange look. He smiled slightly but moved Ruth calmly on. He was familiar enough with looks of that kind.

As they got through the door, Ruth suddenly took off, dancing away from him with a laugh, waving to him to follow. 'Come on then, if you don't want us to have the stuffy old crypt, let's look at the Song School, that's my second option, that choirmaster has far too much space. How on earth can they justify keeping all those shelves full of old music and what looks like a hundred

pianos and things? We'll soon clear that lot
out, we can get rid of the music desks, we'll
put comfortable chairs and they can build a
sort of private room at the end for counselling, then . . .' Stephen could not keep up
with her but he managed to stop her before
she got to the wooden doors that led to the
Song School, taking hold of her arm and
turning her round.

'Ruth,' he said gently, 'why have you done
it again? It's a couple of years since the last
time and you promised me and the specialist that you'd never come off your medication again. But you have, haven't you?'

She made a child's face. 'Oh pooh, Stephen, don't be such a spoilsport. Come on,
I want to get in there and start pulling it
apart. We'll have our shelter for the street
girls right here, you're probably right, this
would be much better than the old crypt,
that's a bit creepy, I can see that now. Clever
old Stephen, always right, darling Stephen.
But you said we could go out for the day —
let's do that shall we? This can all wait.
Where can we go? Let's go to the bank
machine and get some cash and have a
really slap-up expensive lunch somewhere,
treat ourselves. We never have proper treats.
Come on — or no, I'll go to the bank, you
run off and change, I'm not being taken out

by an old crow of a parson in his black suit.'

'Ruth. No.'

'Try and stop me, you do that.'

'Please, come here. People are staring at us.'

'What, do they want me to give them something to stare at? All right then, all right, look those people walking up there, hoy, you, want to see?'

She had started to step out of her skirt, kick her shoes away and now to unbutton her top. Stephen took hold of her and slipped his own jacket round her shoulders, picking up her discarded clothes.

'Come with me now, we'll go back into the house and find your tablets. You have to keep taking them, you do know that. I should have realised sooner.'

'Ha, well, I haven't got any, I shoved them down the pan weeks ago, I hated them, you know what they do, they take my soul away. So what are you going to do?'

Slowly, he managed to half pull, half persuade her around the path and up to the front door of the house, but as they reached it, Ruth gave a loud hysterical laugh and darted away from him again, throwing off his jacket which dropped to the grass and running, barefoot, to where Miles Hurley was crossing towards the building which housed the diocesan offices.

'Miles, wait, hey, I want to see you, just the man I want to see, you'll be on my side, wait, wait.'

She gabbled as she ran, and gave little skips and jumps, but as he caught sight of her, Miles turned and fled, disappearing through the side gate to his bungalow. Ruth stopped dead, shrugged, and sat down on the grass, holding her arms above her head in an odd gesture, as if worshipping the sun which had just come out again.

Stephen went wearily over to her.

'Sit down, it's wonderful, the grass isn't damp. We should sit on the grass more often, we should enjoy the world around us.' It was as if she were drunk, or high, though her speech was perfectly clear and coherent.

'Yes,' he said, 'I'm sure we should. That's why I wanted to go out. We'll go over to the Moor and walk. It will calm you down. Then have some lunch.'

'I am calm. I'm just very happy too.'

'I know.' He held out his hand and after a moment, smiling, she took it.

It had been like this many times before but it never got easier to accept. He knew what to do and exactly what he was dealing with, but somehow, in the periods between, when she was taking the medication which balanced her moods, he forgot — sometimes even forgot that her mental condition was a permanent one. The drugs worked. They were stabilising, and she had gone for as long as two and a half years without deciding to stop taking them. Whenever she did so, it was a few weeks of slow change, which went unnoticed until she tipped over the edge into mania. Strangely, it always went this way. The depressive episodes, during several of which she had had to be hospitalised, seemed not to come as a result of ceasing the drugs. Stephen did not know which was worse, the mania or the depression. He was only profoundly grateful that medication existed and was effective. He had asked her why she stopped taking it and the answer was always the same — that although it stabilised her moods, it took the edge from everything, both enjoyment and sadness. There was no black or white, no light or dark, she had once explained, but a universal muffled grey. Through this, she had to force herself to function, and for most of the time she managed to do so and became competent, even forceful, determined to prove that she was the equal of anyone. He had learned patience, at least when he was with her, though sometimes his patience snapped without warning when he was with others, and over something quite trivial.

It had begun a couple of years after they were married, mildly at first, and she had still assumed they would have a family and that she would put all her energies into it. No children had been conceived, and once the manic-depressive episodes had become more frequent and severe, it had been hinted that having children might not be the best thing for her — though no doctor had ever come out and said point-blank that it was definitely inadvisable. Ruth had been adamant that, on the contrary, babies, several of them, would cure her for good. He had felt trapped between wanting her to be fulfilled and happy, and above all to be well, and fearing the outcome if she did conceive.

She never had. Privately, he had always thought it was God's plan and an answer to prayer, even though he knew Ruth had prayed very differently.

In the car on the way out of Lafferton she hummed and sang and once or twice grabbed his hand as he changed gear. He felt anxious, wanting her to get some exer-

cise in the fresh air in the hope that it would
tire her and calm her down, knowing from
past experience that it might do just the opposite. She had sometimes been awake for
forty-eight hours, kept going on a tide of
euphoria and nervous tension.

He waited until they had left the car and
started to walk up the sloping track in the
hazy autumn sunshine. Sheep grazed in a
field to the west of them, and buzzards
soared overhead on their flat wings. Ruth
put out her arms in imitation and turned
round and round, once almost losing her
footing, now speeding up, running backwards and laughing at him.

But the climb gradually calmed her
enough for her to be willing to sit next to
him, their backs against an incline, and to
look out over the country towards the
cathedral tower which was just visible, rising out of the haze. Stephen felt the warmth
from her body next to his, and the energy
too. She was coiled as a spring, ready to
jerk up and dance or laugh or run. He felt a
thick fog of despair fall on him, almost blot-
ting out the view and the sky, almost pal-
pable. He had forgotten how it could be.

He was loyal to Ruth and knew that he
would remain so, but he also knew that the
years had drained him of love for her and

now he only felt an affinity and a great sympathy, plus the affection born of a companionable daily life and a shared purpose. They saw eye to eye on many things, not least the way things should go with the cathedral and his mission there. But living with her and in the shadow of her mental state was exhausting and he was reminded all over again now how it depleted his energies and blurred his focus.

'Ruth, you need to see a doctor, you know that, don't you? You must get some more tablets.'

'I'm fine. I feel better than I've felt in months, I feel free.'

'I'm worried that if you go on without them for much longer you'll crash down. You know how bad that is when it happens. You don't need me to remind you.'

'It won't happen. I feel quite sure. It can never happen again, I've got it tamed, Stephen. Now, let's go and have lunch, let's order everything we like, why not? Let's eat until we're sick!'

'Ruth . . .'

But she had begun to run down the track, arms outstretched again, as a small child would run, and as it was steep, after a while she ran faster and faster and seemed unable to stop herself. He could see the level ground and some shrubs before the gate to the car park and tried to scramble down behind her and save her from falling, but before he had gone far, she had plunged into the bushes and was sprawled headlong. He reached her in a frenzy of concern. She lay quite still. But as he bent down, terrified that she was badly injured or unconscious, she looked at him and burst into hysterical laughter, shrieking and trying to get to her feet but falling back and laughing more.

Stephen stood up again and waited, not touching her, not speaking, waited for what felt like hours until she ran out of steam and at last fell silent, looking up at the sky with a beatific smile.

THIRTY-TWO

Something was hurting her stomach. She turned over and pulled her knees up and for a moment sank back into the muddy half-sleep she had been dragged from, but then it was hurting her in the small of the back, a regular hard thump of a pain.

Then the noise, low at first, but growing louder, insistent in her ears.

'Maaaaam, Maaaammmm.'

Hayley sat bolt upright.

Now, the noise, which she realised was that of her own son saying her name angrily over and over again, 'Maam, Maaam', was joined by another.

'Jesus, Liam, pack it in, will you? What do you think you're bloody playing at, banging me kidneys like that? Pack it IN.'

Her head was banging too.

She thought that it was not yet morning, then realised that the curtains were still pulled together.

She sat for a few moments, trying to get her thoughts together, wondering why she felt so bad.

'Maaaam.'

Hayley reached out and tried to swipe him but he dodged expertly away.

Yes. Oh Christ.

She'd put the kids to bed and they'd all gone to sleep straight off, but then the telly had packed up, like it often did, snow all over the screen and a sound like an electrical storm coming out of the speakers. She'd twiddled the aerial and shaken it, switched it on and off, but nothing had happened. She'd read an old magazine of Abi's and made a mug of tea. Looked at the kids sleeping.

What she could do with was a can. Or maybe a couple of cans. Nothing else. She'd promised and she was sticking to it. But a can wouldn't hurt. Only Abi had gone out, and Hayley went through all the cupboards but there wasn't anything.

It had taken her a bit of fighting with herself, about going out and leaving the kids alone, but it was only a quick sprint up the road to the pub, she'd be five, ten tops, and back, cans in her pocket, they weren't going to be waking up any time soon.

Only they had always sworn they never

would. Never. Leaving the kids was right out.

Ten minutes.

She'd checked on them twice. Opened the door. Waited. None of them had stirred. She'd put the door on the latch, and run.

That was all she'd done and it was only ten minutes and a few, and she'd got back, racing up the stairs out of breath, but with three cans of strong cider in her pockets and a couple of bags of crisps in her hand.

They'd all been asleep, as she'd left them. Nothing had happened. Of course it hadn't.

She remembered how pleased she'd felt and how she'd tried the telly again and it had worked. It did that. You couldn't second-guess Abi's bloody telly, but it was on and she'd watched *NCIS* and then half of a weird sci-fi film, and drunk the cans one after the other until her mind had gone cloudy.

The next thing had been the pain in her back from Liam's thumping.

Hayley pulled herself out of the bed and across the room. Mia was standing up in her cot, staring at her. Frankie was on the rug with his cars, which he always was, and Liam had joined him. Frankie had no pyjama bottoms on. The day came in. It was bright. Sun.

Hayley looked round.

Twenty past nine.

For a second it didn't register.

Twenty past nine?

'Abi? Frankie, where's your mum gone? She gone down to the bathroom or what? Christ, kid, you're supposed to be at play-group and that.'

Her head was pounding more now she was standing up and she went through the cupboards and drawers until she found the last couple of Nurofen in a pack and took them. She felt the kettle. It was cold. Fuck it, couldn't Abi have even boiled the kettle?

She went to the door, opened it and shouted out onto the landing and down the stairs.

'Abi? Listen, it's nearly half past and the kids aren't even dressed. Abs? You in the bathroom or what?'

'Maaam . . .'

Slowly, Hayley went back into the bedsit and shut the door. Liam and Frankie were still down on the floor, making tyre-scream noises. Mia stared. Huge dark eyes. Pretty. She reached out her arms to Hayley.

Half past nine.

As she lifted Mia up, Hayley felt it, a sick coldness, like water running down her back.

She found her mobile in her jacket pocket,

hanging on the back of the chair, and dialled Abi.

There was no reply and no voicemail. The phone was just dead.

She made a mug of tea and stood staring out of the window, holding Mia, leaving the boys, not dressing them, playgroup the last thing on her mind. Mia smelled of dirty nappy.

The headache had gone and her brain was more focused, only it wasn't somehow, it was like having a running tap inside it, pouring water and rinsing everything from her mind. All she could do was drink the tea and stare out of the window onto the backyards and a white cat sitting on next door's fence in the sun. Mia was quiet, clinging to her.

She had thought maybe the hot tea would take away the coldness down her back and in her stomach and the bitter taste in her mouth, but it made no difference, so in the end, she put the mug in the sink and picked up her phone again.

It was scary how fast it happened. One minute she was pressing the buttons on the phone and what seemed a minute after that, they were there, running up the stairs, and the room was full of them, two in uniform and then another two, a man and a woman, coming in, plain clothes, flashing their warrant cards, crowding the space. Mia was crying with her face in Hayley's shoulder. Liam and Frankie sat on the rug, hands on the small beaten-up plastic cars, but faces turned up to the police, staring, staring.

THIRTY-THREE

Usually, Serrailler ran up the stairs to his top-floor flat two at a time. Tonight, he walked, and slowly, not only because he had been working since seven that morning, but because although he had left the station, he could not leave the case there, it was with him, every step of it going through his mind like a printout as he climbed.

It was just before nine. The building was silent, apart from the sound of his own footsteps, all the rooms on the way up locked and dark. That was one of the many blessings of living in the only flat at the top of a building full of offices. When his work was as demanding and intensive as it had been for the past week or two, the emptiness and the silence were essential for him to recharge his energies. He had spent the whole long day talking and listening to people, even during the couple of breaks he had taken for coffee and a sandwich, and now he needed a whisky and his solitude.

The long sitting room was calm and tranquil as he switched on the lamps which picked out one or two pictures and sent fans of soft light onto the pale walls. He took a deep breath and let it out slowly. To his relief, the light was not flashing on his answerphone, though if he was needed by anyone at work, they would use his mobile.

He wondered whether to take a shower, then pour his drink and relax in his dressing gown, but as he was deciding that he would, the downstairs entrance buzzer sounded.

'Simon? Oh, I'm so glad you're in. I couldn't get a signal from my phone and —'

'Judith?'

'I'm so sorry to disturb you . . .'

His stepmother sounded distressed.

'You're not . . . Come on up.'

She looked unlike her usual composed, cheerful self as she walked into the flat.

'I wouldn't have bothered you, I know how busy you are just now, but Richard's in London tonight and I . . .' She sat down and took a deep breath. 'I was on my way back. I've been playing bridge and then I gave a lift to a friend. As I was coming into town, just at the top by the Lanes, my tyre blew out. The car went all over the place and I hit a bollard. It's all right, that's all it was, but the wheel has buckled, and then my phone wouldn't work so I couldn't call the AA. There were no taxis in the rank and I know it's safe in town but it was very quiet with all the shops closed. I think I panicked.'

'You did absolutely the right thing. Let me sort it out with the AA — have you got the keys?'

'Oh. Simon, how stupid. I left them in the ignition.'

'Don't worry, it doesn't sound as if anyone's going to take it far. Let me get you a drink — I think you could do with it.'

Ten minutes later, the car sorted, he was sitting on the sofa opposite her, whisky in hand.

'This is the most beautiful room.'

For a second he was puzzled and then felt a flush of guilt, that this woman who was his father's wife, his own stepmother, had never actually set foot inside his flat. He guarded his privacy and he had resented her arrival in his family, but he was still ashamed of himself.

'I love it — it's wonderful living up at treetop height and looking down the close.'

'Georgian rooms are so handsome — they

have such a feeling of right proportion. Is that what I mean? I'm not being very articulate.'

'I know you were worried being out on your own, but you shouldn't be. You're probably as safe in the centre at night just now as you'll ever be.'

'It isn't rational, I know. But reason doesn't come into it.' She closed her eyes and leaned back. 'I am rapidly calming down though.'

'What's Dad doing in London?'

'He's gone for a meeting about the future of the journal. I'm dreading what will happen. They may feel it's time he gave up the editorship but it would be a bitter blow to him. He gets such a lot of satisfaction from it and it means he's still in the medical swim. Besides, he feels he has a lot more to give. There was talk of them abandoning the print version and being exclusively online — not that that would trouble him, he's very up to speed.' She took a sip of her Scotch and looked around appreciatively at the pictures. On the wall behind his head was the last drawing he had done of his mother. Judith took it in, glanced at him, and then away across the room.

'I'll finish this and then perhaps you could ring a taxi for me?'

She was sitting close to the lamp, which gave a softness to her features, smoothing out the usual marks of age, and as Simon looked at her, he realised what it was about her that had attracted his father. Judith was not beautiful but she had a warmth and a sweetness of feature and expression, combined with a look of sharp intelligence and a competence, an air of being able to manage things because she'd had to do so. It made it all the more surprising that she had lost her nerve tonight. But in that she was certainly not alone.

He realised that it was the first time he had been able to see her without resentment, discarding everything he brought to his relationship with her of the past and the memory of his mother.

'Have you eaten?'

She shook her head. 'I was going to drive by the supermarket and pick up some things — but I'll just have an omelette once I get home.'

'Let me take you to supper — my favourite Italian is round the corner.'

Her face registered surprise and pleasure — and, he thought, a flash of wariness. But she said, 'I'd like that — if you're sure you wouldn't rather be left in peace — please be honest.'

'Absolutely. Apart from anything else, I've had two canteen sandwiches and an apple since seven o'clock this morning. Give me a couple of minutes to change.'

The restaurant was as usual pleasantly full but the proprietor gave Simon his favourite window table. It was some time since he had been, saddened by thoughts of bringing Freya Graffham here and sitting in the same place, enjoying a Campari and ordering from the long-familiar menu. Now, he looked across and saw Judith. He wondered wryly what Cat would say, Cat who had tried to bring him round to accepting their stepmother over the past year, badgered him and hassled him and argued with him and then simply fallen silent on the subject. And as she would have been the first to concede, saying nothing was far more likely to bring him round in his own time than any amount of argument.

'This is such a treat,' Judith said, smiling at him over the menu, 'I can't tell you. Richard hates eating in restaurants and oddly enough Don was just the same, so unless I go out with a girlfriend or Cat, I just never do it. I'd like Parma ham with figs and the saltimbocca, please.'

He ordered, choosing his favourite *fegato*

296

alla Veneziana and a bottle of their drink-
able house red.

It was as they were finishing their starters
and Judith was lifting her glass that quite
abruptly she put it down again and said,
'Oh Simon, whatever is happening to these
poor girls? Who is doing these awful things?
I can't bear it.'

It sent him back for a moment to a grim
day co-ordinating what was now a major
operation, to the faces of everyone at the
various briefings — serious, disbelieving and
determined — the photographs of the
young women flashed up onto the screen,
the bleak facts from the pathologist.

He shook his head.

'And now another? Is there any chance
this third girl has just gone off of her own
accord somewhere? I'm sorry, perhaps I
shouldn't ask that.'

'Why not? It's what everyone else is asking. Every single person at this afternoon's
press conference, every police officer —
probably everybody in the country. The official answer is that we have reason to be
concerned at the disappearance of a third
girl who was working as a prostitute and we
are asking for any information at all as to
her whereabouts.'

'And the real answer is that you're sure

this one has been murdered too, probably by the same person who killed the other two.'

'More or less. Though there is some doubt about the last part of that — it's possible Marie O'Dowd was murdered by someone who did not kill the other two.'

'Yet all three girls were prostitutes, two of them were found in or near the canal, they —'

'I only said it's possible.'

'I'm sorry.'

'No, you're thinking in the same way most people are likely to be thinking. But in the nature of things, we can't make those sorts of assumptions. We're looking for Marie's boyfriend, who has a history of violence against her, who trashed her caravan shortly before she went missing, who is a drug addict and who has disappeared. We have no reason to suppose he had anything against the first girl who was murdered and we don't yet know if Abi Righton, the third one, is dead. The phrase "serial killer" jumps to everyone's lips — understandably. But we really don't know enough yet.'

Judith looked at him as he spoke.

He smiled. 'You don't believe a word of it.'

'What's your gut feeling?'

He looked at his empty plate for a long time. What was it indeed? If it had not been for Jonty Lewis, he would not have hesitated in taking the view that Chantelle and Marie had been killed by the same man and that it was only a matter of time before the body of Abi Righton was found, to make victim number three of what was most likely the very thing everyone dreaded — a serial killer. But Jonty Lewis was in the picture. He had motive and opportunity and previous form, and he had done a runner. If there had been no other victims, the assumption that he had murdered Marie would have been natural and almost certainly correct. Perhaps he had killed Chantelle. But if they were talking about gut feelings, Serrailler's was that he had not.

Their main courses were set down. The restaurant was quieter — Lafferton did not eat late. Simon relaxed but always it was a relaxation with an edge, in case his phone rang.

'I know some of them need the money to buy drugs but that can't be all of them, can it? They're so young, Simon — they shouldn't be living like that. Doesn't anyone try to get them off the streets?'

He sighed. 'Do-gooding rarely works and I'm always suspicious of motive, you know.

The Reachout van people, for example — yes, they take hot drinks and they have a place where the girls can sit, and there's a needle exchange, but they have a very strong religious agenda. Maybe it's better to do something than nothing, no matter what the motive, but there's a catch and of course the girls know that. Policing isn't the answer — we just move them on. Occasionally someone has five minutes spare to chat, to try to encourage them to get help — but where? You're right, they're not all addicts though many are. There's plenty of trafficking, which we do try and crack down on, but it doesn't get at the heart of that particular problem.'

'I didn't realise it *was* such a problem here.'

'Not many people do. If you never go down certain streets . . .'

'But one night, I happened to be driving home late and I saw a car stop and a girl go to the window, then get in, and I realised . . .'

'What did you think?'

'I suppose I was shocked. Not that I didn't know there were prostitutes . . .'

'Just not in your own town.'

'Then I felt guilty — that they should have to be there at all. I was driving to a nice

300

warm comfortable house and she was getting into a stranger's car like that — and what was her home like at the end of it all? I caught a glimpse of her — I won't forget it. She looked like a made-up child — you know how small girls put on their mother's shoes and lipstick? That was what she seemed like . . . Oh, Simon, why do we always do nothing until it's too late?'

He broke some bread and dipped it into the rich gravy on his plate.

'There wasn't anything you could have done then. You have to be realistic. But I agree there should be a big push to get them proper help. And you're right — it always happens after there's been a tragedy. People slow down for a while after they've seen a fatal accident. Same syndrome.'

Judith looked at him over her wine glass. 'You like your job, don't you?'

'Love it. Not that I don't loathe a lot of the things I have to deal with.'

'You have a good balance — this job and then you always have an exhibition to prepare for. It seems just right.'

'Really? Most people seem to think the art is hobbies department except for those in the art world who think being a policeman is just weird.'

She shook her head. 'I don't think it

would be right for you to have just one — whichever it was. Set aside the question of earning a living — I think you are the kind of person who needs to have two halves to their life — they fit into a whole and complement one another — a bit like the two shells of a walnut.'

He smiled. 'Thank you. I've often wondered — should I just do this, should I give up the day job . . . I never come down firmly on one side or the other.'

'No, and you shouldn't.'

'That makes me feel better about myself.'

'And do you need to?'

'Sometimes.'

He had finished his liver and waited in silence as she ate her last few forkfuls. He had meant what he said. Something had fallen into place and he felt a rightness he had not felt for a long time, because of her few words.

The pudding menu arrived with the usual flourish but Judith shook her head. He ordered coffees.

'Was I being completely irrational in panicking out there tonight, Simon?'

'Of course not. You were alone in a car that had broken down, you couldn't raise a taxi or the AA, and this is a city in which two women have been murdered — possibly three. This is one of our biggest problems — reassuring women that they are safe but at the same time making sure that is really true. I can't tell anyone that the person or persons who killed two young women won't kill again or will only kill prostitutes — it would be irresponsible of me to say any such thing. I think you were safe — I actually do — but there's no proof of that. It's about perception — you perceived yourself to be in danger, so you were frightened. That's perfectly normal.'

'You sound very reassuring.'

'I mean to be. But just make sure you have your mobile phone with you and charged at all times, and don't wander about by yourself at night. Those are common-sense precautions you should always take — like securing the doors and windows when you go out or to bed. I know, I know — I sound like a copper.'

She spooned the foam from her cappuccino. Then she said, 'I know how you feel about your father remarrying and I have wanted to say that I really do understand. It isn't me — it's what I represent. I don't feel I've taken your mother's place and I would never want to. I will never be anything other than Richard's second wife, and he will never be anything other than my second husband. But as far as our children are concerned, any relationship is a new one — a quite different one. My son couldn't care less about my marrying your father because he's a young man who couldn't care less about most things. Vivien did feel troubled by it, but as she's in the States, she can put it from her mind most of the time. It's different for you — I'm in Hallam House, where Meriel was. I'm on your doorstep. And Cat's of course.'

'Cat,' he said, because he did not know how to answer her, nor even how he really felt. He had to take it home with him and think it over, as always when there was something emotionally charged to be dealt with. So it was easier to ask Judith about his sister.

'I think she's struggling and not just with Chris's death. It's tough — three young children, a demanding job, all the other things Cat does . . . I help with the children as much as I can because I love doing it, and Richard enjoys having them over to us — I think a bit to his own surprise. But she's the one who has to make all the decisions, she's the main focus of their lives now. It's a very lonely time.'

'I'd hoped to do more myself, but as soon as I got back from Taransay I was plunged into all this. Maybe I should have come back sooner.'

It had not occurred to him until he said it.

They had finished their coffee. The restaurant was almost empty.

'Now,' Judith said, 'if you'd walk me to the taxi rank, I'll get a cab home.'

The town was quiet, the night balmy and starlit, and Simon had a flashback to Taransay and the beach and the sea beyond the cottage windows. Another world.

'I suppose your people are combing the countryside for miles around looking for the missing girl.'

'Yes. And the divers start on the canal tomorrow.'

'Oh dear God. She's dead, isn't she, Simon?'

They stopped at the taxis.

Simon shook his head. 'I hope not.'

'Hope?'

'If I didn't have it I couldn't do the job.'

'I read that she has children.'

'Two. Quite young.'

Judith reached up and kissed him on the cheek. 'I can't tell you how much I've enjoyed this — it's meant a lot. Thank you.'

'Are you OK about going into the house on your own? I can come with you, see you in and get the cab back.'

'I'm fine. Not in the least worried, I promise you.'

He believed her. But as she got into the taxi, Judith looked back at him. 'I wish I could feel hopeful about her,' she said quietly.

Serrailler walked back towards the cathedral through the deserted streets, wishing the same himself. But in truth, and in spite of what he had had to say to Judith, he knew that by now Abi Righton was almost certainly dead.

The food and wine plus the walk had made him tired, but once in bed and having read for twenty minutes, he lay awake. He never drew the curtains and the moon was almost full. It was not the job, not the thought of another murdered young woman, not whatever the following day would bring, that filled his mind — he could almost always set his work aside when he went to bed. He had to work through what had happened to change his relationship with Judith and disturb his previous, rigid feeling of resentment and rejection. He knew that it had had precious little to do with her as a person — how could it when he had barely given himself a chance to know her? That had been deliberate, a stubborn refusal to admit her not so much into his life as into his mother's place. But what she had said about that had struck him hard. He was not a man who found it easy to admit a fault, or to feel justified shame about something he had got wrong. But now he was forced to confront the fact that he had behaved badly and been guilty of a great unkindness. Above all, he had to admit that the first person who would have admonished him about it would have been Meriel Serrailler, his mother. He would never know the truth about her marriage to his father, never know why they had been unhappy over many years, yet somehow managed to stay together, but he acknowledged that she would have been glad that Richard had found someone with whom to enjoy another chance, a new life, someone who had mellowed him and taken some of the edge off his difficult and austere personality.

He had enjoyed his evening. Judith had been good company. Now, he was faced with a certain amount of emotional turmoil as he came to terms with the way things must be in future.

It was a long time before he slept and it was a light, restless sleep, full of vaguely disturbing dreams from which he woke two or three times with a start, thinking the phone had rung or someone had called his name.

But the house was silent and still and, at last, he turned over and did not stir again until the alarm on his watch went off at seven o'clock.

No one had called him in, no one had rung with any reports. No news, then, good or bad.

No news.

THIRTY-FOUR

After going frantically from room to room right through the house and even down into the cellar he had never investigated before, Stephen Webber grabbed his jacket and went outside. Their temporary house had a small garden with a bare lawn and a few shrubs but there was a shed at the end, which he also looked into before peering through a broken slat of the fence into the garden of the house behind. But the house behind had been converted into offices and the garden to a car park which, at seven in the morning, was naturally empty.

He had woken quietly and lain for a moment coming to, saying his first prayer of the morning as thanks for having been brought through 'the perils of this night'. After this, he always got up first and went down to make tea. In the last few days, Ruth had been even more heavily asleep at his side than usual, a sign he knew was a warning that her manic phase had turned and that she might be slipping down the other side into depression. But today she was not there, nor in the bathroom. The kitchen was empty and it was clear no one had been into it since the previous night.

It was then that he had rushed upstairs, dressed hurriedly and started to search the house. Now, outside in the cold autumn early morning, he stood looking around him in desperation, at the house fronts and paths of the close. A paper boy was cycling from gate to gate at the far end but otherwise there was no one about.

He had no idea where to look next but then caught sight of Maurice, the head verger, crossing towards the Song School to unlock it, which meant that the cathedral itself was now open.

It still took his breath away when he walked in, most of all when the building, its vaulted roof soaring to the heavens, was empty and his own steps sounded so marked and deliberate in the great space. He stopped, unsure if he expected to hear something or to see Ruth, but there was only the extraordinary silence, a breathing silence, it seemed, and the motes of dust glinting gold on the slanting sun coming through the east window. He walked round

310

slowly, up the nave then into the chancel, glanced in the choir stalls, came out and went down each side aisle, into the crypt and the Lady chapel and as he went he looked down every row of pews. But he could tell by the quietness that she was not here — that nobody was here, though Maurice would be back at any minute and soon the few people who came to the early Communion would trickle in through the side door.

In London, when this had happened, he had known several places she sometimes went to and often found her, but he was still not very familiar with Lafferton and nor was Ruth, so had not the faintest idea where she might be.

In London he had been on firmer ground because there had been the psychiatric emergency team to call — whoever was on duty knew Ruth, knew her condition, he could get help from them at any time. And for the last two years she had been well and stable, taking her medication, so that he had relaxed, busy as he was with everything else, trusting her. He did not even know if they had registered with a GP — presumably Ruth must have done so, though if she had mentioned it he had forgotten. But he was sure she would not have made any contact with the psychiatric services. Once well, she always assumed she would never need them again.

As he left the building, he saw Miles Hurley coming towards him, Miles, who knew about Ruth and had supported Stephen through several years of great strain in London.

'Miles . . .'

'What's happened?'

'Ruth. I can't find her.'

'Right. How long has she been missing?'

'She wasn't there when I woke up. She could have just gone or . . . I've no idea.'

'In that case, phone the police.'

'The police? I . . . we've never had to do that, it was always —'

'Stephen, think. There are already two young women dead and one missing.'

'But they . . . that couldn't have anything to do with Ruth.'

'Phone the police, Stephen. I have to go and take the service — I'll come straight over as soon as it's finished, but you must call them, go and do it now. I'm not trying to alarm you, she's probably wandering in the town somewhere, she'll just come back, but this is not a time to take chances.'

But then, as he turned away, a silver Audi pulled away from the forecourt of the house at the far end of the close and drove towards them.

'Stop him,' Miles said. 'Flag him down — you don't need to phone them. This is the Detective Chief Superintendent in charge.'

And as Stephen stood frozen, his eyes full of panic and indecision, Miles stepped out and raised his arm. Simon Serrailler slowed down and stopped his car beside them.

Thirty-Five

There was a blackness, but in the centre of the blackness was a swirling mass like a whirligig. Sparks came out of it now and then and she tried to hold on to those, but they always sputtered out and then there was just the blackness again and she was drowning in it.

When she came round the next time, there seemed to be some light at the edges of the blackness and after a few moments she recognised this as good. But there was also pain, at first so much part of her whole self that she could not separate it as being pain from here or from there, it was simply pain, a heavy, burning pain. She had no sense of time, but in between the bouts of swirling blackness and the moments of light, she began to sense that the pain was centred within the blackness, behind her eyes, around her head, inside her head, in her neck and chest. She thought about the pain.

She was aware of her legs and feet then and the pain did not seem to belong there.

But they were cold. She was cold. Only the pain was burning.

There was no time but there had been darkness and then there was light, then darkness again and a terrible thirst that was part of the pain.

Suddenly, she opened her eyes and there was the sky. She moved her arm and then her hand and beneath the palm of her hand was cold and damp and slippery smoothness. She moved her hand and the cold and damp moved with her. Moving her hands took a long time and she slept again, dropping down exhausted into the black pit.

The next time she woke there was no light, but darkness again, and she was colder. The burning pain was better for a moment, then worse.

She moved her legs. They moved easily at first but then her foot wedged against something, and she could move no more. She moved her hands and the coldness was still underneath them. Cold. Damp. Slippery.

Slowly, hour after hour, perhaps day after day, she spent longer awake and less time down in the blackness, longer moving her hands and her legs, longer feeling the cold and then the burning. Slowly, she began to think that she could move. She did not know where she was or why but she wanted to move. It seemed urgent that she should move, but from where to where she did not know.

She moved. The pain did not affect her legs, so she moved them again, but if she tried to move the upper part of her, the pain burned her up and she had to stop.

Slowly, slowly. It was like learning how to move. She wept the first time she dragged herself an inch forward, before collapsing back again onto what she now recognised as cold ground. But the next time, she felt something new, a determination, a will, and she dragged herself further, an inch or two, a foot, a few feet, and so on and so on, pull, drag, her body following behind, her feet pushing down. It was when she tried to turn her head that she was sick because of the pain, so she kept it down and moved only her body, a little more, a little more.

The thirst was a pain in her throat and the pain in her throat was a burning. Her arms ached but she pulled on and on and then there was wet grass and mud under the palms of her hands and the cold smell of water.

The smell struck a note deep inside her

— a reminder, a warning? She struggled to uncover it but it floated away each time, like a leaf in the stream. But it came back again and then again, the smell of water, the smell of water, and the cold damp grass beneath the palms of her hands.

Now she was on all fours and found it easier to move that way rather than to crawl on her stomach. She could edge her body forward, one knee, then one hand, the second knee, the second hand, and so she went a yard, perhaps, before having to collapse onto the ground again.

And the smell was still there. The smell of water.

The water was near and she seemed to feel thirst throughout her body, not just in her mouth and throat. She wondered if she could find the water she could smell, and drink it.

She had no idea where she was or where she was going, only that she was moving forward, and that that was a good thing, better than lying as she had been in the swirling blackness.

How long was this journey taking her? How long had she been inching along on her hands and knees? Was she entirely alone or were there people, dogs, cats, cars? She heard nothing but the sound of her own laboured breathing, the occasional grunt of pain, and the soft drag of her legs over the grass. Even the water that she could smell seemed silent. Perhaps this was what she would do forever, crawl painfully forwards, stopping to rest, moving a yard, stopping and waiting for the blackness to lighten again. Perhaps.

She subsided into half-sleep, half-unconciousness several times, but always, when she came to, she began to move again, not by her own will, but as if urged on by a machine.

And then the grass ended, and when she put out her hand, it touched against something hard and rough. She felt it slowly, though she could not reach up very high. It was cold but not the cold of metal, a warmer cold. Concrete or stone, she thought, and remembering what those things were gave her a spurt of hope and excitement. Stone. Concrete. Not grass. Not mud.

But there was still the smell of the water.

Her hand slipped down from the stone and fell back as the pain came again, the dreadful burning ache.

And then there were sounds out of the air, somewhere not far away, sounds. Voices. Someone calling. She was confused and she wanted to call back but could not, her voice would not come through the pain. But after a moment, she managed to raise herself up, onto her hands and knees again, and for a second, to raise her head and then, slowly, to lift her arm up, not high, but lift it, lift it.

The sounds stopped and started again and then the voices multiplied, there were many voices, loud in her ear, blinding her so that she closed her eyes against them.

But one said, thunderous above her, 'Over here! Step on it. Over here.'

THIRTY-SIX

The queues had stretched from the desk all the way down the hall and outside the main doors since well before the library opened. New students coming to register at the beginning of term meant that all staff were at full stretch, dealing with enquiries, taking tours, and ushering those who were lost among the shelves to the correct section. There was never any leave for the whole of October, and everyone put in overtime. Some complained bitterly — those who, June Petrie said, would have preferred the library to remain permanently closed to all borrowers so that the books were never disarranged — others enjoyed the buzz of hopeful young people, and the challenge of helping them so that they became dutiful and well informed. Usually, Leslie Blade was inclined to belong to the latter camp. He did not like the attitude of some of the students towards the books, did not approve of the sloppy dress and gum-chewing, but he felt a certain satisfaction in showing them how to behave in an academic library, knowledge few of them arrived with, and when he saw that within a week or so most of them were transformed into quiet, attentive readers and note-takers, occupying the desks in an orderly manner, he felt some pride.

This year was different. This year he went in terror of somehow being known, recognised, pointed out by any one of the line of students, fear of a nudge that would run along them, the turning of heads, the whispers. No one knew, no one had said a word to him about his two days' absence and yet he felt more paranoid by the day. He had suggested he remain in the stacks or the records office, but the librarian wanted him on the desk because he was so familiar with the way this week was organised and there were more students than ever, things had to run smoothly.

He tried not to look any of them in the eye but kept his head down, concentrating on the screen and the factual details, name, address, year, course, subjects, tutor. But at least there was no time on his hands, and none for anyone to talk to him, they were all occupied from the moment they arrived until the doors closed.

Lunch breaks were still sacrosanct though. Without the full hour off, none of them could have coped efficiently. The times were re-scheduled and allocated, not self-chosen. Leslie was given noon till one. He was glad of it. An early lunch suited him and he escaped down to the stacks with his box and the paper as the clock hit twelve.

He had barely unwrapped his first cheese and tomato sandwich when the door above bumped open and he heard the clack of shoes coming down the staircase, high-heeled shoes, woman's shoes. June Petrie was on a later break — it would be someone else. Leslie bent his head and was careful not to rustle the newspaper, but it was his business where he ate his lunch and he thought — though in this he was wrong — that, other than June, no one else knew he came down here.

But it was June, out of breath as she reached him at the far end.

'I had to tell you, I'm sure you've been following it all, apparently they just broadcast it on local radio . . .'

He imagined a knife with a sharp point pinning her to the book stack and then a ball of greaseproof paper from his sandwiches stuffed into her open mouth to silence her.

'They've found her, they've found her alive!'

Her eyes were bulging, her cheeks flushed. Leslie stared at her, not taking in the meaning of what she had said.

'The third girl, Abi, isn't that her name, the one we were all sure had been murdered as well. They've found her alive, hurt, badly hurt, but she's alive! Isn't that wonderful news? Can you believe it?'

Abi. Abi Righton. He had not been able to get her out of his mind. He had had nightmares in which her body had floated in the canal and then been pulled onto the bank by divers in shining black suits and strange helmets. He remembered her face as it had been when they had last talked.

Abi Righton.

'I was sure you'd want to know.'

Why was she sure? In fact, she was right, of course she was right, of course he wanted to know. But why should June Petrie think it worth interrupting his lunch, breaking off her own work, to come down here and tell him? Abi Righton was alive. What made her connect him in any way with that?

'That's very good news,' he said. 'That will be a great relief to . . . everyone. The police. Everyone.'

'They haven't said much — she's in hospital, she's badly injured, nothing about what might have happened . . . Anyway, isn't that good news? I just feel so much better for knowing it, no matter who she is, what she's done, she's just a young woman, isn't she, like the other two, and — she isn't dead.'

She clacked away and up the stairs. Leslie looked down at the bread in front of him, with the border of cheese and the curve of tomato at the edge. Abi Righton. She had children, he knew that, she had talked to him about them. Children and the face of a child herself, a pasty, hollow-eyed child. Thin. Gaunt neck. He had left her the box of tea bags.

He looked at the bread for a long time and, in the end, folded it away inside the wrapping and put it back untouched in his lunch box.

THIRTY-SEVEN

The press had dispersed to file their story, but their vans and equipment were still banked up in the area cordoned off for them at the back of the station car park. From his window, Simon Serrailler looked down and saw the occasional figure emerge from the television van, another two go out of the gate and cross the road towards the pub.

It was rare to be able to walk into a press conference to give good news. He had felt a lift as he had made the announcement and heard the immediate buzz and then a ripple of applause.

'Can you tell us how the girl is now, Superintendent?'

'She was taken to Bevham General where she's in intensive care but there's no report yet. I'll let you know the moment we get anything.'

'What sort of state was she in when she was found?'

'Abi was in a serious condition. She had crawled some distance along the canal bank — we don't know how far — and one of the search team who had been combing the undergrowth spotted a movement. She had wounds to her throat and serious bruising and she was suffering from hypothermia.'

'Did she say anything? Any names? Did she know who had attacked her?'

'She was lapsing in and out of consciousness and obviously the urgent priority was to get her to hospital. No, she said nothing and we won't be able to talk to her until the medical team give us the word. I've no idea how long it will be, sorry.'

'Are her injuries life-threatening?'

'I don't know any more at this stage. I can only repeat that Abi was in a serious condition.'

'Any other news? No sign of the missing man, Jonty Lewis?'

'No, there's a nationwide search for him, as you know, but we have no reports of anyone having seen or heard of him. I'd ask your cooperation on this one please — the more often you show the photograph of Lewis and give out the description, ask people to look out for him, the better our chances.'

'If Abi Righton talks, you'll find the killer

of the other two girls.'

'Not necessarily. We're still treating those as two separate murder inquiries.'

'Are you looking at Abi's case as attempted murder?'

'Until we interview Abi Righton I can't say any more on that. When I have a clearer picture I'll talk to you again.'

'What about any other girls still working on the streets? We know they're out there, last night's news carried an interview with one of them, so what —'

'Yes, I'm well aware of that. There are police patrols out in force, as I'm sure you know, and when girls are seen on the streets, girls we have good reason to believe are working as prostitutes, then officers are speaking to them, advising them to go home, warning them about the risks. They are also advised about safety precautions if they do remain out — we can't force them to stay away — keeping each other in sight, making sure they're carrying mobile phones, that these are kept topped up, they have one another's numbers, our numbers, and so on.'

'Not ideal, is it, Superintendent?'

'Of course not. We would much prefer them all to stay indoors. But we'd prefer that in general, not just in the current situation. Right, that's it, thanks for your cooperation.'

'Superintendent, just one more question.'

Serrailler turned back. The others had started to move but stopped now that Des Ricks, from the *Bevham Gazette,* was on his feet, sensing that this was not just an afterthought.

'Des?'

'Is it true that another Lafferton woman went missing this morning and is it true that this is not another missing prostitute?'

He had wondered whether the news about Ruth Webber's disappearance would get out, though he had warned everyone that for the time being he wanted this kept away from the press.

'I'm afraid I can't comment on that at the moment.'

'Can you confirm that in fact it's the wife of the Dean at the cathedral who's gone missing?'

A buzz ran through the room.

Serrailler looked Des Ricks straight in the eye. 'I have no comment to make at this stage. That's all for now, thanks, everyone.'

He went quickly out, leaving speculation and irritation in the air and a crowd gathering round Des Ricks.

THIRTY-EIGHT

Stephen Webber had come home looking drained. He had given only a skeleton account of Ruth's condition to the police, and had failed to tell them that she had left home on several previous occasions.

'But they need the *whole* picture, Stephen,' said Miles.

'Those other disappearances were in London. And a long time ago.'

'A couple of years, I think. It's nothing to be ashamed of.'

'She's been so much better. It's not necessary to tell them every medical detail.'

'I think you're wrong.'

Stephen Webber stared miserably down at his feet. 'I have to go and look for her, I can't just sit at home.'

'All right, but where do we begin? Where might she possibly have gone? You haven't been here very long, she doesn't know it as she knew the area round All Saints.'

'We went out onto the Moor . . . it was when I realised how — how things were with her, that she was rather . . . hyped up. I thought a walk would do her good, help. It does sometimes help. So we went up there. She loved it.'

'But that's about six or seven miles out of town and she was on foot.'

'Yes,' Stephen said. 'I suppose so.'

'But if you want me to drive you out there of course I will. Until we go you won't rest easy. Did you tell the police about going up on the moor?'

'Should I have? I'm afraid I didn't.'

Miles sighed as he got into the car.

By the time they had walked to the top of the steep bank the wind had got up, tossing the Scots pines on the ridge and sending the shadows chasing across the slopes. Their voices were blown away. They looked about them, moved on, looked again.

'Is this roughly where you were?' Miles shouted at one point.

Stephen nodded and moved away towards some scrub and potholes, scrambling down and looking desperately around. The moor was deserted at this time on a weekday, and the other hills stretched away for several miles, impossible to search themselves.

Miles stood watching as Stephen scanned as far as he could see before coming back, head bent against the wind.

'Come on.' Miles waved his arm and they began the descent, the wind racing across from the west and battering at them so that it was hard to keep upright.

'What should we do now?' Stephen asked once they were back in the shelter of the car.

'I would advise going home. She could well have come back by now, you know.'

'I have a terrible feeling, Miles. Something has happened to her.'

'You need to shake that off. It's unhelpful and it's just going to drag you further down. Nothing will have happened to Ruth, but when you get back, whether she's there or not, you must call her London doctor. You need the support of a team, you know that.'

Stephen listened gratefully to Miles's firm advice. He had always felt that Miles, private and unknowable though he was in some ways, had a much clearer sense of purpose and a more practical nature than he himself. Miles knew what to do, he made a decision and stuck to it, and if he was wrong, it never seemed to trouble him. He should have been in higher office. Canon Residentiary was fine but Miles ought by now to have been a Dean himself — in moments of doubt, of which he had many, Stephen thought Miles rather than he should have had charge of St Michael's. His own appointment had surprised many, himself probably most of all. But Miles had once told him in a rare moment of confidence that he did not have great ambition and that he had always preferred to be second in command. 'Even at school,' he had confessed, 'deputy house captain suited me fine, thanks.'

And he was Stephen's right hand and invaluable sounding board, a voice of reason and sometimes, though not always, of caution.

She was not at the house, and as far as they could tell she had not been back. There were no phone messages. Miles switched on the kettle and looked about him for the teapot.

'Stephen, call your secretary and cancel everything for today — though if I know Aisling she may well have done that already. And then you must see if you can find any medical cards or a local doctor's number somewhere — I wouldn't be surprised if Ruth had registered with someone. When she's well she's very efficient.'

Miles stood to drink his tea, needing to be at a meeting with the Precentor about changes for the Christmas services. Stephen had planned to be there but Miles would now take his place.

'It'll be difficult,' he said now, 'and you're not up to coping with all that today. I'll report back but in the meantime try not to fret too much. Ruth will be back — I know it. And you'll both be in our prayers before the meeting.'

When Miles had left, Stephen prowled round the house, unable to rest, and ended up on the top floor, standing at the window that looked out over the back gardens of the other houses on the west side of the close, autumnal gardens, with shrubs and trees turning in colour and leaves falling and chrysanthemums and Michaelmas daisies straggling about the dying flower beds. He could not pray. It was always the same at times like this, when personal stress took over; he was only able to hand the situation over to God and leave it there, as he had done all his married life.

Because he had almost cried off marrying Ruth. There had been a couple of incidents, minor enough, but a warning, if he had been able to see or heed it, of trouble to come. They had worried him, but afterwards she had been perfectly normal and he had pushed the thought of what her slightly odd behaviour might mean from his mind, knowing that he loved her and that love was enough.

Love was not enough and never had been and, after a time, the guilt had begun to creep in and he had suppressed it, trying to make up for everything that was wrong by indulging her, letting her take over where she wanted to, giving her a say in parish matters that should have been his concern and his alone. It had not gone down well sometimes and there had been a few confrontations, but Miles had always stepped in to smooth things out.

It was quiet. He went downstairs and then up, back down, and out, walked down the close to the main gates and back, and people glanced at him and were uncertain whether to speak or not, a boy on a bike shot past and almost collided with him, he stumbled and nearly fell on the kerb.

He thought that he should go into his office, see his secretary, do some work, but he was so unfocused and troubled, he knew he would be of little use so, instead, he went into the Lady chapel, which was always quiet, and knelt there, trying to pray for Ruth's safe return and asking for guidance in how to deal with her illness, but failing to do more than mumble a few words and then simply crouch there, empty of all feeling, looking at the icon of the Virgin and Child and the ugly Victorian candlesticks.

THIRTY-NINE

'I just want to see her — I brought her these.'

'Are you a relative?'

'I'm her best friend.'

'I'm really sorry but it's strictly no visitors. She's very ill, you know.'

'Can you tell me what's happening? Can you tell me if she's going to be OK? Can't you even just let me put my head round the door, not stay or anything, just see her, I need to see her.'

Hayley wanted to throttle the woman at the desk, wanted to jump over her stupid counter and bang her over the head and find out where Abi was and just go there, just go. Abi would want to see her, she'd want to know about the kids.

The kids.

'Listen, I have to see her, she'll need to know about Frankie and Mia, she'll be worried, can't you understand that, if you got half a brain?'

'I understand you're upset, Miss . . .'

'Hayley.'

'Hayley, but there's no need to be offensive. I'm just telling you the situation. No visitors. I'll take the flowers and get them put in her room, of course.'

'Yeah, right, I bet.'

Hayley turned away. There was no point. She'd met bossy women behind desks often enough. This one had a badge on. *Chris Eames. Reception.* She picked up her flowers and followed the sign pointing to League of Friends Tea Bar. The hospital was huge. Abi could be anywhere. The corridor was full of people pushing things and carrying things and a few others walking along very slowly with crutches or frames. Nobody looked at you.

But the tea bar was all right, full of people, big queue, but brighter than the rest of the place so far, and with a view out to a long stretch of grass in front of another building. A man with white hair and green tabard with BGLOF on it was serving tea. Hayley got a mug full and a cheese and tomato roll. She felt better just for looking at it and then someone got up from a table by the windows.

The tea was hot, the roll fresh, though the

cheese was a bit on the plastic side, and after a few minutes, she calmed down and forgot about *Chris Eames. Reception.*

She didn't forget about Abi though, Abi was in her head night and morning, Abi, who'd been near-dead and had crawled God knows how far, to get to help, Abi, who everyone had assumed was dead, and wasn't.

The one thing Hayley knew was that Abi would want to be told about the kids, no matter what state she was in.

But she didn't see how she was going to get to her. Maybe she could write a note. No. She didn't know if Abi was up to reading, and besides, she wanted to explain, say that she hadn't had any choice, that the kids had just been taken into care because fucking social services had arrived and hadn't believed she was capable of looking after Frankie and Mia as well as her own. And now where were they? With people they'd never set eyes on in a place they'd never been to, and what was that going to do to them? They could have been with her in their own place, she'd have taken Frankie to playgroup with Liam and had Mia all day herself. She loved Abi's kids, and was some foster-carer going to love them?

She ate her roll and felt upset, imagining

338

what it would be like to be taken off in a
car away from everyone and everything you
knew, when your mum had just vanished,
and left with strangers, not told for how
long or why, not told bloody anything if she
knew social services. She'd had run-ins with
them in the past and they'd been worse than
schoolteachers, a million times worse.

Abi had to know.

There were people coming in and out of
the tea bar all the time, and after she had
been there five minutes, a woman in a white
coat came over.

'Hi. Do you mind if I sit here? Only there
aren't any free tables.'

'No, you're all right, I can move over.'

'Thanks. Sorry to barge in.'

'You're not.'

She was young. Her badge said *Dr Esther
Gilman.* Nice face, Hayley thought, funny
eye, a bit turned in somehow. Lovely skin.
Peachy. Long neck, bit like a mushroom
stalk.

Hayley glanced at her, glanced away,
drank some tea, glanced again.

'You a doctor then?'

'Junior doctor, yes.'

'Right.'

'Are you visiting, or an outpatient?'

Hayley hesitated. She didn't want to tell

all her business, but on the other hand, maybe this Dr Esther Gilman could help.

'Complicated,' she said. 'See . . . can I tell you?'

'Sure . . . unless it's a list of symptoms.'

'God, no, I bet you get a basinful of them without over your tea break as well. It's . . . do you know about this girl, she's my friend, Abi, the one they thought was murdered only she's alive?'

'I heard it on the news. She was pretty lucky, wasn't she? Maybe it'll give them what they need to catch the bastard. Hope so.'

'Yeah, right, and me. Only, the thing is, she's here, she's in this hospital.'

'She would be, yes.'

'And I'm her friend, she'd . . . I had her kids, when she disappeared, and I've got to tell her about them, she'll be going mental worrying, but I tried to get to see her, find out what room, and they wouldn't tell me a thing, won't let me near.'

'She's probably in intensive care and under sedation. They would only let in next of kin.'

'She said, the woman on the desk. But Abi doesn't have anyone, her kids are her family, and I think she ought to know what's going on, nobody else will tell her. You couldn't . . .'

She shook her head. 'I'm on obs and gynae at the moment, it's nowhere near where she'll be, I'm afraid.'

'Oh. Right. Sorry then.'

'The only thing I could do . . .'

Hayley looked at her, willing her to go on, to say she'd do something, help, get her in to see Abi.

'I could probably find out where she is and how she is and if it was possible I could get a message to her. I mean possible, as in, depending on her condition. I can't do more than that — can't smuggle you in under a blanket.'

'Aw, that'd be great, that'd be better than just leaving it, just letting her worry. Thanks, thanks a load.'

'You're welcome. OK, let me write it down. What's your name?'

'Hayley.'

'Hayley what?'

'She'll know.'

Dr Gilman wrote it on the back of her hand with a biro. There were other things written there already.

'Tell her . . . lots of love and the kids are fine. I don't know if I ought to get you to tell her any more really, maybe not, maybe better waiting till I can see her. They took

341

her kids into care, the buggers from social services.'

'I think you're right then. It would be best for her just to know they're fine for now. OK, Hayley.' She got up, swallowing the last of her milk.

'I've got to run. But I promise I'll try . . . don't know if I'll succeed, I've got no idea . . . but when I have a minute, I'll do my best.'

She will, Hayley thought, if she can she will. You know who to trust.

There was an hour before she had to fetch Liam from playgroup. She went to the counter and got another cup of tea and an iced bun from the man with the green tabard, thinking what a treat it was, sitting here, looking out of the windows onto the green, watching people, looking at what they had on their trays, wondering about the man in the tabard. It was normal and she didn't often do normal.

When she got outside, it had clouded over and was starting to drizzle, and by the time the bus came her fleece was damp and she was cold. Another wet night on the street then, and she had to go, she had almost no money and her giro wouldn't come for another four days. One of the women in the other flats would listen out for Liam. Hayley told her she had to work a night shift sometimes, no choice, and that her friend was ill. All of which was the truth. Sort of. She would go out for no more than an hour, hour and a half, and then, if she'd taken enough, get back to Liam. He never woke up anyway, except for the time they'd all been sick.

She changed buses in Bevham and the bus to Lafferton took her to the end of Abi's road, which was near enough her own, so she got off there. The rain had stopped again. She wondered if the doctor woman had seen about Abi yet, how she was, whether she knew what had happened. Hayley had no idea what Abi's injuries were, the news didn't say, the police wouldn't when she rang them. Why did everyone clam up? What harm could it do to tell a best friend? Why was it some dark secret? It was habit, she decided, they said nothing because that was what they did. Said nothing.

It came to her as she got near Abi's that she had left her black skirt drying in front of the electric fire and that it would be all right to wear now, she could do with putting that on tonight, it was newer than her other stuff. She had time. It was only fifteen minutes to the playgroup. Besides, she probably ought to check out Abi's room.

It was quiet and empty and weird. It smelled of the kids and Abi's hairspray. Hayley sat on the bed for a minute. She didn't know what she felt most — scared was a lot of it, scared for Abi, scared for herself, scared, but she also felt shaky and sick. She had to go out tonight and the only way she knew how to make herself was a hit, either that or vodka, but she didn't have money for either.

Abi sometimes had a quarter-bottle in the back of her cupboard, though it hadn't been there for ages. Abi didn't drink much, it was no good with the kids, she'd said, once you started you could get pissed and they'd need you and how was that looking after them properly? She'd lost it with Hayley enough times.

There wasn't a lot in the cupboard — a box of opened Ritz crackers, Nescafé, the kids' tomato sauce, a tin of beans, matches. In the next were the crocks. Hayley felt round behind. No bottle. There was a tin though. She pulled it out. *Highland Shortbread.* If there were any biscuits left, she would move them to the other cupboard. She shook the tin. Something made a soft sound. Not biscuits.

Sixty-five pounds in rolled-up notes. She knew Abi had a post-office book and that she put as much as she could into it for the kids and for when she was giving up the street, though Hayley never believed she would or could, but Abi liked her dream. Sixty-five pounds. Hayley took it to the bed and sat there counting the notes two or three times. It meant a hit. It meant she didn't have to go out that night. It meant she could get a couple of spliffs and some cans and just stop in with Liam and a pizza, which would be better than leaving him, even if somebody was listening out. It was better.

That's how it seemed to her, as she put the money in her purse and slung her bag across her front. Anyway, if this place was going to be empty it might get nicked and she'd pay Abi back, once she got home. If she ever did.

FORTY

'Come in.'

'Guv? Do you have a minute?'

Simon leaned back from the computer. He had been at his desk for the past three hours and he was not a desk man by nature. The downside of promotion was that, at least when he was not on a SIFT job, he had to spend far more time than he wanted to in his office. He had talked to the Chief about it and indicated that he was going to make a change to his working pattern, spend more time out in the field, more time with the others, more time doing what he knew he was best at — being hands-on and leading from out there, not in here, even if the main planning and control was in the station. The Chief Constable, Paula Devenish, sympathised but cautioned him about retaining distance and authority. Simon had used a short sharp word about both.

'Hi, Ben, yes, it's fine, I've gone glassy-eyed staring at that bloody screen.'

He stood up and stretched to his full height. Apart from anything else, sitting for too long was bad for his back. He looked at the young DS, still smartly suited and with quite a sharp tie — he had not yet adopted the Lafferton CID dress-down casual-to-scruffy look. Simon suspected that he never would.

'What's on your mind?'

'To be honest, I'm sick of hanging around, guv. I've been told to go up to the hospital again, see when Abi Righton might be able to answer questions, but it's pointless at the moment.'

'You take that up with DI Franks, Ben, as you well know.'

'I do know . . . I just feel a bit frustrated. It's going nowhere.'

Serrailler looked at the young sergeant. Of course he knew what he should do — give Ben Vanek a bollocking for having the nerve to come complaining to the Detective Chief Superintendent. Most bosses would have done so but he was not most bosses and he recognised Ben's frustration and his eagerness too, and eagerness to get on with the job was a quality that ought not to be sat on because of a senior officer's misplaced desire to maintain hierarchical self-importance. Simon required order and discipline in his team but he gave protocol low priority.

'We all feel like this, Ben. It is frustrating. It grinds you down, it wears you out, your patience is thin, but police work goes like that, you should know. You get the buzz, the excitement — Abi Righton being found alive for instance — and then you get the routine again, questioning, waiting, sifting through the CCTV tapes and, if you're uniform, handing out leaflets and knocking on doors. I can't make the lights come on again.'

Vanek shrugged. 'I just wondered if there was anything you had for me that I could get my teeth into, but I suppose I shouldn't ask.'

'No, you shouldn't, but I tell you what. I'm not staying in here any more today — I've been at this bloody desk all afternoon. I'll go up to BG, see if I can get any more out of the medics about Abi, so you come with me in case there's the slightest chance of having a word from her. There won't be but we've got to keep at it. Then I want to go down to the canal area, have a nose round. I like to spend time at a crime scene, and it's good for the uniform who are standing around and manning the vans down there to see my face. Come on.'

'That's great, thanks, guv.'

In the forecourt, DI Franks was getting out of his car.

'I'm out and about,' Serrailler said, keeping moving, 'taking DS Vanek, if that's all right with you.'

He nodded to Ben to get quickly into the passenger seat and swung out of the car park before the DI could protest.

'Thanks, guv.'

Simon knew that Vanek was keen — some would have said overkeen, but in his book there was no such thing. The corners would get rubbed off soon enough but he wanted to make sure that cynicism didn't set in at the same time. He had seen too many young CID officers lose enthusiasm and ambition, settle for the easy routine. He thought of Nathan Coates, and a picture of him flashed into his mind — hair like a yard broom, face that looked as if it had been hit by the flat of a shovel, bright, hard-working, an ordinary young man who was rising in the Yorkshire force to which he had gone from Lafferton and who would make DCI in a couple of years. Nathan had never lost his edge and his almost schoolboy relish for the job, even the humdrum routine of dull patches. It was not within the official remit of a detective chief superintendent to take interest in a new young sergeant and try to ensure he did not lose his shine, but that didn't trouble Serrailler.

'Right, Ben, what's your take on all of this?'

'Which particular bits, sir?'

'Two prostitutes dead, both murdered, one prostitute left for dead. Same MO. Same killer?'

'Oh, no question.'

'Why? You should question everything, *everything,* until there's no shadow of doubt.'

'You mean you think there's more than one killer, sir? You can't really think that.'

'Can't I? Why can't I? You've heard of copycat murders, I presume.'

'Well, yes, but . . . All right, to copy the first murder a second murderer would have to know a hell of a lot more detail about exactly what was done than has been given out.'

'True.'

'There isn't a full medical report on this Abi Righton yet so we don't know exactly how she was attacked.'

'We know she had severe throat injuries.'

'Points to the same man then.'

'On the other hand, strangulation is a

common means of killing, especially killing of women by men.'

'Right. I'd still put a lot of money on this being the same bloke.'

'This isn't a game, Sergeant.'

'No, sir.'

Serrailler put his foot down and the Audi surged forward to overtake a lorry. Ben Vanek gave a low whisle of appreciation.

Simon grinned, 'You're right. Love this car,' he said. 'What about Marie O'Dowd's missing boyfriend?'

'He'd been violent to her before, he trashed her caravan in a fury, he's a user . . . If it was *just* her, I'd say open-and-shut. But . . . He lost his temper with his girl. He had a history of losing his temper with her. What reason would he have to kill other prostitutes?'

'What about the one who isn't a prostitute?'

'I feel as if I'm being grilled for the job all over again. Give us a break, guv.'

Serrailler laughed. 'Speak your mind.'

'Mrs Webber's just a missper — only everybody's twitchy because of the others. She doesn't fit the pattern.'

'Meaning she isn't a prostitute?'

'She wasn't around the canal area, she —'

'How do you know?'

351

Ben Vanek sighed.

'All right, you're off the hook,' Serrailler said, swinging into the entrance to Bevham General. 'I'm not being sadistic, just using you as a sounding board, helps me get things straight in my own mind.'

Abi Righton was in a side room on the ITU with a uniformed constable outside the door.

'Hang on here,' Serrailler said to Ben, 'I'm going to track down the Sister on duty.'

A few years earlier, when he had come in to see his sister Martha, Simon had known a number of the medical staff, but the present ITU Sister was new, and unimpressed by his police status.

'I'm sorry, she's sedated and we can't have you people barging in.'

'Sister, I do understand, but I know you also understand that Abi may well have some vital information for us. The moment she's up to it, we must talk to her.' He gave her his most beguiling smile. 'I know you have your patient's best interests at heart, of course I do — she is your priority — but can you see it from where I'm standing?'

But his smile and the way he pushed back the flopping ash-blond hair that fell over his forehead and every ounce of charm he could muster had no effect whatsoever.

'When she is fit — *if* she is fit — to talk to someone, you will be told. And now, if you don't mind — one copper cluttering up this ward is more than enough and three is definitely a crowd.'

She turned and went away.

Serrailler made a face to Vanek. 'Nothing doing.'

But as they left the ward, a doctor Simon knew slightly was on his way in.

'Roger — can I possibly have a word?'

'Let me guess . . .'

'This is my colleague, Detective Sergeant Vanek. I know the official score but can you give me any idea when Abi Righton is going to be well enough to talk to us? It's urgent.'

'Talking is the problem. She was nearly strangled, you know — her vocal cords, her windpipe, her larynx are all pretty badly bruised and inflamed.'

Simon groaned. 'Any brain damage?'

'Not so far as we can tell — the MRI scan looked OK. But we'll know more later. She isn't out of the woods. She was dehydrated, hypothermic and in deep shock, quite apart from her physical injuries. I can't let you see her.'

'Maybe we could just ask her questions to which she could nod or shake her head . . .

perhaps even write something down on a pad for us?'

'Possibly. But not yet.'

'When? Come on, Roger, help me out here. I'm probably dealing with a serial killer. We have to get to him before he kills again. I promise you we'll be sensitive, there'll be no pushing her, I'm happy for you to be there to monitor the whole thing.'

The doctor rubbed his chin. Then he said, 'I take your point, but I'm still not going to commit myself. If there is a chance that you can talk to her I'll ring you, but you've got to leave it to me.'

Abi Righton surfaced from a mist of images which neared her and receded, changed shape and broke into small pieces like shards of glass, and the white ceiling and the dimmed light through the slatted blind confused her. She did not know what she was looking at when she opened her eyes and there was a strange hum that went on around her and beside her and through her head, and a tick like a clock or a machine. The instruments recorded many things but not what was happening inside her head, not her tangled feelings and the images she could not grasp. But once or twice, she felt as if the cloudiness was evaporating and

354

when she opened her eyes she almost knew who and where she was, though never why, and not why she couldn't swallow or why her tongue felt huge inside her mouth and her neck and throat and jaw burned.

The moments of being awake grew longer and she reached out and grabbed at them, as if grasping them like a bar and holding them fast would somehow rescue her and make everything clear, and then she would know. Know.

The doctor looked at her charts, at the instrument recordings and then at Abi, pale as a moth against the pillow, her eyes sunken, body thin and oddly flat beneath the tubes and clips and wires.

But for the first time since she had been brought in, he had a hope, faint and thready as Abi's pulse, that she might recover.

FORTY-ONE

At twenty past eight, Serrailler was parking his car on the slip road by the main gates of the printworks. Further up, a police mobile unit, identical to the one he had just visited in the town centre, was stationed on the verge, with arc lights and a couple of television vans making the whole area look as artificial as a film set. In town, uniformed officers had been leafleting passersby; here the purpose was different. The unit was there to act both as a base for the beat officers and search teams and as a deterrent to the prostitutes and their punters — and also to the killer.

He had intended to bring Ben Vanek, but the sergeant had been called back by his DI after a reported sighting of Jonty Lewis, so Simon was alone.

'Evening, everyone.' He climbed the steps into the police van, in which a couple of officers were taking a tea break and another was manning the phone. The place was cramped but useful, with CCTV, a screen giving them updates on all the cases, and a side area for interviewing anyone who called in with information or concerns.

There was a general shuffling to order and murmurs of 'Sir'.

'Relax, I'm only dropping in to see how things are going.'

'Quiet.'

'The toms are pretty fed up, guv. They're out there but they don't want to be anywhere near us for obvious reasons, so they're much further down the main road and the punters are pretty wary.'

'We've killed off their trade.'

'You're also making the world a safer place for them, guys, tell them that.'

'Yeah, right, as if they listen, sir.'

'No info from anyone?'

'Not really. Couple of people came and had a look in, took a leaflet.'

'Any news of the Righton girl, sir?'

They stood round, chatting, offered him tea. It was a good exercise in boosting morale, if nothing else, Serrailler thought. He liked to get among the rest as much as possible, and the Chief had always backed him. 'I like coppers who don't like their desks,' was how she put it, though they both knew that an officer in overall charge of major cases often found it difficult to escape the station.

He stayed for a few minutes, asking questions and listening carefully to their answers and opinions. They were all familiar with the area and the girls on the street; their eye for detail and for anything unusual was far superior to his.

'Right, I'm off to walk the towpath.'

'Come with you, sir?'

'No thanks, I'm fine. Meanwhile, try to get the girls to see that we're only moving them away for their own good — not that they'll believe us.'

They didn't. They were prepared to risk even an encounter with a killer because they needed money, usually money for drugs, sometimes just money. They were not stupid, most of them tried to be careful, they knew the score and they looked out for one another, but they were still out there working the streets, hoping for punters, praying that the ones they went with were 'normal'. If you were desperate enough, Serrailler thought, walking towards the towpath, you took any number of risks.

It was a damp, mild October night with a thin mist drifting away over the black water of the canal like a spirit departing a dead body. The air smelled green.

There were officers on both sides of the bank near the lighted area around the second police van and a couple further down, but after a few words Simon went on past them, walking slowly and stopping every few yards, looking around into the murky darkness, smelling the air. Why did some girls hang around on the towpath? Most of them kept to the roads, and got into their punters' cars. Perhaps someone had *wanted* to come here . . . someone whose car might be recognised? A punter on foot? There were a couple of wooden seats, without backs, on the towpath. And under one of them was a wet dark shape. Simon shone his torch, his heart beating ridiculously fast. With his gloved hand he pulled it out. A sodden plastic carrier. It contained a large packet of tea bags.

He walked on, to the footbridge. Yellow-and-black crime-scene tape cordoned it off and a constable was standing at the bottom of the steps.

'Sir.'

'Evening. All quiet then?'

'Very quiet. Gives me the creeps, to be honest.'

'I'll duck under and take a look.'

His torch lit up the small dank space

beneath the steps where Marie O'Dowd's body had been. Forensics had marked out the area and put up a cordon of tape here too. What had happened? Who had been lurking here waiting for her? The boyfriend? Or someone else?

The ground was damp earth with a few weeds at the edge, a bit of shale. He imagined a girl coming down here with a punter for sex. Likely or not? Anything was possible in that fetid world.

They had traced the route Abi had taken, dragging herself along or crawling. It had ended just below the bridge steps, not quite fully underneath them but there were also marks in the scrub area behind the towpath. The courage and sheer bloody-minded willpower of the girl was humbling. Had her attacker left her for dead, or had he been surprised and run away? But no sign of a person leaving the area in any haste had been found, and if he had raced up and across the footbridge, rain and the general traffic — the footbridge was well used by day as a short cut — would have obliterated his tracks.

The more he thought about the three girls, the more Serrailler believed that they had not been attacked by the same person, but that was only a hunch, he had no real evidence other than the fact that Jonty Lewis's DNA had only been found on Marie, not on the others. Forensics had already taken away and tested the clothes Abi Righton had been wearing. They bore traces of DNA but it did not match that of Lewis.

Simon gave the tea bags to the constable, with follow-up instructions. He then walked into the darkness. Once out of the way of the police activity it was very quiet.

If Lewis had not been in the picture, it would have been easy. The same killer, with a hatred of or a grudge against prostitutes, had murdered two, and left the third for dead. It was Lewis who put the whole thing out of kilter. Find Jonty Lewis . . .

He turned round. Find Lewis and pray that Abi Righton would be able to talk.

It was only as he reached his car that he remembered the fourth woman. Ruth Webber, who, until an hour ago at least, was still missing.

Ruth Webber. Wife of the Dean, twenty years older than the other girls and not a prostitute.

What the hell had Ruth Webber got to do with it? Anything at all? Or was she, and coincidentally, as Ben Vanek had said, 'just another missper'?

He was about to head to the station and then home, but he knew he would be caught up in the spider's web of the cases and he needed a break, so he made for the country road and Cat's farmhouse. He didn't ring ahead on his mobile, but it was not a choir night. She would be home. Apart from the lunch after he got back from Taransay he had been too occupied to see any of them. He had missed them — until he pulled into the drive and saw the lights on, he had not fully realised how much.

Cat came running down the stairs calling his name.

'You can never know how glad I am to see you.'

For a second he thought she was going to burst into tears.

'I've been trying to put a light bulb in the holder on the top landing but it's really high, I've never been able to reach it, and I need to get into the old filing boxes up there. Chris always had to do the out-of-reach lights and . . .'

He put out his arms and gave her a hug. 'It's OK. I'm here and I'm tall. Come on.'

She half laughed, leading the way upstairs,

but the laugh was one of relief.

'It's things like this, you know — not big stuff, just stupid things like not being able to reach a light fitting . . . that sounds pathetic.'

'Not to me.'

'And Dad was here earlier, I could have asked him, but I didn't think.'

There was enough light from the floor below for him to replace the bulb.

'I needed to find some old stuff about palliative care — I've got my interview for the course at King's soon. Maybe I don't need to read up on all this but I want to be properly prepared.'

She opened a file drawer, glanced into it, opened a second, slammed it shut.

'God knows where they are. I don't think I can face going through this lot tonight, and anyway, I'd rather talk to you. Are you drinking? Eating?'

'I haven't eaten — sandwich will do.'

In the kitchen, he put on the kettle and found the cafetière.

'I can't drink, I might be called in.'

'I can and I won't be.' Cat got a bottle of wine from the fridge.

'Mushroom omelette? There's some left-over apple crumble as well.'

Simon sprawled out on the old sofa and closed his eyes for a second, savouring the warmth and the familiar kitchen smells.

'I'm sorry I haven't been up before.'

'For heaven's sake, I hardly expect to see you at all when you've got this sort of job on. Any breakthroughs?'

'Not really. Waiting for the girl he didn't manage to kill to be able to talk to us. She's bloody lucky to be alive. Abi Righton. She's a courageous one.'

Cat thought of the thin, fiercely protective young mother who'd sought comfort in her surgery. Yes, Abi was indeed courageous. Cat felt a terrible sadness. She would never fully understand the lives the prostitutes led. And nor would any of the Magdalene Group.

'And now Ruth Webber,' she said. 'She's not led a life struggling to break free, to give up the streets, to do better for her kids.'

'Might be unconnected. You know Ruth — do you have any take on why she'd go missing? Voluntarily?'

There was a long pause. Cat sliced mushrooms, cracked open three eggs, took bread from the bin and butter from the fridge.

'I don't know much about the cathedral set-up,' Simon said carefully, 'but I gather it isn't a happy ship at present.'

'Understatement. The place is riven by faction — new Dean and his gang on one side, old guard and most of the congregation on the other. It's a mess.'

'Where does Mrs Webber fit into the picture? Anywhere?'

'Very much so. She's the Mrs Proudie of St Michael's.'

'Trollope doesn't explain her disappearance.'

Cat was silent again, swirling butter round the pan.

Simon knew his sister's thoughtful silences. He made his coffee, poured it. The beaten eggs sizzled into the hot pan.

'Can you tell me if she's your patient?' he asked.

'The Dean and Mrs Webber are both registered with the practice. Can't tell you any more.'

'Could be a murder inquiry.'

'Come on, Si, you know the rules. But I will tell you one thing — I've never actually seen them as patients. Either they've never been to the surgery or they've seen Russell. And that's your lot. Now you tell me — do you think there's any link between Ruth Webber's disappearance and the others?'

He shrugged.

'Doesn't look likely, does it?'

'Open mind. I just hope she turns up somewhere alive and well and we can get on with the real job, because if you ask me, unofficially, I'd say she's just a distraction. God knows we get enough misspers — had another this morning, teenage boy, probably run away from an angry dad, no conceivable link to the killings.'

'But Ruth Webber is a woman.'

'Yes, but how do I know the killer hasn't started on teenage boys? Or respectable middle-aged women? Or the killer *is* a teenage boy? Answer, whatever my gut feeling is, I don't know.'

He changed the subject to the children.

'I suppose they think I'm gone from their lives, what with Scotland and now all this. I did manage to send Sam a cheery text the other day.'

'He didn't tell me. Get any reply?'

' "Hi Si luv u Sam." That sort of thing. Is he all right?'

Cat's face had clouded. 'Ask me how Hannah is, answer, great. Fine. Busy being Hannah. Ask about Felix — robust and well and busy being nearly three. But Sammy . . .'

'Remember his age — and the new school.'

'Yes, I see boys of eleven, twelve who are

366

definitely adolescent. Sam isn't there yet. To start with he's still quite small for his age. School seems all right, in so far as I can get anything out of him. That's the thing — I don't. I don't get a word out of him about most things . . . He isn't rude, he's just silent, and Sam was always a gasser, you know that.'

'It's his age, the new school and he misses Chris. Nothing worse.'

'Those are quite a lot all at once.'

She looks older, Simon thought, though perhaps what he saw on her face were the indelible marks of grief, and the more temporary ones of tiredness.

'He buries himself in a book or a computer game. He used to fight with Hannah, now he just ignores her completely. It makes me wonder whether I ought to give up the idea of doing this palliative care course.'

'Of course you shouldn't and you know it.'

Cat poured cream into a jug. 'I think I'll have some of this crumble. Comfort food.'

'Tell me about the course.'

She outlined the King's College diploma and what difference it could make to her work at the hospice. 'Judith has said she'll have the children when I go to London. I couldn't do it without her — well, without them.'

Simon wondered if she knew that he and Judith had had dinner. If she did, she gave no sign of it. He guessed that Judith had tactfully thought it should come from him if he wanted Cat to know.

He leaned back. 'I'm not going to stay too late, I need to sleep.'

'Did you sleep well in Scotland?'

He had not told her about Kirsty McLeod.

'Air's like chloroform.'

'You're welcome to stay here.'

'Thanks, but I need my own bed. Besides, if anything happens, I'll get called and that'll wake everybody.'

'Do you think anything will?'

He got up and stretched. 'It's what we're all afraid of.'

'Meanwhile, I guess the girls are still out there.'

'A few. They don't seem to be bussing the foreign girls over from Bevham — the pimps don't want any trouble.'

'Aren't they afraid of the killer going over there?'

'He won't. This is a local thing. He's got his patch.'

Cat shuddered. 'You know, when we had

that first meeting — the Magdalene Group thing — people were talking about the risks involved in prostitution, about STDs, violence, drugs, general risk of being ill if you spend your nights out on the street — and "the moral risk", as Ruth Webber kept saying. "The moral risk." But nobody dreamed of this.'

'Maybe you should have done. It's happened before.'

'The whole idea seemed a bit naive, and Ruth was so evangelical about it — but then, she is. And now she's missing. Why would a woman like that just — go off? Have you talked to Stephen Webber?'

'The sergeant who interviewed him felt he was being a bit cagey — something he couldn't quite put his finger on. He didn't refuse to answer any questions, he wasn't unhelpful — there was just something. But this sort of thing takes people in funny ways. They clam up, they panic, they babble on about nothing, they're sick in front of you, they get hysterical. It's unpredictable. Are you likely to see him?'

'What, Stephen Webber? You mean professionally?'

'No, around the place — cathedral?'

'I try not to. He makes himself scarce on choir nights and if I go to the early service,

369

it's usually Miles Hurley taking it. You're more likely to bump into the Dean than me, given that you live a hundred yards away.'

'Right. Do you think the marriage is sound?'

'I'd say it was an — unusual marriage. No children. I think her determination to run the cathedral after she has turned it upside down and put it back together her way is maybe a bit of displacement activity — but that's cod psychology. For all I know they didn't want any children. They don't seem at odds with one another though — I doubt if she ran away after a row.'

FORTY-TWO

Someone was flashing a light into his eyes and kicking him in the ribs, not very hard but persistently, shove, shove, shove, flash flash flash. He rolled away and buried his head in his arm, but the kicking went on in the small of his back. At least he couldn't see the light any more.

His head was the usual painful fuzz and his body ached, his mouth tasted foul.

'GERRUP.'

Shit. He rolled further away and came up against something hard.

'You're outta here, GERRUP.'

He managed to open his eyes. He had rolled up against the wall.

The next kick hurt low down.

'Fuck you!' Jonty Lewis sat up suddenly and lashed out with his left leg, but whoever it was jumped away.

'Gerrup and fuck off, Lewis.'

He had come here a few nights ago — two? Four? He hadn't much sense of that. He'd walked and hitched and hitched again and been thrown out of a lorry onto the verge. He remembered that. Then he'd found his way to the edge of the town and the waste ground behind the car park where he knew they all fetched up. It had been dark and wet but they were there. He'd nicked a wad of money from the first lift. The driver had gone for a leak and he'd stayed in the cab, and there it had been, under a roll of greasy rag in the door pocket. He'd almost laughed out loud. The guy had come back, even bought him a can of Coke, and then dropped him at the roundabout.

He'd no idea how much money there was but enough. He'd found them and bought a fix, and another, and said he'd pay to sleep on the floor of the squat. That was the last he remembered apart from some blurred memory of a lot of noise and his head spinning.

Now the light was in his face again. Flash, flash, flash.

It wasn't daylight — it was a fucking torch shining into his eyeballs.

'What the fuck . . .'

Next thing, he was banged up against the wall in one swift move, hands were round

372

his throat and someone with snake's breath was yelling in his face.

'You're gerring out, right, cos we don't want fuckin' stranglers here, right? Now shift it.'

'What? What you talking about? Who's a strangler?'

'You are, ent you, you're the fuckin' strangler, you killed your girlfriend, you did them others in, you're scum.'

Jonty managed to shove him back using his knee. The man yelped and swore.

'OK, what the fuck are you on about? Who's been strangled? Whose girlfriend?'

'Yours, shithead. What's her name, Marie? That one. And the others.'

Jonty shook his head to clear it and a pain shot up the back of his neck and over the top like a lightning bolt.

'Jeez, man, I got no idea what you're fuckin' on about. Marie? What about Marie? Marie's all right.'

'No, she ent, she's dead and you strangled her, they said, it's all over the fuckin' news, man, she's dead, and there's other toms dead, right, it was all over the fuckin' news.'

'Listen . . .' He rubbed his head now. He couldn't take it in. 'Listen . . . Marie. How do you know?'

'I just said, it's —'

'Marie O'Dowd's my girlfriend's name, it wasn't her.'

'That's it. Knew it. Some Paddy name.'

'She's not dead.'

He rubbed his eyes, then his face, then round his head and neck, as if he could rub himself to some sort of normal thinking. The room smelled foul. He looked at where he'd been lying, on a strip of dirty foam with a rolled-up newspaper for a pillow, and at the piles of rubbish on the floor, needles and broken glass and old bloody bits of towel and mugs with mould growing out of them.

'Shit,' Jonty Lewis said.

'Yeah, right.'

'You sure?'

'What would I make it up for? How'd I know anything about it?'

'Shit.'

'Anyway, you're out.'

'I haven't strangled anybody.'

The man shrugged. Jonty had no recollection of ever having seen him before but presumably he had, presumably he'd been here all along. He followed him downstairs, pulling his belt together round his jeans. The stairs were broken here and there and the banister was coming away from the wall.

'Jacket,' he said, everything becoming

crystal clear for a flash moment. He looked around the dark hallway, then turned and ran back up the stairs, mistaking the room and barging into one where three or four people were lying passed out on the floor, going into the next, and there was the foam and the newspaper pillow. And his denim jacket in a heap near the skirting. He grabbed it and felt in the pockets, all of them, and in the top right, where the button had come off, his fingers touched the roll of notes. Nobody had bothered to go through his stuff. Nobody.

Three minutes later he was out on the street and walking fast. He had no idea where he was. He didn't recognise anything, houses, shop, road ahead. Nothing. It was dark and he was cold. He walked faster, wanting to clear his head, and wanting a drink and wanting a fix and wanting to find out if what he'd heard, or thought he'd heard, was true. Every few minutes, he put his fingers into his pocket to touch the roll of notes. And then, quite suddenly, he turned a corner and saw the pub, the Cotsworth Arms, and everything went click.

There were only a couple of people at the bar but one of them moved away as he went up and the barman gave him a look.

'Pint of Strongbow and a Scotch.'

The man held out his hand. Money. Fuckers, he'd got money, did he look like he hadn't got money? Maybe he did. Yeah, right, he did. He guessed he did anyway.

He turned and headed for the bogs. It was only when he got inside a cubicle smelling of creosote that he took out the roll of notes and pulled two off, folded the others and put them back in the inside pocket. There must have been a couple of hundred there.

Back at the bar he handed over a tenner and picked up his drinks. There was a table in the far corner with a newspaper on one of the seats.

'HUNT CONTINUES FOR MISSING CATHEDRAL DEAN'S WIFE.'

He read down fast. Every paragraph there was a reference to other women who had gone missing and been found dead. Marie was named four times. Towards the end there was his own name. Police were continuing the search *for 27-year-old Jonathan — Jonty — Lewis, boyfriend of murdered Marie O'Dowd, wanted for questioning in connection with her murder'*.

He finished his cider in three gulps and went back to the bar for more. A couple of people had come in but nobody looked at him and the barman served his drinks with barely a glance. So maybe there hadn't been a photograph then. Though maybe the reason people weren't looking at him and were moving away was the state of him, his clothes, his hair, his unwashed state. He knew what he looked like.

Marie. So the other guy had been right. He hadn't believed it but it was here in the paper, and he knew why the police wanted to see him. Because he had form, because he'd trashed the van . . . only he hadn't killed her. Hadn't set eyes on her since he'd kicked the place to bits. Funny that. He couldn't remember a lot about the last few days but he remembered everything about that night, how he'd felt, what he'd said and done, it was clear as a film in his head.

But he hadn't killed her. So what bastard had? Some creep preying on women for kicks, some pervert. Not him. And that was so clear and straightforward that it wasn't difficult to decide what he was going to do. Marie. He couldn't get his head round it. She'd just come waltzing back, herself. Marie couldn't be cold dead.

Two minutes later he was out in the street and looking to hitch a lift to Lafferton.

FORTY-THREE

Even though Leah Wilson always put her alarm clock under a cushion on the carpet beside the bed it never failed to wake Geoff. This morning he groaned as usual, turned over and pulled the pillow over his head while she slid out and into the bathroom in a few quiet movements to try and give him a bit longer. She closed the door quietly too because once the boys heard the slightest sound they pinged awake and were up and roaring about and there was no chance of Geoff getting an extra fifteen minutes asleep. Fifteen seconds would be asking too much.

She felt guilty enough that she was the one working now without making Geoff's life any worse by having to field Alfie and Jake at half past five in the morning, when it would be three hours of racket before they had to set out to walk Alfie to school. At least Geoff could leave Jake a couple of doors away with his mother while he did that — gave him and Alfie a bit of time alone together. Molly would give Jake his breakfast, and feed Geoff, too, when he got back. Over his bacon and sausage he would start the usual business of going through the local paper to see what jobs there were, which would be none, or at least none suitable for him, before he headed into town and the jobcentre. Where there would be more no-jobs.

It was still dark. These mornings it was dark all the way to work and for an hour after she got in, which made it feel as if it was the middle of the night. Spring and summer were best, when she loved the bike ride down through the quiet streets, sometimes in warm early sunshine — and even when it was grey and raining, the fact that it was light made all the difference.

Three months ago, she had left for her cleaning job at the printworks only half an hour before Geoff followed her for the first shift there, but they never met at work now, of course, never had the chance for a quick early cup of tea and a bacon roll and a catch-up about the boys. They still couldn't believe how many had been laid off at the same time. Geoff had been at the printworks thirteen years, so when the rumour had gone round he'd thought his job was safe enough — he was one of the most skilled there, he'd come to it straight from school, knew nothing else apart from a paper round. But it had meant nothing. He'd had a reasonable pay-off but there were no thanks and no efforts to help any of them get another job. For a couple of weeks, he'd stood staring out of the living-room window like someone war-wounded, trying to get his head round empty days, after thirteen years of routine in one work place. He had started getting the paper and tramping down to the jobcentre but even before he went he knew there'd be nothing — nothing in printing, that went without saying, but nothing of anything else either. He had no IT skills beyond using the computer at home, he had no trade other than printing, and even when he got to the stage of knowing he'd accept anything at all, anything, he was without pride, he still found nothing. Leah had her cleaning job, which had always been for the extras, Christmas and a holiday and presents, and running her own small car, but now it was what kept them, that and the Jobseeker's allowance. Her car had gone straight off and the money was in the bank. She'd got out the old bike and Geoff had sorted it out and after a week she'd started enjoying it, as well as noticing that her waistline had shrunk a bit. He was happy looking after the boys till she got back at eleven, and later, when she went to do her shift in the pub, and there was always Molly. But Molly wanted to stick her oar in too much about how the boys were brought up, so Leah didn't want Molly having them more than was necessary.

It was hard though — not so much doing two jobs, as doing one early shift and one late, so she never got her full sleep except on Saturday night when she didn't do the pub or the cleaning and could have a lie-in. Geoff was brilliant about that. He got the boys up and took them out to do the shopping and then gave them the treat of the week, the supermarket breakfast. If it was fine they went somewhere else, the park or over to his brother's, so Leah could sleep in till half eleven, and there was still time to get the dinner on ready for them coming back. Without Sunday morning, she couldn't have held it all together.

The house was still quiet. She made her tea and had two slices of bread and marg. She used to have cereal with the boys but now they got the cheapest brand she'd given it up because it tasted of sawdust. The boys didn't notice. She left the kettle full and laid the table quickly. She liked to have the radio on in the morning to keep her going but it wasn't worth risking the boys hearing it — let Geoff have as long as he could get. Only Geoff walked into the kitchen as she was ready to go, hair on end, unshaven. Leah turned and lit the gas again under the kettle.

'That'll only be a minute. All right, love?'

'Yeah, I didn't go back again.'

'What's wrong?'

'I was worrying, if you want to know.'

'Well, don't — worrying won't get you a job. Something'll turn up, you couldn't be looking harder.'

'Not that.'

She took her jacket off the back of the chair.

'Look, don't go the canal way. You know why. I don't want to think of you going over that bridge. Go the long way round, doesn't matter if it makes you a bit late.'

'That's just the kind of thing gets people the sack, being a bit late without a good reason, and if I get the sack —'

'It's not without a good reason, is it? If they don't know that . . .'

The kettle started to whistle. He dropped two strong tea bags into his mug.

'Can you try doing with just one of those?

I know tea bags aren't that dear but we get through a heck of a lot.'

'No, I can't. There's some things I can't do and having weak tea first thing is one, as you bloomin' well know. Only we weren't talking about that.'

'I've got to go. Look, I tell you one thing. I'm safer going that way at the moment than I've ever been. Have you seen what it's like down there? Police cars, coppers walking in twos along the towpath, great big lights, police van at the entrance to the works. You'd be more at risk inside Scotland Yard.'

Geoff sat down and stirred his tea. 'If you say so.'

'I'm not daft.'

'No.'

'But I am going. Just in time . . .' She kissed Geoff on the back of his neck and went for the back door as she heard the sound of footsteps running across the landing. Geoff groaned. Then he said, very quickly, as if he'd had the words ready and been unable to find the right moment to say them, 'If I don't get a job soon, you know, we'll have to sell the Sprite.'

Leah stopped dead on her way out of the door. 'I'll go out and do twenty cleaning jobs if I have to before we get rid of the caravan. It's the one thing we've got, Geoff, the one thing we —'

'I know. Only —'

'Only nothing. It's not even worth much.'

'Thousand or two.'

'In your dreams. Anyway, dream on, because no way are we selling it. Besides, there's a job out there with your number on it — you wait.'

'That's the trouble. Waiting, bloody waiting.'

The boys hurtled into the kitchen. Leah fled.

Unless it was pouring with rain or there was a gale, she enjoyed the quiet bike ride to work. She was happy pedalling along and thinking, even if the thoughts were too often fretful ones, about the absence of jobs and money, about Geoff's morale, about the future. This morning, she tried to put what he had said about selling the caravan out of her mind but it wouldn't go. They had bought the Sprite the year they were married and been everywhere, almost every weekend, taking off to the sea, the hills, to festivals. In the Easter and summer holidays they'd gone as far as Ireland and the Scottish lochs, though once the boys were born, it was generally to the seaside. It wasn't only cheap holidays, it was family holidays, it was fun and an adventure and it was freedom.

When Geoff had spent his days in the din of the printworks, to get away somewhere quiet on Friday afternoon for two whole days and nights was the best way for him to unwind.

She had meant it. If there were more cleaning jobs, she would take them. Anything, so as not to have to sell the caravan.

Geoff had been fretting for days about her riding along the towpath, but as she pedalled down the side street that ran towards the canal, she saw the police van that was now stationed permanently at the top. One morning, there had been dogs with their handlers sniffing along the bushes — not this morning. She liked the smell of the canal, a green, watery smell that reminded her of something from her childhood — maybe the old ponds they had spent so much time at during the long summer holidays. You wouldn't do that now, let your own kids play beside deep water miles from anywhere, but things were so different then. They'd looked out for one another. Nothing had happened. Only she wasn't about to let her boys go off on their own the way she and her brother had.

She was thinking about how it had been then, messing about by the ponds, when she felt something pull sharply on her back wheel from behind. She looked quickly round, thinking she'd got it caught in a tree root or that somehow the wheel had buckled, but by then she was off the bike and something was pressing round her mouth as she was dragged away from the towpath under the footbridge. She kicked her feet hopelessly but the arm, which she knew it was, tightened. The last thing she heard was the sound of something splashing into the canal and the last thing she saw was the darkness under the bridge.

A couple of hundred yards away, on the hard-standing area above the canal, the police van was steamy with half a dozen uniform, logging off and getting ready to hand over to the day shift.

In the printworks the others in the cleaning team walked and biked and drove in through the main gate.

At home, Geoff Wilson cleared the breakfast dishes from the table and went upstairs to try and persuade both boys to clean their teeth and wash their faces rather than jump from the top bunk bed onto the floor and climb up to do it again. Until he had been doing it every day, he had never realised how much went into turning two small children from animals into civilised human

beings on a daily basis or wondered how
Leah managed it in half the time he did and
apparently with half the effort.

FORTY-FOUR

'Show us dealing.'

'*Yesss!* I'm going doolally hanging round here.'

The patrol car with the two PCs span showily round and headed towards the bypass, away from the street in which they had been parked up near the printworks, waiting for something to happen.

'Hang about, what was it, a Code Red?'

'Naw, but anything to get the adrenaline flowing.'

'Better cool it though . . . I heard a rumour the DCS was on the block.'

'Serrailler's always on the bloody block. I thought a Super was supposed to be safely tucked up in the station out of harm's way.'

'Since when did Serrailler ever do what he was supposed to? He's a maverick, he likes to get his hands dirty. I think it's good — he knows where the real work gets done, unlike some. He's never been a desk man.'

The bypass was busy with heavy goods vehicles, and the morning school and work rush, but Louis Wills overtook everything in the fast lane. He liked driving and he liked getting on with something.

'You think he's gay?' Nick asked now.

'What, the Super? No chance.'

'Not married, pushing forty . . .'

'Plenty of men aren't married at forty — doesn't make them shirtlifters. What does he have to be married for?'

'Didn't say that.'

'Anyway, I heard he'd been pretty near getting hitched to that DS who was murdered.'

'Never knew that.'

'Here we go. It'll be a false alarm.'

'Right.'

The supermarket was busy, but the sight of two uniformed policemen always made people glance around either curiously or with a flicker of anxiety, and the customer services desk had them escorted off the floor and up to the manager's office in seconds.

'Mr Meacher? I gather someone here reported a sighting of a missing person?'

The manager was young and wore a Bart Simpson tie the PC hoped his children had given him.

'That's it. Came in an hour ago, night-duty manager had left a note . . . One of the till staff thought they'd recognised this Mrs . . . Warren, is it? Or Wilson. The one who has something to do with the church.'

'Webber. Yes? What time was this?'

'She was on the tills at about two this morning — we're open twenty-four hours as you probably know. Marlene DeAddio . . . till number 7. It was fairly quiet — always is at two o'clock, though we do get people stopping off from the bypass and so on — so she'd more chance than usual to think she recognised this woman — well, from the newspaper pictures and the television, I suppose.'

'Why didn't someone call us then?'

'Marlene didn't say anything till she was clocking off just after six. She'd been thinking about it and she went to the staff canteen and found a paper with the picture in it, and it made her decide yes. So she reported to the duty manager, who left me the note.'

'Still, it would have helped if we'd been called as soon as. Right, is this lady still here?'

'No, no, she's gone, be in bed, I expect.'

'Well, we'll need her home address please. Do you have CCTV of the shop floor?'

The manager picked up a tape box from his desk. 'This covers the floor from ten o'clock until six. I knew you'd ask for it — I don't watch *The Bill* for nothing.' He grinned, showing bad teeth.

'We'll also need a CCTV tape of the exit and the car parks.'

'Whoops. Course you will. I'll organise that. Can I get you a coffee? Bacon roll?'

'No thanks, Mr Meacher. Just the lady's address and the tapes. Did anyone else recognise the woman?'

'Nobody else has said. But there wouldn't be — except maybe a shelf stacker if she happened to pass by one. None of the other till operators reported seeing her.'

'All the same, we'll need a list with the full details of everyone who was at work here around two this morning please, doesn't matter where they were.'

'Okey-dokey. All this will take ten, fifteen minutes . . .'

'We can wait.'

'Sure about the refreshments?'

The PCs glanced at one another. 'Thanks then, a tea would be good.'

'And a coffee thanks. Both milk, both sugar.'

'Muffin? Slice of toast?'

'No thanks. Just the drinks would be good.'

'We could have gone down to the café,' Nick said when they were on their own in the small, windowless office.

'He won't want us visible down there, putting the wind up people.'

'Can't understand that. Sight of us ought to be reassuring.'

Louis gave him a look.

Geoff Wilson took the bus into town. He hadn't used the bus for years, until he'd been made redundant, but now the car stayed parked up most of the time, the price of petrol being what it was. The bus was fine, the stop not far away, but the timetable was unreliable and he'd missed a couple of appointments as a result. When you were job-hunting, you had to be there, they didn't give you a second chance if you weren't on time. Now, he went half an hour before he needed to, just in case.

This morning, though, there was no delay so he got to Hunt Square and the jobcentre with so much time to spare that he wandered around for a bit and then went to get a cup of tea in the manky café on the corner. Why did jobcentres operate out of the cruddiest part of the town? Nobody came to Hunt Square for any other reason — even the charity shop was boarded up now. But the café was full and the sort of people in there were not the usual jobcentre dossers, they were ordinary blokes like him, including a couple he knew from the print-works, and even some smarter types in suits. The downturn had hit everywhere, there was nothing for skilled people unless they were in IT and even those jobs were getting thin on the ground. Geoff got his tea and looked around him, thinking of how much training and skills and education were probably packed into this café right now and all of it going to waste. How could you tell your kids to stay on at school, do their best, achieve, give up this and that so they could have a great future, when they'd got this place to point to and call you wrong?

He sat looking out of the window through the steam. Someone had decided in the seventies that Lafferton needed a cheaper shopping precinct and had built the place quickly out of concrete, with a multi-storey car park taking up one side. That was the only part still used, other than this café, a pound shop and the jobcentre. The square itself was weedy and the slabs broken where kids had taken over with skateboards. Lafferton had always been the wrong place for this sort of down market dump — but where was the right place? Ugly was ugly, wherever.

He was ten minutes early for his appointment, though why he didn't know, given that he expected it to be the same as every other one — a pleasant chat with a young bloke with acne and a string tie, who then told him there was nothing for him and even the shelf-stacking vacancies were all filled. But today, the young bloke was replaced by a woman in a bright yellow jacket and too much lipstick whose badge read *Yvonne Moon* and she gave Geoff a broad smile as she looked down the paperwork in front of her.

'Now, Mr Wilson, how are you?'

'Fine thanks.'

'Keeping your spirits up, I hope? I know how depressing this job-hunting can be.'

He wondered if she did.

'Still, it's all just a question of time, you know.'

'Time is what I've got plenty of, isn't it?'

She grinned again. Then she said, 'I think it's just possible you won't be having so much in future, Mr Wilson, because I may have something for you.'

Binman? Painting white lines on the road?

Cleaning toilets? OK, OK, he'd do any of those.

'You have a lot of experience in printing.'

'Yes. Like a good few other people.'

'Right. But you seem to have been the longest time in the business of any of our clients, as far as I can see. Surprisingly.'

'Why surprisingly?'

'Well, you're not too old.'

'I went there straight from school.'

'Good.' She turned a sheet of paper over and back, read the one underneath it, turned that over. Then looked up and grinned again.

'Have you heard of Delf and Wimborne?'

'Yes, they do the small stuff — we used to pass things on to them that weren't enough for us — leaflets, parish mags, letterheads, all that sort of thing.'

'Well, they have a vacancy. It came in just this morning and I matched it up with you straight away.'

Geoff sat up straight in his chair.

'They want a general machine operator who can also double as a van driver if needed. Have you got a clean driving licence? Yes, it says here.'

'As a whistle.'

'Van driving?'

'Small vans. I don't have an HGV.'

'Wouldn't be necessary. Now, there's a list here of the sort of machinery they have . . . best if you just look down it yourself really.'

She pushed a sheet across and Geoff read slowly down it, checking off everything. There was nothing there he couldn't handle in his sleep. He felt his throat tightening and his heart begin to thump. He was as qualified for this as anyone in the country, it was a few steps down and sideways from what he'd been doing, but it wasn't toilet cleaning either.

'And it's still vacant?'

Her grin flashed on and off like a neon sign.

'As I said, only just came in. I'd like to set up an interview today, if you can manage that?'

'Oh, I can manage it all right.'

He waited for the grin to flash and grinned back.

Two hours later, he walked on air out of the industrial units belonging to Delf and Wimborne Printers. He had taken two buses out here, to the far side of Lafferton, and then walked for fifteen minutes — he would definitely have to drive to work — but it had been worth it, he'd have walked a hundred miles for the reception he had,

Tony Delf saying they were lucky to get him, everyone looking pleased. The unit operated across the ground floor of two units, with the graphics people and office upstairs. The place had been humming, machines turning out thousands of brochures and theatre programmes, leaflets and orders of service for a wedding. The noise wasn't anything like the racket inside the big printworks but it was a familiar noise and to Geoff it was music.

He did a little dance in the yard outside; then, as he was walking towards the main road, he rang Leah's mobile. He had thought, for a nanosecond, of waiting till she got home to tell her, see her face, but he couldn't wait, and her voice when she heard his news would be almost as good.

And when he'd told her, he'd be back to tell his mother, and then the boys — not that they'd understand much — and see what they could do for a celebration, get something in, or all go out to Pizza Hut maybe. The boys would enjoy that, and if they were happy, he and Leah were happy. One of the best things would be her giving up one of her jobs — he knew which it would be, the pub. She didn't mind getting up early, she didn't mind cleaning, the gang of them seemed to have a good laugh at his old works. The pub was just graft and having to be pleasant to unpleasant people. She could hand in her notice tonight.

FORTY-FIVE

Jonty Lewis leaned back in the metal chair and closed his eyes. His head hurt. They'd left him for what felt like a day and a night in front of a plastic cup of cold tea. The interview room had only one window — a narrow slit high up in the wall — and it smelled, though he couldn't work out what the smell actually was, and anyway, he was past caring. He wished he'd stayed in the squat or else gone walkabout.

All the same, Marie being dead was a facer. He hadn't believed it, even the newspaper report, hadn't believed it till he'd come into the station and said who he was and they'd grabbed him like he was going to turn straight round and out again. Next thing, he was dumped in here, a couple of people had come in and gone and now he was waiting. Waiting. Waiting. It gave him time to think — too much time. Think about Marie. He panicked because he tried to recall her face and couldn't, there was a line drawn round her but it was blank inside, like one of those weird cut-outs. Marie. The last time he'd seen Marie . . . But his head had stopped working. He took a swig of the tea. Cold tea.

Disinfectant. That was the smell. Disinfectant and ancient cigarettes. He'd give anything for a spliff.

Only here they were again, the Irish bloke and the CID woman with the fat face.

'All right, Jonty, let's wrap this up. You had a fight with your girlfriend, Marie O'Dowd. She went off to work — she was a regular prostitute, probably keeping you in drug money, isn't that right? You kicked her caravan to bits because you were drunk or high or both, and then you hadn't finished, you went and found her on her patch and you got her down to the canal towpath and you strangled her. Right?'

'No. Not fucking right. I didn't kill Marie, didn't even know she was dead till this morning.'

'What made you come in to the station now, Jonty? Bad conscience? You couldn't live with what you'd done?'

'No. I wouldn't have if I'd done it, only I didn't.'

'Or just thought, if I give myself up it

might get me a better deal, is that it? Lighter sentence? Well, maybe that sometimes works for petty theft but it doesn't work for murder, Jonty.'

'I told you. I didn't murder Marie.'

'I suppose you're going to tell us you loved her too much.'

He shrugged. He didn't know. Love? Love Marie? What was that? But he'd liked Marie well enough and he didn't go in for killing, strangling. He couldn't even think about that, someone's hands tightening round Marie's neck. He felt sick.

'Tell us why you trashed Marie's caravan, Jonty.'

He was silent, working it out. How did they know he had? Wasn't difficult. They'd obviously have gone there and found it and who was the first person they'd think of? He'd got previous for all that sort of stuff, Marie's mother would tell them he'd done it, she'd put anything on him, and her friends. If he said he had, then what? One thing led to another with them. But if he said he hadn't and they'd got proof . . . could they have proof? Probably. He hadn't been careful, he'd probably put his hands all over everything and left prints, or cut himself and left blood. He couldn't remember much about it.

'I was mad.'

'Why?'

'Had a row.'

'What about?'

He couldn't remember. That night was a fog in his brain.

'Jonty?'

He shrugged.

'Did you have a lot of rows?'

'On and off. Like people do.'

'But this one was more serious. Was she threatening to kick you out, had she got someone else, was that it?'

No. He knew that hadn't been it — not that he remembered, but Marie wouldn't have done that. Wouldn't have dared.

'No.'

'What then? Come on, Jonty, get it over with.'

'What? All right, I trashed the van but then I left it, I went.'

'Where did you go, Jonty?'

'Don't remember.'

'Bad memory yours, isn't it? Where did Marie go?'

Go? Had she gone? He had a vague sense that he'd been on his own in the van but he couldn't be sure.

'To work? Did you make sure she'd gone to get you drug money before you wrecked her home? Was that it? Only then you worked yourself up into such a state, you wanted more, you wanted to go on hitting out, so you went and found Marie again. You were mad with Marie, weren't you?'

Shrug.

Now the woman took over.

'Listen, Jonty, we know an awful lot about you, we know a lot about what happened that night. Now we just need to know about Marie. What happened exactly? Did you follow her? Did you maybe find her by chance, and when you saw her, something clicked inside your head because you were still in a rage?'

'I didn't kill her.'

'All right, did you do anything to her? Did you beat her up? Maybe just intending to give her a good seeing-to but it all went wrong, you got out of control?'

'No. I didn't see her. I did the van but I never saw Marie. She . . .'

'She what?'

Suddenly, the fog cleared and he remembered watching her go out of the van, in the different clothes, that was it, she changed into her working gear, short skirt and that.

'Jonty? Come on.'

'We had a fight, I don't remember what about, that's the truth, I don't remember anything much only I do remember now, her getting changed and going out.'

'Going to work?'

He nodded.

'Convenient this. Just remembering. Why didn't you remember before?'

He didn't answer.

'And then you trashed the caravan?'

'Must have.'

'Then you went after her.'

'No. I didn't see her. I told you. I never saw Marie, I never touched her, I never killed her, right?'

'Did you know Chantelle, Jonty?'

'Chantelle who?'

'Chantelle Buckley.'

'Never heard of her.'

'Or Abi? Abi Righton. You must have known Abi, she was a friend of Marie's.'

'Yeah, I know Abi.'

'What did you do to Abi, Jonty?'

'Abi? Christ, she isn't dead as well, is she? Jesus Christ.'

'Come on, Jonty, where've you been?'

'I swear to God I didn't know that. Marie and her as well. Can't get my head round all this, I tell you.'

'Where have you been the last week, Jonty? We've had TV, newspapers, all with your photograph, radio's been asking you to contact us . . . Someone must have seen you even if you've been living rough. Which it looks as if you have.'

'Been in someone's house.'

'Great. Whose? Address?'

'Somewhere off the motorway. North.'

'Big area, Jonty.'

'I dunno the address.'

Fat face sighed.

'You stayed there for — how long? Days? Over a week — but you don't know the address? Funny that.'

'It's a squat.'

'You mean a crack house?' The man.

'Squat, like I said.'

'And how long were you in this squat?'

'I came out this morning. Came here, didn't I? Soon as I heard.'

'Heard?'

'About Marie.'

'So you came to tell us you'd murdered her and give yourself up.'

'NO! No, I didn't touch Marie, I didn't see Marie, I told you . . . Look . . . Ah, forget it. Just fucking forget it.'

'All right, Jonty. We'll leave it there for now. Interview terminated at eleven twenty-five.'

'Can I go?'

'No, you can't go, what makes you think

we arrest people on suspicion of murder and then let them go?'

They went out.

Five minutes later he was banged up.

At twelve o'clock, the small conference room had Serrailler, the two DIs heading up the separate investigations, and the DS heading up the team looking into the disappearance of Ruth Webber.

Serrailler looked round the table. They were tired. He could see it on their faces — tiredness and frustration, a sense of futility, that whoever it was, one killer or more, they were not ahead of him, not even close.

'Right, before I get your reports, listen up. I know exactly how you're feeling, believe me, because I feel the same. This is the sort of thing that drives good coppers to drink and despair. I know. I also know you're giving it everything, I know the guys on the ground are working their socks off and right now it seems as if we're getting nowhere fast. I still want to keep the investigations going parallel but going separately. However, I've little doubt the two murders and the near murder of the prostitutes are linked. Same area, same MO, probably the same motive, whatever that might be. I'm sure Mrs Webber's disappearance has nothing to do with any of it, and now we've had a probable sighting, I'm even more sure, but she still hasn't turned up. And until she does, we can't know if there's a link to the others or not. What's going on with Jonty Lewis?'

Franks shook his head. 'I've just had a listen to the interview tapes, guv, and a quick debrief. He isn't confessing to anything, he didn't see Marie after he trashed the caravan, he didn't even know she was dead till this morning. If he's lying — and there's no liar like an addict — he's convincing. Gut feeling is, he didn't do it but if he did chances are it was only Marie, and as we think the same person killed Chantelle as well, it looks dodgy. Why would he kill Chantelle? He didn't know her, never met her, as far as we know.'

'He did know Abi Righton.'

'True — but what does "know" mean in this context? She was a friend of Marie's, they worked the same patch. Jonty was Marie's on-off boyfriend. They didn't spend cosy threesomes together. And when he heard Abi might be dead he seemed genuinely shaken.'

He leaned back. 'I don't buy it, guv. I wish I could, it would fit nice and neatly, but I don't.'

'Doesn't sound as if we've anything to hold him on.'

'Circumstantial. All of it. I don't see why he would come in here at all if he'd killed her and Chantelle and attacked Abi. He's been stoned and holed up in a crack house, somewhere off the motorway, sleeping it off. He came in here to clear himself.'

'He's got form, of course.'

'Aggravated and GBH, true — and possession and dealing. Doesn't make him a killer.'

'Makes him violent.'

'Not enough, guv. We just don't have enough.'

'Right, put Vanek and Mead back in there. Have one more go at him and pull out all the stops . . . If he's guilty I want him broken down.'

'Guv.'

'OK. Moving on, I want to look back at this other guy we had in — the librarian. We sure about him?'

'Honestly, sir, all we had to even start questioning him was the fact that he had this weird thing about the girls . . . being their friend, taking the food and drink and so on. Peculiar way to spend your evenings but it isn't a crime. On the other hand, he fits.'

'The profile?'

The DI nodded.

'Loner. Not married, no close relationship, not now, not ever, so far as we could discover. Lives with his elderly mother. Keeps himself tucked away. Apparently shy. Bit of a cold fish. Odd habit he has, don't you think? If you want to do good and help the girls on the streets, you go with the Reachout vans or join the Sally Army or something. Did we get anywhere with him at all?'

'No. The boys said it was like interviewing a ball of string — tight packed, but when you unwound it there was yards of — well, string, and a hollow middle.'

'Someone's been doing the psychology course then! No forensics?'

'No motive, guv.'

'I disagree. I think there could be a motive. Dislike of women, fear of women, fear of sex, hatred of prostitutes coupled with guilt about them being out there . . . OK, don't look at me like that. I know, I know, it's another case of "Who's been doing the psychology course then?" Still, I think I want another go at our librarian, but this doesn't need a tough interview, it needs softly-softly. Put someone clever onto it, not one of your bull-bar lot.'

'Guv?'

'You know what I mean. All right, Andrea?'

'Guv. We've gone through the CCTV tapes from the supermarket and —'

There was a tap on the door and someone thrust a piece of paper towards Serrailler and retreated. He read it quickly, frowning, then pushed his blond hair back with the unconscious gesture he made when under stress.

'We've another missing woman. Leah Wilson, twenty-nine, morning cleaner at the printworks. Didn't arrive at work, husband tried to call her at eleven ten, mobile switched off. And she cycled to work from the Cherrywood estate, via the canal towpath.'

There was a brief, total silence.

'Andrea, let's have your rundown and then I need to go.'

'Guv. CCTV, as I was saying, shows what we think is Mrs Ruth Webber, but it isn't a good tape, and the one outside the supermarket only catches the back of the woman thought to be her. The till operator who recognised her gave a better description, to be honest. We're getting her husband in to look at the tapes, we're doing house-to-house and car checks in the entire area of the supermarket, we've got a trace on anyone who was in there at the same time as this woman — some traced through their loyalty cards — which wasn't many as it was two in the morning. Everyone cooperative. And we're doing shops and anywhere else this woman who could be Mrs Webber might have gone. Blank so far, but local radio is doing a request for any drivers on the roads round there at that time, and there's a new photograph of Mrs Webber being printed and going out this morning. We've got a team going to the cathedral to talk to people there — that's aside from the Reverend. Or the Dean . . . I don't know how he styles himself.'

'The Dean. Thanks, Andrea, good work. It's a lot to handle but I want to stay right on top with this one. Somebody has got to have spotted a woman on her own walking from the supermarket at 2 a.m. and then going somewhere or other. No stone unturned and all that. I'll be around later, talk to the teams on the ground.'

He went out. The others followed him in silence.

FORTY-SIX

Cat woke from a deep sleep, puzzled by the sound she was hearing, before realising that it was the buzz of her phone. She was not on call to the hospice and the days when she had done night duty for the surgery were over, so that it took her a few minutes longer than usual to come fully awake. It was half-term and the children were away for four days with Chris's parents in Derbyshire. They saw too little of his side of the family, she thought, so they would be having a mighty catch-up with uncles, aunts and several cousins. For the first time, she was feeling content at having time in the house entirely on her own.

'Dr Deerbon.'

There was a long enough silence for her to repeat her name and 'Hello — who is this?'

'Cat . . . I'm so sorry . . . I know this is . . . very early.'

'I'm sorry, I don't . . .'

'Stephen Webber. I do realise it's, what, not five o'clock I don't think, I am so sorry, I . . .'

She sat up. It was ten to five, still pitch dark. Stephen Webber sounded distressed, as if he was unable to catch his breath properly.

'Stephen, what's happened? Is it Ruth?'

'Yes. No. Oh God.'

'Take a deep breath. Slowly. Good. Now . . . what's happened?'

'Thank you, thank you, Cat. That's it — nothing. Nothing at all has happened.'

'She hasn't come home?'

'No.' He sighed a long, exhausted sigh. 'No, and there's no news from the police. But . . . There's something I . . . I think you should know. That I should tell you.'

'Me?'

'Yes, please . . . I need to talk to you about this. I can't talk to anyone else. That is, because you're a doctor, a doctor I know . . .'

'Do you want to come into the surgery first thing? I start appointments at nine but if you can come, say, at half past eight . . .'

'Oh.'

'Is that a problem?'

'I was wondering . . . I'm not sure if I can

face coming to a surgery. I feel . . .'

'Right. Listen. I was half thinking of getting up for the early Communion service, so I'll do that . . . I could come to your house straight afterwards — that's still only half seven or so, it gives us plenty of time. I can perhaps take a cup of coffee off you?'

'It's Miles taking the early service you know, I won't —'

'I know, but you'll be at home?'

'Yes, I suppose I shall.' Stephen sounded hopelessly confused.

'I'll see you then. Now, try and get a couple of hours' sleep, Stephen.'

'Thank you, so much. I am grateful. Thank you. I will try, yes, but . . . thank you.'

She had to ring off, sensing that he would have stayed helplessly on the other end of the phone for some time.

After another twenty minutes of failing to get back to sleep she got up and went downstairs. The warmth of the Aga when she lifted the lid to put on the kettle was comforting, the catflap banged as Mephisto came in from his night's hunting. She hesitated about booting up her computer and doing an hour's work but settled for the sofa, on which Mephisto soon joined her, and Marilynne Robinson's novel *Gilead*.

But now and then, as she sipped her tea, she lifted her head and looked at the curtain shifting slightly in the autumn wind, thinking about the children, wondering if Felix was worried about being away in a house he barely remembered, worrying herself about Sam, and disturbed by Stephen Webber's call. It was a distressing start to the day. But as she was getting into the car for her drive to the early service, it occurred to her that one thing she had not been doing was brooding about Chris. She was at a loss to know if that was a good thing or not.

'Almighty God, unto whom all hearts are open, all desires known and from whom no secrets are hid: Cleanse the thoughts of our hearts by the inspiration of thy Holy Spirit, that we may perfectly love thee, and worthily magnify thy holy name, through Jesus Christ our Lord . . .'

Miles Hurley had a good voice, Cat thought, kneeling in the second row of the Lady chapel, clear, without any sing-song, well modulated. And voices mattered, especially in the main body of the cathedral, whose acoustic picked up every word and lifted it up into the great roof, so that the wavering, the reedy or the booming made no impression. There were a dozen people in the small chapel, the same ones who were usually there — an elderly lady who walked slow as a snail from the Almshouses, on two sticks, a couple of people coming in from night shift, others who started work early. She knew most of them by sight, a few by name. This was the service more than any other which had sustained her during the dreadful months of Chris's illness and the bleak time after his death. Often she had repeated the responses mechanically, too numb to pray properly, but simply needing to be in this place that had been the backdrop to her life for so many years, in which she had been married, her children christened, her mother and sister laid to rest. She had sung in dozens of concerts here, listened to others. She loved the cathedral, and the changes that were being forced through with such haste were distressing and unsettling. She wondered now, as she listened to Miles Hurley say the prayer of repentance, how much he was committed to those changes, for she suspected that though he had worked with the Dean so closely in London, he was less of a moderniser and charismatic evangelical than Stephen. Apart from anything else, he seemed to be more cultivated, have better taste, a greater sense of the importance of quality in the liturgy and the music. Stephen Web-

ber did not take any of the early Communion services, or the occasional evensong, in
which the 1662 prayer book was still used
— though whether any of them would
survive for much longer was anyone's guess.
He had said that he could not bring himself
'to utter archaisms which were so little
understood'. But they were understood by
many more than he imagined — certainly
by most of the regular congregation —
understood and greatly loved.

Usually, even at such an early service, the
celebrant greeted people as they left, but
this morning Miles hurried away so that Cat
was at the Webbers' front door just before
half past seven.

She was well used to seeing people in
shock, people in states of distress, their
worlds turned upside down by an accident,
a death, some appalling news, but she was
still surprised by the change in Stephen
Webber. His face was grey, he had the deep
hollows of sleeplessness beneath his eyes,
which seemed to have sunk back into his
skull, and those eyes were wary and with
the odd blank look she recognised in someone who was trying to keep things together
without much success.

The kitchen was in chaos. Cat wondered
if they had any sort of domestic help be-

cause Stephen was clearly not managing. He was looking around for the kettle and cups, and as he found the latter on a tray, knocked the whole lot off the worktop.

'Stephen, if you clear that up — mind you don't cut yourself — I'll make us some coffee. Do you have a dustpan and brush?'

He looked about him helplessly, so that in the end, she made him sit at the table and found everything herself. It took some time.

'Thank you. I'm afraid I'm in a mess. I can't function normally, I don't quite know what I should be doing, but I shouldn't ask you to come here and then expect . . .'

She set down a cafetière and two mugs. 'It's fine. Are you taking this time off work? I hope so. As you say, you can't function, which is entirely normal. Just take everything quietly, don't put any extra stress on yourself.'

'Miles has taken over some of my work for now. I'd be nowhere without his help — and everyone else's . . . People are very good.' His voice was toneless and infinitely weary and when he picked up his coffee mug, his hand shook.

'Stephen, you said there was something you wanted to tell me.'

He stared at the table, rubbing his forefinger round and round the wood in a small circle.

'Is it about Ruth or about you?'

'I'm not sure what . . . if I should say anything.'

She waited for a long time, sipping her coffee. His hair was thinning and had wisps of grey, she saw. He had arrived only a few months before as a young-seeming, vigorous, energetic new Dean. Now, the energy and purpose had gone.

'Ruth,' he said at last, looking up at her. 'Ruth is a manic-depressive — has been for some years. No, that's untrue. Many years. Perhaps she has always been so. I married her without fully realising the extent of her condition and I have often asked myself if I would have done so if . . .'

He told her the full story quite coherently, as though, having started, he gained confidence and a certain strength. Cat listened carefully, listened to accounts of hospitalisation, Ruth being sectioned after bouts of manic behaviour which had put others at risk as well as herself, and of suicidal depressions, even a couple of attempts, one of them almost successful. The story followed a familiar pattern of someone gradually learning about their condition, accepting help and medication, slipping back when that medication was stopped because it made life, as a patient had once said to her, 'like grey flannel'. There had been a crisis team, a good London GP, average-sounding hospital care. And, through it all, Stephen had battled to keep her on an even keel, and to hide her condition from others. It was clear that he felt it was a burden he should bear alone, clear that he was both afraid and ashamed of it.

He came to a halt, drank his cooling coffee all at once, and shook his head several times, as if trying to clear it. But the inevitable relief at having talked himself out was evident in the way his shoulders dropped and he slumped in his chair.

'Stephen, have you told this to the police?'

'No. I couldn't . . . somehow, it felt . . . it seemed wrong.'

'Absolutely not. You have to tell them, you have to do it this morning. I'll drive you down to the station.'

'No, please, I can't do that, I can't go in there . . .'

'Why not? They need to know, urgently. This is very, very relevant to Ruth's disappearance.'

'It might not be.'

'Yes it is. Two young women were murdered, another almost killed, and then your wife disappeared . . .'

'But it isn't the same, she isn't — like that.'

'Of course Ruth isn't a prostitute, but the police know nothing about her mental state, her health, so they are mounting a major search with, always in their minds, the fact that she could be dead too. They can't assume the person is only ever going to attack prostitutes. But if they know what you have just told me it alters the way they'll deal with this. They already know someone answering to her description was seen in the supermarket in the middle of the night —'

'It can't have been her.'

'Why can't it?'

'They asked me to go in and look at the CCTV tapes . . .'

'And did you?'

Stephen looked at her. His eyes were full of tears. 'I couldn't face it yesterday . . . I said . . . I told them I had . . . that there was . . . I said I'd go today.'

'Right. I'll take you. You'll look at the tapes, and then you'll tell them. Stephen, you have to. You have a duty to.'

Now the tears were running down his cheeks, but silently. She reached out and put her hand over his. 'It will be all right. They'll understand and they'll help you. But you can't hide this.'

He shook his head again violently. It was clear that his normal ability to think clearly had deserted him.

'Listen, Stephen. You know my brother is in charge of the police investigations? Would it help if I asked him to come here and talk to you — just him? He's probably still at home — I can get him to come now. That would be easier for you and he'd probably drive you in to the station so that you can look at the tapes. You know this is what you need to do.'

'Can't you . . . would *you* tell them?'

'No,' Cat said gently. 'You know I can't.'

Fifteen minutes later, Simon was sitting opposite Stephen Webber, looking at him calmly and with understanding, leaning back as if he had all the time in the world to listen. Cat left for the surgery, after suggesting that Stephen come to see her, or her partner, Russell Jones, to get a medical check-up himself. She made a mental note to book an appointment for him later that day, as a matter of urgency.

As she was getting into her car, Miles Hurley came through the side gate of the Precentor's House opposite, hesitated, then walked quickly over.

'Is something wrong? Should I go and see him?'

'No. He just wanted to ask me about something and as I'd been in to the service it was a good time.' She had no idea how much Miles knew but it was not her business to tell him anything at all, and she did not want anyone interrupting Stephen in his talk with her brother.

'If you're sure . . .'

'I am.'

He hovered. 'I have to see the head verger but I'll be about here today. If Stephen needs me.'

Cat smiled non-committally and drove away.

FORTY-SEVEN

Ben and Steph were at the house by eight. Their arrival on the doorstep coincided with Hilary's.

'Can I help you?'

'DS Vanek, DC Mead, Lafferton CID. We're hoping to talk to Mr Leslie Blade.'

Hilary frowned. 'Well, he won't have left for work yet. Have you rung the bell?'

'We were just about to.'

She put her key into the lock and glanced round. 'If you'll wait a moment, please, I'll ask Mr Blade.'

She did not invite them in, and pushed the door to until it was almost shut.

Vanek shrugged. 'Just wonder about this, to be honest.'

'Did you say?'

'To the DI? Yes. Came from above apparently.'

'I think he's floundering, me.'

'Who wouldn't be?'

'Well, I would, but then I'm not a DCS and the officer in charge, am I? And I wouldn't want to be either, would you?'

'Certainly would. Let me get my hands on a big op like this. One day . . .'

Steph Mead rolled her eyes.

'What's she doing? Letting him escape over the back fence?'

'You want me to go round?'

'Nah, he hasn't got the bottle. Mother's boy, this one.'

It was several minutes before Leslie Blade came to the door, dressed in his grey trousers and sports jacket for work.

'Good morning.'

'Morning, sir. I wonder if we could come inside for a moment?'

'Not really. It isn't convenient. What can I do for you?'

'It would be better inside, Mr Blade . . . you know what neighbours are like.'

'I'm quite happy to speak to you here.'

'Very well. We'd like you to come with us, if you would.'

'Where to?'

'The station, sir. We have a few questions we'd like to go over with you again.'

'I've told you everything I know, absolutely everything. There is nothing more I can possibly say because there is nothing more I

425

know, officer. Nothing has happened since I came to the police station, as far as I know. Nothing to do with me, that is. I'm sorry I can't be of more help, I wish I knew something about these poor women, I wish I could lead you to whoever is committing these terrible acts, but I can't.'

'That's understood, but we still want to go over your statements, Mr Blade.'

'Are you arresting me?'

'No, sir. You would come with us voluntarily.'

'Then if I am not under arrest, I would be grateful if you would leave and let me go to work.'

Vanek was about to open his mouth but Leslie Blade raised his voice slightly.

'On the understanding that at the end of the day, I will come into the station and go over whatever you wish me to go over. But I have nothing more to tell you, I cannot have yet more time from my work, we are quite short-staffed at present and it's our busiest time of the year. If that's acceptable?'

Vanek hesitated, and again Blade raised his voice slightly. 'You need have no fear that I will fail to appear, Sergeant.'

No, Vanek thought, I have no fear. You'll turn up. You're a decent bloke, even if you're a bit weird, and you didn't have anything to do with these murders. If it was down to me, we wouldn't be here at all.

He said, 'Thanks, Mr Blade. That's fine. What time do you think you'll get to the station?'

'I'm working split shifts this week. Ten till two, then six till ten tonight. So it will be somewhere between two thirty and three o'clock.'

In the car, Steph Mead said, 'Wasn't that a bit of a risk?'

'He'll turn up. He's that sort of bloke.'

'Hope you're right. So now what?'

'Canal. They've got the divers going in this morning.'

'Reckon they'll find anything?'

'Not Mrs Webber, that's for sure.'

'Not if she was doing midnight shopping. Odd though.'

'The whole thing's odd, all of it. It's going nowhere, Steph, and unless and until we get to talk to Abi Righton it'll stay this way. It's bloody frustrating.'

Thirty seconds later, Vanek's phone rang. He listened, said 'On our way' and turned to Stephanie Mead who was driving. 'There is a God.' He was smiling. 'We can have five minutes with Abi Righton.'

■ ■ ■ ■

Stephen Webber had identified the CCTV
footage as almost certainly showing his wife,
both at the checkout and then leaving the
store, on foot, with two plastic carrier bags.
The grey coat she wore was the same as one
Ruth had and though the images were
blurred, everything about them, her hair,
her movements, left him in no doubt.

'Thank God,' he kept saying, 'thank God.
That is so good, that is such a relief, thank
God.'

Serrailler had come in to look at the tapes
again himself, and to look after the Dean,
concerned about his fragile state after his
long and anguished confession early that
morning. Cat had spoken to him quickly as
she left, warning him that Webber was close
to breakdown. Now, Simon escorted him
back to his own room, where tea had been
provided by his secretary — tea in a pot
with the cups and saucers, reserved for
special visitors.

'Thank you very much for doing that,
Dean. I'm very grateful and you do realise,
don't you, what good news this is? I know
you can't take that in yet because we still
haven't found your wife, but the fact that

she was caught on camera shopping in Lafferton, albeit in the early hours, means that she was alive then and that was several days after she disappeared. In all the other cases, where the young women have been murdered, or almost murdered, they were killed very shortly after they went missing. We knew your wife didn't fit the profile of the others and this does confirm that she has very probably gone of her own accord. Given what you told me earlier that seems even more likely. So you do have reason to be optimistic.'

'I have always had reason, Superintendent, I trust in God, God doesn't fail us.'

Simon said nothing, only wondered that such confident faith had not been apparent before now. He looked at Webber as he sipped his tea. He seemed strained, anxious and tired, he was strung up, he was the picture of someone who entirely lacked trust and optimism and hope and faith in anything whatsoever. But living with a manic-depressive wife, trying to keep it a secret while holding down a demanding new job, would put years on anyone. He would talk to Cat later. She would tell him in more detail exactly what Ruth Webber's mental condition meant in terms of her behaviour and her relationships. For now, he waited until the Dean had drunk a second cup of tea and looked slightly restored, then had him driven home.

Half an hour later, he was in his own car, heading for the canal, and as he pulled into the lay-by and looked round, he thought that it resembled nothing so much as a location film set. The entire area had been cordoned off and onlookers were being turned away, or at least held back behind the tapes, by a large number of uniform. But he could see people looking from the back windows of the printworks. Nobody could prevent them seeing whatever they could see.

He went down the grassy slope and onto the towpath, but as he was about to go over to where the divers were making their preparations near the footbridge, someone called his name. The Chief Constable was also on her way down the slope, with a constable hovering, as if unsure whether to treat her as a woman and take her arm, or as a police officer and leave her to her own devices.

Simon Serrailler wondered how the teams would feel, watched by both their commanding officers.

'Simon.'

'Morning, ma'am. I'm sorry, I didn't get any message that you were coming down.'

'I didn't send one.'

She stood beside him on the towpath, looking across at the three men in their black rubber suits now putting on the diving masks. He did not glance at her. He could tell from the tone of her voice that she was not there to hand out praise.

There was a splash as the first diver dropped into the water, then another and another.

It had gone quiet as everyone watched and waited.

'How deep is it?' Paula Devenish asked.

'It's one of the deeper canals in the country — about fifteen feet.'

A diver resurfaced but went under again at once.

Serrailler felt uneasy. Finding nothing would mean he had to make a decision about how much further downriver the divers were asked to look, how much time he could justify keeping them. If the missing woman, Leah Wilson, had been murdered as she was cycling along the towpath near the footbridge, then the attack would have happened right under the noses of the police surveillance. Surely the killer would not have taken such a risk?

'Can I get someone to fetch you a coffee from the van, ma'am?'

'No thanks. I was wondering if you'd thought of bringing in a profiler?'

'I have thought, yes.'

'I know you're not keen on them, but at this point it might tie up some loose ends, focus everyone, give the investigations a new sense of direction. It needs someone from outside, don't you think?'

'Yes. We've had an excellent young woman with SIFT a couple of times — she gave us a pretty exact profile of the arsonist in the West Country. She works from Liverpool — she'll know something of all this already of course.'

'Nobody could fail to, could they? We're getting some very bad press, Simon.'

'Yes.'

They were. The media was becoming increasingly hostile, demanding results, arrests, answers, reinforcements, new leadership, increased public safety measures, more police on the streets, and whipping up the public into a frenzy of fear and suspicion and anti-police feeling. The press officer at the station was under extreme pressure and it would only get worse until an arrest was made. If another woman was found to have been murdered, the headlines would not make pretty reading. Television vans were camped outside permanently now, every movement in and out was recorded, and Serrailler was hassled morning and night. He believed in keeping them onside at all times but now he was losing them and he knew it. An ITV special on the killings and disappearances and lack of progress was being threatened and posters were appearing demanding 'Women of Lafferton have the right to walk safely'.

At the beginning, though people were shocked and their sympathy genuine, the murders were of prostitutes and they did not identify closely with what had happened. Once Ruth Webber disappeared, they did. Serrailler had made sure the press were given copies of the CCTV footage showing her in the supermarket, but at the last press briefing he had been made uncomfortably aware that the reaction would not be wholly positive. A sighting did not make a finding.

Now, standing by the canal in the chilly autumn morning, under a bright blue sky, Simon was suddenly transported to Venice. It was the smell, of course, the faint green smell, and the sleekness of the dark water. He had not been to the room he rented from Ernesto for some time, and he promised himself now that when all this was over he would take himself off for a few days there, before the winter mists and chill descended on the city. He could taste the coffee, hear the extraordinary silence of that car-less city where you could make out the sound of footsteps on the stones and individual voices floating up through an open window. He was in a trance of recollection when at the same moment as the Chief murmured and went past him, he heard a splash and a shout from one of the divers who was surfacing. He was being helped by another to carry something.

FORTY-EIGHT

The machines bleeped and hummed but otherwise there was a great quiet in the small side room. Ben Vanek and Steph Mead sat on either side of the high hospital bed, a nurse at the end of it. The consultant had said that because Abi had regained consciousness three times, and had indicated some alertness, and because the readings were improving, albeit only slowly, he was prepared to let them come in, wait, and if the right moment came, talk to her.

'But no aggressive questioning, absolutely no pressure, do you understand? Otherwise you'll be out and I won't let you back for some time. She won't be able to speak, you do realise that? Her throat is badly damaged. But if the moment comes, it's possible she could make some gesture in reply — sometimes it's a good idea to suggest one blink for yes, two for no, that sort of thing. But keep your questions to an absolute minimum and don't tell her anything that's likely to distress her.'

They had been sitting there for fifteen minutes, drinking lukewarm coffee and waiting, listening to the machines, looking at Abi. She was the colour of the sheets. Her hair was brushed back from her face, she had tubes from her nose, and tubes and clips and drips from various veins. Her throat was bandaged from the chin. They could see nothing of her injuries. But it was very peaceful in the room, and now that it seemed likely Abi would survive, the mood was upbeat as well as tranquil.

Vanek had gone outside to take a couple of calls, but now he had returned, everything was the same, and their wait took on a feeling of unreality, as if they were suspended in time. Only the machines went on monitoring, recording, monitoring, recording.

Abi woke quite suddenly, opening her eyes which for a split second were blank and then filled with fear. She moved her left hand slightly. The nurse went to her, checking the readings, touching her gently.

'Hello, Abi, you're fine, you're in hospital.'

Ben Vanek put a restraining hand on Steph, who had made to get up.

Abi did not move her head but her eyes looked round carefully, taking in the nurse, the ceiling, the bed, the machinery and slowly, slowly, came round to the police. Ben smiled but did not move.

'Hello, Abi,' he said quietly. 'I'm Ben. This is Steph.'

Nothing, for a moment, then a slight twitch of her lips, something in her eyes which was not fear.

Vanek glanced at the nurse who nodded.

'Abi, you can't say anything, but can you raise your hand? Or your finger?'

She did both.

'Great. Abi, do you know where you are?'

Her hand moved.

'Don't be worried at all because you are absolutely safe. Do you remember that I just told you my name?'

The finger was raised at once.

'I'm a police officer, so is Steph. We're not here to cause you any anxiety, we're here to ask if you can just possibly help us. If you don't want to, we can come back. If you'd rather we didn't ask you any more questions now, just lift your finger again.'

No movement.

'Thanks. Abi, can you remember anything at all, the tiniest thing, about what happened to you?'

Her eyes clouded and she moved her head fretfully on the pillow.

'Can you lift your finger for yes, please?'

After a long pause, during which she closed her eyes, then opened them and looked at the nurse, who smiled at her, Abi lifted her finger.

'Good. That's terrific. Abi, you were attacked. You were by the canal somewhere and someone attacked you. Do you remember anything about that?'

Again, the agitation, the closed eyes. The nurse looked at the monitors and said, 'Three or four minutes, no more.'

'OK,' Vanek said. Stephanie Mead glanced at Ben with respect. He was getting this so right she thought she should stay out of it, not cause Abi Righton any more confusion or distress.

'I'm not going to tire you out now, we'll come back later. But just one more question. Raise your hand or your finger for yes, OK? Did you see the person who attacked you? Did you see them, or hear them, or recognise them in any way at all? This is really important.'

Abi lifted her hand and looked straight at him.

Vanek waited but Abi was still. Into the silence, he eventually said: 'Thank you, Abi. That is a big help. Right, we'll go now and come back when the doctors say you're up to it. I'm sorry we have to ask you more questions but we need to catch this person, you understand?'

Suddenly, she started to shift her head about, to raise her hand and try to shake it, to look at him with an expression he could not fathom but which he did not think was fear. He glanced at the nurse.

'Is something wrong, Abi?' she asked, but it was Ben Abi was looking at, the hand still agitated on the bed, and now she tried to raise her head.

'Do you want to tell us something?'

She nodded anxiously.

'Is it something to do with the attack?'

She moved her hand and tried to shake her head.

'Don't get upset, Abi, it's all right . . . I don't know how to help her,' Vanek said. But Steph, looking into the girl's desperate face, had a flash of realisation.

'Abi, are you trying to ask us if your kids are all right?'

Relief, distress, delight, a strange amalgam of emotions fled across Abi Righton's face one after the other.

'Yes?'

The hand tapped the bedclothes.

'Well, they're both absolutely fine, they're really well and being looked after. You don't need to worry about them at all.'

The girl's eyes filled with tears.

'Right, we'll go and let you get some rest. You just concentrate on getting well, OK?'

Again, the flicker of a smile.

'Tell you what,' Steph said, and for a moment she put her hand on top of Abi's, 'I'll find out about your children today and when we come back I can give you an update. The hot news. But I know they're fine. No probs.'

'I'm glad you told her that about her children,' the nurse said, 'but her memory still comes in fits and starts because she already knew . . . a doctor called in yesterday to say they were fine. She'd seen a friend of Abi's apparently. But she hasn't remembered. I'll make a note. "Memory unreliable." '

Outside in the corridor, Ben touched Steph's arm. 'Well done,' he said. 'Telepathic or what?'

Steph grinned. She was pleased.

'So, she remembers a bit about the attack. It was someone she recognised. All we need to find out now is who.'

As they reached the hospital car park Ben's mobile rang.

'Vanek . . . Yes . . . Ah. Interesting.

Whereabouts exactly? . . . Is someone down there? OK, we'll find it. On our way.'

'What?'

'Do you know some allotments behind Grange Meadows — up where the canal joins the river?'

'I certainly do — my grandad had one of those allotments till he died, I used to spend hours up there with him.'

'You drive then.'

'What's up there?'

'Old boy was going to do some clearing on his allotment first thing and saw a woman near one of the sheds on the other side — more or less answering to the description of Ruth Webber.'

'Bet it isn't her. What would the wife of the Dean of St Michael's be doing living in an allotment shed?'

'So where is she then?'

'In the canal,' Steph said.

The allotments were looking gone-over and ragged at the end of the season, with bean wigwams bare and some of the earth already dug over ready for the winter. The huts seemed deserted apart from a couple of people standing by their open doors looking across to where the constable was hovering in front of a shed at the far side. The patrol car was parked on the track nearby, but there was no other sign of police activity.

'Right,' Vanek said, 'what have we got?'

'Forensics are on their way so best be careful.'

Vanek gave him a dirty look, but pulled out a packet of latex gloves from his pocket, put one pair on and handed the others to Steph Mead. The PC stood aside as he opened the shed door.

It smelled of something slightly sweet, and of wood and soil, but it was clean and tidy.

'Apparently this allotment's been vacant this year so nobody's used the hut. There was a bolt on the outside of the door but no padlock.'

Inside, at the back, was a rough bed made of sacking and an old red blanket, with a cushion. An old but whole wooden chair and small table stood under the window which looked as if it had been wiped clean recently. A carton of milk, a china mug, tea bags, a couple of plastic plates and a torch were on the table. There was also a Bible and a biro.

Vanek picked up the Bible and opened it but there was no identification. He smelled the milk, which was not sour.

'Nothing to eat,' he said. 'But if this is where Ruth Webber has been, where's the stuff she bought? We know she had a couple of carrier bags.'

'Maybe she ate it.'

'Doesn't add up. There's no leftovers, no carrier bags — and another thing, there's no heat of any sort in here and it's turned pretty cold at night now.' Vanek stripped off the gloves and went outside. 'Thanks,' he said to the duty constable, 'we don't need anything else.'

As they left, the forensics van was drawing up behind Vanek's car and he stopped the young woman as she went to get her gear out of the back.

'Hi. DS Vanek. Can you get me any prints, asap? We've got a set of Mrs Webber's from the house so we can try for a match straight away.'

'Do you think there'll be one?' Steph Mead asked as she started the car.

'Doubt it.'

'Back to the station?'

'Yes. I want to go over what we say to Leslie Blade before he comes in.'

'Think he'll show?'

'Yes.'

'You seen the governor today?'

'No, I think he was off down to see what the divers were doing. Why? Do you fancy him?'

'Serrailler? Never thought about it.'

'Course you have, every woman in the station has.'

'How do you know — you've only just come. Anyway, you're the one who was all eager-beaver to work with him.'

'Still am. He's a great copper.'

'Not doing so great right now, is he?'

'Think you could do better?'

'No. Sarge? Can you play darts?'

'Used to. I wasn't bad either, but I haven't played for ages. Why?'

'The station team's got a friendly tomorrow night and we're a man short.'

'What, do you play?'

'When I said "man" . . . I'm team captain actually.'

'Bloody hell.'

'What?'

He laughed. 'Are you asking me on a date, DC Mead?'

She flushed crimson, but he couldn't tell if it was with embarrassment or anger.

'No, I am not, I'm asking you to play on a darts team, Sergeant Vanek.'

'Where? The station?'

'No, we play at the Cross Keys in the Lanes. Seven sharp.'

'Who's it against?'

'Area drug squad.'

'OK, you're on.'

Steph Mead banged the steering wheel and accelerated.

A date? Ben Vanek wondered. Or just a darts match? He realised that he'd be quite happy either way.

FORTY-NINE

Leslie Blade assumed that Hilary knew nothing whatsoever about his late-night visits to the girls on the street. In fact she had long known, ever since she and Cliff had been driving back from the cinema once and seen him. She had assumed then that he had been going with one of them for sex and it had not particularly shocked or even surprised her. Leslie was a single man, he had a difficult life with a disabled mother, he'd never had the opportunity to find a wife or even a girlfriend so far as she was aware. It seemed quite likely that he would occasionally feel the need of a prostitute.

Hilary was a realistic woman, and quite non-judgemental. But she had semi-deliberately taken the same route back a few weeks later, on the way home from an evening out with a couple of girlfriends, and then she had seen Leslie again, under the street lamp by the printworks, in full view of any passers-by, and pouring something out of a flask for one of the girls who was holding out a cup. Hilary had gone on, round the roundabout, and doubled back, and there he had been still, handing out what looked like iced buns from a carrier bag, and this time there had been three girls, all standing round, smoking and talking.

After that, Hilary had put two and two together about all the food that appeared in the fridge and the cupboards — far more than Norah and Leslie could surely eat. So, he might not be using the girls after all, unless they paid him in services for the food and drink. He was looking out for them from the kindness of his heart and she knew him as a kind man.

When the first girl had been found murdered, Hilary had been as horrified as the rest of Lafferton, but with the second body she had begun to worry.

And then Leslie had rung her from the police station.

Hilary had thought about it, about nothing much else in fact, night and day, as she had looked after Norah, driven to and from her own home, sat over breakfast and tea, watched television, lain in bed . . . She had

447

not been able to believe the killer could be Leslie, not for a split second, he was not capable of any sort of violence, but she could understand perfectly well why the police had had to question him. It would have been bad if they had not. He spent time with the girls, he chatted to them, he was in the area, he was a man on his own. Of course they had to interview him. But he hadn't done anything. Hilary would have laid her life down on it. You might as well suspect her own gentle husband, Cliff.

Norah had said nothing, not a single word. Did she know? She watched the television news twice a day, so she certainly knew about the murders, but she had not mentioned them to Hilary. Once or twice they had watched together, but when the item had come up, again Norah had said nothing. Leslie had been different when he came back from what he had called his 'work trip'. He was never loud or chirpy, but he had been even more subdued and quiet than usual, and there had been something about him, a nervousness maybe, that Hilary had noticed. He had only spoken to her about domestic things and she had not pressed him to chat.

Why he went to talk to the girls on the street, why he took them sandwiches and

448

cakes and tea and coffee, she had no idea. But when the two detectives had arrived she had been surprised at how angry she felt on Leslie's behalf. Had they not asked him enough the previous time? And if anyone had been looking out or going past the gate, they would have recognised them as coppers — they stood out a mile, even the plain-clothes lot.

When she had gone in and told Leslie quietly that two detectives were on the doorstep to see him but that she had not felt she should ask them in, he had just nodded, snapped his lunch box shut, and gone to talk to them, pulling the door behind him. Norah was having her tea and listening to the radio but she must have heard the door. Hilary had gone straight in to her, asking if she was ready for her second cup. Norah had said that she was not, but otherwise, nothing.

Leslie had gone off as usual, saying goodbye to his mother, asking Hilary if she wanted him to do anything, shutting the gate carefully. So far as their conversation had gone, there might never have been anyone come to the front door at all. He had not referred to them, nor had Hilary. But she had heard some of what had been said, enough to know that he had agreed to go in to the police station later that day. Enough to worry her.

She had made an egg salad for lunch with warm potato in mayonnaise, and took hers in to eat with Norah, as usual. They watched the one o'clock television news.

'Oh no!' Hilary said involuntarily. They had retrieved the bicycle of the missing mother-of-two, Leah Wilson, from the canal. There was an intensified search for her body. 'I don't understand it,' she said, putting her fork back on her plate. 'I don't understand any of this. What is going on in our society?'

'But,' Norah said very quietly, 'she wasn't a prostitute.'

Hilary looked at her sharply but Norah had her head bent over her food, cutting a piece of potato into smaller pieces. She did not glance up.

When he worked split shifts, Leslie sometimes picked up the car and spent the free hours doing whatever shopping they needed. Hilary gave him a list, and he went to the largest of the three Lafferton supermarkets, having a snack there and then going on to do any jobs he might have in town. Knowing that he was due at the police station, Hilary had hesitated at first about giving him any shopping list at all, then realised that it would seem odd, and compiled a short one, of things they needed but not urgently. If he didn't have time, it wouldn't be important and she wouldn't ask questions.

The day passed as usual. She cleaned, cooked, washed up, helped Norah have a bath, took her for a slow walk round the back garden, looking at the Michaelmas daisies and the roses that still hung on into the depths of autumn. Norah had her rest. They played a game of Scrabble, they did the crossword, they watched television.

Hilary stayed until six on the days when Leslie worked late. Even so, she wondered if Norah minded the hours when she was left alone. But she always had a couple of library books, her word search puzzles and the television. Perhaps she enjoyed being alone. She had a panic button which would call a centre, which would alert both Leslie and Hilary that something was wrong. But Norah had never had to use it.

Hilary realised that she had been worrying most of the day, and she was not a worrier, she was even-tempered, cheerful, and things did not easily upset her. But now, she was not cheerful, she was anxious, and her mind kept returning to Leslie and the police, Leslie and the girls on the street.

Ben Vanek and Steph Mead had had a small bet that Leslie Blade would not show. At three twenty, the desk sergeant rang to say he was there.

'Ha. You owe me tea and a Danish pastry,' Ben said, as they went down. 'Knew he'd make it. If he says he'll keep an appointment, he'll keep it.'

'There are appointments and appointments, Sarge.'

Leslie Blade was calm. His face looked slightly pinched, his eyes were dull. He sat straight-backed, not glancing round the room, not looking at them, but somewhere in a vague middle distance across the table.

The line of questioning was, to begin with, the same as before — why did he go to talk to the girls and take them food, did he have sex with them, had he been by the canal on the nights when Chantelle, Marie and Abi had been attacked, had he talked to them for long on those nights if he had, how well did he know them all. His answers were the same, spoken firmly in a low voice. There was no discrepancy in his story, they'd checked with his mother, and they got no sense that he was trying to hide anything.

Then Ben Vanek said, 'You're not married, Mr Blade, is that correct?'

'It is.'

'May I ask why?'

'I have never wanted to marry. And I look after my mother.'

'Well, your mother also has a carer. Would your mother object to your marrying?'

'I wouldn't imagine so, no. If she approved of the — the lady.'

'What do you do for sex?'

He flushed and looked angry but did not reply.

'Come on, you're a man, you have normal needs, we all have normal needs. Have you ever been with a prostitute?'

'No. I haven't.'

'Would you?'

'No.'

'Do you disapprove of what they do? They sell sex. Do you think that's immoral and disgusting?'

'I think — it's a very unhappy life for the girls who do it.'

'But it doesn't disgust you?'

'The people who prey on the girls . . .'

'Yes?'

'Make me angry.'

'Do the girls make you angry?'

'Oh no.'

'Do you think they should be punished

for what they do?'

'No. It's not our — my — business to judge them.'

'What about the other women? The two missing women?'

Leslie looked blank.

'Did you ever talk to them?'

'Not to my knowledge. I'm sure I didn't.'

'Do you know where they are?'

'No.'

'One of them rode a bicycle, and that bicycle was found in the canal this morning. Did you throw it there?'

'Of course I didn't. Why on earth . . . ? No, I didn't. I wasn't anywhere near the canal. I haven't been near the canal . . . since . . . the girls disappeared.'

'Why not?'

There was a pause, then Leslie said in a louder voice, 'Because the girls are not there . . . because they were my friends and two of them are dead . . . out of respect for them . . . because the entire area is crawling with your people and if I so much as showed my face down there . . .'

'Yes?'

But he went quiet again, shrinking back into himself as if afraid of his own outburst.

The interview went on for thirty more

minutes. Afterwards, Steph Mead said it had been like interviewing a wall. They took a break outside the door, exhausted.

'He's not going to crack,' Steph said.

'Because there is nothing to crack about. We'll get nowhere because there is nowhere to get. I'm done. He walks.'

'Agree.'

They went back into the room. Leslie seemed not to have moved at all, barely even to have breathed. He sat forwards in the chair, arms on the table in front of him, face now paler, but quite expressionless.

'All right, Mr Blade, I'm happy for you to go. We won't be needing you further.'

Leslie Blade looked at the sergeant, as if not entirely sure what he had said or of its meaning. Then he sighed, and put his hands over his face. They waited.

'Mr Blade? Can I get you a cup of tea? Some water?'

There was a jug of water on the table and plastic cups, but it was, as always, tepid and tasted of drains.

Leslie Blade shook his head.

'OK. I'll show you out. Thank you for your cooperation. And if there is anything at all you remember about the dead women — anything they might have said to you, especially about their punters, please call me.'

He held out his card. Leslie Blade took it without a word and put it in his pocket.

As he turned the corner of the road, he took it out again and dropped it into a waste bin.

FIFTY

Each time Serrailler gave them an update, there were more press in the room than ever. This afternoon, it was packed, with several standing at the back. There was the usual buzz, and then silence as he came in. They were not in a forgiving mood. He ran through the arrest and questioning of Jonty Lewis, 'a twenty-seven-year-old Bevham man'.

'This man was released without charge yesterday afternoon. We have again questioned a fifty-three-year-old Lafferton man, who was also released without charge.'

'Superintendent, do you —'

'Questions to follow, please. I have no more information to give you for now on the missing Lafferton woman forty-three-year-old Mrs Ruth Webber, but there has been a development regarding the other missing woman, twenty-nine-year-old Mrs Leah Wilson. This morning, police divers retrieved a bicycle from the canal in the area of the footbridge, and it has been confirmed as belonging to Mrs Wilson, and on which she was last seen cycling to her job at the printworks — she was caught on CCTV on the corner of Freeman Avenue and Corley Road at approximately 5.47 a.m. We have not found Mrs Wilson and at present we do not have any information as to her whereabouts. Right, anyone?'

'Are your divers now looking for Mrs Wilson's body in the canal?'

'We have a team of police divers and various other search teams along the whole canal and towpath area — and we have drafted in police from elsewhere to ensure we have as many people on the ground there and —'

'There were plenty of coppers on the ground when Mrs Wilson went cycling past. And now she's vanished.'

'Do you presume Mrs Wilson is dead, Superintendent?'

'I never make presumptions of that kind.'

'Come on, you've got the bike, the woman was on it, she hasn't been found . . . this is another murder, isn't it?'

'I am not jumping to any conclusions, sorry. Don't try and put words into my mouth.'

'Superintendent Serrailler, you've now arrested and released two men without charge. Is anyone else in the frame for any of this?'

'Not at present, no, but obviously we are following up every possible lead.'

'What's that mean, exactly?'

'What it says. We are studying CCTV footage of traffic in the whole of the area used by the prostitutes, we are interviewing any of the prostitutes still working on the streets, though obviously we are doing our best to persuade them to stay away.'

'Have you talked to Abi Righton again?'

'No, but the doctors have said she'll be well enough to give another interview tomorrow. I am hopeful that she'll give us vital information in due course, but obviously she is in a serious condition and we can talk to her only when the doctors allow.'

'Superintendent . . . let's face it, you've got nowhere. Will you admit that? You haven't a clue about the murders, the attempted murder or about the missing women. It's a mess. Would you accept that?'

'That we have not yet charged anyone with murder, true. That it's a mess, no.'

'And that you haven't a clue?'

Serrailler made a dismissive gesture and turned to the next questioner.

'Do you think the disappearance of these

other two women and the murders of the prostitutes are connected? I know you've been asked this before but in the light of the sighting of Mrs Webber?'

'I don't like to speculate. At the moment all these cases are still being looked at separately.'

'I wonder if you've got any idea what the public mood is out there, Superintendent? People are pretty wound up.'

'I fully appreciate that people are concerned, that they're worried for their own safety and very anxious for a result — or results — and an end to all this. I assure you that I am too. Don't underestimate how well the police are aware of all this. I am determined to get results, my teams are working round the clock under great pressure. But we will find the person or persons who committed these terrible crimes against the young women.'

'And what if you don't? Your head's on the block, isn't it, Chief Superintendent?'

The Chief was on the phone two minutes after he had got back to his office and he had an uncomfortable ten minutes, though she stressed several times that she was giving him and the teams her full support and wanted him to know that she had every confidence . . . But her underlying message was the same as the one that had come across in the press conference — she wanted results, she wanted to know why there had been none, if everything possible was being done, every single officer properly deployed, every stone turned. 'The public are on our backs, Simon.'

As if, he thought as he put the phone down, he was unaware of that fact.

He turned and looked out of the window, down into the station yard and at the media pack outside and as he did so felt an over-whelming weariness, as if all the energy and resilience, mental and physical, were drain-ing out of him. He hadn't eaten properly for several days, only grabbed sandwiches and coffee and the occasional apple, and he knew that he was being foolish and, what was more, ignoring his own advice. He lectured the others about eating and drink-ing properly, taking refs, not filling them-selves up with too much caffeine. He was walking evidence of the soundness of the advice.

An hour later, he went into the CID room, asking every head of team to come in also.

'We're all tired, we're all frustrated, and it doesn't help to have the press on our backs.

I understand entirely, believe me. We seem to be getting nowhere, we've put in the hours but not only have we not had the reward for painstaking work, we haven't had any luck either. Luck does happen, though we can't ever rely on it, but it's deserted us for the time being. Right, I want everyone, as far as possible, to take a break. When your usual shift finishes and unless there's been a development, go home. Go home, eat a proper, nourishing meal, have a drink but only one, and chill. Go to bed early, and tomorrow, you'll feel a different person. It's very important. I'm knocking off soon. Tomorrow, let's hope we get a break, but I want to look at everything, everything, afresh. Try and put whatever you've been working on and the whole lot right out of your mind. Play with your kids, talk to your partner, go for a good walk, watch a bad film . . . do not watch the news. I have full confidence in every single one of you and absolute conviction that we will get there. We will find who has murdered these women, find what has happened to the ones who are missing. We will nail this. OK, thanks, guys. Now home as soon as you can.'

Normally, at the end of each day during a major inquiry, he left feeling tired, sometimes exhausted, but always keyed up, always ready for the next morning, always optimistic. But over the past few days he had become increasingly frustrated and downbeat as he left the station for home. Nothing was worse than things not coming together, and Simon had the feeling that he was pushing against a door while someone else, much stronger, was pushing back from the other side.

He did not feel like going straight to the flat, he wanted company — his sister's sofa to stretch out on with Mephisto purring beside him, a drink in his hand and the smell of cooking. But when he rang Cat he got the answerphone. He tried a couple of times, surprised that she was not there, but gave up and did not bother to leave a message or try her mobile. One by one, the teams were leaving the station, doing as he had suggested, taking time out. The vans were still on the streets, uniform and vehicle patrols still thick on the ground, the area by the canal now with double police numbers, but for tonight, the CID teams needed this break. For tonight.

He sat for some minutes. Ben Vanek and Steph Mead went out together, got into the same car and drove away. DI Franks and his wife, a civilian who worked as a SOCO, left on foot with a couple of others, probably bound for the pub. He knew they wouldn't object to his joining them, but he was sensitive to their need to let their hair down among themselves, talk about work or ignore it, talk about him if they felt like it. He wasn't about to cramp their style.

There were very few times when he felt at all troubled by lacking a wide circle of friends. Those he did have were far away from Lafferton, scattered not only round the country but round the world. For the rest, he was happy as he was, and with his family.

Family.

He picked up his phone again.

Judith opened the front door of Hallam House to him wearing a blue scarf tied behind her ears, jeans and what seemed to be an old shirt of his father's. She had a couple of splashes of white paint on her face.

'Oh good, now I can stop and get us something to eat. How lucky.'

'What on earth are you doing?'

'Painting the smallest bedroom. Felix usually sleeps in there now, though tonight he's in with Hannah, and he deserves better than the old mushroom walls.'

'Why are you doing it?'

'Can you see your father?'

'Of course not, but you could get someone in.'

'What a waste of money. I always did the decorating when Don was alive. I even did ceilings and wallpaper, but I was a tad younger then. I enjoy it. I listen to interesting programmes on Radio 4 about philosophy and life in Croatia.'

They were in the kitchen. 'I shall have to get someone to do the ceiling though. I know my age limitations.'

'Will I do?'

'Can you paint ceilings?'

'I did my entire flat, ceilings and all. I even sanded and stained the floorboards. Let me do the ceiling for you — it's only a tiny room, I can do the first coat tonight.'

'In exchange for supper?'

'Deal.'

'You can't wear your work suit.'

'Dad's more or less my size. I can wear this shirt if you find me a pair of his old trousers. Those cotton ones he wears in summer would do.'

Within ten minutes, he was on the ladder, white emulsion beside him, pushing the paint roller in broad sweeps to and fro. It made a soft silky sound and the autumnal night air coming through the open window mingling with the smell of the paint added to the pleasure the job gave him. Just after nine, Judith called him for supper. He finished the final few strokes in the far corner, and went downstairs.

'That's done. It'll be dry tomorrow morning and tomorrow being Saturday, unless something kicks off at the station, I'll come and finish it. I'll wash the roller after I've eaten.'

'You won't, you leave that to your assistant. Thank you, Simon, that's much appreciated. Now, I'm going to have some wine. For you?'

'Do you have a beer? Pray I don't get called in.'

'I cooked a ham yesterday, so this is leftover, but the chips are not.'

She handed Simon his lager and the bottle opener.

'It isn't Cat's choir night,' he said. 'Is she at the hospice?'

'No, she's gone with a friend to Bevham City Hall to hear Mozart. Richard's at a Masonic, so it's nice to have some company. I'm glad you feel you can invite yourself, Simon.'

Judith did not ask questions or press him to talk about work, or anything at all personal, accepting that if he wanted to he would. He felt easy in her company now, though his relationship with his father was still not easy and he supposed that it never would be.

They ate companionably, talked about politics and paintings. He mentioned Taransay. And then, he heard himself say, 'There was a rather nice girl up there. Kirsty McLeod.'

Judith topped up her wine glass, but said nothing.

'It was a very pleasant time. No strings, uncomplicated.'

If he had been telling this to Cat she would now be asking if he had any conscience at all, why he let women think they meant anything to him when they never did, what he thought he was doing taking yet another one for granted, whether he was ever going to let himself be serious about any woman . . . Judith simply let him talk. He finished his beer. There was some chocolate mousse and Judith peeled and sliced kiwi fruit and added some lychees. 'I do like scratch meals,' she said, 'they often turn up wonderful new combinations quite by chance.'

'They do. Not sure if chocolate mousse and lychees is one of them, though.'

She laughed and then looked at him for a

moment, her face suddenly thoughtful.

'Don't ever let anyone try to persuade you that life is insupportable without marriage or a similar long-term relationship. I've never believed that, you know. When Don died I didn't want or expect to marry again. Apart from missing him so terribly, I was actually quite content on my own. I wasn't looking for anyone else but it happens. Or it doesn't. I sound like one of those awful agony aunts. I apologise.'

'You needn't.'

'Thank you.'

'I'd rather you didn't tell anyone else though. I can do without the family pressure.'

'Absolutely. And you'll get none from me, Simon — even supposing I had a right, which I certainly don't.'

He cleared the table, Judith made coffee and they went with it into the small sitting room. The heavy curtains were drawn, the lamps on.

'It feels like winter,' Judith said. 'Which I rather like.'

They sat opposite one another. The house was very quiet. Simon thought of the three children, sleeping upstairs, children he dearly loved and about whom he sometimes felt great concern.

468

'How do you think Sam is?' he asked. 'Cat was fretting about him.'

Judith sighed. 'I wish I knew. I think he's a troubled little boy and it's probably a reaction to Chris's death — that wouldn't be at all surprising. He never talks about it, though Hannah does. She finds it easy to say she loved her daddy and she doesn't want him to be dead, to have a good cry and feel better. Not Sam. Perhaps there's something else, but what else, I've no idea. He is on the cusp of being adolescent of course, and I'm not sure how well he's settled at St Michael's. But he used to chatter away and now he doesn't. He is perfectly polite and pleasant but a portcullis has come down.'

'I must take him out for a day. He likes to go walking with me. But right now there's no chance.'

'I wonder —'

Judith got no further. There was the sound of Richard's car in the drive, and Simon's phone rang.

'Serrailler.'

He listened, holding up his hand to his father as he came in.

The call was brief.

'Oh, Simon, not some more dreadful news?'

'On the contrary,' Serrailler said, relief flooding through him. 'Ruth Webber has just turned up at her own house. Husband called the station ten minutes ago.'

'Is she all right?'

'As far as they know. Someone will see her in the morning.' He slipped his phone into his pocket. 'Judith, do you think there's a chance of another coffee before I head home?'

'I'll join you,' Richard said. 'Surprised to find you here at all, Simon.'

'Yes,' Simon said, 'so am I rather.'

FIFTY-ONE

Stephen Webber stood at the window of his study among the boxes that were not to be unpacked until the move into the Deanery. It was twenty past midnight and he had left Ruth upstairs, in bed but not asleep and almost completely silent. He had come down because he had felt tears welling up and knew that, if he was to cry, he must be alone. He had not put on the lamp but there was a moon enough for him to see a little way down the garden, to where the white fencing gleamed like bone. A cat, not their cat, an unknown, ginger cat, sat in the middle of the grass facing towards him, topaz-eyed, impassive.

He took off his glasses and wiped his eyes. His tears were tears of anger, relief, frustration, and they came mainly because he had not been able to find words to use, and, in any case, what he felt could not be expressed to Ruth. She had tapped so softly on the kitchen door, while he was making a pot of tea, that at first he had not fully realised what the sound was. When he opened the door, she had said nothing, simply walked past him, looked around the kitchen for a moment, as if trying to familiarise herself with it, then had sat down at the table. She wore an old mackintosh which he did not recognise, and she was dirty, her hair greasy and flattened to her head, her hands grubby. Her shoes were soaking wet.

He knew at once that she had descended far down into her depression. Her facial expression was dead, her eyes without any light in them, her shoulders slightly hunched. She said nothing, she did not look at him.

He had put a cup of tea in front of her but she made no attempt to drink it.

'Ruth,' he had said. 'Oh thank God you're alive.'

She glanced up at him, a flicker of bewilderment crossing her face.

'They've been looking for you . . . there . . .' But he could not tell her any more, she would not take it in, did not need to know about everything else that had been happening.

'Drink your tea. You look cold.'

She shrugged.

'You're exhausted . . . have you walked a long way?'

She pulled the cup nearer to her and stared into it but made no attempt to lift it.

It was then that Stephen realised he must ring the police and also that if he did not leave the room he would burst into tears — either that or lose his temper. Once, that was what he had done when she had been missing in London for more than twenty-four hours and been brought home eventually by a neighbour who had seen her walking along a main road in the dark. He had shouted at her but it had been like shouting at a deaf mute. She had not reacted to him in any way.

It had been the same now but he had not shouted. He had persuaded her to drink half the cup of tea, then taken her upstairs, filled the bath and left her. When he had phoned the police he had gone back up, to find the bathroom door open, wet towels on the floor and the light still on. When she was well, Ruth was meticulously tidy. Tonight, she would not have noticed how she had left the bathroom.

She was in bed, lying curled on her side and turned away from him. He knew that she was not asleep but the tears had overcome him and he had come back downstairs to stand at the window in despair.

Half an hour later he was still there, numb and barely thinking, when there was a soft knock on the side door.

'Stephen, I saw your light still on . . . Is everything all right?'

Miles Hurley came in, his clothes wet. Stephen hadn't noticed that it had been raining for much of the time he had been standing at the window.

'My dear man, you look as if you've had a terrible shock.'

Stephen suddenly felt as if his legs might give way beneath him and he sat down heavily on one of the kitchen chairs.

'Yes,' he said, 'Ruth's back.'

'Oh, thank God! When? Is she all right? Stephen, if I may say so, I think you should have a whisky. Can I get you one?'

'You may be right. Yes.' He started to get up but Miles put a hand on his shoulder and made him sit back. 'I know where it is. So what happened?'

'She just walked in. Exhausted. Very depressed. She looks as if she's been living rough, which, if the police are right about the allotment shed, she has. But you know how it is, Miles. She said nothing. She can barely speak when it's like this.'

'Have you phoned a doctor?'

'No, no. I will. Tomorrow. I will. But she's in bed. She won't go anywhere now and she won't come to any harm overnight. I can't start getting out a doctor and risking her being distressed . . . it won't help just at the moment.'

Miles set two glasses with generous measures of whisky on the table, and found a jug to fill with water.

'Perhaps you're right. What did the police say?'

'Nothing much. Thanked me for telling them. They'll send someone round in the morning. I suppose they have to check it out.'

'Certainly. But it's no longer their concern after that.' He drank. 'I'm very relieved, Stephen, but I'm sorry it's come to this again. It is such a dreadful strain for you. I really thought she was stable now — I thought the move here had done her good.'

'So did I. I don't know what to do. I feel I've failed her. Perhaps we should never have moved, perhaps she hasn't settled.'

'She seemed more than settled. Don't blame yourself.'

Stephen swirled his whisky round the glass, watching it catch the light. 'In confidence, Miles . . .'

'That goes without saying.'

'Yes. Of course. In confidence, I am utterly weary of it all. I simply cannot bear the thought of this going on and on into the future, of having to catch her the whole time, of not trusting her, of trying to do this job, trying to . . . to make a real impact here . . . while my heart is in my mouth all the time about her. I feel drained, absolutely drained.'

'Look, why not take a few days off? Even go away somewhere? Once she's seen the doctors and so on. I can look after things here.'

Stephen shook his head. 'She wouldn't come, and it may be that they think she needs a spell in hospital. I don't know if . . . dear God, I hope if they think it necessary that she agrees to it. Having her sectioned is . . .'

'I know. But if she does go in, then you have a break. You need it, Stephen. Everything will run perfectly smoothly.'

'You have enough to do. I can't dump my workload onto you as well.'

'You can and you must. I'm very resilient. You should know that.'

Miles got up and finished off his drink. 'Now I'm for my bed. And so should you be. Don't try and battle on, Stephen. I'm here. Everyone will pitch in. But tonight, let

476

us thank God Ruth is back home. Just at the moment that is what the young would call a result.'

FIFTY-TWO

It was hopeless now. Police were thick as blowflies all over the area so that even if any of them went down there they got moved on — 'friendly warning' and all that. Hayley had tried for four or five nights in the town centre, then moved out towards Hunt Square, but that was dead, and creepy as well. It was where the winos hung out. The centre had been OK for the occasional punter but several of the streets were now pedestrians only which cut the numbers down, and the police were there too, handing out leaflets with pictures of the dead girls on them, which gave you the creeps.

Besides, she hadn't been happy with the arrangement for Liam. The woman who listened out for him had taken to nipping out to the pub. That scared her. She thought of how it had been with Abi. They could trust one another.

So now she stayed in and had no money

apart from the child allowance and her benefit which never lasted. The money she'd taken from Abi's tin had long gone.

She was watching a rubbish soap on the afternoon telly when her mobile went. She only just about managed to keep it topped up now.

'Hello. Is that Hayley? Hayley Duncan?'

'Who wants to know?'

'This is Gwenda Mayo from social services. Is that you, Hayley?'

'It's me.' She almost clicked off. She hadn't anything to say to that cow who'd taken Abi's kids away.

'Good, thank you. Hayley, I was wondering if I could come and see you?'

'No thanks. You're not having my boy as well. Liam's fine.'

'Hayley, listen, of course I don't want that. But something's come up and I need to see you.'

'What sort of thing?'

'It isn't ideal to talk on the phone but it's about Abi Righton's children, Frankie and Mia?'

'I know their names. What's happened to them, what have you done now?'

'Nothing's happened to them, Hayley, but I need to talk to you about them, please.'

If it was about them, she'd have to see the

bloody woman.

'OK. Come now if you want.'

'Thank you, Hayley. I'll be there within the next half-hour.'

It was less. She had started to clear the table and put the dirty pots into the sink, not because she thought social services were so important but because she wasn't about to be judged on how tidy her flat was. They could probably use any excuse to take Liam away, even dirty coffee mugs. But when Gwenda arrived she didn't even glance round.

'Can I sit down?'

Hayley pushed some stuff off the chair.

'Now, you know Abi's children are in care.'

Hayley said nothing.

'Well, the people who are looking after them, Brett and Louise, are very good foster-carers and they are looking after Frankie and Mia really well. They love having them and they're very experienced. But they have found it difficult to settle the two of them, especially Frankie. And he keeps asking to see you. You and your little boy. And when he says your name, it's quite clear that Mia understands too.'

Hayley felt a wave of something rising from her gut to her throat. She wasn't sure if it was distress or anger, tears or the desire to kick the door down.

'I said I could have had them, didn't I? They'd have been great with me, and now look what's bloody happening, poor kids. Well, if they want to see me, me and Liam, you've got to let them, it's what Abi'd want and you've got no right to stop them, you —'

'Hayley, that's why I'm here. Because I think it would be a very good idea, I think they should see you. I can take you there later today if you'd come. Brett and Louise thought you could go and have tea and Liam could play with Frankie for a bit . . . and if it worked out well, then you could go again, re-establish contact with them. Especially in view of their mum being so much better.'

'What, you mean if she'd been dead they wouldn't have let us?'

'Well, she isn't dead. She's responding to treatment now, so although it will probably take some time, if she goes on improving there's every chance she will eventually have the children back home . . . obviously all other things being equal.'

'What's that supposed to mean?'

'It means it depends on a lot of factors — such as whether there would be a suitable flat or other accommodation available for them, how long it would be before she could look after them on her own or if she'd need help to begin with. It isn't just my decision, I can't say yes or no — as I said, there are a lot of factors. Anyway, will you come? I think it would be a really big help.'

'I love those kids like I love my own. You try and stop me. You change your mind and I'll kick up, I mean it.'

'Nobody's going to stop you, Hayley — nobody wants to. Quite the opposite. I'll come about three thirty, if that's all right with you?'

Maybe she'd been unfair, Hayley thought, after the woman had gone. Maybe she wasn't as bad as some of them. One thing she hadn't done was mention anything about what she or Abi did. It was about the kids, it was about making sure they were OK, and that was in her favour. No judgement. She raided all the jars and tins and mugs in the flat, and with what she found and what she could spare, she got together four pounds seventy. She'd ask if they could stop off, get Frankie and Mia a comic and some sweets and then there'd have to be something for Liam.

Before she went to collect him from

nursery, she was suddenly feeling so good she put the radio on and then cleared up, washed up, put everything away, wiped the windows, vacuumed, dusted round until it all looked good. She felt full of energy. If there was the chance of Abi getting a decent flat from the council, maybe they could get one together. Abi would need help when she got out of hospital, though Hayley wasn't sure how much damage had been done. She'd bought the local paper a couple of times, and kept listening to Radio Bevham, to try and find out more, but they had only ever said 'serious injuries'.

She wasn't sure what to expect from the foster-people. She'd never met any. The house was smaller than she'd imagined and the woman, Louise, a bit younger. Friendly.

'Hi, Hayley, nice to meet you. I'm really glad you could come — Frankie's been asking and asking after you, it got quite upsetting. I didn't tell him you'd be here today, hope you don't mind, only if you hadn't been able make it at the last minute or anything . . . well, you know.' She bent down. 'Hello, Liam. There's a surprise for you . . . do you want to go through?'

There was one long room that had been made out of the original two, with the sitting part at the front and a play part at the back, in front of some doors that looked out onto a long narrow garden. Hayley saw a swing and a slide. But then she saw Frankie beside a car track on the floor. For a split second, his face was a blank, a complete blank, as if he didn't dare react in any way to anyone. And then he saw Liam. She had never understood before exactly what it meant when you said someone's face 'lit up', but now she knew. Frankie hurled himself towards her, grabbing her round the knees, and at the same time Liam gave a lurch onto him, so that all three of them were together in a huddle, with Hayley crying and the others laughing.

'And here's Mia,' the woman said, and picked up the little girl from where she had been playing with a plastic dog on the floor.

'Hi,' Hayley said, through her tears. 'Hi, Mia, hi, sweetheart, it's me, it's Hayley and Liam.' She reached out and Mia clambered into her arms and clung with her legs as tightly as a monkey gripping a tree trunk.

The boys separated themselves and were soon brawling affectionately on the rug, laughing and yelling.

The three women looked on, unable to stop smiling. Lou took several photographs with her mobile phone. She made tea and they sat at the table, watching the boys play-fight and race toy motorbikes across the floor, Mia on Hayley's lap and looking at her anxiously every so often for reassurance. Hayley fed her sponge cake.

'God, I just wish Abi was here. I just want her to see them like this. It would do her more good than all the hospital stuff.'

'You could take these pictures in to show her. I'll load them onto the computer and print them off for you.'

She's nice, Hayley thought. Ordinary, nice eyes, gingery hair, jeans and a sweatshirt. What kind of people could take in someone else's kids, not knowing how long they'd stay, not knowing what they were like? She couldn't. She'd have Frankie and Mia but that was because she'd always known them, they were like her own.

She wished they were her own.

Lou had opened the doors and the boys charged out into the garden and started roaring round making plane noises. Mia watched and laughed but still clung to Hayley.

Gwenda Mayo was looking at her. 'She's fine, you know,' she said. 'She's very happy here.'

'Only it still isn't the same, is it? It's strangers. I'm not a stranger.'

'No.'

'Abi's going to be fine to look after them. She'll be OK once she's out of hospital, she's tough, Abi, she'll fight for her kids.'

'And nobody's saying anything different, Hayley. I just want to make sure they're well and happy while they're here.'

'Right.'

But she hugged Mia tight. She liked the woman and the kids were fine, she could see that. It was the social services who needed to know.

Louise printed off four pictures, really good, fun pictures of the kids, and gave them to her.

'Can I come again, bring Liam?'

It was Louise she'd spoken to but Louise'd had to glance at the Mayo woman, as if she couldn't decide for herself, which made Hayley mad, and it was the Mayo woman who answered.

'I'm sure we can arrange that, Hayley, but let's see how things go.'

'They're going fine, look at the lads, look at this little one. Why wouldn't it be OK? I want to be able to tell Abi all about them more than just once, I'm, like, standing in for her here, you know?'

'Well, I have an appointment, so we'll have to leave it there for today.' Gwen Mayo stood up.

'I wonder . . . perhaps Liam can stay for the rest of the day? He and Frankie are having such a good time. Maybe you could come back for him later?'

'I don't think we could make that work, Louise. I can't fetch Hayley, I'm tied up for the rest of today now, and she hasn't got a car. This is quite a way from where she lives. It just isn't convenient.'

You don't want it, Hayley thought, that's why it's not convenient. You're scared of letting me come here without you in case I snatch them or something daft like that. Control freaks is what you lot all are.

The worst was peeling Mia off her. She clung and clutched and then Liam wouldn't move from Frankie. It took a lot of hassle and at the end of it Hayley was in tears herself. Lou looked pinched and upset. Only the Mayo just carried on, urging them out, saying goodbye, not bothered about how they all were.

In the car, Liam sat with his thumb in his mouth and said nothing. Hayley knew how he felt. She didn't trust herself to speak either, just kept hold of the photos in case the Mayo wanted to confiscate them.

At Hayley's door, Gwenda said, 'It's been good for the children, good to see one another. It was worth doing.'

Hayley took Liam by the hand. 'Right,' she said, 'and if it's worth doing once it's worth doing more times. So I'll be ringing you.'

She went inside and closed the door without looking round.

FIFTY-THREE

The late shift was always unpopular because the library was packed with students, and at the start of the college year, they caused more work because they didn't know their way around the stock or the systems, queued at the desk to ask endless questions, were unfamiliar with, ignored, or complained about the rules, dumped their bags in everyone's way and generally prevented the staff from getting on with what they all regarded as their real work. A younger colleague who had more sympathy with the students once accused June Petrie of being much happier when the place was full of books and empty of people. June Petrie shared this with Leslie and for perhaps the only time they were instinctively in tune with one another.

Tonight was more crowded than usual because there were late lectures midweek and the students piled in at the end of those.

June and Leslie were both on the desk and at one point Leslie had told a youth sharply that if he continued to stand in the queue with his iPod in his ears emitting tinny noises, to the irritation of everyone around him, he would bar him for the rest of the term.

'You can't do that. You haven't got the authority.'

'Oh yes I can and oh yes I have and oh yes I will. Now please be so kind as to turn that thing off.'

June Petrie glanced at him. It was unlike Leslie to be irritable, let alone to raise his voice. He was always even-tempered and patient even when annoyed by something. But he had not been himself for the past few days. He had spoken little, either to her or the other staff, he had made one or two errors, forgotten a few things, which was entirely out of character. Leslie Blade was a meticulous man with an almost finicky insistence on correct detail. Now, he seemed either distracted and worried, or simply absent, as if he were only half conscious of the world and others around him.

June was well aware of the rumours that had been circulating and had dismissed them loudly, out of a natural loyalty to a long-standing colleague and because she simply did not, could not, believe them. Leslie, a suspect for the murders of several women? Leslie, a suspect for any violent or even simply illegal activity? It would be laughable if the whole business had not been so upsetting and frightening. When the murdered women had been prostitutes it had been lamentable but seemed far removed from her life, the lives of most people in Lafferton. Now, it had been announced on the news earlier today, they had found the body of a married woman and mother of two children, a woman simply on her way to work, and that had changed everything. If Mrs Leah Wilson, whose body had been in the canal, could be attacked and strangled and dumped — and within yards of a mass of police officers and their vans — then it could happen to anyone. June Petrie would not even cross the car park at the college on her own if she was on the late shift.

The police had questioned two men and later released them, and then one of them had been questioned again. That was when the rumour about it being Leslie had started buzzing around. No one knew why. No one knew anything. But the rumour persisted and Leslie was given odd looks. People kept their distance. Only June behaved in the same way as ever towards him simply because the whole thing was completely incredible.

Leslie. He looked thinner in the face. If she could persuade him to join the Savoyards it would do him a great deal of good, introduce him to new people, give him something of a social life. She was sure he had none and his excuses always sounded half-hearted. She would have another word about it; not now, the place was still seething with students — she would find him out when he had his break.

'Where are the maps?'

'Maps? If you mean the geography section, that's in the Sir Geoffrey Cass building which is on the other side of the square, you take the —'

'I'm not doing geography, I'm doing physics. I just want a map of the place.'

'The place?'

Leslie Blade's voice was tightening.

'Lafferton, this place.'

'Young man, if you need a map of Lafferton, I suggest you —'

June slipped in between them. 'You could take your break now, Leslie. Now, you said you wanted a map?'

Leslie stepped back but when June had sent the student away with the address of

WH Smith in the town centre, he touched her arm.

'I am perfectly capable of managing to explain to —'

'I know you are, of course you are, you just seemed a bit weary. I do understand, silly little queries which really we shouldn't have to deal with. I thought you might want a bit of peace away from them.'

'I'll take my break when it's time.'

He spoke so sharply that June moved away to the other end of the desk and decided not to approach him when he went for his break, and certainly not to suggest again that he would enjoy membership of the Savoyards.

The students thinned out after nine o'clock and the library became calmer, though there was still the residue of forgotten jackets and pens, and the mass of books to put away on the trolleys ready to be re-shelved on the following day. They should have finished at ten but were rarely away before half past and though June saw Leslie go through the door that led to the stacks on the precise minute when his break began, she did not take one herself. They were a member of staff short, not because of sickness but because one had left and was not being

493

replaced. Cuts were cuts. The library was always one of the first to suffer.

She did not notice at first that Leslie had not returned at the end of his break. A last-minute queue at the counter and a student who had been sick all over one of the tables meant that the other two in the main reading room were running round trying to sort everything out well after the closing bell.

'June, did Leslie go home early? He hasn't been back since his break.'

'Not that I know of, and in any case, he would have come through here on his way to the staffroom. I didn't see him.'

'Nor did I.'

June Petrie and Melanie looked at one another in silence for a moment.

'I'd better go and check.'

'Do you want me to come with you?'

'No, no, you finish tidying up.'

The stacks were in darkness but the stair lights were on — Leslie must have put them on when he had come down. June hesitated and then called out his name. There was no reply and the silence ahead was so complete that she felt unnerved and went back to ask Melanie to come with her after all. They went carefully, switching on every light. It was still silent. Their footsteps echoed through the stacks.

He always took his break in the window facing the last bays of books and that was where they found him now, his flask and packet of biscuits untouched. He was sitting on his usual high stool and his head was resting on the ledge in front of him.

'Oh,' June said softly. 'Leslie?'

She put out a hand but then drew it back.

'Best not touch,' Melanie said. She leaned over Leslie and listened. Then she looked at June.

'Get someone over here,' she said, 'and call an ambulance.'

FIFTY-FOUR

Stephen Webber seemed to have aged thirty years, Cat thought. He was ashen, his eyes had a dead glaze and his expression was lifeless.

He brought in a tray with two cups of coffee and a plate of biscuits. Ruth was curled in a ball on the chair opposite Cat, her face turned away, her arm up as if to protect herself. Stephen glanced at her and then at Cat. He said nothing, simply half-shook his head and went out. He had told her that it had taken an hour to persuade Ruth to get up and have a shower and dress, longer to agree to see Cat. She had twice tried to walk out of the house rather than accept a visit so that in the end he'd had to lock the doors. His eyes had filled with tears when he had admitted as much. Cat was as concerned about him as she was about Ruth. Medication would restore her to stability, but the effect on Stephen was deeper and might be less easy to treat. He'd had too many years of the strain, and the combination of a recurrence of the nightmare plus his new job was putting him under tremendous pressure.

After a long time he had managed to get Ruth to come into the sitting room where Cat was waiting, but Ruth had refused to look at her, had simply gone to the chair and huddled in it.

Beforehand, Stephen had said that he would do anything, give anything, not to have Ruth go through the anguish and humiliation of being sectioned and sent to hospital against her will.

'I don't know anything about the psychiatric facilities here,' he said, 'but she was incredibly distressed in the London unit, she hated it. I was terrified she would kill herself, even though it's something they're on the lookout for the whole time.'

'If she's judged to be at risk of harming others or of harming herself, then hospital is the safest place for her. You do know that, Stephen.'

'But if it makes her so desperately unhappy . . . if she finds it intolerable?'

'We need to find out why that is, which I will try to do. A psychiatric team would come in and assess her too before the decision was made.'

'Once she gets back on her medication, it will be fine.'

'But not immediately. It takes a while to kick in properly — perhaps a couple of weeks — and I want her to be in a place of safety while that happens.'

'She isn't going to harm anyone.'

'Other than herself.'

He rubbed his eyes and turned away.

Cat had been at odds with him, with both of them, since their arrival. She did not like his brand of churchmanship or Ruth's lack of sensitivity, she hated what they were doing to the cathedral and their plans for the future. But she could set all of that to one side, and then she was deeply sorry about an illness that was always hard to bear, and sad for the anxiety it caused him. She thought that, aside from her opinions about St Michael's, he was actually not the right person for such a job while having to care for such a sick wife. The fact that Ruth had been stable for a couple of years meant nothing. Her condition was incurable and she was always likely to come off her tablets without warning. It was almost a given of her illness.

The sitting room had the bleakness of a room which did not belong to its occupants, the furniture slightly ill-assorted, the book-shelves empty, the walls without pictures. The Deanery renovations were due to be completed within the next couple of weeks but it seemed unlikely that Ruth would be in a fit state to oversee it all or even to move house.

Cat sipped her coffee and waited. The house was silent. Ruth did not move. A bright shaft of golden autumn sunlight lay like a lance across the carpet. Cat was about to say something when Ruth uncurled her body and looked across at her.

'It's pretty pointless,' she said.

'What's pointless?'

'Your being here. I know you mean well.'

'Ruth, I'm here as your doctor. I want to help.'

Ruth shrugged. 'People are kind.'

'I'm not here to be kind, I'm here to help you get better. You understand that, don't you?'

Silence.

'The thing is, when you disappear, as you did for several days, it's very distressing, not only for you but for Stephen too, and it causes a lot of problems.'

Ruth sighed. 'I don't mean to cause problems.'

'I know that.'

'You see? That's why it would be better for everyone if I wasn't here at all.'

'I don't think Stephen would want to be included in that.'

'If he told you the truth he would.'

'Would it be better for you? Is that how you feel about yourself?'

'Of course it is.'

'And you've often felt like it before?'

Silence.

'But it isn't your normal state of mind, is it?'

Ruth let out a short, bitter laugh. 'What's that?'

'Think of your moods as a pendulum. I'm sure you've been told this before. You've swung down — how long have you been down? Days?'

'I've never been anywhere else.'

'Yes, you have. It's hard to remember but you have. Can I pass you this coffee?'

'No thanks.'

'Biscuit?'

'I'm not hungry.'

'When you swing up, are you hungry then?'

'I told you, I never do.'

'Can you remember what triggered your need to leave home?'

'No.'

'Do you know where you went?'

'I found a place. A hut. It was cold at night. But I liked it there, you know — can you understand that? It was quiet, I was — there wasn't anything I had to think about or do. Nobody else. I thought I might stay there.'

'What made you come home?'

'Cold. And then I heard voices.'

'Do you know whose they were? People looking for you?'

'God, I shouldn't have said that, should I?' Ruth got up and began to walk agitatedly around the room, rubbing her hands together, then swinging her arms and shaking her head. Despite being thin, she was strong. Tall, with muscular arms. 'Why can't I keep my mouth shut? Voices telling me to do things. I'm so stupid. I'm rubbish. I deserve to be dead.'

'Ruth, you'd feel calmer if you sat down.'

But she went on pacing the room.

'There were murdered people,' she said as she walked, 'did you know? Women. Those poor girls on the streets, the ones we were going to do something about. They've been murdered, all of them, did anyone tell you? Isn't that a punishment, isn't that justice? We said we were going to help them and we didn't. But they're better off. It's a pity they

501

had to die like that, it's a pity they didn't choose. I can choose. I'm very lucky.'

'Did you see any of them? The girls on the street?'

'They were being hounded.'

'Hounded?'

'The police. They whisper behind their backs. They persecute those girls.'

'Ruth, there are a lot of police out on the streets because of the girls who were murdered. It would be more disgraceful if there weren't. Do you feel happier pacing about?'

'I don't know what "happier" means?'

'Calmer then.'

Ruth stopped dead. 'Yes,' she said. 'I know calmer. Sometimes when I'm at the top, I'd give everything to be calm.'

'You see, what you're telling me shows that you have a good insight into your own feelings and how they change quite dramatically. If you had to choose, where would you like to be, ideally? Calmer? Full of energy?'

Ruth sat down, this time on the very edge of the chair, and leaned forward, looking at Cat intently.

'You mean, dead or alive?'

'Is that how it seems to you? One or the other of those? I was thinking perhaps of high or low — or maybe somewhere in between?'

For a long time Ruth was silent, staring ahead. Cat could not tell whether she had gone into the inert, emotionless state which was part of her deep depression, or whether she was trying to make her brain function enough to consider those choices.

At last she said, 'I know what you're trying to do.'

'What's that, Ruth?'

'Make me say I want to be living in that grey place where nothing has any edges and there isn't any music and the colours have drained out of everything. If I say that's where I want to be, you can make me agree to take your tablets. But I'm not going to say that because I couldn't stand it, grey, grey, grey, no feeling, no happiness, no anything. If it's that or dead, I want to be dead.'

'Ruth, it isn't that or dead. We should be able to balance your medication so that you are simply normal . . . calm and normal, not too high, not too low.'

'But you never can, can you? No one ever can. Don't pretend.'

'Will you let me try?'

'What will you do if I don't?' She laughed. 'Don't bother to tell me, I know. What's this one like? Beige walls and people shouting or green walls and zombies? Have you ever been in one of those places?'

'Yes.'

'What, to stay for weeks at a time? Don't lie.'

'No. Not that. I don't want to have to send you into hospital, Ruth, but if you won't let me prescribe medicine that you will promise to take, for your own safety I'll have to. I know you understand that.'

'You sound like all the others.'

'I'm sorry. I'm giving you a chance, and by doing so, I'm taking a chance. I wonder if I should do that or if you'll let me down.'

Cat stood up and went to look out of the window, partly to weigh up the risks, but mainly to give Ruth a moment to understand and to try and choose. She thought it was worth it. If Ruth rejected this one lifeline, Cat would have to call the crisis team and an ambulance. Ruth would be sectioned and would have to go to Bevham psychiatric unit.

Cat waited. Maybe one of the reasons she had never wanted to specialise in psychiatry was just this — the waiting, coaxing words out of someone reluctant to speak them.

Perhaps Ruth was about to agree, perhaps she was not, but there was no chance to find out because Stephen Webber came in, looking anxiously first at Ruth then at Cat, who cursed his inappropriate entry but could do nothing other than smile.

'I should go out, I have a meeting with the verger and then I have to go to the diocesan offices. I wondered . . . if I ought to . . .'

'Yes, I think you should carry on, Stephen,' Cat said quietly, hoping that he would simply leave. But he stood, looking from one to the other again, his face anguished.

'I'm doing as I'm told,' Ruth said, 'like a good girl. Go to your meeting.'

But he was clearly unable to make up his mind. 'Yes,' he said but still did not move.

For a moment, the three of them did nothing, said nothing, but seemed to be suspended in some sort of dreadful limbo of uncertainty. Then Ruth stood up and went over to her husband, touched his face gently and said, 'Stephen.'

He put his hand on hers.

'I've told you, I'm going to do as Cat says. It's right. Please don't worry.'

It was the first time since Cat had arrived that Ruth had shown she was in control of herself, and Cat was suddenly hopeful.

Stephen left. Cat had brought some of the drug that was needed with her, the rest she would prescribe, Ruth followed her into the kitchen, where Cat poured a glass of water and handed her the tablet. 'Eat something as well — a couple of those biscuits.' She watched as Ruth did everything as obediently as a child.

'Good. It's going to be all right, Ruth. I know how tough this is but you'll get through it. I'm here to help. What are you going to do now? It isn't good for you to be alone for long.'

'I'll go to bed. I feel as if I haven't slept for a year.'

In fact, Cat guessed that in this phase she had probably been oversleeping, but for now, if she slept she was safe.

'I'll call in this evening. Meanwhile, here's my mobile number. If you need anything, if you want me to come back or just to talk, ring it. Now, until Stephen gets back, is there anyone else you can ask to come and be in the house?'

'I don't need anyone. I'm going to sleep.'

'I'll come upstairs with you then, see you safely to bed. You haven't had this medication for a while, it may make you feel groggy.'

Ruth made a face. 'Yes.'

Her movements were still slow, as if her limbs were heavy. Cat waited until she had been into the bathroom and undressed, then watched her slip deep down under the bedclothes as if she were burying herself.

Cat left a note for Stephen and, in the car, phoned the psychiatric unit and alerted them that they should visit later that day, before her own next call. She sat for a few minutes, wondering if she had got it right, worried about what might happen if she hadn't. But she hated sectioning a patient unless it was unavoidable. Ruth had been desperate not to go into hospital and perhaps her capitulating and going back onto her medication would be the beginning of a slow return to stability.

Instead of driving away, she got out of the car and walked across the grass to the side door of the cathedral. The organ tuners were in, making their succession of odd-sounding, apparently unharmonious noises as they worked. Cat slipped into a pew at the side, bent her head and prayed, for Ruth first and then for her brother, for a break-through in the spider's web of investigations.

As she left the cathedral her phone rang with a message that a psychiatric team would call to see Ruth in a couple of hours, and as she had her mobile in her hand, she rang Simon.

'Serrailler.'

'Hi, it's me, only a quick word.'

'Has to be. Everything all right?'

'Fine. I just rang to say chin up and cheer up and whatever and if you want supper I'm in every night this week except the usual Thursday choir.'

'God, if I could take a night off.'

'I know. But the offer's on the table along with the meat and two veg.'

'Thanks. Kids all right?'

'They are. Keep smiling.'

Simon had sounded more downbeat, more weary than he usually did in the middle of a complex case. He enjoyed being in the thick of things, he relished being in charge and motivating everyone, keeping morale high so that they all worked harder and willingly until they got a result. What he hated most would be this frustration, the endless going round in circles and the very real and ever-present dread that something else would happen.

FIFTY-FIVE

As Stephen Webber came out of the Chapter House Miles Hurley came down the corridor and raised his hand.

'Good. I hoped I'd catch you.'

'Miles, I'm on my way to the diocesan —'

'No you're not, Aisling just gave me a message for you — they want to rearrange.'

'Oh.'

Stephen stopped dead and seemed to lose all sense of where he was or what he should be doing. He had been moving from one job to another in a straight line because that was what he had programmed himself to do. Now he was thrown.

'And there are a couple of things I want to talk about . . . now you've got a free half-hour.'

'I should get back to Ruth . . . I'd better do that.'

'I'll come with you. How is she this morning?'

'Cat came to see her . . . she seems . . . she's agreed to go back on her tablets . . . I think it should be all right. I don't know.'

Miles put a hand on his shoulder briefly. 'Cat Deerbon knows what she's doing but I am slightly surprised they didn't have Ruth in hospital for a day or two, just until she's stable again.'

'She hates it — she'd do anything to avoid that.'

'But she's had a bad relapse, Stephen, and frankly, if I may say so, it's very unfair on you.'

'No, no. I can care for Ruth. I wouldn't want to put her in hospital against her will, never.'

'You're a good man, Stephen, but you do need to think of yourself. Still, perhaps some of us can do a little of that for you. That's partly why I wanted to talk to you.'

They went into the house and at once Stephen started to go in and out of rooms looking, before saying, 'I must just check the bedroom,' and took the stairs two at a time.

When he came down again a moment later, Miles was in the kitchen, filling the kettle and setting out a couple of cups.

'She's asleep, thank God.'

'Good. Now, Stephen, let me get to the point. I think you need to hand over the reins for a while. Frankly, you look worn out and you have your hands full. I want to take some of the burden off your shoulders. There's this whole question of the launch of the fund-raising for a visitors' centre — it's terribly important and you simply cannot take that on just now . . .'

They went into the sitting room where Stephen listened to Miles Hurley confidently outlining what he proposed to do, and felt a sudden rush of gratitude and relief as well as a realisation of his own inadequacy. Miles was so much more competent, so organised, so able. He should be the one in charge. Perhaps this was a God-given opportunity for him. The thought of struggling with the vast amount of new initiatives, while worrying about Ruth in her present highly vulnerable state, had been pressing on him. Now he saw a door by which he might escape, and honourably, at least for a time.

'You need to be able to concentrate on looking after Ruth. Perhaps you could go away for a few weeks, once she's feeling better. It would do you a power of good.'

Stephen sighed. 'I'm not sure. Ruth might not want . . . I think we may be better staying quietly here. And we have the move into the Deanery coming up.'

'Well, I'd think about it. It's not fair on everyone else. If you're weary and only half focused on the job it's almost worse than if you're absent altogether.'

'And is that how I've seemed to you, Miles?'

'In recent days, frankly, yes. I know you'd prefer me to speak the truth.'

Easy for you, Webber thought, easy for a man who has only his work, is without ties and responsibilities. Easy for you. But Miles had always supported him, even if he had also sometimes tried to lead from behind.

'This job should have been yours,' he said now.

'Oh no. I like things as they are.'

It occurred to Stephen that he was either pushed by Miles or by Ruth, that he was not and never had been his own man. He felt impotent and frustrated, as so often.

Ruth was lying on her back, awake, but did not turn her head or acknowledge Stephen as he went in.

'Can I get you anything? Tea? Are you hungry?'

'It would have been better if I hadn't come back.'

'Better for you or for me?'

'You should have let me kill myself years

ago. Whatever has happened since has been your fault.'

Stephen sighed. He sat down on the chair beside the bed and tried to take her hand but she pulled it away.

'This isn't you talking, Ruth, this is your illness. You aren't yourself.'

'Oh. Who am I then? Not this person lying here. Not Mrs Dean? Not Ruth Webber?'

'You're ill and you're depressed . . . you don't really want to die, you never have, and when you're well again you'll understand that.'

'You should have let me kill myself.'

'Suicide is a sin. I believe that. Though I'm sure if it's committed when the mind —'

'— when the balance of the mind is disturbed. Ha.'

'Yes. Then of course that's different. But you'll come up from this dreadful pit, you'll be able to see life clearly again. It just takes time for the medicine to work — only a little time.'

They were both silent. Then he said, 'Miles suggested he could take over if we went away — had a holiday somewhere. He feels things would carry on fine and God knows I think he's right. I'm beginning to believe he should have had my job in any case. Would you like to go away? We had a wonderful time in Switzerland, if you —'

'I haven't lost my memory.'

'We could go by train, spend a week in Wengen, move on down, go to . . . go anywhere you'd like. Or perhaps further afield? You wanted to go to New Zealand.'

'Did I? I wonder why.'

'Shall I say yes to Miles?'

Silence.

'It's difficult for me, Ruth. I want to help you and you won't let me.'

Silence.

'I don't know which way to turn.'

Silence.

After a few moments, he went quietly out.

FIFTY-SIX

Abi was propped up, her eyes closed. A couple of the machines had gone, and one of the tubes. As Hayley went round to the chair on the far side of the bed, Abi opened her eyes, looked concerned for a moment, but then smiled. She was less pale, and her eyes didn't seem to be so sunken into her head.

'Hey, Abs, you look so much better!' Hayley leaned over and gave her a gentle hug. Abi lifted her hand and touched her arm.

'I'll be back in a minute,' the nurse said. 'She can't talk but she's much brighter, you're right there. She gets tired though so take it easy.'

'I've got something to show you,' Hayley said, 'and you're gonna be so pleased, you'd better believe it.' She opened her bag and took out the envelope in which she'd put the photos Lou had given her.

'Here.'

She put it on the bed by Abi's hand.

Abi looked at it for a moment, then slowly lifted the flap and tried to reach inside, but in the end Hayley had to take out the contents for her.

'What have you been saying to her?' The nurse came through the door to see tears rolling down Abi's cheeks.

'It's her kids. Photos . . . She didn't know if they were happy or anything and now she's got their pictures. You'd cry.'

'I think I would. Let me have a look.'

'Abs, I've seen them, I took Liam. They're great, they're really great.'

The tears went on spilling down as Hayley told her everything she could remember about her visit, the smallest thing about Frankie and Mia — what they'd had on, what they'd said, how they'd seemed, the house, the people . . . she talked until her mouth was dry and Abi watched her face, as if by staring into it hard enough and then back at the photographs she could somehow conjure up the children into the room.

Hayley was still talking when the door opened. She knew it was a copper. They thought because they weren't in uniform nobody could tell.

'I might have to go but you keep those,

they're for you. I'm going to see them again, Abs, and I'll get some more. And listen, once you're out of here there might be a flat, the social woman said you'd get a priority now. God, don't you bloody deserve it?'

Ben Vanek and Steph Mead saw at once that Abi had taken a step forward, though they had been warned that she was still very ill and that there could be permanent damage to her throat. The nasogastric tube feeding her had not been taken out.

'She's had some photos of her children brought in . . . that's done her a power of good, can't you tell?' said the nurse.

Abi moved her hand towards the pictures that were still on the bed and Steph went to look.

'These are great, Abi. They look really well.'

Abi nodded and smiled, but her eyes were brimming with tears.

'Don't tire her — she's had one lot of excitement and I don't want her blood pressure up.'

The detectives sat next to one another on the chairs beside the bed.

'Abi, do you remember the last time we were here?'

Abi hesitated, her eyes clouded.

'The first time we came you were pretty much out of it but if you can remember back to a couple of days ago . . . Do you know what we want to ask you about?'

After a second Abi nodded slowly.

'I know you can't talk but you can nod and shake your head. I want to find out if you remember anything at all about the night you were attacked. Is it any clearer in your mind?'

Abi hesitated and her face was shadowed with anxiety.

'Don't get upset . . . just do your best. Now, try and picture what you can remember. You're out. It's dark. Are there any of the other girls out on the street?'

Abi had closed her eyes. Now, she frowned. Opened her eyes, but her expression was blank.

'Is anything coming back to you?'

Gently, Vanek pressed on, asking if she remembered whether it was fine or wet, if she was wearing her leather skirt, her anorak, had she stood on the corner by the entrance to the printworks, had the Reachout van been round? There was no response until then but at the words 'Reachout van' there was a flicker of something . . .

'You remember the Reachout van?'

A long pause.

'You know what I'm talking about?'

A slight nod.

'Good. The last time you were working, that night, the one when you were attacked, had you seen the Reachout van?'

Another long pause, then a slow shake of the head. Vanek was pleased. They knew that the van had not been out that night.

'Well done. OK, if the van wasn't out what about Leslie? What do you call him — Loopy Les?'

Nod.

'Was he around? Did he bring you girls sandwiches and a drink that night? Can you picture him? Under the street lamp, where he usually is, near the works? Was he there?'

After a moment, Abi shook her head. She had closed her eyes and her face had gone pale. Vanek needed to get as much out of her as he could now before she was too exhausted.

'Not many punters that night?'

Abi shrugged.

'Any? Do you remember anyone stopping? Any cars at all?'

They pressed her about car makes and colours, tried to describe men — tall, short, fair, dark, fat, thin, old, young, regular, new. But Abi could not answer.

The nurse put her head round the door, glanced at Abi, then said, 'Five minutes.'

'Do you remember where you were? Was it on the street?'

A pause. Then a headshake, quite firm, and a sudden expression of fear.

'Was it down by the canal then?'

Abi looked agitated.

'Yes?'

Nod.

'Good girl. You were on the towpath?'

Nod.

'Were you by the bridge?'

Abi looked around her, eyes flicking about, clearly still afraid.

Steph Mead said, 'It's OK, Abi, it's all over and you're safe. But the more you can remember the more it will help us to catch whoever did this. Now, did you see anyone? I know it was dark but did you see a man?'

Pause. A nod.

'Was it someone you know? Did you recognise him?'

A slight nod.

'Someone you'd met there before?'

Nothing.

'A regular punter?'

Nod.

'Had you met him on the towpath before?'

Nod.

'I'll give you some descriptions — if you're too tired to nod, just raise a finger for yes, and keep still for no. Is he young?'

Nothing.

'Older?'

Nothing.

'Is he tall?'

Nothing.

'What about his voice? Do you remember his voice?'

Abi raised a finger at once.

'Is it an English voice?'

Yes.

'A loud voice?'

Nothing. Then Abi started to make movements with her hand which they could not understand. She closed her eyes again.

'We can't go on much more,' Ben muttered.

'What is it, Abi?' said Steph, quietly.

Abi moved her hand about again, then her finger on the sheet, before picking up one of the photographs and tracing her finger over it.

'Oh, she wants to write something down,' Steph said. She turned to a new sheet in her notepad and handed it to Abi, with her pen. Abi smiled, hesitated, then wrote a word slowly. Her writing was weak and slow but when she turned the pad they clearly read *'Whispery'*.

'He talked in a whisper?'

She nodded several times.

'Thanks, this is really helpful, Abi, try and keep going a bit longer. Now, did you see his eyes?'

Nothing.

'Did he have any facial hair? A beard or a moustache?'

The finger did not move.

'What about his hair? Does he have dark hair?'

Suddenly, Abi's eyes lit up and her face was bright with a flash of recognition.

'Fair hair?'

Shake.

'Curly hair?'

Now she was agitated. She pulled the pad towards her and hesitated. Closed her eyes for a moment. Then she drew something and turned the pad round for them to see it.

Vanek looked. Frowned. Passed it to Steph.

'Is this his head? The shape of his head? Oh, I get it, he's bald?'

Abi took the pad back.

She drew the outline of a head, with a primitive face, such as a child would draw. Ears, nose, mouth. But then she drew a shape on top of the head, and the shape came down low.

'Is that a hood? He was wearing a hood of some sort — a hooded jacket?'

Violent shake of the head. Abi drew something again.

'I can't work it out, Abi. It's a shape but . . .'

Abi wrote under the shape slowly. 'BEANIE'. And then, the writing tailing off as her hand weakened, 'BEANIE MAN'.

Vanek got up and put his hand over Abi's. 'That is absolutely great, Abi, you're a star. Now you have a good rest. You've done so well.'

He nodded to Stephanie Mead. 'Let's move.'

FIFTY-SEVEN

The room was crowded and everyone was attentive. For days and days they had been sifting through details. Appeals to the general public had brought in hundreds of phone calls.

'And don't dismiss anything that seems a bit off the wall as a crank call,' Serrailler had said. 'If in doubt, follow it up. Sometimes, the cranks have the one vital piece of information even if they don't realise the fact.'

House-to-house calls had been made again and again, leaflets distributed, the press encouraged to keep the cases on the front page even though there was no news.

But it was difficult to keep up morale when every lead came to a dead end, the force was stretched to breaking point and everyone was exhausted and out of temper. Serrailler had taken to going for a run early every morning just to work off some of his own tension.

'Right, listen up. And look.'

On the screen was a blow-up of the drawing Abi Righton had done, with her writing. BEANIE. BEANIE MAN. Later that day, Vanek was going back to the hospital, this time with the identikit specialist in the hope that they could get a clearer picture of Beanie Man.

'The drawing isn't meant to represent him, we don't think — that was just Abi Righton's way of showing us her attacker's type of headgear. This isn't going to be easy because a lot of young men wear beanies. But this drawing is going out on the media and we are asking anyone who knows a man who wears a beanie, to contact us. When we get a photofit with the beanie that will be up on posters straight away. It may not seem much but we've nothing else and it's a bit better than being told he wore trainers. Of course the minute this is public every single guy who's ever worn a beanie is going to stop wearing it — but it's what people remember *before* today. Someone who often did wear a beanie, even if he's now chucked it in the bin. Next, three of us are going into a session with the profiler in half an hour's time. If we get anything out of that, I'll ask you to come back in here later.

Meanwhile, please don't forget there could be another lead — something quite different — so don't exclude everything but the beanie hat. Last point, Leslie Blade, the librarian from the CFE, had a heart attack not long after he'd been interviewed for the second time . . . he's in Bevham General and it was a close shave but he should be all right. We can't talk to him again for the moment, even if we have reason to, but we haven't wiped him off the board just yet. OK, that's it, everyone, keep smiling, keep at it — and I have a good feeling today. Either by a lucky break or by painstaking police work, or most likely a bit of both, we're going to get him.'

Five minutes after the information about Beanie Man had gone out on the television news, one of the team took a call from someone who would not give her name.

'Can you give us a contact number then?'

A pause, then, 'No. If you're going to want all that I'm not saying anything.'

The girl sounded hesitant and suspicious.

'OK, that's fine. You say you have some information for us?'

The calls were all traced anyway. Better to get people to talk.

'Yeah. I just saw it on the news, you know,

about the murders and what Abi said.'

'Yes. Do you know Abi Righton?'

'No. Yeah. Well, sort of.'

'Right.'

'Only, you know the Reachout van? It comes — it goes round at night from some church or something.'

'Yes, we know about it.'

'There's a guy on that . . . Damian. He's generally on it. Most nights.'

'Yes?'

'Well . . . he wears a beanie. In winter anyway . . . not every time but quite often he wears one. A beanie hat like in that drawing.'

Ben put his head round Serrailler's door, unable to contain the excitement in his voice as he passed on the information.

Serrailler looked at him quietly for a moment.

'You serious?'

'Guv?'

'The young man from the Baptist church who runs the Reachout van sometimes wears a beanie hat?'

'Apparently — you were right, this is our bit of luck.'

'What is, the beanie? The van? The guy wearing the beanie in the van?'

Ben Vanek fiddled with the door handle, floundering for a reply. There were times when he couldn't read the Super at all.

'Don't faff around in the doorway.'

'Sorry, guv.'

'Right. Have you thought this through? Has anyone?'

There was a silence.

'Damian Reeve is in charge of the Reachout van. Right? He drives it, he's the team leader, he's generally serving at the counter, and he always has time to talk to the girls or whoever comes up to him.'

'Right.'

'And where does it park?'

'In the red-light area? Either at the entrance to the printworks or in Back Street just above the canal.'

'How many people are generally working in the Reachout van on any one night?'

'Two, guv. Occasionally I think there may be three, but generally it's two.'

'So Damian Reeve would easily have been able to stop making hot drinks and cutting sandwiches and microwaving sausage rolls, leave the van with his companion doing all the work, and this on several occasions, then walk down to the canal, along the towpath to . . .'

'I see what you're getting at.'

'I should bloody well hope you do see what I am getting at.'

'Guv. Sorry.'

Serrailler sighed. 'As you're here — is there an update on Leslie Blade's condition?'

'I'll check.'

'And while you're about it, send up a prayer that he's on the mend because heart attacks are frequently brought on by extreme stress and there'll be questions asked about whether our interviews put him under such a stress.'

The DS slid out, closing the door quickly behind him, and went to spread word round the CID room about Serrailler's foul mood.

Serrailler knew it. Damian Reeve might have been able to create an opportunity. Just might. But unlikely. All the prostitutes knew Damian, and some of them had seen Beanie Man hanging around. But none had linked Beanie Man with Damian. And none had been able to identify Beanie Man, or even to describe him. The police were clutching at straws . . . Simon would go along and apologise to Vanek and give the teams a boost. They needed it. They would be trawling through a hundred thousand emails and phone messages about men who sometimes wore beanie hats, dispiriting enough without being bawled out by the boss.

FIFTY-EIGHT

June Petrie had no idea what Leslie Blade's home would be like. None. She tried to picture it as she drove carefully across the lights and turned right. She knew the sort of houses they were from the outside, roads of semis with the odd small detached between. But what would it be like inside? Very neat and clean? A bit of a tip? Old-fashioned? She decided the latter. Leslie lived with his mother, it was doubtless her house, her furniture. There was a carer, she knew that much, but whether the woman, Hilary, did any sort of housework or whether that was left to Leslie she had no idea.

She crawled along looking for the numbers, which were oddly arranged so that she had to double back once before she found the one. It looked right. Neat curtains. Nothing much in the way of a garden but what there was seemed orderly. Paintwork was neither old and peeling nor new. Looking at the house you would not be able to guess who lived in it except that it was not likely to be people with children.

She had brought a card signed by everyone, a chrysanthemum in a pot and a CD. She hadn't telephoned. If it was not convenient, she would simply leave them. But Leslie had left hospital, she knew because she had phoned Bevham General to check, and that had to be a good sign. They didn't let you out if they feared you were about to have another heart attack.

It was Hilary who opened the front door. Leslie, she said, was with his mother.

'He'd like a visitor but maybe not for too long this time, if you wouldn't mind? Only he's just out of hospital and he's quite tired.'

The house was neat and tidy and the furniture was old-fashioned. It seemed exactly right for Leslie, now she was there, seemed so right she wondered how she couldn't have pictured it exactly.

He looked different, she could see at once. Older. Strained. A sunken look about his eyes. His mother was sitting opposite to him, a heavy woman, her hands gnarled and swollen with arthritis.

'No, no, don't even think of getting up, Leslie. I just popped in to bring these from us all . . .' She put the card and the plant on a small table. 'And this is just from me. I do hope you can play it — let me know if not, I can lend you a CD player — I know it'll cheer you up no end.'

The CD was of *The Mikado.*

'I think,' Norah Blade said, leaning forward slightly, 'that we have to thank you, Mrs Petrie. If it hadn't been for you finding Leslie and getting help, well . . .'

'Yes,' Leslie said — and June noticed that his voice sounded different, hesitant and frailer — 'indeed. We do have to thank you.'

'Well, thank God I noticed you were a few minutes late back from your break, a thing you never are . . . Anyway, let's not dwell on any of that, you're here and you're obviously going to make a good recovery and I know everyone at the library will be very glad to hear it. We can't do without you, you know.'

Leslie gave her a strange look, and then glanced away towards his mother.

'It may be,' Norah Blade said, 'that you'll have to. It may be that Leslie will want to take early retirement, after . . . after all this.'

'Oh, but surely —'

'Nothing's decided,' Leslie said quickly, 'nothing's decided.'

■ ■ ■ ■

When June Petrie had gone, hastening back to the library to report everything about Leslie, Leslie's state of health, Leslie's house, mother and general situation, Leslie sat with his eyes closed. He was tired. The smallest thing exhausted him and apparently this was quite normal and would continue for some time. But he was not asleep. He was thinking that this was what it would be like if he did indeed take early retirement, sitting in the chair opposite his mother for hour after hour, playing a game of cards with her, watching television, going to change his own library books along with hers, having Hilary as his carer too.

He opened his eyes and saw the plant. And the CD. June Petrie's determination to force him into the Lafferton Savoyards would follow him to the grave. June Petrie. He had always wanted to kill her. He had thought of pushing her down the steps into the book stacks and shoving her head through the plate-glass window of the staffroom. Yet she had saved his life. If she had known of his thoughts would she have done that? But she did not know, could not know, and his thoughts had no power.

He had no power.

'Leslie . . .'

He turned to his mother who was leaning forwards and looking at him.

'I wanted to tell you . . .'

The door opened and Hilary brought in a tray of tea, and a china pot in which to put the chrysanthemum plant, and asked if they would like the small window closed, and then there was a conversation about Norah's chiropody appointment. Leslie closed his eyes again. When he felt stronger, he would go upstairs to his room and lie on the bed, but climbing them was exhausting and he didn't feel up to it yet.

Hilary and his mother chattered on, the diary was fetched, some confusion discussed with much giggling, and then the tea was poured and the sugar spilled and more laughter and joking and Leslie opened his eyes and thought that he would like to kill them both, to hurl them over a precipice and dash their bodies on rocks below, to push the wheelchair into the fast lane of the bypass, to pour sulphuric acid into the pot of tea, to . . .

'Leslie?'

Hilary was holding the cup out to him, smiling.

She had a sweet smile.

'What we would ever do without dear Hilary, I just don't know,' Norah Blade said wonderingly several times a week. 'Wasn't it lucky that it was her and no one else?'

He would have to sit every day listening to it, the same little saws, the same innocent silly jokes between his mother and Hilary. The alternative was to be fit enough to return to work and perhaps he would be. Perhaps. What else was there?

He went on thinking of ways to kill them both until Hilary left, having said goodbye twice, and then it was only Norah.

'Leslie . . .'

He kept his eyes closed but she knew he was not asleep. She knew everything about him.

'There's something I want to say to you. I've wanted to say it for some time but I didn't know how . . . or if I should. And of course for a time, I wasn't quite sure. But since all of this dreadful business with . . . the young women, and the police . . . They questioned me, you know, the police. I've spent a lot of time going over things and now I'm sure. When I'd gone to bed, when you left me and said you were going upstairs, or working on your computer . . . and the house was quiet . . . you used to go out again. You crept out, so that I wouldn't hear you, and then the car would start up and I always knew you were going . . . somewhere. I never mentioned it. You're a grown man, Leslie, you're entitled to a life of your own. But it worried me. I have to tell you that. It worried me. It was so late and you came back so late . . . and you kept it from me.'

He said nothing. He was thinking about the girls, about their pale faces, bad skin, the dark shadows beneath their eyes, their legs sometimes blue with cold, the way they held their cigarettes, the way they came for his sandwiches and the flask of tea, the way they had become his friends.

'But it would never have mattered, not really mattered, until all this dreadful business and . . . and the police.'

The silence in the room was like a deep well into which they both stared and the well got deeper the longer they looked. He was not going to interrupt that silence. She was looking at him and he was looking away across the room at nothing at all.

'Leslie, did the police . . . come to ask you questions? About the . . . these dreadful things? Is that where you went? To the police station?'

She looked at him and waited but he could not reply. He could never answer

537

those questions, never tell her the truth.

'Leslie, I understand men, you know. I have been a married woman. I do understand.'

He glanced to the side table and saw the plant in its new pot and the card propped beside it and the CD of *The Mikado* to which he would never listen. But he did not look at his mother and he did not speak.

'Did you — go with those girls?'

He had so little strength, that was the trouble. If he had only part of his old strength he could have killed her. He could have simply hit her over the head with the heavy plant pot, or picked up her own stick beside the chair. He could have strangled her.

But he was too tired to do more than stare at the plant and the hideous card and the CD of *The Mikado* and say nothing. And in the end, Norah leaned back in her own chair, and after a while, closed her eyes, and the two of them slept, opposite one another in the quiet room.

FIFTY-NINE

Hayley bought a couple of cans of cider on the way home, and a frozen toad-in-the-hole, and some ice cream. She hadn't treated herself for a while and she'd earned a good whack the previous two nights, when one of the girls who hadn't been around for a while offered to have Liam. Hayley hadn't been sure, so Carmen said she'd come and stay with him at Hayley's, not take him to hers, so long as she could bring her little girl. It had been a bit strange because she was used to doing this with Abi, but it had seemed to work out, Liam hadn't objected, and she'd been able to go out for longer than usual. They'd all moved away from the canal area, down to Hunt Square and the surrounding streets, which weren't crawling with police and which felt safer.

Tonight, though, Liam had gone to be with Frankie and Mia, to stay over. It had all been worked out, the social services woman had agreed, though it made Hayley mad the hoops they had to jump through just to get the kids together and make it all above board. Still, it was done and Liam and Abi's kids were over the moon.

She wasn't going out tonight. She was going to enjoy her feast and a horror film which she'd rented and sleep in late tomorrow. Then she'd go and see Abi again. They'd put her funny little drawing of Beanie Man in the paper, on television, on posters, and Hayley had looked at it quite often, without being able to see how anyone could ever spot whoever he was from it. She'd always seen him in the dark, the beanie pulled right down almost over his eyes, and there was precious little else to go on. Beanie Man. He could be anybody.

Hayley turned into the gate and up the steps, humming.

'Wondered when you were going to show.'

She jumped so hard she dropped the cans. He was sitting on the steps, with a roll-up hanging out of the corner of his mouth and his usual cocky expression.

'Jonty fuckin' Lewis, you scared the bloody daylights out of me,' she said, grabbing her cider. 'What the hell are you doing here? I don't want you on my fuckin' step, thanks.'

He shrugged. He looked as if he'd slept under a hedge, and when she got closer, she smelled his filthy smell.

'Thought you'd done a bunk. Well, as you haven't, do it now. Bunk off.'

'I'll have one of them cans.'

'You will not.'

But he reached out and wrenched the pack from her hand, pulled the ring off a can and downed it in one.

'Look, I just bought those, they're mine for tonight, what do you think you're fuckin' playing at?'

'What's happening tonight then?'

'Nothing. I'm having a night in. So you can bunk off, like I said.'

'You got any money?'

'If I had, you think I'd give it you?'

She stood facing up to him but he wasn't about to let her past him and she knew she didn't stand any sort of chance if it came to a scrap.

'What do you want, Lewis?'

'That's friendly.'

'I'm not your friend. I was Marie's friend. Did you do her in?'

'Don't you start, I had enough of that. No, I fuckin' did not.'

'OK, well, I still don't want you round me. Can I get into my house, please?'

'Oooh, my house, my house. My one-roomed slum.'

'Look, I don't know what you want, only —'

'Cash.'

'You're out of luck then.'

'You got cash?'

'Nope. Even if I had, would I give it to a lowlife like you? I don't bloody think so.'

'Got a spliff then?'

'I don't do drugs.'

'You fuckin' little liar.'

'Not any more. I'm clean, I've got my kid, I'm getting a nice house with a friend and I can do without you on my step.'

'Got a fag then?'

'Don't smoke.'

Suddenly, before Hayley realised what was happening, Jonty launched himself off the step and onto her, knocking the cider and her carrier bag onto the ground and shoving his hand into her pockets, first one, then the other, holding her round the neck from behind. But she didn't smoke, hadn't for years, and when he didn't find anything he shoved her hard so that she fell face down onto the step, the edge against her forehead, and, just before she blacked out, she screamed.

Jonty grabbed the other cider can and ran.

SIXTY

Ruth had felt a lot of different things over the years. The pills blunted the edges of what she felt but the feelings were always there. She sometimes thought of them as a poisonous jellyfish floating about helplessly under the great swell of the sea, the ability to sting, hurt and even kill still wound up but powerless because of the press of grey-green water on top of them. So she could be raving or suicidal, resentful, passionately jealous, or high as a kite with an ecstatic happiness, but these feelings were coiled up uselessly inside her and she was under the grey-green water which was her medication, drifting to and fro, but never able to surface, never able to release the pent-up emotions.

When it all reached an unbearable point, when she was boiling under the surface, then the only way she knew to get release was to stop the pills so that the water receded in a slow tide and she could float upwards until she was above it.

But over all the years she had never known this particular feeling. It was anger. Rage. Fury. It was nothing to do with being down in the black pit nor to do with shooting up towards the sun. It was quite different. She had been angry as normal people were angry, of course she had, but that was anger over something that had happened, or not happened, often something trivial. This was very strange. It was an anger unrelated to anything or anyone, and it was both ice cold and like the raging core of some great conflagration. She felt as if she had the strength of ten, and as if her skin were prickling, as if she had ants crawling beneath it.

Perhaps they had changed the composition of her pills in some way and this was the cause, though usually re-starting them only made her feel nauseated and slightly disconnected.

She had no way of dealing with this pent-up rage. Stephen was constantly hovering over her, trying to ensure that she was improving, trying to persuade her that they should take a month or two away. Irritability was her symptom then, and a restlessness. She could not sleep or be still or read, watch television or sit through a service in the cathedral, she prowled about the house and waited, waited for the sting to be drawn from this thing.

Stephen came in late. She had gone to bed but was still awake.

'I'm sorry, I didn't mean to disturb you,' he said. How kind Stephen was, how often he shouldered the blame, assumed something was his fault when it patently was not, and how little he deserved to be saddled with a wife like this, she thought, sometimes a shrew, sometimes a depressive, sometimes a maniac, never equable and pleasant and supportive.

Why had he married her? She had been pathetically grateful for it, always felt entirely undeserving, never repaid him generously. But he should have a better wife.

'I'm just going to sleep,' she said.

But the restlessness would not be stilled in her. Stephen fell asleep; and after another half-hour, she slid out of bed, dressed in the dark and went downstairs and out of the side door.

It was cool but not cold. The autumn had been mostly mild. There was a full moon and the Close was full of silvered spaces with deep shadows between. Now that she was out Ruth felt better, she could breathe more freely, and walking along the paths between the dark houses calmed the feelings. She had on jeans and a pair of soft-soled shoes that made no sound so that she felt like a ghost or a shadow herself and the idea was pleasing. No one could see her, no one knew her, no one could identify her. She was entirely alone. She had felt happy with the same idea when she had been in the shed. Although she had been sliding down and down, there had been something comforting about curling up there on her own, without being watched, without Stephen fretting about her. Alone had been good. She did not like herself, she was a person she would never wish to know, she hated having to live with the person she was, and yet for those days and nights she had begun to come to terms with this woman, Ruth Webber, and to accept her own dislike, and the knowledge that others disliked her.

But there was this anger now. Inside her head. Deep down in her head like the core of a smouldering bonfire.

But walking in the cool night air was helping. She reached the end of the Close. She knew Simon Serrailler's car. It was parked there but all the lights in his flat at the top of the building were out. She looked up. It was a good building, handsomely proportioned, sitting well in its place, looking down the grass avenues towards the great bulk of the cathedral.

She turned back towards Stephen, towards the house, but then walked past it, to where the real Deanery stood, empty, windows like hollow eyes, but waiting for them. It would be better when they were there. A new start. It might be better.

Only there had been something . . . one thing. It came back to her now, but like a feather tossed by on the wind, and out of reach. Some sound or sense. Something.

She shook her head. She would stay out here. She was feeling better.

She crossed the grass and it was when she was only a few yards away from the door that she heard it. Stopped. And then saw, and as she saw, she drew in her breath sharply and everything came together in a terrible, blinding flash of realisation and disbelief. But she had no time to piece it all together because there were sudden footsteps and something lashing out at her. She fell and in falling opened her eyes wide and knew. Knew. But knew nothing more.

SIXTY-ONE

'No, Grandpa, you have to, you have to blow when we sing.'

'Actually, he blows after we sing,' Sam said.

'Same thing.'

'Of course it isn't the same thing — how can "at the same time" be the same as "after"?'

'All right, you two. This is Grandpa's birthday and you don't squabble.'

'I would be perfectly happy for you never to sing,' Richard Serrailler said.

'Don't be silly, how can you have a birthday without people singing? You can't. You have to. You're forced to.'

'Right, stand back a second.' Judith lit the candles on the chocolate cake with coffee icing, which was Richard's regular choice.

The candles flickered briefly, then the flames steadied.

'Go on, Grandpa, close your eyes and

make your wish.'

'Wish,' Felix said, 'Wish fish.'

Richard groaned slightly, closed his eyes briefly and blew. The candles went out as one.

'Happy birthday to yoooooooooo . . .' Felix sang.

'Happy birthday, dear . . .'

'As the last note died, Hannah shouted at the sound of a car. Felix raced to the door.

'Sorry, sorry — Oh no! Have I missed the singing?'

Richard Serrailler shot his son a look.

'Many happy returns, Dad. Sorry, I couldn't get away. You know.'

'Oh, I do know indeed. It was ever thus.'

Simon put a bottle of malt whisky on the table and hugged Hannah who was dancing beside him, then bent to Felix who had grabbed him round the knees. Sam stood back, silent, watchful.

'Hi, Sam. Did you win?'

'Yes.'

'Did you score?'

'Twice.'

'Top man.'

Sam had been playing for the St Michael's under twelves hockey team. But now he wandered out of the room without saying anything more. Simon glanced at Cat but she was cutting up the birthday cake and helping Judith to hand it round. He had promised to take Sam out for a day, promised to talk to him, promised . . .

'And are you any nearer to resolving these investigations?' Richard asked, his tone as cynical as ever when talking about the police. Simon stuffed a forkful of cake into his mouth in order not to have to reply. 'I imagine this drawing of a man in a strange hat hasn't got you very far.'

'What man in what strange hat? What kind of a strange hat?' Hannah pulled at Simon's arm.

' 'At,' Felix said, out of a chocolate-smeared mouth, ' 'at.'

'Richard, have you opened all your parcels?' said Judith, giving Simon a conciliatory glance.

'I have, apart from Simon's munificent bottle which I will open later. Unless you'll join me now, Simon, or are you wanted by the police?'

'He can't be wanted by the police, he is the police.' Sam had come back into the room with a Sherlock Holmes book. 'Would I like this?'

'Certainly you would,' Richard said. 'It's about a highly successful detective.'

'All right, Dad, I get the message.'

'Darling, you haven't even had a cup of tea. I'll make some fresh. Richard, could you possibly get a piece of kitchen roll, damp it and wipe Felix's face and fingers?'

'No, I —'

'No, Cat, you sit down and enjoy your cake, Richard is quite capable.'

Simon marvelled at how his stepmother managed to calm every wave that threatened to engulf a family gathering, to smooth and distract and restore order, and he wondered again how he could have got it so wrong and not recognised her qualities from the beginning. Because, he thought now, it wouldn't have mattered if she had been a canonised saint, I wasn't ready for anyone at all to replace my mother. Not that Judith has ever behaved like that. He watched her now, handling his father, Cat, the children, smiling, calm. It has taken a long time, he decided, but now I love her.

Cat was sitting on the edge of the Windsor chair in the corner, watching everything. She was very tense. Simon caught her eye. He did not want to talk shop in the middle of the party, but he needed a word about Ruth Webber.

A couple of minutes later, Cat slipped away into the side garden, and Simon followed her.

'Stephen rang me,' she said. 'I know Ruth's bunked off again. I should have insisted on her going into hospital. I'm kicking myself. But I thought, and the psychiatric unit did agree, that it was worth giving her the chance . . .'

'You made a judgement call — you'd have done the same thing again.'

'Probably. No word?'

'We went straight back to the allotments but she hasn't been there. We've got all the searches going on, but given what happened before I don't feel we need to start dragging the canal. Not yet anyway. Was she suicidal?'

'It's possible, yes. She sent me a text message saying she should have killed herself.'

'We've got a full alert on the canal and right along to the river. If that's where she's gone, we'll find her.'

'My guess is, she won't be far away, alive or dead.'

'No.' He sighed. 'Any other time . . .'

'Poor you. Your teams must be a bit demoralised.'

'You can say that again. But determined. Still absolutely determined.'

'What about Beanie Man?'

He shrugged. 'We got an identikit from Abi Righton this morning but to be honest it gives us very little. I don't think we'll put it out. There's no facial detail. She just remembers what she calls a whispery voice and the hat, otherwise it's more a question of what he isn't — not fat, not thin, not bearded, not very tall, not very short, nothing — just the hat.'

'Needle in haystack then.'

'Pretty much. But at least we know this time that Ruth has probably strayed of her own accord. There haven't been any more killings, though there was a nasty bit of violence on one of the prostitutes. We know who did that, we've got yet another search on for him. But if he murdered the others we haven't been able to pin it on him.'

'And did he?'

Simon sighed. 'Honestly? No. I doubt it. Nasty piece of work, but this man is different. He's clever. He's devious. He's cunning. He's stealthy. Jonty Lewis isn't any of those things, he's just a druggie with a habit of violence.'

'Is the girl all right?'

'Cut her forehead, knocked herself out. But she's OK. Listen, if Ruth Webber turns up, what are you going to do?'

'Try to persuade her to go into the unit, until the medication kicks in properly and she's a bit more stable. It might be necessary to section her this time. I also need to talk to Stephen for longer. I don't think he knows which way to turn.'

'I know the feeling.'

They started to go in. 'Sam's quiet,' Simon said.

'I really hope you can get this day away with him. Maybe it'll all be sewn up by half-term.'

'Which is?'

'Next week.'

'No chance.'

'Heigh-ho. By the way, I'm glad about you and Judith.'

'What about us?'

'You know perfectly well. I'd say not before time, if I was feeling like it.'

'No, you'd say you told me so.'

In the kitchen, Felix was sitting at the table removing the candles from the cake and laying them out in a neat row and Judith was putting the tea things into the dishwasher.

'Supper?' she said. 'There's plenty for everyone — I just need to know how much veg to do.'

'Judith, I won't, I have a lot of reading for my course and a report to start on the day-care unit whose principal function nobody seems clear about.'

'Simon?'

He hesitated, half waiting for Cat or Judith to tell him how much his father would appreciate it. Neither of them did.

'I'd like to,' he said. 'Just pray I don't get a call.'

'We seem to have been praying that rather a lot recently.'

'I'll round up the gang.'

But when it was suggested that they get ready to go home, Hannah set up wails of protest and Felix watched for a careful moment, then joined in, though unsure what they were wailing about.

'I want to stay, please can I, pleeease . . . ? Granny Jude, please . . . and Felix wants to.'

Felix wailed more loudly, though completely dry-eyed.

'What are they making that din for? I can't hear myself read,' Sam said, coming in.

'Cat, we're more than happy for them to stay as you know, but it's your call.'

'If they're sleeping here I want to come home,' Sam said.

'All right, you do that, and Hannah and Felix will stay.'

'Good.'

Cat raised an eyebrow at Simon. But the thought of a peaceful drive home with Sam was pleasing. They spent too little time together without the other two and perhaps if there was something he did want to say to her, it would give him the chance.

SIXTY-TWO

Stephen Webber sat with his head in his hands at his desk, sobbing. Miles looked at him with concern.

'I probably shouldn't say this,' he said, 'but ill or not, Ruth is being grossly unfair on you. It was her duty to go into hospital and get herself better. As it is, you're a wreck, you can't function as Dean or anything else while this is going on, and when she is found you really are going to have to be firm. We've known each other a long time, Stephen, I have great respect for you, but I have to say this is not doing us any favours. I'm going to call a Chapter meeting if you won't, and you must formally ask for three months' leave of absence. Now, drink this.'

He held out a measure of brandy. Stephen did not move. His shoulders remained hunched and he continued to sob. Miles set the glass down beside him.

'Stephen, pull yourself together. This is very difficult, I understand, but you have to face things. Hold fast.'

Stephen lifted his head and took out a handkerchief.

'Now drink that.'

He drank.

'Right. Now, presumably the police are looking for her again? Perhaps she's gone to her previous hiding place. She won't be far away. It was more worrying the last time when it seemed possible that she was a victim of this madman, but now that her mental condition is known, there won't be that confusion.'

'Dear God, Miles, I should have recognised that she was in such a bad state. I should have insisted.'

'Well, you did as you thought best.'

'No. That's the point. I knew perfectly well what was for the best and I was too afraid to stand firm. How could she have slipped out without my even waking up?'

'Oh come, that's something easily done. Ruth is very determined and she is not a noisy person by nature — even more when she is trying not to disturb you. That's not your fault.'

'I feel at fault. I feel entirely guilty.'

'Yes, but that's not very productive. Accept that the worst you have done is make an error of judgement. Now, will you call an extraordinary meeting of the Chapter or shall I? I have authority but it would be better coming from you, obviously.'

'Yes. You're quite right, I'm of no use to anyone just at the moment. Perhaps ever.'

'Don't be ridiculous. Now, may I make a suggestion? That you and I go into the cathedral and pray together that Ruth returns home safely and accepts the need to be admitted to hospital? It would help, you know.'

Stephen wiped his eyes, and put his hand on Miles's arm for a second.

'You are a rock,' he said. 'It's always been the case but now . . . Bless you, Miles.'

SIXTY-THREE

At seven thirty Hannah rang to say good-night and the call went on as she gave a detailed account of the programme she and Judith had just watched, then of Felix having hidden the bath plug.

'Let me speak to Felix.'

'Heyyyylooo.'

'Felix, where did you hide Granny Jude's bath plug?'

There was a pause then shrieks of laughter before Felix put the phone down.

Cat sighed and went back to making herself a salad sandwich. Judith would coax the information out of him. Judith could coax Felix to do anything. She wondered if Simon was still there or whether something had happened to call him back to the station.

Sam had said little on the way home but that little had been enlightening. She had not spoken herself, determined not to make him clam up, and for a while there had been silence in the car. But she had taken the longer route home and as they had left the outskirts and got onto the country road, Sam said, 'Does it make you gay if you play hockey?'

'No. It makes you a hockey player. Why?'

'Just wondered. Does it make you an orphan if your dad died?'

'No, only if both your parents die.'

'Does it make you a wuss?'

'Does what make you a wuss?'

'If . . . your dad died.'

'Absolutely not. Of course it doesn't. Whatever a "wuss" is. What is it?'

'Not sure. A coward, I think.'

'How could anyone think that? Is that what people have said to you, Sam?'

'Sort of.'

'Right, well, that makes them much worse than a wuss, it makes them cruel, mean, thoughtless and unkind.'

For a second Cat's eyes filled with tears, tears of rage more than of distress, that Sam should have had to bear this sort of bullying. She brushed them away with her hand.

'It's OK,' Sam said in an odd little voice.

'No, Sam, it isn't OK. It's very not OK. Do you want me to talk to them at school?'

'No! No, please don't, don't do anything.

Please say you won't.'

'All right, I promise I won't. If you promise to tell me if anyone says that sort of thing
again, Sam. I have to know. If they're cruel
and mean to you they'll be cruel and mean
to other people — you have to stand up to
bullies.'

'I know. I do. But you going in to school
isn't me standing up to them.'

'That's true. All right, but please remember. How's school otherwise?'

'OK.'

Something in his tone of voice warned her
not to push any further.

'Look!' Sam whistled as a barn owl
swooped ahead of them, skimming low over
the hedge.

'Uncle Simon said he'd take you with him
on one of his walks, once he's got some free
time.'

'I wish he'd take me to that Scottish place.
That island. I really want to go there. Did
you know they sometimes see golden eagles?
He didn't. But they do.'

'Maybe next year.'

'Could I?'

'You'll have to ask him obviously but I
think it would be great, yes.'

Sam let out a long sigh.

■ ■ ■ ■

At Hallam House, Judith found the bath plug in one of Richard's slippers, Hannah lay in bed reading her Barbie comic and Simon sat with Felix on his lap trying to put him into his pyjamas and remember more than one verse of 'The Wheels on the Bus'. Richard was in his study reading the paper, a glass of Taransay malt beside him.

'You're good at this,' Judith said.

'No, I'm not, he's got his pyjama top on inside out.'

'In general.'

'If this is heading to "wouldn't you love to have your own children?" territory the answer is no.'

'It wasn't. I wouldn't presume.'

'No,' Simon said looking at her with affection, 'you're the one person I know who never would. Cat used to presume the entire time until we had a row about it, but she still sort of hovers around the subject.'

'Ignore her. OK, are you putting this young man into his bed or am I?' Felix slithered out of Simon's grasp and went racing out of the room. Downstairs, Richard heard the small footsteps go across the landing, the adult protestations, and took another sip of whisky. Family life again. He had never enjoyed time with his own children when they were as young as this, partly because, as a hospital doctor, he had seen little of them, partly because he simply had not liked the early stages of childhood, partly because of Martha. Martha had been different.

He loved his grandchildren and thought that he tolerated their presence around his house very well. He had more time, he was more relaxed, and it was all because of Judith. But his plan for him and Judith to spend a year driving round America had not been abandoned. He wanted to get away, and he wanted her to himself. Cat, he decided, was ready to stand on her own two feet, and if she was not, their absence would see to it. When the children had gone back home tomorrow, he intended to raise the subject again.

SIXTY-FOUR

Vanek and Mead stared at the blackboard menu in the pub they had found six miles out of Lafferton, and which nobody else in the force seemed to know about. It had become their own place.

'Soup and ham and eggs,' Ben said.

'You'll be full up.'

'I want to be full up.'

'Crab salad and a fishcake.'

'And chips.'

'No.'

He gave the order across the bar. 'And chips twice.'

Steph stalked across to a table by the window, even though it was dark. The fire was lit in the bar and there were stubby candles on the table.

'You can eat mine then.'

'Be a pleasure.'

Steph took a long draught of dry cider. 'If I have to look at one more CCTV tape this week I quit.'

'No you won't.'

'Shut up or I'll buy you a beanie hat.'

'That isn't funny.'

'No,' Steph said, 'it's not. Sorry.'

'Let's talk about something else.'

'What else is there to talk about?'

'Can you ski?'

'Yup. Black runs.'

'OK, come skiing with me. We'll both have leave after Christmas, if not before.'

'Is this a proposition?'

'Yes.'

Steph smiled. But she was uncertain if she wanted to go as far as taking a holiday with him. Not yet. She liked Ben, they worked well as a team, they'd enjoyed some good nights out. Anything further and she panicked.

'I'll think about it.' She would. And then say no.

'How long before one of two things happens?' Ben asked now. 'Another of the girls is murdered — or they're not and the whole thing gets downgraded.'

'It won't get downgraded, it can't.'

'There are a hell of a lot of resources being thrown at all of this, Steph — look at the overtime alone. Dogs. Divers. Permanent manned vans by the canal. Leafleting.

It can't drag on for ever getting nowhere and costing what it's costing.'

'It won't go on getting nowhere.'

'Says who?'

She finished her drink. The starters came, with a basket of fresh bread.

'I didn't ask for bread.'

'I did.'

'You eat too much bread. All those canteen sarnies.'

He threw a bit at her.

'The other thing people are starting to worry about is the gaps in policing elsewhere . . . it was always going to happen. Look at the car thefts, look at that spate of burglaries on big country houses. The only people not involved in the murder investigations are the drug squad.

'I thought we weren't talking, er, shop?'

The piece of bread came back.

'Still think Serrailler walks on water then?'

'I never did.'

'Liar. He isn't cracking this one, is he?'

Ben was silent. He was not about to agree with her, not about to admit that his idol had feet of clay. But there was something in what Steph was saying and she was not the only one saying it. He wiped his bread round the soup bowl.

'Man U for the triple,' he said.

Steph snorted. Football talk was one more nail in Ben Vanek's coffin.

Hayley lay on Louise's sofa covered with a duvet, under which Liam and Frankie were also snuggled, watching an old *Batman* film. She had come home from the hospital feeling terrible, and called Louise to ask if she could keep Liam just one more night. Within half an hour, Gwenda Mayo had come round and fetched her and she was tucked up with the kids, a mug of tea and a couple of painkillers.

'You're just so kind,' she kept saying 'why are you being so kind?'

Lou looked surprised. 'You're only on the couch with some tea,' she said. 'It's not a lot to do and you'd have been miserable on your own, it would have felt a whole lot worse. If those two are bothering you chuck them off.'

'They're not.' The boys wriggled and started to try and shove each other until Frankie fell off the sofa.

Leslie Blade had slept much of the afternoon, in the chair opposite to his mother, slept and had tea, and felt that he should begin to do what he had been told, and walk. 'Half an hour a day,' had been the recommendation, which sounded little enough and he had left Norah watching the evening news. Even putting on his coat and outdoor shoes seemed strange, as if it had been years since he had done such a thing. Half an hour. Perhaps he would extend it day after day until he felt able to walk to the library and then to go into work, help out for an hour or so, and then half a shift and so on until life was normal again.

Normal life would mean that he could start to pack the sandwiches again and make the tea, take out the car and drive down to the printworks. Normal life. But Norah would hear him, and now Norah knew and had spoken to him, nothing would be the same because he would feel anxious, self-conscious, wondering if she would be awake when he got back and wanting to ask him questions.

He closed the gate. There were lights on in the houses, cars going up and down the street. People were coming home, eating tea, watching television, getting ready to go out. He hesitated, then turned left. After fifty yards, he was exhausted. Half an hour would take him almost into town and he had not walked for more than a couple of minutes. He was out of breath, he felt nervous about going further, and his legs

569

would hardly hold him up. Normal life. He sat on the low wall of a house and waited until he felt stronger, wondering if there would ever be any normal life for him again.

SIXTY-FIVE

Cat went upstairs. It was almost nine but Sam was still reading the Sherlock Holmes.

'I have to finish it, I can't sleep if I don't.'

'How far to go?'

He flicked forwards. 'Nine pages.'

'OK. Then . . .'

'I know. Can you go now please?'

Cat laughed. 'Are you all right?'

'Why shouldn't I be all right?'

She leaned over him, wondering if he was going to turn his face quickly so that her kiss landed somewhere at the back of his head. But instead he dropped his book, put his arms up round her neck and pulled her down. He said nothing at all.

'Love you, Sambo.'

As quickly, his arms dropped and he was deep in his book again.

It was quiet. Mephisto was out hunting by the light of a full moon. Cat made herself a cup of coffee to see her through her course notes, and took it into the small study. Of all the rooms in the house, this was the one in which she missed Chris the least, simply because he had rarely done more than put his head round the door. It was her room. He had never left a letter or a book in it, his mark was simply not on it at all. It was the same as it had always been. She did not need reminders of him but she got them, sometimes sharply, when she found an item of his clothing still left in a drawer or saw his writing in the margins of a book she consulted. She had felt his presence in the house strongly in the weeks and months after his death, had walked into a room and known that he was there. But never in this room.

She switched on the desk lamp, opened a folder and settled down to work. She was deep in an article about drug dosages in the final hours of a dying patient when she saw car headlights as someone drove in through the gate. Simon possibly, though he had said he would be staying for supper at Hallam House. There was a single ring at the front doorbell.

'Am I calling at a very inconvenient time?'
Miles Hurley stood slightly back from the

door, his coat collar pulled up.

'Oh. No, no, you're not. I was just doing some work. Sorry, Miles, come in.'

He smiled and unbuttoned his coat.

'I was going to make some coffee.'

'That sounds delicious. I expect you make coffee as well as you do most things.'

The compliment sounded genuine enough and yet Cat instinctively recoiled from it. It made her feel uneasy. She supposed she wasn't used to compliments from men since Chris — given that her father and Simon did not go in for them, and Russell, at the surgery, gave out praise only sparingly, though she knew he appreciated her.

Miles followed her into the kitchen.

'You heard about Ruth Webber, I imagine?'

'I did.'

Miles held up a hand. 'I realise you can't discuss a patient, of course, but it's a great strain on Stephen, indeed on all of us, I'm sure you understand.'

'The police will have a much better sense of things this time. They can separate her disappearances from the murders . . . Do sit down, Miles . . . if you don't mind the kitchen sofa, or we can go into the sitting room . . .'

'No, this is perfect. Cosy. Thank you.'

Cat spooned coffee into the cafetière, noticing that in fact Miles remained standing.

'I came past the police vans just now . . . they've set up quite an encampment near the canal, haven't they?'

'Yes. If there are any girls in that area they'll feel safer.'

'Those wretched young women. But I didn't see any. I hear they've moved on. Hunt Square, that dismal place nearer the centre.'

'Is it about the Magdalene Group you wanted to see me, Miles? I haven't had it in my mind, I'm afraid. I've had a lot of other things going on and I rather thought that with all this business of Ruth . . .'

'Well, it was something we could discuss. Yes.'

'I meant to ask my brother if perhaps there could be a police representative in the group. I'm not sure if they could spare anyone at the moment but in the future.'

'Ah yes, it must be interesting having such a senior detective in the family.'

'Interesting? I'm not sure it's that.'

'So he doesn't come to you to offload his work problems then?'

'Absolutely not.'

Cat poured milk into the saucepan and

574

went to the dresser to take down two mugs. After a second, she put her hand on the smaller ones. She did not particularly want to have Miles linger over a large beaker of coffee. She liked him well enough, it was just that she minded having her work interrupted, and she suspected that he had in fact come to discuss Stephen Webber, in spite of paying lip service to Cat's commitment to patient confidentiality.

'I wonder,' he said now, 'if you agree with me that Stephen should take a sabbatical? He has been under great strain, you know.'

'That's understandable.'

'I have strongly advised him to go away, take Ruth, unless of course she has to go into hospital once she returns. He's a wonderful person, you know. I was hoping you would back me up on this.'

Cat set the coffee down on the table. He was still standing.

'Miles, I really can't get involved in Stephen's work. It wouldn't be right, as I'm sure you understand.'

He looked at her carefully for a long time, but it was a look she could not read.

'Please, do sit down.' She filled his mug. He picked it up but then began to wander round the room, looking at the children's drawings pinned on the cork board, reading a couple of notices, looking at a photograph.

'Is this your husband?'

She nodded. She wanted to rush over and take it down, turn it to the wall, anything to stop him scrutinising it.

'Tell me, what was his view of the scourge of prostitution in our city?'

'Of . . . ? I don't think it was something we ever discussed. I think he would have felt much as the rest of us — and wanted to do something to help the girls get off the game and try to get decent jobs, live normal lives. He'd certainly have been concerned about their health. As I am.'

'Yes. Sexual diseases, I suppose.'

'Not only those. Their general health is usually poor — their diet is bad, a lot of them are on drugs, they smoke, they get cold and wet and . . . all of that.'

As she spoke, she had turned to reach for a teaspoon on the worktop behind her so that she had her back to Miles when he said, 'Ah yes.' And then, after a pause, 'Poor wretches.'

And in that split second something struck her, some sort of reminder, or recollection, something . . . But what was it? What? An alarm bell rang in her mind. As Miles Hurley had spoken, there was that and also . . .

He said again, 'These prostitutes really

have to be dealt with.'

Cat froze and then a great shiver ran down her back. She realised what it was. The newspaper and the television reports. Abi. The girl who had survived, the one who had done the drawing of the man in the beanie hat. Abi who had been half strangled so that she was unable to speak, unable to do more than draw and nod and shake her head. Abi Righton. Her own patient. Abi who had said she was going to 'get out of this'.

Abi had not been able to do more than draw the rough little sketch of her attacker, and write two things. 'BEANIE MAN' was one. The other was that he'd had a *whispery* voice.

It had not stayed in Cat's mind, or she thought it had not, until Miles Hurley had just spoken, in a tone quite different from his normal one.

These prostitutes really have to be dealt with.

A whispery voice.

She could not turn, could not speak, she remained as if paralysed, reaching for the spoon.

It was nonsense of course. What had gone through her mind could not be, but then, into that mind came the identikit picture of 'Beanie Man'. He had no distinguishing features, no beard or broken nose, no exceptionally thin or fat lips, no scars or marks. Just a middle-aged man wearing a dark-coloured beanie hat pulled well down. And that man could be Miles Hurley who also had an unmemorable face without any distinctive features. She saw the picture steadily. But it simply could not be the case.

She turned and as she turned she looked at him. He was a few paces from her, and what she had suddenly thought, in absolute disbelief and horror, must have been written on her face.

He came round the table and stood beside her.

'Poor girls,' he whispered. 'What did Abi say, Cat? How much did Ruth tell you?'

She opened her mouth to ask what he meant and could say nothing, it was dry and her jaw seemed to be locked.

She looked into Miles Hurley's eyes, just for a second before she had to look away, but it was enough. She had seen madness there, the steady, assured, arrogance of a certain sort of madness, emotionless, intent, focused. And then he smiled, a thin, pleased, mad sort of smile, and took a step closer to her so that she was trapped between him and the worktop. With some strange instinct for self-preservation and knowing that she could not get past him, she half turned away from him. Miles raised his arms with his hands outstretched.

'Mum, I can't —'

Cat looked round in terror. Miles did not flinch or drop his hands or stop staring at her, did not seem to have been startled at all by Sam, who had come a step or two into the kitchen and then stopped dead. She saw the expression on her son's face change from enquiring to bewilderment to terror like the swiftly moving pages of a flicker book.

There was no thought, no plan, nothing but pure gut reaction as she screamed, 'Sam, phone —' before Miles lunged forward to grab her round the neck.

Sam did not think and afterwards did not remember. He could see Cat's mobile on the hall table, ran for it and pressed 3, her automatic dial for Simon, who answered within a couple of rings.

It was Simon who recalled in detail and who never afterwards forgot the voice.

'He's in the kitchen, he's killing Mummy, please come, please come . . .'

The phone was knocked out of Sam's hand by Miles Hurley who swung at him twice, catching him on the side of his head, before opening the front door and racing to his car, starting it, turning it so fast it kicked up the gravel and the smell of burning tyres drifted in through the open door.

'Mummy,' Sam said, and stumbled towards the kitchen door, his head smarting but not bleeding, not seriously hurt.

'Mummy . . .'

Cat lay on the floor where Hurley had left her. Afterwards she remembered more than Sam, remembered the terrible pain in her throat and the pressure of trying to breathe, and then breathing again as she fell, remembered the odd sound that came out of her mouth and another sound, a grunt or a gasp that came out of Hurley's, remembered hearing the car, hearing Sam, feeling Sam's small warm body pressed against her own, his face against hers, hearing him trying to breathe and say her name through his panic and tears, remembered reaching up and holding him, holding him. Remembered a hundred years or five seconds and then the sound of sirens and more cars, more spraying gravel, and the blue of a light whirling round and round somewhere. Remembered footsteps, voices, and holding tightly to Sam. Remembered Simon's voice, Simon, talking to her, talking to Sam, talking to the others, shouting at the others. Remembered

more sirens, more lights, more confusion.
Remembered relief.

SIXTY-SIX

Serrailler was waiting at the entrance to the station at nine when the Chief's car turned into the gates.

'Morning, Simon, how are you feeling now?'

'Morning, ma'am. Where do I start? Shock, relief, fury, satisfaction . . . but my reactions are nothing to what the teams are feeling this morning.'

They headed up the stairs to his office.

A tray of brewing coffee was waiting, cafetière, hot milk, best cups, chocolate biscuits. Paula Devenish glanced at it.

'Hmm. Guilt offerings.' But she smiled. 'You've nothing to beat yourself up about Simon, none of you has. But I know what you're thinking — it's been down to luck. Never despise luck. Your policing wasn't at fault. Look how many unsolved murders there are on the national police books and thank God these are not adding to them.'

'I'm just kicking myself . . . surely there was something we should have known, something . . .'

'Why? Did he ever come within a mile of your radar?'

'He fitted the profile.'

'Along with how many other men in Lafferton? Loners. You'd already questioned one loner twice, and if you think about it, you had far more reason to suspect the librarian.'

'I know, I know.'

'How's your sister?'

'She's fine, thanks. They kept her in overnight, and she's still shaken. Sam's the one I'm worried about. He was a hero but he also had a horrible experience. He needs to get it out of his system. I'm planning to take him away for a weekend, go walking. He'll talk to me.'

'Has Hurley talked?'

'Can't shut him up, apparently. He asked to see the MO and was assigned psychiatric time. He's talking to the shrink.'

'It's not unusual, you know — this sort of split personality, half the man of the cloth, the pillar of the community, the other half . . .'

'A man with a dread of prostitutes and a hatred of them, yes. In a way, you know, if we hadn't been all over the area and frustrated him, huge police presence, broken the pattern, he would have gone on killing the street girls. Instead, it changed and Leah Wilson died just because she was there and he couldn't stop himself killing. If we hadn't —'

'Come on, Simon, what are you saying? That if he'd found another prostitute to murder if would have been better?'

Serrailler sighed and finished his coffee. 'No,' he said. 'Sorry. Of course I'm not.'

'He was very cunning, you know. So the ends are tied up?'

'Well, no . . . Mrs Webber is still missing.'

'Have you spoken to the psychiatric team?'

'Yes. They think suicide a strong possibility but that doesn't mean we're not looking out for her alive too — all the usual, railway station, bus station, there's a photo out in case there is even a remote chance she hitched a lift somewhere.'

'I imagine the cathedral's in shock — are we liaising with them?'

'Yes. People carry on, but Stephen Webber is distraught.'

'Tell me, how have you found young Ben Vanek?'

'Impressive . . . still a bit green, still not quite confident enough to strike out on his own, but that's understandable. No, he'll do well.'

'Perhaps for the next week you could pull him into the debriefings, get him to do some analysis of the way the policing was organised, what worked, what was less successful. Assuming that everything goes quiet enough for that sort of luxury.'

'Pray for quiet, ma'am.'

There was a knock. Serrailler frowned — he had said no interruptions — but the Chief nodded towards the door.

'Guv, ma'am . . . sorry, but you need to see this.'

The sergeant put a piece of paper into Serrailler's hand and disappeared.

Simon glanced at it quickly.

'Trouble?'

'Hurley's made a full confession. Ruth Webber.'

'Oh *no*.'

'Uniform's already searched his bungalow. First place they went . . .'

Paula stood up. 'Let's go.'

They took Vanek, Mead and a couple of uniform. Paula Devenish went with Serrailler in his car.

'Mad or sane?' she asked as they turned out of the yard.

'Hurley? Evil.'

'Try to stand back a bit, Simon.'

'Stand back? The man tried to strangle my sister! If Sam hadn't been there, if he hadn't had the presence of mind to —'

She held up her hand. 'I know. That's precisely why you need to detach emotionally, and you know it. I think getting this last piece of the puzzle solved will help. How well do you know Hurley?'

'Hardly at all. Cat knew him a bit better but not well — she didn't much like him, which is quite rare with her, but she doesn't let an instinct get in the way. They were on a committee together, and she's a pillar of St Michael's congregation of course. She just gets on with it.'

'So you haven't an opinion about his mental state? Could you slow down? This isn't a blue-light job.'

'Sorry, ma'am.' He eased his foot off the pedal and leaned back slightly. 'This sort of obsessive serial killing is never the work of a sane man, is it? He had a fascination with prostitutes and a loathing of them. He clearly has sexual hang-ups. But he's a priest, canon residentiary of a cathedral. There's the split. He probably thought he was doing God's work or carrying out a sacred plan — ridding the world of harlots.

586

But then things changed — and he discovered he liked killing women, any women. Jesus Christ, I haven't got my head round it properly but one of them was almost Cat.'

'Do you think you need to talk to someone?'

'No,' he said shortly. 'I sort myself out. Always have. Thank you.'

'High horses are difficult to climb down from, Simon.'

He did not reply. He meant what he had said. He sorted himself out. He did not need to talk to the HQ shrink.

The side door of the bungalow was open and a PC stood on guard.

Serrailler halted in the passageway. There was a dreadful silence, the sort of silence he was used to, a silence that over the years he had come to recognise as different from that inside a merely empty house. Early in his police career he had scoffed at one of his first sergeants who had drawn his attention to the silence of death, assuming it was a fading old police superstition. Then he had experienced it for himself.

He went into the rooms one by one — bedroom, bare as a monastic cell; study, orderly, papers neat, books carefully aligned, laptop covered. Sitting room. Bare. Pleasant enough. Bland. This was the house of a man who gave nothing away, whose personality had left no mark.

Kitchen. Clean. Immaculate.

The Chief was at his shoulder. 'Smell,' she said.

It was there, faint, but unmistakable, the smell of death and early decomposition.

They found the body of Ruth Webber, pushed into the small broom cupboard, off the kitchen. She had been strangled and her face had cuts and abrasions.

Serrailler looked at it for a long moment. It was impossible to get the other image out of the way, the one that was super-imposed on what was in front of him, the image not of Ruth Webber, but of Cat.

Simon was the first to see Stephen Webber, standing opposite the gate that gave onto the Close, ashen, his face crumpled into grief and distress and a terrible sort of bewilderment.

Simon went over to him.

'What's happening? Have you heard something . . . ?'

'Would you wait just a moment? I'll be straight back.'

Simon ran back to the bungalow. 'Ma'am, the Dean is outside wanting news, he hasn't been told anything. I'll take him inside, tell him myself. He might want to identify the body, see his wife, but later. I don't want him anywhere near here. We'll get the tapes up, he needs to be out of the way while forensics are in and then when they remove the body. Shall I phone your driver, get him to fetch you from here, or will you wait for me?'

'You go and talk to the poor fellow. I'll call my car. Thank you, Simon.'

Stephen Webber sobbed, head in his hands, body shaking. Serrailler offered to make him coffee, get him brandy, but in the end simply poured a glass of water, set it beside him and waited. He had been the bearer of bad news often enough and everyone's reaction was different but he never got used to it or became hardened. He doubted if any of them did.

After a long time, Stephen wiped his eyes, sipped the water, and then began to talk, to pour out everything, about his marriage, about what he now saw as a grave mistake in coming to St Michael's, about himself and his own perceived inadequacies. But above all about Miles Hurley, a man he had liked, worked with, trusted, relied upon, yet never, he now realised, known at all.

'It's the betrayal,' he said several times, 'and the fact that he's a stranger to me. I can't begin to understand.'

'I doubt if anyone does.'

'No. But it is wickedness. A mind like that — he is possessed by some dreadful evil.'

'Or else deranged. Madness takes some strange forms.'

Webber shook his head.

'I'll resign, of course.'

'Don't make any decisions immediately.'

'I have made my decision. It is irrevocable.'

He stood up and put out his hand. 'Thank you, Simon. One thing — I would like to see Cat. I owe her some sort of explanation — though I have none. I owe it to her not simply to disappear. Would you ask her, if she has five minutes she could spare me in the next week?'

'I'm sure she will. She's staying with my father and stepmother for the time being. I'm going there later. I'll tell her.'

'Thank you.' The Dean looked around him as if puzzled, uncertain where he was or why, and not knowing what he should do next. 'Thank you,' he said again.

'Do you have someone you want me to ring? Family? Someone to come and stay with you?'

'I have a sister.' He smiled suddenly. 'But please don't trouble — I'll ring her.'

As they walked to the door, Stephen Webber said, as an afterthought, 'Geraldine — my sister — never liked Ruth, you know. From the beginning. It was — a sadness. People didn't understand her, you see, and they didn't always find her easy. But I loved her. I realise it now. And that is the secret, you know.'

He watched from the door as Simon walked slowly to his car, past the forensics van and cars which had already taken over that side of the road, where the crime-scene tapes were in place, cordoning off the gate and the path that led to Miles Hurley's bungalow.

Sixty-Seven

'Darling, you don't have to go home until you're good and ready, you know that.'

Cat and Judith were sitting in the conservatory with coffee. The late-autumn sun was bright on the garden and through the windows, though outside it was cold after the first frost of the year.

'I ought to go back.'

Judith sighed. 'I sometimes think the words that have caused most harm and unhappiness to the human race are "should" and "ought".'

'You've been fantastic and being here has given me time to steady myself again. The children have loved it, needless to say, but they have to get back to a proper routine.'

'Yes, I can see that. Well, up to you, of course. You do have to face the house and what happened there. There isn't any need to hurry it, but once you've done it, you'll have pulled the sting.'

'Yes.'

'I hear the Dean's resigned.'

'And most of me feels extremely glad about that. Perhaps now they'll make a sensible appointment — he was never going to be the right man for St Michael's. But I feel so desperately sorry for him. I can't think where he'll go or what he will do.'

'On the other hand, perhaps he woke people up just a little and that's never a bad thing.'

'Oh, undoubtedly. The words baby and bathwater applied but he had some fresh ideas which we needed. The new visitors' centre, his plans for reaching out to the students — not just sitting there smugly waiting for everyone to come to us.'

'The Magdalene Group?'

Cat shuddered. 'There does need to be something — the problem isn't going to go away.'

'If you think . . . well, it's something I feel I'd like to be involved in if I could be useful.'

'You could be extremely useful . . . thank you. I'll hold you to it.'

'When we get back from the States.'

Cat lowered her coffee and looked at Judith with alarm. Judith looked steadily back.

'We are going,' she said. 'Your father so wants to do it and at his age you can't so easily say "maybe in five years". I owe it to him, you know. He needs me to himself for a while.'

Cat swallowed her panic. She'd had Judith to help her cope in the aftermath of Chris's death, and now, with the trauma of Miles Hurley's attack, she had come to rely on her, she had done so much with and for the children . . .

'Yes,' she said at last, 'he does. And I have two feet. Time I stood on them again.'

'It's only six months, darling, and you'll have Simon.'

'I also have my diploma course, a job and three children. But one thing I did wonder about and that's taking a lodger — maybe a medical student or a junior doctor from Bevham General? What do you think? Heaven knows we have enough room. It's either that or an au pair which I don't really need and I'm not sure I want.'

Cat looked across the garden, put to bed for the winter but with the last few blooms on the climbing iceberg rose catching the sun, and had a sudden vision of her mother, gardening trousers and apron with the pockets full of twine and plant ties, secateurs in hand, hair pinned up. The garden meant Meriel. Judith did what had to be done but she was not the gardener her mother had been. Cat felt her eyes fill with tears, as they seemed to do easily at the moment, as always when she looked at Sam.

Judith was quiet. I love her, Cat thought, and she is absolutely right for my father. But of course it's different.

'Simon will miss you,' she said. 'You, as in you.'

Judith shook her head. 'No, he won't. But it's all right between us now and I can't tell you how good that feels.'

'It pleases Dad too.'

Judith laughed. 'I think you may be right.'

'Simon's taking Sam walking in the Brecon Beacons next weekend. I want him to make sure Sam is really all right with all this — he still hasn't said much to me.'

Not said much, she thought, but he had not let her out of his sight since, he had come into her room every night and climbed into her bed silently, had rushed to find her the moment he got in from school and brought his homework to whichever room she was in so that he could do it with her beside him, had been reluctant to go anywhere with anyone else, and if he did, could not wait to be back. He needed someone to talk to without fuss until he had cleared everything, feelings, anxieties, confessions, problems, and a healing could begin. Cat knew that she was not the right person. Simon would be.

'I wonder if I'll ever again be able to think of Miles Hurley as one thinks of a normal human being? I'm supposed to forgive him but I can't . . . I think I can forgive what he did to me — after all, he didn't succeed in killing me, I'm here, I'm fine, unharmed. But Sam . . . he'll never forget that, he'll have the memory of those few moments of terror for the rest of his life. Hurley murdered four women and left one for dead. He was evil, he was a liar and a deceiver and "he hid his evil in the robe of righteousness". He's ruined Stephen Webber's life and totally betrayed Stephen's trust and friendship . . . what good is there to say?'

Judith was silent.

The sun moved round, slanting through the bare branches of the old walnut tree onto the grass.

'What can I do?' Cat asked in sudden distress.

After a pause, Judith said, 'I think all you can do is wrap it up in a metaphorical bundle and lay it down.'

'But where?'

'Are you going to Ruth Webber's funeral at St Michael's?'

'Oh yes. I must.'

'So, maybe you could lay it down there?'

'Yes,' Cat said. 'Maybe.'

'I'm going to make a lamb casserole.' Judith got up.

'I'll come and do the vegetables.'

Ordinary things, Cat thought gratefully. Washing up the coffee cups. Making a lamb stew. Chopping vegetables. Ordinary life. That's what saves us.

'By the way.' Judith looked at her with a smile. 'Simon rang. He said he might go back to Taransay. In the early spring.'

'For another holiday?'

'Not quite. Apparently he's had an invitation to a wedding.'

SIXTY-EIGHT

Stephen Webber could not even find the telephone because of the packing cases, boxes, suitcases, detritus. Even the table he'd been using in the temporary house, instead of his own desk, had already gone to storage. The telephone was on the floor behind a pile of books for the charity shop. He lifted the receiver on about the twentieth ring.

'Stephen Webber.'

'Good afternoon. This is James Penman.'

The name meant something. Nothing. Yes.

'Solicitor. My office is on the other side of the Close.'

Something. A shadow fell.

'I wonder if I might come across? I need to have a word with you about something.'

'Something?'

'Not for the telephone. I can be with you in a couple of minutes.'

So it wasn't yet over. Even now, even the

week he moved out, moved away. Not over. Why wasn't it over?

'The house is in chaos.'

'You're packing up, yes, I know. But I think it better if I come to you, all the same.'

A couple of minutes, as he had said.

Miles Hurley's solicitor.

'The kitchen is the only clear room downstairs. Sorry.'

'Fine. How sad that you didn't even get a chance to move into the new Deanery and enjoy some time there.'

Stephen said nothing. Spooned coffee into the pot. He had only spoken to James Penman once, a formal word, meeting by chance in the Close. There had not seemed reason for anything more.

He had nothing to say to him about Miles.

He stood waiting for the water to boil. The kitchen was filled with thin sunlight.

'As you will know, Miles Hurley has the services of a barrister, and he has asked me to see you.'

Stephen set the coffee and milk on the table. He could think of nothing that either lawyer might have to say to him. Nothing he had to say to them. To anyone.

James Penman had a pale face, shadow of a beard. An intelligent face. He looked steadily over the top of his coffee cup at Stephen.

'I know what your response may well be,' he said. 'It would probably be my own response. But I am obliged to put this to you, and ask you at least to consider it.'

Stephen had a sudden flash of memory, back to the last time Ruth had left the house, the last time he had spoken to her, the last night. She had gone out into the Close and met Miles Hurley.

He took a gulp of coffee. It was hot. His tongue smarted. He had not learned how to divert his mind, how to let the flashes come like pictures in a film but simply not to look at them, as a child closes its eyes before a frightening image.

'Miles Hurley has asked to see you.'

The words meant nothing. They were gobbets of sound hanging on the air between the two of them. Miles. Hurley. Has. Asked. To. See. You.

'Because he's a remand prisoner until the trial, he doesn't need to send a visiting order. You simply telephone the prison and book a time.'

'Why?' Stephen touched his scalded tongue to the roof of his mouth.

'He — has things to say to you. I imagine that he feels he needs to say.'

'There is — nothing. Nothing to be said. How could there be?'

'I understand. Of course I understand.' James Penman stirred his coffee. Waited.

Miles. Hurley. Has. Asked. To. See. You.

'Might it — perhaps if he spoke to you it could help towards some sort of . . .'

'Understanding? Forgiveness? Sympathy? What? Towards what?' He heard his own voice, strident in the quiet room.

'I know.' Penman's voice was calm. Not strident. Stephen felt embarrassed. 'There is absolutely no reason why you should agree to this request. He has asked to see you. You are at liberty to send back a simple refusal. No. You don't have to give reasons. Just "no". Or you can go. Your call.'

'Why does he want to see me? Does he say?'

'No. I asked. Do you want me to call back, see if I can find out a bit more?'

Stephen got up and went to the window. The sun was still pale through a film of cloud. The brick of the high garden wall was rose-red.

He thought of Ruth, complaining about the garden at the Deanery. 'I don't want to have to do the garden thing, I'm not a garden woman. It's huge. Can't we let it off or something?' But the Deanery was weeks off being ready for anyone, even now. He need never worry. She need never worry. Whoever came would move straight in there. Would they want a large garden? Who would they be?

He turned round and — before he had allowed himself time to let the subject worm its way back into his mind and burrow there, so that he had to consider it — he said, 'Yes. I'll go. Tell me where I have to go. Tell me what I will have to do.'

He was grateful to Penman for taking in what he said at once and without querying it, without asking him if he was sure.

He was not sure.

'The best thing will be for me to get the Brief to telephone you, run you through the procedure. It's quite straightforward. You need photo identity — passport is fine. And be prepared to be searched.'

He stood up.

Searched?

Stephen, standing briefly at the door, watched Penman cross the Close on his stork-like legs, shoulders bent.

Would they expect him to be trying to take in drugs? Money? A weapon?

He did not think about it again. It was the only way he could continue to function, to see people, pack books, eat, sleep. He turned a switch off. It surprised him how easy it was to do so.

James Penman offered to drive him to the prison, seventy miles across the county, but he preferred to go alone and by train and taxi, not trusting himself at the wheel. He knew that he could think of other things on the way there, keep the switch off. But on the return journey?

He had imagined that he would wear a tie but, when he dressed, he reached for his clerical collar.

'Chaplain, then?' the taxi driver said. 'Some tough nuts for you to crack in there, I tell you. Only a lot of them get God inside. Kiddy-fiddlers do it, I tell you, then come out with haloes, all forgiven, job in the church youth club, off they go again. You know that, do you?'

If he had allowed himself to imagine it, to think of it at all, he would have known what the prison would look like.

'Supposed to be knocking this lot down, getting a nice comfy new one only there's no money. Still, I daresay you know all about that.'

There was a side door. They checked his name off. Perfectly pleasant. The search didn't take long. He had to empty his pockets.

Keys. The sound of footsteps. More keys. He had visited a parishioner in Wandsworth years ago. Nothing had changed apart from the security electronics.

The only way was not to think. Follow behind.

He had expected to join a queue of other visitors in line. There was no one.

'This is a one to one, Reverend, you know that I expect, Brief will have explained. Special Perm. But there'll be an officer in the room. It's twenty minutes.'

Stephen felt panic like nausea coming into his throat. The switch went down and he knew where he was and why. Realisation flooded in.

It was the usual sort of room. If he had allowed himself to think ahead he would have been able to picture it.

'If you'd like to take a seat, Reverend.'

The table was bare. Room bare. Walls bare apart from *No Smoking* and a fire assembly points map. The warder who had brought him went away. Sounds from somewhere, voices, footsteps on metal stairs.

Stephen felt suddenly calm. He had not prayed but his prayer was anticipated. Answered.

Footsteps.

Stephen simply sat, staring down at his own hand on the table top because — having glanced at him once, as he was brought in — he could not look at Miles again. It was worse than he could possibly have imagined. His feelings were so confused, so turbulent, so violent that he had to press his feet against the floor to stop himself from . . . he did not know.

But then the chair opposite to him was pulled out and he was sitting down, quite close, because it was not a big table. Stephen could feel his warmth, smell an institutional soap, see his wrist below the prison uniform sweat shirt.

The warder stood back against the wall. But watching, watching. Ready. The silence was terrible.

'Thank . . .' Miles's voice went husky. He coughed. Cleared his throat. 'Thank you for coming Stephen,' he said.

Stephen could say nothing. Could not look up.

Silence.

Miles cleared his throat again. 'I could have written this, but that . . . but I needed to see you. Tell you.'

You needed, Stephen thought. Is this right? I have come here because of what you need?

Stephen looked up and straight into Miles Hurley's face.

His skin was pale, with a blue shadow round his jaw, dark streaks beneath his eyes. He had lost weight. His eyes were dull, apart from points of piercing brightness in the centres. His thinning hair was combed back from his forehead.

This is the man who killed my wife, Stephen thought calmly. These hands, in front of me on the table, gripped her round the throat. This is . . . this . . .

'There is no forgiveness,' Miles said. 'I know that. I understand that. I don't expect to be forgiven. But perhaps you don't understand.'

Stephen realised that he had not spoken a single word since entering the room. He had thought that he had none to speak. But he had.

'Understand? How can I understand?'

'No. Of course. But . . . not the others. Not the — the women. Ruth. I need you to understand the Ruth part of it.'

The Ruth part.

Stephen wanted to walk out but he had no strength to move, his legs would not have held him.

Miles stared at his hands and did not speak again for some moments. The warder shifted his weight but did not take his eyes away from them. Noises. A door clanging. Footsteps. A burst of distant laughter echoing down a stairwell.

It was Stephen who broke the silence between them.

'You killed her because she knew. She came outside and saw you and she knew, and so you killed her.'

'Yes. No. No, that isn't all. That . . .'

He looked up. The bright pinheads stared into Stephen's own eyes. His thumbs were working to and fro against his forefingers.

'I did it for you,' Miles said. 'Can't you see? Don't you understand?'

And then the room was filled with a mad babble of words.

'You had to put up with her, that woman, you were so good, so caring, you were . . . All that madness, that abuse, that mania, those weeks of . . . all of that. She went missing, you went after her, you always brought her back, she pushed you into this, into that, and I knew you didn't want it, I knew it was always against your judgement, we all knew it, but you, your kindness. Your loving of her. You were chained to that, she was tied to you and she would never have let you go, shackled, yes, that's what I mean, shackled. Why did you marry her? I never understood it, no one did. She held you back, she embarrassed you, she was of no use to you at all but you went on and I saw that nothing would change. If you couldn't make it change now you would never . . . it would have gone on. And I so respected you, so admired you, I so wanted you to do great things. You should have done great things, Stephen, and now you can. Understand that, please. *Now you can.* I don't matter. I . . . what happens to me isn't relevant. You see? It is you, now, only you. I did it because of that. Surely you see, surely you understand. The others were different, they were nothing. That was someone else, the man who . . . not this man. But Ruth. Yes. Yes, Ruth. I killed Ruth for you, so that . . .'

The moment Stephen was on his feet the warder was beside him.

Miles remained seated, silent now, but looking up at him, an urgency, a desperation in his eyes.

'I want to leave,' Stephen said. He was shaking. He faced the door and waited the

608

few seconds it took for someone else to come. Did not look round or back. Within three minutes, he was standing in the street outside the prison gates.

That night, he lay awake and the images in front of his eyes clicked on and off, on and off, one after the other but always returning to the image of Miles Hurley, his eyes bright, bright, peering urgently across the table, and talking, talking. I did it for you. I did it for you. I did it for you.

He had no way of knowing if he would ever understand, ever forgive, though he was certain that he would never forget. He could not think or sift out the madness from the sanity, the delusions from the truth. He could not pray and yet he knew that simply lying there in the darkness was some sort of unvoiced petition. But for whom? Miles Hurley? Ruth? For himself?

He left Lafferton two days later, without seeing any of his former colleagues again.

It was early in the morning, bright, cloudless, but there had been rain in the night and, as he drove away, the soft grey stone of the Cathedral, the roofs of the houses, the

609

cobblestones of the lane beyond the arch gleamed.

ABOUT THE AUTHOR

Susan Hill is the author of four other mysteries starring Chief Inspector Simon Serrailler: *The Vows of Silence, The Various Haunts of Men, The Pure in Heart,* and *The Risk of Darkness,* as well as the stories "The Woman in Black" and "The Man in the Picture." www.susan-hill.com